BABY IT'S COLD OUTSIDE

CYN ALEXANDER

KINGDOM LIT PUBLICATIONS

To my grandma. Christmas has been my favorite holiday since before I can remember. Spending the holiday with you and grandpa made it that much more special. I will cherish those memories forever. Rest In Peace, Grandpa. You are missed.

ATTENTION READERS

*Thank you guys for supporting me! It means the absolute **WORLD** to me! I want to make sure that you don't miss out on any of my other books, so please be sure to look out for books by my other pen name **Queen Pen**. I love you all so much! Many, many thanks to you!*

TRIGGER WARNING

CHAPTER 1

CHRISTMAS MUSIC COULD BE HEARD THROUGHOUT TIMES square. It was packed with people, and the holiday spirit was overwhelming. Kids tugged on their parents' hands, leading them closer to the stores with the coolest toy displays. Couples marveled at the lights and snuggled up to their loved ones to keep warm. Even the dogs that were out with their owners for a nighttime walk seemed to be in high spirits as they galloped through the snow. The date was December first, and the energy was magical. The holidays in New York were the most wonderful time of the year for most people, but for Jade Lawrence, it was the worst time of year.

She sat huddled in a dark spot beside an alley as she tried to stay warm. It was only six o'clock and the shelter she wanted to stay at that night wouldn't open until eight. She started walking towards it anyway, to help keep her body warm. The thin long sleeved t-shirt did nothing against the harsh twenty degree weather. She shivered severely as she dragged herself up into a standing position, her breath coming out in small white puffs.

Jade would not complain, though. Believe it or not, freezing her ass off was a step up from the situation she had been in a couple of weeks ago. She would gladly endure this weather and live on the streets if it meant she was safe, and that was saying a lot because living on the streets in New York wasn't exactly danger free, either. Especially with these weather conditions.

The further she walked, the quieter the streets became. The shelter was about an hour walk and set away from all the shops and people. It was all the way in Manhattan, set right in the middle of the hood, but it was the nicest shelter she had found so far and the biggest, too, which meant that she had a better chance of getting in.

Away from all the lights, noise, and people, Jade was forced to be alone with her thoughts. She tried not to wallow in self pity, but having nothing to her name or nobody to turn to left Jade lost. She couldn't pinpoint when her life had taken such a turn for the worse. Growing up, she had a wonderful childhood and great parents. As the only child, she was spoiled and doted on. Her parents were killed in a car accident a few years back, when she was only twenty-two years old, and depression seeped in.

As an up-and-coming artist, she spent her time in her loft painting her emotions away. Lonely, with no family left, she let her feelings spill out onto each canvas that sat in front of her. Painting was her solace, her escape, and it was the sole thing that got her through the depression of losing her parents.

It was at an art fair that she met her husband. He bought every piece of her art at the exhibit and then asked her on a date, which she accepted. Six months later, she was head over heels in love with him and she really believed that things were turning around for her. How wrong she was.

As she finally approached the shelter, Jade shook the thoughts from her head and groaned out loud when she noticed the line was already long as hell to get into the shelter.

"Why the hell is it so busy?" she asked nobody in particular.

The line was a block long, and she silently prayed that she could get a bed tonight. The next closest shelter was five miles away, and she didn't have a dime to her name to take a bus or a cab. It would take her entirely too long to walk to that shelter, anyway. All the beds would be taken by the time she got there, so this really was her only hope. In this weather, she would freeze her ass off if she had to spend the night in the park nearby, which she had done before, but tonight it was entirely too cold for that.

At least I came early, she thought as she found her place at the end of the line and prepared herself for a long wait.

A few minutes later, a woman around Jade's age stood in line behind her. The girl popped her gum loudly and said, "shit, ain't no way we getting up in there."

Jade turned to look at her. The woman looked like she was Latina, with light tanned skin and long curly brown hair that was pushed over one shoulder. Jade knew she was cold with her skin tight grey sweatpants and white t-shirt. She pulled her arms into her shirt in an attempt to keep warm. She was only a couple inches taller than Jade, who was five feet two inches. Her nose was bright red and Jade could have sworn that her lips were blue, but she couldn't be too sure in the dull lighting of the street lamps.

"I hope we get in. I don't know what the hell I'll do if I have to sleep out here tonight." The thought of it made tears pool in Jade's eyes, but she reminded herself that she had survived much worse. Cold weather would not break her. It couldn't.

"You and me both, sis. Shit, if I'm going to be living on the streets then I need to move my ass to California or some shit. At least it's always warm. My name is Mia, by the way."

She spoke fast with a Spanish lilt as she held her hand out for Jade to shake. Jade smiled and shook her hand. "I'm Jade."

"Jade. Cute. I used to know this girl named Jade back in high school. She was a complete puta, but you aren't her. I can tell you're way nicer than that girl. You have a soft aura about you, you know? How old are you anyway?" she asked as she hopped from foot to foot to stay warm.

"Twenty-five," Jade answered. She wasn't sure why, but she liked the fiery Latina standing before her. She was the complete opposite of Jade, who was shy and quiet, but Jade knew firsthand that it was rare as hell to find someone so friendly, especially in New York. There weren't a lot of kind people that lived here, but Mia genuinely seemed to be one of them.

"No shit? I just turned twenty-six a few weeks ago. In November. It was the worst birthday I'd ever had. I moved here from Florida a few months ago to be with my man, Kenny. He's a major baller, you know? My parents disowned me and shit because I moved here with him, but love makes you do dumb shit. Would you believe that gillipollas left me on my damn birthday? I don't have shit to my name. He moved me out here on his dime and the little bit of money I had was gone after a week of sleeping in hotels. My parents won't even answer my calls. It's some bullshit. So, here I am. Sorry, I talk a lot. Kenny hated that about me, but I'm not changing for no man. Anyway, when is your birthday?"

Jade's head was spinning. Mia was talking a mile a minute and changed subjects at the drop of a dime. It was a nice distraction for her, though. It was nice to have someone to talk to. It felt like it had been weeks since she had a normal conversation with someone.

"December 28th," Jade said and then before Mia could pick up the conversation again , she said, "I'm sorry about your parents and everything. That has to be rough."

Mia shrugged her shoulders. "Can't be any more rough than what you're going through, Chica. What's your story, anyway?"

Jade shifted uncomfortably and Mia peeped her unease. "I'm sorry. I shouldn't ask no shit like that. Just because I shared my life story with a complete stranger doesn't mean you have to."

"Let's just say I'm running from a bad situation. I don't have anyone or anything to run to...so here I am." Jade pushed her long honey brown braids over her shoulder so they hung down her back. It had been awhile since she had them touched up, so they weren't looking as neat as she preferred, but that was the least of her worries.

"Say less, mama. You're preaching to the choir. I get it," Mia said, now running in place.

The line in front of them moved, and Mia let out a small cheer. "Thank God."

"Looks like they're opening the doors early," Jade said as she peeked over the various heads in front of her, trying to get a look at the front doors.

"Good. I don't know how much longer I can stand it out here in this cold," Mia said.

Jade nodded as she cupped her hands over her mouth and blew hot air into them. The line steadily moved forward as the two women subconsciously migrated closer and closer to each other to stay warm. They watched the person in front of them sign in and head into the building when a woman stopped them from doing the same.

"Sorry, ladies. We're full tonight," She said.

"Just my fucking luck," Mia grumbled.

Jade just stood there, trying her hardest not to cry. *What the hell am I supposed to do now?* She thought as she shivered from the cold breeze that kicked up.

"Please, just wait here for a moment. We are bringing out some things to help you all out for the night," the woman said sympathetically.

Jade nodded her head while Mia huffed loudly, producing thick white clouds in front of her. A few minutes passed and two men came out carrying boxes of items and trays of sandwiches. The woman looked at Jade and Mia, but spoke loudly enough for everyone remaining in the line to hear, "I know it isn't much and it isn't the same as having a bed to sleep in, but we have some items for you all to take to help you stay warm. Coats, mittens, and hats as well as blankets and sandwiches. Please stay warm and safe tonight and we hope to help you all tomorrow."

Jade wasted no time rifling through the box of secondhand items, glad that she would at least have something more to keep her warm tonight. By the looks of it, this supply wouldn't be enough for everyone in the ever-growing line and she felt bad for them, but it was a cold world and she had to help herself first.

Finally deciding on an olive green coat in a size small that would fit her perfectly, she slipped it on and grabbed a pair of mittens, a hat and a scarf along with a blanket. The mittens were a little small for her, but again, Jade wasn't one to complain. The coat was fuzzy on the inside and she already felt warmer. She slid the hat over her braids and flipped her hood up before wrapping the scarf around her face to warm up her nose and mouth. Last, she grabbed a sandwich and a bottle of water, her stomach growling. She wanted to grab another sandwich, but the thought of all those poor people behind her in line stopped her.

Jade was about to walk away as she thought about where the hell she would sleep tonight when she stopped, remembering Mia. It felt wrong to just leave the girl without saying goodbye. In the last twenty minutes, they had really bonded, and she didn't want to be rude.

She turned around and spotted Mia walking up to her, looking much more warm with a hot pink oversized jacket on along with a hat, mittens, and a blanket wrapped around her. She was clutching a sandwich and water in her hand, and they almost fell as she approached Jade. "Shit, I am so damn clumsy. I get that from my mother. She was always tripping over her own feet or dropping something. One time, she fell down the stairs and scared my papa and I half to death. She was okay, though. Only a sprained wrist."

Jade giggled at her blabbering, feeling much better now that she was more prepared for the cold. "Where are you off to?"

"There's this place I know of. It's a few blocks from here. Kind of like a low-key safe haven for homeless people. They call it the trench. They make bonfires and shit, and the people are surprisingly nice there. We look out for our own, you know? I've stayed there a couple times when I couldn't get into the shelter, and it isn't all that bad. You should come with me, Chica. You know what they say...two is better than one."

Jade didn't have to think about it much. She hated being all alone at night while she was on the street. It was terrifying and made for long, sleepless nights. She didn't know Mia at all, but she felt she could trust her. "Okay, let's go."

They started in the opposite direction of where Jade was originally going. While they walked, they tore into their sandwiches, which turned out to be turkey and cheese. That was it. Just bread, turkey and American cheese, but both women were grateful for the food. Jade realized that this was the first thing she had eaten all day, and when she was done she was left wanting more. She had always been a small person, but the last few weeks living on the streets had left her skinnier than ever. She knew it wasn't healthy, but there wasn't anything she could do about it.

Finally, they made it to the trench which looked like it used to be a baseball field, but was now abandoned. It was kind of in the cut, set behind the King Projects, and there were dozens of people scattered around the field. A big fire was burning in the middle, and that was where the pair headed. As they walked passed, people nodded at them or offered small smiles, but mostly everyone kept to themselves.

About five feet from the large bonfire, the two women stopped, relishing in the warmth emanating from the flames. "Let's set up right here. We can use one blanket to lie on and one to put on top of us. That is, if you don't mind sharing. I don't mind, but if you do, then we can always wrap up separately," Mia spoke quickly as she looked at Jade.

Jade smiled, "I don't mind."

They got to work, making their pallet on the dirty ground.

"You don't talk much, do you?" Mia asked as they got situated on top of the blanket. They huddled close together, facing the fire. The floor was frozen solid, sending a shiver through their bodies, but the fire made up for the coldness of the ground.

"No. I pretty much just keep to myself," Jade responded.

"Well, Chica, if you ever need someone else to listen to those thoughts up there," Mia tapped Jade on her hood that was shielding her head from the cold, "then I am your girl. I talk a lot, but I never tell secrets. I'm a good listener, is all I'm saying."

Jade looked at Mia and nodded, "thanks. That means a lot to me."

Mia smiled, and Jade couldn't help but smile back at her. Jade noticed for the first time how gorgeous Mia was, despite being homeless. The light from the fire illuminated her features. She had big hazel eyes and a cute button nose. Her hair was thick and curly, held down from the hat on top of her head. Her skin was smooth and perfect, and her lips were full and pouty. Jade wondered how beautiful she would look after a hot shower, some makeup, and a brush for her hair. Not only that, but Mia's whole personality was magnetic. Jade couldn't understand how Mia could be in the position she was in and keep such high spirits. Granted, Jade made it a point to never complain, but that didn't mean she was in a good mood day in and day out. Her situation was shitty, and it didn't seem like it would get better anytime soon.

"No problem, girl. Now, I'm tired as hell from all the walking I did today. I'm going to get some shuteye. Be warned, I snore. Not like, loud, but my ex hated it, anyway. I hope you don't mind," Mia chirped as she laid down.

"No, I don't mind," Jade smiled down at her before laying down beside her.

The two laid side by side, facing each other as they listened to the quiet chatter around them and the crackle of the fire. It didn't take long for them to drift off to sleep.

CHAPTER 2

NOAH BENNETT HAD BEEN POURING OVER DESIGNS FOR SEVERAL hours without a break, which wasn't unusual. He was only thirty years old, and he owned one of the top architecture firms in New York. He didn't achieve that status from being lazy. Noah worked seven days a week and no less than eighty hours a week. He was the best at what he did because of the hard work that he had put into it. His family and friends were always on him about living more and working less, but to Noah, his career was his life.

Being the youngest black man to own a successful architecture firm in New York made the journey ten times harder for him than his competitors. Noah sacrificed a lot to get in this position, and he found that he had to continue sacrificing in order to stay on top. That meant long days, sometimes sleepless nights, and no social life. The only reason that he and his best friend, Kenyon, still saw each other was because Kenyon worked at the firm.

Noah and Kenyon had been friends since Junior high school. They were thick as thieves and always getting into trouble. They were just two knucklehead outcasts that found friendship in each other. Their main common interest was drawing. They would fill notebook after notebook with their artworks, comparing and collaborating on each piece. As they grew older, their interests shifted slightly. They both still loved to draw, but instead of cartoon characters they drew houses and buildings. Each time they put their pencil to paper, they created amazing structures that rivaled the ones they walked past every day on their way to school. All throughout high school they had an ongoing competition on who could draw the best house. The drawings were endless and were comprised of exterior and interior layouts.

In the end, the day before graduation, the pair agreed that Noah had the best design in all four years they had the competition going. The house was beautiful and sprawled across a breathtaking plot of land. The outside was a baby blue color with white trim, and double doors graced the front. There was a long winding driveway that opened up to the wrap-around porch. The backyard had a stone path that led to an outdoor kitchen with a brick oven stove and grills, and of course there was a swimming pool.

Inside, there were two levels and an underground basement that served as a home theater. There was a skyway that separated the upstairs. On one side was the master suite with a bedroom and walk-in shower with a jacuzzi. On that side of the house there were also his and hers closets that were the sizes of full rooms. Noah even went as far as to layout the shelving and shoe racks for the closets. On the other side of the upper level there were four more bedrooms, all with their own three quarter bathrooms.

On the main level was the kitchen, dining room, living room, workout room, half bathroom, laundry room and a man cave. The house was off the chain, and Noah still had those drawings. When the two went off to Columbia for college, they majored in architecture and Noah vowed that he would build that house one day when the time was right. For now, it was too much house for just him to live in.

Where Noah was motivated, Kenyon was lazy as hell. Noah did

exceptionally well in school while Kenyon barely made it. When Noah started his architecture firm, Kenyon was extremely supportive, but he wanted no parts in running it alongside Noah, like Noah had originally suggested. Don't get it twisted, Kenyon loved the finer things in life and he was willing to work to get what he wanted, but he would do the bare minimum.

Aside from Kenyon, the only other people in Noah's life were his younger brother, Roman, and his mother. They were the only family he had, and he loved them both dearly. Mrs. Darlene Bennett was a tough cookie, and even more so when the boys' father passed away several years earlier because of a senseless act of violence. Always the hero, Murphy Bennett intervened when he saw a man beating on a woman on the street and got himself killed in the process. The woman lived, and the man went to jail, but the Bennett's were left with a gaping hole in their family. Since then, Darlene made sure that her boys stayed on the right path and that they didn't end up another statistic. In Darlene's mind, her only job in life was to make sure that her boys were successful black men. Nothing more, nothing less. She really was a sweetheart, though. Now that she was retired, she filled her time hosting charity events and traveling when she wasn't spending time with her boys.

Roman was the baby of the family and a troublemaker. He was the one that Darlene had to constantly keep her eye on. She knew that he was into illegal activities, and she tried daily to set him on the right path. Not that he was a bad person, but the streets constantly called his name. They were alluring to him and there wasn't anyone, not even his mother or his older brother, that could deter him from doing what he wanted. He was smart, though, and made sure to only associate with real bosses of the streets. Nobody knew for sure what he did, but his family knew that he was careful and that was all they could ask of him at this point.

As closed off as Noah had become trying to run a successful business, he always made time for his family. Those three were the only people in the world that kept him sane, and that was saying a lot because each and every one of them was a handful in their own ways. Kenyon was a certified playa that had a different woman in his bed every night. Not only that, but the nigga cracked jokes and played all damn day. Mrs. Bennett was overbearing and protective, damn near trying to run Noah's life, and Roman was hard-headed as hell.

"Yolanda, bring me the Anderson file!" Noah belted from his office.

A moment later a tall slim woman with skin the color of dark chocolate and as smooth as satin came rushing in. "Here you go, Noah."

Noah glanced up at her quickly as she set the file on his desk before looking back down at the stack of papers in front of him. "Thank you."

"You are so welcome," Yolanda purred as she eyed Noah.

It was no secret that Yolanda was crushing on her boss, and it was also no secret that Noah never gave her the time of day. He barely paid her any mind and never gave her any indication that he was attracted to her. Yolanda was a very attractive woman with slanted brown eyes, a thing straight nose and heart-shaped lips, but Noah didn't have time for dating, and that was exactly what Yolanda wanted from him. He would also never date an employee. That was bad for business, and his business meant everything to him. He'd talked to Yolanda about her mannerisms around him and how he expected her to keep the flirting for after work and with someone that wasn't him. He was very blunt and straight to the point, so there was nothing else for Yolanda to do besides agree with him.

Noah monitored her, though, and would have her demoted to an admin for one of his other architects if she stepped out of line. It wouldn't be the first time he'd had to to it. Like clockwork, his administrative assistants all had to be demoted or fired for their inappropriate behavior. His first assistant was transferred for repeatedly asking him out on dates. His second assistant admitted that she was in love with him after working for him for two years. Noah was surprised because she was never anything but professional, and he told her he didn't feel the same. She quit out of humiliation. He hired a male the next time around, but he was fired after making a pass at Noah. Kenyon never let Noah live that one down, clowning him for not being able to tell the man was gay. Before Yolanda, Noah hired an older lady who was happily married, but she was fired when Noah walked into his office one morning to her sitting on his desk butt ass naked.

It wasn't hard to understand why this kept happening. Noah was handsome as hell and could grace the cover of a GQ magazine with ease. His milk chocolate colored skin was smooth and blemish free. His black hair was always cut in a caesar and lined to perfection. His goatee was trimmed close to his face and always looked freshly lined. His almond-shaped eyes were brown, and his lips were big and full. He was six feet tall and the early morning trips to the gym gave him a muscular build. The one thing that set Noah apart from other niggas was his style. He would never be caught in public without a custom suit, and with every suit, he had a fly ass pair of sunglasses to go with it. It was his signature, and the ladies damn near drooled at the sight of him. Some actually did.

He was definitely the most eligible in New York, but the only problem was, he wasn't looking to date. He'd tried a relationship once, and it ended in disaster. His ex girlfriend, Alana, was too needy and far too clingy. She didn't understand that Noah was trying to run an empire and that it took a lot of his attention. Alana became borderline obsessed with Noah, which only drove him further away until he finally broke it off with her. That had been five years ago, and he was content with never going down that road again.

"Do you need anything else, boss?" Yolanda asked.

"No, you can go for the day. I'll be here late," Noah said, never taking his eyes off the papers on his desk.

"Okay, but don't forget you're hosting that charity dinner at the women's shelter tonight," she said.

"Shit, I forgot. Thanks for reminding me. What time is that at?" Noah asked as he looked at the time on his phone.

"Five," Yolanda said. "I can accompany you if you'd like?"

Noah looked up at her, "that won't be necessary. I'll have Kenyon come with."

Yolanda fought the urge to sigh out loud as she walked out of his office. *One day I will get his ass*, she thought as she gathered her things from her desk and made her way towards the elevator.

Noticing that he only had an hour to get to the shelter, Noah shut down his computer and grabbed his briefcase, tossing his phone and wallet inside. He grabbed his coat and then sunglasses off their holder on his desk and flipped the lights off in his large office with floor to ceiling windows. The view was spectacular, and he got his best work done when he stared out at the New York streets, vying for inspiration.

He stepped to the office next to him and knocked before entering. Sitting with his feet on his desk, Kenyon was staring at his computer and laughing, not bothering to look up at his friend. Noah smirked and shook his head when he saw that Kenyon was watching Kevin Hart's latest stand up special on his laptop. "Come on, man. We have to go to that charity dinner for the women's shelter."

Kenyon glanced up at Noah, "Can't. I'm working."

Noah walked behind the desk and slapped Kenyon on the back of his head, "Get your ass up, fool. You told me you would come with me."

Kenyon rubbed the back of his head and sighed, "Fine, man. Just give me a second."

Noah watched in amusement as Kenyon dragged his feet off his desk and begrudgingly shut down his computer before gathering his things.

"You're a fool," Noah chuckled.

"Yo mama," Kenyon joked as they walked towards the elevator.

"I'm telling her you said that shit, too," Noah said.

"Aw shit, man. Why you gotta do me like that?" Kenyon asked. "Mama Darlene will tear my behind up."

Noah grinned, "That's what I was hoping for."

Kenyon grabbed at his heart and acted offended as the pair stepped off the elevator and onto the busy streets of New York. A company car was waiting for them outside of the Bennett & Co. building. They got inside and cracked jokes the entire way to the women's shelter.

CHAPTER 3

"I'M FREEZING MY ASS OFF," MIA COMPLAINED. "WHEN ARE they going to let us in?"

Jade shrugged her shoulders, "I don't know. You're the one that insisted we come here instead of to going to apply for more jobs."

Mia rolled her eyes, "Because! When was the last time we had a hot meal?"

"We just had some McDonald's yesterday morning, remember?" Jade asked, exasperated.

"I'm not talking about no damn McDonald's," Mia sucked her teeth. "You know Tessa from the trench?"

Jade nodded her head as she adjusted her scarf on her neck while Mia continued, "She told me that every year some big wig throws this big ass dinner and it's off the chain. Food fit for a queen! I'm talking ham, turkey, mashed potatoes, mac and cheese, and greens. The works. They don't turn anyone away and you can have as much as you want. It's like the food is endless or some shit. You know I'm going for seconds *and* thirds. Shit, I'll sneak some in my pockets, too."

Jade's mouth watered. She hadn't eaten that well in over a month. Her and Mia had been attached at the hip for the past couple of weeks and had become fast friends. They shared everything and looked out for one another. They were glad they'd found each other because it made being homeless a little more bearable. Sticking together had been a good choice, and the two found it a little more easy being homeless with a friend by their side.

"And," Mia sang as she danced around, "I heard the brother that hosts this every year is fine as hell. Apparently he mingles with the women as they eat."

"Girl, I am not worried about nobody's nigga. I just want to eat and then apply to a couple more places before the sun sets," Jade replied sternly.

"Give it a rest, sis. We already put in dozens of applications today. The sun will be down by the time we get done eating, anyway. Chill," Mia scoffed.

"Fine, but tomorrow morning we are waking up early to check in on our applications and to fill out more," Jade warned.

"Whatever," Mia waved her off. She wasn't worried about that when she was about to eat good as hell and go to bed on a full stomach tonight. That was all that mattered to her in that moment.

Ten minutes later, the doors to the shelter finally opened. Mia made sure that she and Jade were there early as hell so they would be one of the first ones in line, and they were. Grabbing Jade by the arm and squealing in her ear, Mia shouted, "Ohhh I bet that's him, Jade. He is fine as hell. That has to be him! Oh my God and look at the man next to him. Those are some fine ass men, Jade. You can't tell me they aren't. Look how they're dressed! Money is dripping off them."

Jade wasn't paying attention to anything Mia was yapping about. Her eyes were locked on the handsome stranger in front of her as he gazed at her. He had the most beautiful eyes that Jade had ever seen. They were kind and framed with the longest lashes Jade had ever seen. Mia was right, everything about him screamed money, and that intimidated Jade. While he was decked out in the finest threads, she was sporting the same disgusting clothes she had been wearing for a month and hand-me-down winter gear with a dirty blanket wrapped around her shoulders. Despite the cold air, Jade felt her cheeks warm and diverted her gaze, embarrassed. She could still feel the strange man staring at her, and when she glanced back in his direction, he spoke out loud to the crowd while still looking at her.

"Ladies, thank you so much for coming. We have some good food here for you tonight and some goodie bags to take when you leave. Please, eat as much as you want and enjoy the warmth of the shelter for the next few hours. For those of you that cannot get inside, we have a tent outback with warming heaters for overflow. Think of this as a party. Mingle, dance, eat, and just have a good time."

The women in line cheered and some of them whistled and shouted out their compliments to the man, Mia included. Jade stood still, avoiding the strangers stares. When he moved to the side and held his arm out for the ladies to enter, Jade walked past him and got a good whiff of his cologne. It turned her legs into jelly, but she refused to react as Mia grabbed her arm and made a beeline towards the buffet.

"Holy shit, Mouse," Mia said, calling Jade by a nickname she'd come up with a few days ago, due to Jade's shyness. "This looks better than I ever imagined."

She grabbed a plate and began piling it high with everything on the long buffet table, and Jade did the same, not really paying attention to what Mia was saying as she babbled on. "And there's cornbread? Oh! And rolls? Oh, my God. I think I love that man. My mama used to cook her cornbread just like this with little corn all up in it. Jade, look at the mashed potatoes! Look at all that melted butter right on top!"

Mia was like a damn kid in a candy store, but who could blame her? This shit right here was rare as hell for homeless people. The best they got was the occasional fast food and even that could get tiring, but it was better than nothing, which was what they got most days. A big fat serving of nothing. On those days, Mia and Jade would huddle together and talk more than usual to keep their minds off the hunger pains. Those were the days they bonded the most, huddled together and thwarting off the cold. It was them against the world on those days as they lifted each other's spirits and kept each other warm.

When they were done filling their plates and getting their drinks, they scoped out an empty table near the food and sat down. They dug into their food, and before long a few more women joined their table and even a little girl. Jade's heart broke at the sight of the small child who was huddled up against her mother. The girl ate happily though, and Jade could tell that this food was sure to make a change in everyone's mood. There was something about a good meal that made everything okay, at least, until the hunger pains returned.

They were about halfway finished with their second plates, laughter ringing through the room along with Christmas music playing softly in the background, when the man hosting the event came to their table and sat down. Jade had just taken a big bite of stuffing when she saw the handsome man from earlier sit beside her. She almost choked on her food and she coughed loudly as Mia patted her on the back, "Damn, Mouse. Slow down before you get sick."

"Mouse?" The handsome man grinned down at Jade.

Jade quickly swallowed the rest of her food and then peered up at him. "That isn't my real name. It's just a stupid nickname my friend gave me. My name is Jade."

"Jade, that's beautiful. Do you have a last name, Ms. Jade?" He smiled so sweetly, and it made Jade blush.

"Lawrence," she replied.

"Jade Lawrence. It's nice to meet you. I'm Noah Bennett," he stuck his large hand out to shake hers.

She slipped her dainty hand into his and shook it. She smiled at the warm embrace and Jade's cheeks flushed to a deeper red.

"Nice to meet you, too. Thank you for all this," she said, gesturing to the food on her plate.

He simply nodded his head with a smile and asked, "Why Mouse?"

Before Jade could respond, Mia jumped in. "Oh, that's easy. She's quiet and just as shy as a damn mouse. I told this girl my whole life story the first day I met her, but I barely know anything about her. Not the good stuff, anyway. It's okay, though. She's a great listener and the best friend I ever had. Even though I've only known her for a few weeks. She isn't like other bitches, jealous and manipulating. She's as sweet as they come and all about her business, too. She's a real go-getter. You might not think it because, well, we're here, but you can't ever judge a book by its cover. That's what my mama taught me, anyway. Do you know that she made my ass apply to fifteen jobs today? In one damn day. Who does that?"

The more Mia talked, the more Jade blushed. Noah was hanging onto Mia's every word. He wasn't sure why, but he wanted to know more about the pretty girl with the long honey blond braids. When he first saw her outside, she was completely covered from head to toe in winter gear, but her eyes caught his attention. They were big and brown and held so much pain and sadness that he wanted to hug her and tell her that everything would be okay. He refrained, though. He didn't want to scare the young lady away, especially since she was about to get a nice hot meal. There was no telling what she had been through, and a simple hug from a stranger might send her running for the hills.

When they were outside, Kenyon joked around with the crowd of ladies as they passed by and into the building. Noah stood there and smiled pleasantly, half listening to Kenyon as he conversed with the women. He had a way of making them feel welcome and beautiful, even in their situation. It was one reason Noah brought him along every year. Kenyon had his faults, but he was a crowd-pleaser and knew the right things to say in any situation.

When the building was at full capacity, Noah led the remaining ladies around the back where there was a huge tent with another buffet of food. The outside heaters made it so it didn't even feel like it was only twenty degrees outside. Every year he splurged on this event. He had never been homeless before, but that didn't mean he couldn't empathize with what these ladies went through. He had a good life, and he knew he was blessed, so because of that, he wanted to be a blessing to others. His parents had taught him and his brother early on to always do what they could to give back to others less fortunate than them. Both Noah and his brother lived by that to this day, and this was only one of several events that his firm put on for people in need each year.

After mingling with the ladies outside for a while, Noah made his way inside and instantly spotted the woman from earlier. She'd taken her coat off and was eating next to her friend, not saying much, but nodding every once in a while, which told Noah that she was paying attention. Without her coat on, he could see that she was a tiny little thing. Her white long-sleeved shirt hung loose off her body, and her light colored jeans were baggy on her slight frame. Her braids hung down her back and almost to her ass, and when she turned her head up in laughter at something her friend said, he noticed how beautiful she was.

Her eyes crinkled, and her full lips turned up, showcasing her perfectly straight teeth. Even without makeup, she was the most beautiful woman he had ever seen. He'd had several flings with women in the past few years, but none of them put him in a trance the way this woman had. He didn't know what it was about her, but he knew that he wanted to know more about her. Noah stared at her as she ate until Kenyon clapped him on the back, "You gonna get out there and mingle, or what? I'm trying to get this thing over with. I got a hot date tonight."

"Man, you have a hot date every damn night," Noah grinned at his best friend.

"Don't hate the playa, hate the game." Kenyon popped his collar and grinned slyly as he looked around the room.

"Who the hell does that shit anymore?" Noah laughed.

"Me, nigga," Kenyon replied confidently. "Now, let's go talk to some ladies. I see a couple fine ones in here tonight."

Noah chuckled and led his friend into the crowd. He made a beeline towards the woman's table and Kenyon went in the opposite direction. Now that he was sitting at their table, he was happy he came to chat with them first. Her friend talked a lot, but he didn't mind because she was giving him more information about Jade than he thought he would ever know. Noah laughed when Jade and Mia began bickering back and forth.

"Why are you telling all my business," Jade hissed under her breath, but Noah could still hear her.

Mia waved her off, "Girl, there ain't shit to tell. I don't know enough of your business to tell it."

Noah watched as Jade shook her head slightly and turned back to him, "Sorry about her. She really doesn't know when to shut up."

"I don't mind," he smirked down at her. "You know, my company has a couple of job openings, if you're interested," He lied.

He didn't have any openings in his company, and he wasn't sure why he was telling them he did. Scratch that. He knew exactly why he was spewing bullshit from his mouth. He wanted to see her again. He wasn't sure what it was about her that had him so captivated, but he was damn sure ready to find out. Now all she needed to do was say yes to his offer.

Jade perked up instantly. It was so hard getting a job with no contact information. She had to physically go back to each place she applied to and check on the status of her applications. It made for long days and a lot of walking. Mia complained the whole time, but Jade knew she was just as desperate to get a job as she was. Their first goal was to get a little place to share. It didn't have to be all that, just somewhere they could feel safe. Somewhere to call their own, and they figured that two incomes would be better than one, so they vowed to move in together as soon as they could.

"What kind of job?" Mia asked skeptically. As much as she talked, she wasn't one to trust so easily. She was the type to talk someone in circles but shut all the way down if it meant getting her hopes up. Her ex and her parents taught her that even the people that were supposed to love you the most could turn their backs on you at the drop of a dime. If Noah was offering jobs to two homeless women he didn't even know, you better be damn sure Mia would find out what the catch was.

"A couple of my agents need assistants. It's office work, like handling schedules, taking phone calls, emails...stuff like that," Noah responded.

Jade looked hesitant. "I've never had an office job before."

She cast her eyes down and played with the food on her plate. The only work she had ever known was her art. She used to be a free spirit that way. Living off her creations and setting her own schedule. It was crazy how much that had changed. Now, here she was, looking for work and not having any experience. She felt stuck, and it was getting a bit discouraging.

Seeing sadness seep into her eyes, Noah wanted to take his finger and nudge her chin up so she was looking at him. Instead he quickly said, "It's okay. They are both entry-level positions."

"So," Mia eyed him, "you're just handing out jobs to anyone?"

Noah chuckled, "Nah, it isn't like that. I'm just trying to help my sistah's out."

"There are plenty of sistah's in this place. Why us?" Mia asked.

"I see potential in you," Noah responded. He was speaking to them both, but his eyes were dead set on Jade and as she picked her head up to look at him, she gave him a weak smile.

"When can we start?" she asked quietly.

"How's tomorrow?"

CHAPTER 4

"Come on, Mia. We're almost there," Jade said as she crossed the street, looking behind her to make sure Mia was keeping up. The two women had been up early as hell so they could make the long trek from the shelter to their new job in lower Manhattan. They were lucky enough to have been one of the first people at the shelter last night, because it guaranteed them a spot to stay the night.

Noah wanted them to be at work at nine in the morning, which meant they had to wake up at six so they could start their two-hour walk. Their feet were killing them, but they knew it would all be worth it in just a few weeks when they got their first checks. Maybe then they could splurge on an Uber from time to time when they were too tired to walk.

"Come on, let's go in here," Jade gestured to the McDonald's restaurant they were walking up on. Mia followed her friend inside, thankful for the warm air that greeted her, and they both ducked into the bathroom and locked the door behind them.

"I'm fucking cold," Mia complained. Her nose was red and running, and she was shaking from the chilling temperatures outside.

Jade looked at her sympathetically, "I know, Mimi. It'll be worth it, though. Aren't you excited to have somewhere warm to stay all day long? And don't forget about the checks."

Mia nodded, "You're right, but can we please try to find a shelter that's closer tonight? I don't think I can make that walk again."

Jade thought about it for a moment as she slid her backpack off her shoulders, "Yeah, you're right. As soon as I get in front of a computer today, I'll look up some other places to go. The shelter from last night was nice, but I don't think it's worth the walk."

"Cool," Mia said, and it didn't miss Jade that she wasn't her normal talkative self.

"You good?" Jade asked quietly as she slipped off her dirty white shirt.

"Yeah. I'm just tired as hell already, and our shift hasn't even started. Living on the streets is hard as hell, Jade. I haven't had a good nights sleep in weeks because my guard is constantly up and don't get me started on the walking. My damn feet are one big ass blister at this point." She plopped down right on the filthy floor and put her hands in her head as tears slipped out of her eyes. "I'm just fucking tired."

Jade was on the verge of tears herself because everything Mia was saying resonated with her. She was tired, too, and she also couldn't remember the last time she had slept through the night. Both physically and emotionally, Jade was exhausted. Most days, the women would talk to distract themselves from their problems. They would joke around and laugh, and when it was too damn cold to even speak, they would hold hands or lean on each other. Those silent forms of communication, when times were really hard, became the only thing that kept them sane. It had only been a few weeks, but they'd formed a friendship that bonded them for life. It was strange how being with someone at their lowest moments could bond you to them in a way that others wouldn't understand. Mia was the rock that Jade needed to keep pushing forward, and Mia felt the same. It was by pure fate that the women met, and they were happy they had.

With only her dirty bra, pants and shoes on, Jade sunk to her knees in front of Mia, ignoring how gross the floor was and the stench coming from one of the stalls. Jade lifted Mia's chin, so she was looking into her eyes. "Mimi, you have to be strong, sis. Today is the first day of our new beginning. I know you're tired. So am I, but we have to keep fighting. I need you to push through this with me. One foot in front of the other, okay?"

Mia took a deep breath and wiped her tears before nodding her head, "Okay."

Jade stood up and held out her hand to help Mia up as she grinned, "Besides, we have some new clothes to try on."

Mia's eyes lit up. As if the food weren't enough last night, Noah organized a clothing drive, so the women had brand new clothes, shoes, and plenty of other accessories and toiletries to choose from. The selections were endless and even after each woman taking as much as she wanted, there were things left over that the shelter held onto for other women that would come by. Mr. Bennett's generosity floored jade, and it touched her heart that he was kind enough to do all of this for women he didn't even know. She would forever be grateful to him for offering her and Mia a job, and she vowed to do something nice for him when she got her first check.

The two women quickly peeled off their clothes and shoved them in the bottom of their large backpacks. They made quick work of running the warm water and taking bird baths in the sinks with dove body wash before putting on deodorant. Jade washed Mia's hair with the shampoo and conditioner they had been given the night before. Mia opted to part her hair on the side and let her hair air dry while Jade threw her long braids into a professional-looking bun at the top of her head. Feeling clean for the first time in weeks, Jade smiled at herself in the mirror after washing her face and brushing her teeth.

"Come on, Mouse. We're going to be late," Mia hurried Jade, breaking her out of her trance.

Jade noticed that Mia was already dressed in some plain black slacks and a black turtleneck with a pair of black flats to match. It wasn't exactly business chic, but it was the best they could do with what they had and to Jade, she looked stunning. Above anything else, they were ecstatic to have something else to wear aside from the same dirty shit they had on for weeks.

Jade carefully pulled out her outfit of choice along with a fresh pair of panties. She had to wear the same bra, and she cringed when she put it back on her clean body, but she really couldn't complain. She had three new outfits and five new pairs of panties, along with toiletries and a big backpack to carry everything in. She was happy as hell and couldn't nothing steal her shine today. She quickly put on her black leggings and grey sweater dress along with an identical pair of black flats that Mia had on.

"Okay, I'm ready," Jade said as she put her coat back on and packed up the last of her things.

"Let's go, then," Mia said as she unlocked the door and pushed her way out of the bathroom.

Any other day, the smell of the fast food would have had Jade's mouth watering, but since she ate so well last night, she surprisingly still felt full, and she was thankful for that. She glanced at a clock that hung on the wall and saw that they only had ten minutes to make it to work.

"Come on, Mimi. We're going to have to walk fast," Jade said as she zipped her coat up to her mouth.

They made quick work of the few blocks to the Bennett & Co building with only two minutes to spare, huffing and puffing from the brisk walk. When they pushed through the doors to the building, they were thankful for the blast of heat that welcomed them. Their feet were frozen from the flimsy flats and Jade's ears were cold as hell too, since her big ass bun wouldn't fit under her hat or in her hood.

"Hi, ladies. How can I help you?" A pretty blonde haired girl with blue eyes asked from behind the reception counter. Jade noticed that the plaque on her desk read *Lyla Walker*.

"Hi, we are here for our first day. I'm Jade and this is Mia," Jade gestured at herself and then towards Mia.

Lyla smiled warmly and was about to speak when the elevator

dinged from behind them and a baritone voice said, "Jade, Mia. Happy you could make it, and right on time, too."

Noah checked his watch as he strode towards the women, smiling. Jade noticed that the same man that was with him last night was trailing along behind Noah with his hands in his pockets and a smile on his face.

"Hi, Mr. Bennett. How are you this morning?" Jade asked as she extended her hand towards him.

He laughed as he took her hand, loving the feel of it in his own. "I'm doing well, Jade. How are you?"

"I'm great," she smiled.

Noah noticed that her hands were as cold as ice and her face was red. She even shivered a bit before he let go of her hand from his embrace. His brows furrowed as he wondered if they had walked all the way from the shelter to get here this morning. He silently cursed himself for not thinking to have a car pick them. He'd tossed and turned last night, not able to sleep in his five thousand dollar bed knowing that Jade was sleeping in some shelter, or even worse, on the streets. As soon as he saw her, something in him wanted to protect her and he was already failing.

As Noah beat himself up, Kenyon held out his hand to Mia, "Good morning, Ladies. I didn't get the chance to meet you last night. I'm Kenyon Hughes."

"Hi, Mr. Hughes. Are you Mr. Bennett's partner?" Mia asked, eying the tall handsome man with a smile on her face.

Kenyon chuckled, "Oh, no. I'm just his best friend and his best architect. This whole place is all his."

"He's half right about that," Noah smirked.

"Which half did I get wrong? Being your best friend or best architect?" Kenyon playfully elbowed Noah and everyone laughed.

"Don't mind him, ladies. He was always the class clown and not much has changed since we graduated," Noah chuckled as he turned and gestured towards the elevators. "Shall we get started? I'd like to give you a tour and then we can get started on your paperwork."

"Sounds good," Mia chirped as they followed the two men onto the elevator.

The building had fifteen floors, and they stopped at every one of them. Kenyon and Mia talked the whole time, making everyone laugh, which was good because Jade was feeling extremely nervous for some reason. With each floor they stopped on and every new person she met, she felt more and more out of place and underdressed. She knew nothing about architecture, so the terms being thrown around intimidated her. Everyone was nice, though, which put her at ease, but only a little.

Then there was Noah. She could feel his eyes on her whenever they were in the elevator, and she tried hard not to look at him. She sneaked a few glances when he was talking to an employee or joking around with Kenyon, though. He was wearing another suit that fit him to perfection. This one was black with a navy blue button up underneath. She noticed a pair of Ray Bans peeking out of his suit breast pocket and his ears were gleaming with diamonds. He was fly as hell and so damn sexy. It was intimidating to Jade, and she almost felt ashamed to even be in his presence.

"Alright, floor fourteen is our company cafeteria. It's available to all employees during work hours. They serve everything from tacos, and pizza to a fried chicken dinners. There are snacks and drinks available over there for free," he pointed to the right where two employees were digging through the bags of chips and cookies and grabbing drinks from the coolers. "For any food you get from here, you can pay with cash or have it taken out of your paycheck. Just a little perk for my employees and I might be biased, but the food is pretty good, too."

Jade and Mia glanced at each other slyly and grinned. This place was like a sanctuary for them. Nice and warm and they could eat on a daily basis? Shit, at this rate they might never leave.

"This place is so nice. Did you design it yourself?" Jade asked.

Noah nodded. "I did. With Kenyon's help."

"You two are very talented," Mia said. "Maybe Jade can help if you ever need any ideas or something. She's an artist. I guess it's different from what you guys do, but I'd like to think art and architecture go hand in hand. I wish I could draw. I can't, though. I'm convinced I don't have a creative bone in my body. I'm good with numbers. Always have been."

The group moved back towards the elevator, and Noah hit the button signaling it. Mia and Kenyon were engrossed in a conversation about math as Noah turned towards Jade, "You're an artist?"

Jade smiled and gave a polite nod. "I am, but Mia was right. It's nothing like what you do. I mostly paint. I mean, I used to anyway."

Her smile fading, Jade thought about how long it had been since she picked up a paintbrush and made something beautiful on a blank canvas. Painting was her solace. Her escape. It had been since she was young and her heart ached from being without it for so long, especially in such a dark time.

Noah noticed the frown on her face and wondered what caused it. Then Noah realized how he would feel without his drawing pad and pencils. He couldn't remember a time where he wasn't able to draw for comfort or escape, or even just for fun. If she was as into painting as much as he was into drawing, then he could understand where that frown had come from.

"I'd love to see some of your work sometime," Noah said and then cringed when her frown deepened. He could have kicked himself for being so stupid. He didn't know what her living conditions were, but if she was at the shelter the night before, he was willing to bet that she didn't have a home. If she didn't have a home, she probably didn't have any of her artwork just hanging around.

"Maybe someday," she whispered down at the floor, but Noah could tell she didn't mean it. Thankfully, the elevator dinged, breaking the awkward moment between the two.

"Ahh and now for the fifteenth floor. The executive floor, or as I like to call it, the good-looking people only floor," Kenyon grinned as they piled onto the elevator and went up a level.

When the doors opened, both Mia and Jade were in awe. The top level differed completely from the rest of the building. The natural light that filtered in from the floor to ceiling windows gave it a different feel. Jade looked up and noticed that they made the ceiling of thick industry cut glass. It was breathtaking.

There were just a handful of offices through the vast open space with a reception desk in the middle. A beautiful dark-skinned woman with high cheekbones and a long weave ponytail was sitting right behind the desk eying Jade and Mia as they stepped out of the elevator.

"Hey, Noah. Kenyon. And who do we have here?" The woman arched a perfect eyebrow and looked between Jade and Mia.

"Yolanda, this is Mia and Jade," Noah said, gesturing to the two women. "Mia is Kenyon's new assistant and Jade will work closely with you as my other assistant. I have a lot of new jobs coming on and it'll be very busy around here."

Jade noticed that Yolanda slit her eyes at her just a fraction of an inch before turning a smile on Kenyon, "I thought you didn't want an assistant."

Kenyon shrugged, "I didn't, but I think Mia will be a great asset to the company. Now, if you all will excuse me, I have a couple of phone calls to make. Mia, please knock on my door when you are finished with your paperwork."

Mia nodded and gave Kenyon a little wave. There was a conference room next to the reception desk and Noah gestured towards it. Mia and Jade made their way into the room as Noah asked Yolanda to bring the new hire packets in that were sitting on his desk, along with some bottled waters.

Jade and Mia took off their winter gear and laid it across the backs of their chairs before sitting down and getting comfortable with their backpacks at their feet. On the other side of the table Noah noticed they were wearing new clothes, and he smiled realizing they were from the clothes drive he had as a surprise to the women at the shelter with last night. His heart warmed knowing that he could help so many people last night. Seeing Jade in brand new clothing did something to him. She had been beautiful before, but now she was stunning, and that was saying a lot because she was still wearing the bare minimum and no makeup with braids that needed to be touched up weeks ago. Still, she was breathtaking in his eyes, and Noah had been around a lot of women. He'd had sex with supermodels and fashion icons, and none of them held a candle to Jade's beauty.

Yolanda came into the conference room with the items that Noah requested and frowned. Noah was staring at Jade as she and Mia chatted happily back and forth. It wasn't the fact that he was looking at her, but how he was looking at her. His features softened as he looked at her, and he had a smile playing at the corner of his lips. Yolanda whipped her head back towards Jade and realized that the heffa didn't even notice that Noah's fine ass was checking her out. Noah was so engrossed in their conversation that he hadn't heard Yolanda enter the room. She cleared her throat once, and then again when he didn't look up.

Startled, Noah finally realized Yolanda was in the room as he pried his eyes off Jade and looked up at his assistant. "Thank you, Yolanda. Please close the door on your way out."

"Are you sure you don't need me to stay? I can take notes." Yolanda replied. She wasn't trying to go back to her damn desk so she could pretend to work. She wanted to stay her ass right in this room and figure out who this Jade person was.

"No," Noah shook his head. "This isn't that kind of meeting. Please finish getting the Pennington file together and make copies of the contracts. We'll be finished here soon."

Steaming with envy, Yolanda turned on her heels and closed the office door. She would be damned if some broke bitch came up in here and took what she had been working so hard to get for the past year. Noah was one hell of a catch and one that she planned on capturing herself. She didn't need this two dollar hooker coming in and fucking up her groove.

Yolanda had fallen in love with Noah the first day she met him. He clarified that he didn't date employee's, but she wasn't trying to hear that. She cooled it on all the flirting because she didn't want to get fired, but she knew that Noah would eventually give in to her. It was only a matter of time.

She sat back down at her desk and tapped her foot impatiently, staring straight through the glass walls of the conference room at Jade. *Who the hell are you?* She wondered. She didn't know the answer to that question, but she was damn sure going to find out.

Inside the conference room, Mia and Jade began filling out their paperwork. They were thankful that they each had two forms of ID, although Jade was a little nervous to use hers. When she handed her driver's license and social security card over to Noah to make copies, he scrunched up his face.

"It says here that your last name is Willis. I thought you told me it was Lawrence last night?" Noah asked. He knew he remembered correctly because there was no way in hell he would forget her name.

"Willis?" Mia asked with the same scrunched up expression on her face as Noah had on his.

Jade's whole face got red, and she began to sweat. "Willis is my married name."

"Married?" Mia and Noah asked in unison as Jade cringed.

"We're...separated. It's complicated, but is there any way that I can go by Lawrence here?" Jade asked in a panic. Using her married last name would make it too easy to find her. She couldn't be found. She needed to stay low key and hidden.

Noah noticed the panic on her face and wondered what it was all about, but he nodded. "Yeah, that isn't a problem. Just fill the paperwork out however you want and I'll make it work. Don't worry about it."

He passed her ID and social security card back to her without making the copies and Jade stared up into his eyes and after a moment, she nodded, feeling relieved. She looked down at the paperwork in front of her and whispered, "thank you."

"No problem. Mia, are you okay with your name as it is?" Noah asked, wanting to be sure. He did not understand what situation these ladies were in, but if he could help, he would.

"Hell yeah! I mean, yeah," she blushed as Jade glared at her for using that kind of language in front of their boss. "My last name is Reyes and I am proud of it."

Noah chuckled, "Cool. I'll be right back."

As soon as the door closed behind him, Mia whirled around on Jade.

"Married? You're married?" She screeched.

Jade cringed before hissing, "Not now, Mia. Please."

"Okay, but you better fucking believe I will ask again later. I can't believe you're married. I want to know all the details. Where the hell is he, anyway?" she gasped. "Oh, God. Don't tell me he's dead. Oh, you poor baby. No wonder you barely talk about yourself."

Jade held her hand up to stop Mia from creating a whole fake ass scenario that didn't exist. "He isn't dead."

Mia opened her mouth to say something, but Jade held her hand up again. "Later, Mia. I promise."

Jade pleaded with her eyes for Mia to drop the subject for now. Seeing how uncomfortable her friend was, she shut up and went back to filling out her paperwork. By the time Noah came back into the conference room, they were finished and ready to start their day. Noah sat back in his chair and clasped his hands together. "Alright, ladies. First of all, I want to officially welcome you to Bennett & Co. I'm excited to have you two on board."

"Mr. Bennett, thank you so much for this opportunity. You don't know how much this means to us," Jade said.

"What she said. This job will help us out more than you know," Mia smiled.

"My pleasure, and please, call me Noah. All of my employees do." The ladies nodded, and Noah continued. "I'm sure you're wondering what your day-to-day operation will look like. It's pretty simple, really. I got you both set up with company emails and laptops. You'll be scheduling meetings and responding to emails, mostly.

There will be the occasional need for you to take meeting minutes or mail out company letters. You will also answer phones and direct calls. As I mentioned earlier, Mia, you will work closely with Kenyon and Jade, you will work with me and Yolanda. I will split my projects down the middle. You will be the contact for half and she will be the contact for the other half. This week, Kenyon and I will take you two under our wings and showing you the ropes. Unfortunately, there was only one office available up here, but I had an extra desk added and I think you two will fit comfortably in there."

Mia nodded slowly, "That's cool. I don't mind working side by side with my bestie, but tell me, what's that money looking like?"

Jade blushed furiously and elbowed Mia in the ribs. Noah chuckled and said, "Forgive me, I forgot to include that information in your hiring packet. I was a bit rushed in creating them. We will pay you each twenty dollars an hour to start with full benefits if you want to include them. Schedule will be nine-to-five Monday through Friday and you get all major holidays off and paid."

"That's what the fuck I'm talking about!" Mia cheered.

"Mia!" Jade screeched and then looked at Noah. "Please forgive her. I promise I'll work on her and that mouth of hers."

Noah laughed deeply, "It's okay. I'm sure you could tell earlier that Kenyon and I are laid back, and that is exactly the kind of work environment we provide. Please, feel free to be yourself."

Mia grinned and nodded her head. "I like you, Noah. You and I will get along just fine."

Jade shook her head furiously, "Trust me. You do not want to give Mia free rein to act however she wants."

"Hey, what's that supposed to mean?" Mia snapped.

Noah intervened, still laughing at their antics. "How about this? Be yourself when you are just in the office conversing with one of us, but when you are dealing with a client, try to reel it in a bit and be professional."

Mia thought about it for a moment and nodded, "You have yourself a deal."

"Great, now, there is just one more thing I wanted to discuss and please forgive me if I am being too forward," he paused as he looked back and forth between them. "I couldn't help but notice how cold and out of breath you two were when you got here this morning. I have to ask, did you walk all the way here from the shelter?"

Jade felt so embarrassed, she could have died right there in the conference room but Mia nodded, her eyes big. "Hell yeah, we did. It took two whole hours to get here, and my feet are killing me. Don't get me started on the cold. I thought I would pass out by the time we got here."

Jade kicked her under the table to stop her from saying anything else.

"Ouch! What was that for?" she eyed Jade.

Jade placed a tight smile on her face and turned to Noah, "It wasn't that big of a deal. We're used to it."

Noah sighed as anger seeped into his veins. It had hurt him when he found out that Jade was married, but now he was just pissed off. What kind of man was okay with his wife living like this? He wasn't sure, but he knew that he wasn't okay with it. "Listen, it's only your first day, but you've shown great dedication to this job already. I appreciate that more than you know, but I don't want you two to get burnt out. That much walking mixed with those weather conditions and then an eight-hour workday would burn the toughest of people out. I take care of my employee's here and I would love to allow you two access to our car services. Please, allow me to do this for you."

"Noah, you've already done so much," Jade said with her eyes wide. She had never in her life met someone as generous as Noah. In less than twenty-four hours he had given her the best meal she had in weeks, a job, clothing, and now a car service. She would definitely make good on her vow to do something nice for him as soon as she got some cash in her hands.

"Girl, shut up. Now is not the time to act too proud to accept someone's help. Talk to my aching feet if you have a problem," Mia said to Jade before turning to Noah. "We absolutely accept that. Thank you, really. This means a lot to us."

Noah smiled at the ladies. "Great. I'll make sure you have one of our driver's numbers before you leave today. Mia, you can go ahead to Kenyon's office to start your training. He can show you to your office."

Mia stood and gathered her things. Before she left she said, "Thanks again, Noah."

"No problem," he nodded at her as she closed the door.

Jade stared at Noah, trying to figure him out. He looked back at her and smiled. "Penny for your thoughts?"

"Why are you being so nice and helping us?" she blurted out and instantly wished she hadn't.

Noah shrugged, unsure about what to say. How could he explain the magnetic pull he felt whenever he was around her? He couldn't, without sounding like a creep, so instead he said, "When my dad died I made a vow to help as many people as I could while I was on this earth. Not only did he instill that in me as I grew up, he died trying to save a complete stranger. He was my hero, and my mom always told me I got my good heart from him. It's just in my nature to help people."

Jade nodded. "I'm sorry to hear about your father. I lost both of my parents, so I know how it feels. I don't know you very well and I never knew your dad, but I'm positive that you're making him proud."

It surprised Noah to hear about Jade's parents, and it only led to more questions. He wanted to know every single reason behind the sadness in her eyes. He wanted to know so he could make it better. He had to stop himself from reaching out and grabbing her hand. *What the hell is wrong with you? Get a hold on yourself,* he thought. He couldn't understand what was happening with him, but he knew that it had everything to do with Jade.

It surprised jade herself that she told him about her parents. There was something so pure and genuine about him that made her comfortable, but not even Mia knew about her parents being dead.

She felt a twinge of guilt that there was still so much that Mia didn't know about her, but she decided to fix that, starting tonight.

Realizing that they were just staring at each other, Noah cleared his throat and began collecting the papers on the table. "I'll take you into your office so you can stash your things and then we can get started with training."

Jade stood, shaking the odd feeling that came over her in Noah's presence off, and gathered her things. Ready to officially start her day.

CHAPTER 5

"U<small>GH, </small>I <small>AM SO DAMN TIRED,</small>" M<small>IA WHINED AS THEY GOT</small> situated on the flimsy mattresses.

"Tell me about it," Jade replied as she stifled a yawn.

"But I can't lie, Chica, that job is a God-send. Better than a stupid ass restaurant or some shit. Twenty dollars an hour makes the shit well worth it, too. How did we got so damn lucky?" Mia wondered out loud.

Jade shrugged underneath the stiff blanket that was lying on top of her. The thin material making her itch. Still, the two women were happy that they found a shelter closer to work, and that they could get into it for the night.

"I don't know, Mimi, but I'm happy as hell. Noah is such a kind person, sometimes I wonder if it's even real or if it's all a facade."

Some woman laying in the bed next to theirs shushed them, Mia rolled her eyes and flung her blanket off her before climbing into bed with Jade. The bed was tiny, so Jade had to scoot all the way against the wall and lay completely straight, but she was used to Mia being in her personal space by now. It had even become a source of comfort to her. Even while they were at work today, they found themselves huddled together, sharing one computer at several points. Some people might find it unhealthy that they had become so close in such a short amount of time and that they literally did everything together, but what other people didn't understand was that their friendship was all they had. Mia's family refused to speak to her, and Jade didn't have anyone. They were all each other had, and it wasn't a crime for them to draw comfort from one another.

"Uh huh, don't think I haven't peeped the way you two look at each other," Mia whispered. "Y'all like each other." She grinned wickedly, referring to Jade and Noah.

Jade laughed out loud and then covered her mouth, when more shushing sounds came from around the room. She hated staying in shelters and couldn't wait for the day that she and Mia could rent out their own spot. They could stay up late talking and doing whatever the hell they wanted, without there being a curfew or other women telling them to shut up. She felt like a child with all these stupid ass rules, and she couldn't wait to get back on her feet again.

"It isn't like that, girl. Noah is nice, that's all. Like I've said before, I am not worried about a man. Especially not my boss," Jade breathed.

"You might want to tell him that, then. He could barely take his eyes off you all day," Mia giggled, getting a kick out of her friend's discomfort.

Jade shook her head, "in case you forgot, I'm married."

"I was wondering if you would bring it up or if I would have to. What's up with that, Mouse? You have a whole ass husband somewhere and you failed to mention that to me? What the fuck?"

"It isn't as simple as it seems," Jade said somberly.

"That's obvious. What kind of man has his wife living this way, anyway? That's real foul, Jade. Real fucking foul."

"It isn't like that. I mean, yeah. He is foul, but he has no idea where I am and I need it to stay that way. He's dangerous, Mimi."

Mia laid perfectly still as she asked, "How so?"

"He used to beat me, and I'm not talking about a slap here and there. Elijah is a big man, and I'm already so tiny. I've broken more bones than I ever care to admit. He would force me to do sexual things that I don't even want to mention. If I refused, he would beat me and then do it, anyway. The last time he almost killed me. I was in the hospital for weeks. I'd lost so much blood, and I was really banged up. I finally confided in one nurse about what happened and she begged me to stay so I could fill out a police report and get the help I needed, but I refused. Elijah is a powerful man. He's an attorney, and he knew his way around legal situations and the courtroom. I'm terrified of him and I would rather run and never face him again than stay and get dragged through the courts and get my ass beat in the process."

Jade couldn't stop the tears from falling and Mia wrapped her up in a hug, heart aching at her friend's story. "Fuck him. You have a new life now, and as shitty as it has been for the last few weeks, it will only get better. You're alive, Jade, and I am so damn thankful for that. I'm thankful for you. We'll get ourselves out of this situation. Wait and see."

Jade sniffled and nodded. She hated talking about her past life. She couldn't figure out why her life had taken a turn for the worst. She had so much promise growing up right along with a loving family and a great life. As soon as her parents died, it was as if someone had snatched her perfect life from her and replaced it with nothing but heartache and grief. Elijah sniffed her out like a wolf would a sheep. He treated her right through their brief courtship, and Jade really thought she had found some happiness amidst all her grief. For the first time in a long time, she felt as though her life had purpose again.

That was snatched from her the moment they said *I do*. It was on their honeymoon to Florida that Elijah had first hit her. Jade was shocked and cried for hours afterwards as Elijah carried on about his business, ignoring her and acting as though nothing had happened. Finally, he told her to get up and iron his clothes so they could go to dinner. Too scared to disobey him, she got off the floor and headed towards the bathroom so she could clean the blood out of her nose.

He got real mad then. "Bitch, didn't I tell you to iron my clothes? I ain't said shit about cleaning your face off."

He hit her again. This time in the back of her head and so hard that she saw stars for days, and that wasn't all that had changed about him. Before they got married, their sex was on point. It was the best Jade had ever had. He was so careful and loving in the bedroom towards her. Once they got married, that changed, too. Elijah did anything he could to hurt and humiliate her. He would ram his ten inch dick up inside of her with no warning and nothing to lubricate her. She would be so sore and scuffed down there that it hurt to pee for days after. One of his favorite forms of torture was anal sex. Jade had never had any desire to try anal sex, and Elijah knew that, but do you think he cared? He would ram his dick straight up her asshole as she fought and screamed from underneath him. He took pleasure in her pain and would go at it for hours. That wasn't mentioning the various objects he would penetrate her with. He was as sadistic as they came, and Jade had endured it for far too long.

On the outside looking in, they were the perfect couple with the perfect home, but to Jade it was a living hell. She wasn't allowed to have friends, she couldn't speak unless spoken to, and she damn sure didn't have anything to her name. Elijah made sure of that. All of her money from her art was automatically transferred to his bank account. He would give her a weekly allowance, just enough to get her hair, nails, and waxing done, but everything else was his to keep. He claimed it was so he could pay the bills in the big ass house they had, but Jade knew that he made more than enough to cover all that and he didn't need the chump change she was bringing in. No, Elijah keeping her money was just another form of control.

The night that he beat her so badly that he panicked and brought her to the emergency room was the last straw for Jade. He spun a tale about her getting jumped on her way home from work. As he talked, he was squeezed her kneecap underneath the hospital blanket, almost crushing it, as she lay there in bed, daring her to say anything that conflicted with his made-up story. The nurses didn't seem all that convinced, though, and as soon as Elijah left to handle a court case that he couldn't miss, Jade broke down and confessed that her husband had beaten her. She had been there for a couple of weeks by that point and her fractured ribs were still sore, but her face was healing. She was still black and blue all over and barely able to walk, but she looked a hell of a lot better than when she came in.

The nurses were frantic and yapping about calling the police, but Jade said she would refuse to talk to them. She knew she fucked up by telling them when they told her they were legally obligated to call the police. As soon as they left the room to make that call, Jade grabbed the outfit that Elijah brought her from home for her afternoon walks and threw it on. The only reason he had even been nice enough to bring it for her was because he didn't want people looking at her backside as she walked around the hospital. No matter the reason, Jade was thankful for it because it would do a lot better against the cold than a flimsy hospital gown. She didn't have a jacket or anything else besides her wallet. Slipping her ID and social security card out, she tucked them safely in her pocket and left everything else. She stealthily slipped out of that hospital and never looked back.

"I sure hope so, Mia, because I can't go back there. He will kill me," Jade whispered as she shook the thoughts from her head.

"I wouldn't let him," Mia said as she hugged Jade to her. "Now get some rest."

Jade cried herself to sleep that night as she thought of the horrors her husband had put her through and Mia held her tightly on that little ass bed, never leaving her side.

CHAPTER 6

THE WEEK FLEW BY, AND IT WAS NOW THE WEEK OF CHRISTMAS. Jade and Mia were excited because they would get their first checks today. Typically, they got paid every other Friday, but since the holiday fell on a Friday, they would get their checks today, which was a Wednesday. Subsequently, today was their last work day for the week.

Their first check wouldn't be for a full two weeks since they started in the middle of a pay period, but the few days they had on those checks would put a couple hundred in each of their hands and they were ecstatic.

"What do you want for Christmas, Mouse?" Mia asked as they tapped away on their laptops. "My family was always big on Christmas. I used to be spoiled as hell. As an only child, I guess it's understandable. I remember one year my mom took all my presents away because I failed a class in high school. She was strict like that, but papa sneaked them to me. I was always a daddy's girl. My mom was so mad when she found out papa gave me those gifts. Anyway, I was thinking I could get you some clothes or something. What do you think?"

Jade stopped what she was doing and turned in her chair so she was facing Mia's back. She was used to Mia's long tangents by now, and Jade always listened patiently until she was done before speaking. "I don't want anything. I just want to have a night with you in a hotel or something where we can be as loud as we want to be and I want to have a hot meal. That's it."

Mia turned around to look at Jade, "Okay, and we'll have that, but there has to be something small that you want."

Jade thought about it for a moment and said, "A tube of lipstick. It's been so long since I've had makeup on, and I miss it. I used to be fly, honey!" Jade laughed as she snapped her fingers.

"I guess you had to be since your man beat you every chance he got," Mia quipped. She didn't say it in a mean way and Jade knew that. Mia was just speaking matter-of-factly like she always did.

Jade knew not to be offended, so she waved her off, "yeah, I guess so."

"Awww, I'm sorry I brought that up. I'm an idiot," Mia said once she realized what just slipped out of her mouth. "I just hate him, Jade. I hate him so much."

Jade gave a small laugh, "You never even met him."

Looking at Jade like she was crazy, Mia put her hand on her hip and twisted her neck, "I don't have to know him and he better be happy that I don't. He deserves to have his dick chopped off and shoved down his throat."

Jade busted out laughing. "I won't argue with you there."

"Really, though. What kind of man puts his hands on his own wife? I'll never understand that."

Jade grabbed Mia's hands. "It isn't for us to understand. I don't want to think about that now, anyway. It's almost Christmas, and it has been too long since I've actually enjoyed the holidays. I'm looking forward to it."

"So am I," Mia smiled. "Let's go shopping after work today. We can get a couple of things for each other, nothing big, and then find a hotel to crash at for a couple of days."

Jade smiled at the idea and nodded her head. It would be nice not to worry about where they would sleep or how they would eat for the next few days.

A knock at the door interrupted them. Noah stuck his head in the doorway of their office and saw the ladies holding hands. "Sorry, am I interrupting?"

"Last I checked this was your building, Noah. You can interrupt us anytime," Mia smiled. Noah shook his head as he entered the cozy office with a grin, and Kenyon followed closely behind.

"I have your checks here for you ladies," he said as he handed them each an envelope. "We wanted to see if you two wanted to grab lunch?"

Jade glanced at the time on her computer screen and was amazed that it was already noon. "I didn't even realize it was lunchtime."

"Shiiit, I'm ready. Let's roll," Mia said as she tore open the envelope. Her eyes lit up at the amount showing, and she stood up, happily rubbing her belly.

Jade still wasn't used to the fact that Noah was okay with Mia swearing while on the clock, but since they'd started she could see that Bennett & Co was like a big ass family. All the employee's were cool as hell, except for one. Yolanda had hated Mia and Jade from the minute she met them and wasn't shy about making sure they knew it. The girls steered clear of her as much as possible.

Kenyon laughed and looped his arm around Mia's shoulders. He was a tall brotha, although not as tall as Noah, and he had high yellow skin. His jet black hair was curly at the top and cut close at the sides, and his eyes were a pretty grey color. He was a handsome man and when Jade asked Mia if there was anything between the two of them; she laughed her ass off. After catching her breath, she said, "Hell no! I see him as more of a friend or a sibling. He is not boyfriend material at all, Mouse. Get with the program. Half the women that work with us have slept with that man."

Mia continued to giggle about it for the rest of the day and Jade never brought it up again. Seeing them together now, Jade could see that they really bickered like brother and sister and there weren't any stolen glances or lust filled awkwardness between them. She couldn't say the same for her and Noah, though. The four of them had been eating lunch together every day and while Mia and Kenyon were joking around, Jade and Noah were pretending not to glance at each other and fumbling over awkward conversation. Jade didn't know what it was about Noah that made her so nervous whenever he was around, but she wished she could shake it off.

Normally, Jade would be more reserved about something like this, but she was also dying to see how much her check was, so with her back turned to everyone else as they talked, she slid the check out of the envelope and smiled. Tears pricked her eyes at the six hundred dollar check. Together, she and Mia had twelve-hundred dollars. It wouldn't be enough for them to get their own place just yet, but they could start paying those application fees and they could also afford to get a couple more outfits for work and some odds and ends that would make life living on the streets a little easier. She put the check safely in her backpack and then did the same with Mia's when she noticed that the girl had just discarded it on her desk before getting up and following everyone else out of the office. Jade locked it up with the key Noah had given her on her first day before joining the others.

Yolanda caught them as they were waiting for the elevator. She had just come back from getting coffee and noticed the four of them heading down to lunch. Again. She was fuming, but she put a fake smile on and said, "Hey, Noah. I cooked my famous lasagna last night. I brought some for you for lunch since you liked it so much last time."

Noah glanced at her before setting his eyes back on Jade who was standing next to Mia. "No thanks, Yolanda. I'm having lunch with these guys. Thank you for thinking of me, though."

The elevator arrived, and they piled on as Yolanda glared at them until the doors closed, whisking them down to the cafeteria. She was livid. Ever since Jade started working for the company, Noah had his nose right up her ass. He was wide the fuck open for her and Yolanda couldn't understand why. Jade was one of those poor bitches that desperately needed her hair and nails done. She was so homely and soft-spoken. The complete opposite of Yolanda who was confident, sexy, and always in prime condition. Her weaves were always laced just right, her nails on point and her makeup flawless. Yolanda knew she looked ten times better than Jade, so why the hell couldn't Noah see it? That was okay, though. In due time Yolanda would make sure that both Jade and Noah knew who belonged on Noah's arm, and it damn sure wasn't Jade.

Down in the cafeteria, Jade was the first at the table they occupied every day for lunch. She slid into the booth and began devouring her chicken club sandwich and fries. She'd gained a couple of pounds since last week because the cafeteria fed her really well. Mia and Jade made sure they got to work early so they could eat breakfast before work. They had everything from bagels and cream cheese to french toast and sausage. They ate lunch with their bosses and at five o'clock each day after their shift ended they would be back in the cafeteria to grab a quick bite for dinner and to stock up on snacks for the night. They would share their snacks with some women in the shelter or other homeless people they saw on the streets. They really didn't mind, and they were no longer stingy with their food because they knew that the next day they would eat good again.

The only time they felt a little hungry was on the weekend after their snacks and sandwiches had run out, but it wasn't near as bad as when they'd gone days without food. The weekend wasn't nothing but two days and Monday came around real quick. They were so blessed and they never took for granted the safe haven they had been given in the form of a job.

Noah slid into the booth next to her, and the warmth from his muscled body sent Jade into a tailspin of anxiety. He looked down at her tray of food and noticed it was almost gone. One thing about Jade that he loved so much was that she always finished her food. Her eyes were never bigger than her stomach and she always got just enough to satisfy herself.

"Was it good?" He grinned down at her, and she blushed.

"Yeah. The food is always good here," she replied.

"Yeah, I'm happy I had this place added. Before this cafeteria was here, it was just more offices, which was fine, but I work so much that I would literally forget to eat all day. I figured if I had a place just one floor below me, there wouldn't be an excuse not to eat. It's been working so far," he grinned before taking a bite of his burger.

"I wish I could forget about food. Sometimes it's all I think about. When my next meal will come or how I'll pay for it or if I will even be able to eat..." Jade blushed again ash she trailed off, realizing what she was saying. "Sorry, I didn't mean to—"

"No, it's okay. You can speak freely with me. I'm always here to listen," Noah said. He felt bad that he was so insensitive to her situation sometimes. Jade was so good at hiding that part of her life that he sometimes forgot that she was homeless.

She thought about what he said for a moment. "It's embarrassing, you know? Nobody wants to admit that they don't have a home and as ashamed as I am about my situation, I'm also thankful for it for many reasons. I won't get into most of them, but one of them is that by being homeless, I take nothing for granted. Not food, not warmth, not money, friendships, clothes, shoes, soap, or even something as simple as a hairbrush. It's taught me how to survive and how to be more empathetic towards people that live on the streets. A lot of them didn't have a choice, like me. It's either be homeless or die."

She glanced up at Noah and then stammered, "or, you know, their home was taken away or they were laid off. It could happen to anyone."

Noah was in awe of her. He had never touched on her situation because he didn't want to offend her, but he was in complete awe over how she could turn such a shitty situation into something positive. Noah wanted to ask more, but they could hear Kenyon and Mia nearing their table. They tore their eyes away from each other and focused back on their plates.

Kenyon and Mia weren't stupid, though. They knew their friends were feeling each other, and they had just come up with a plan to hook them up. Mia wanted Jade to be happy and Kenyon had never seen his best friend so infatuated with a woman, so both Kenyon and Mia were more than happy to set them up.

"What are you two over here talking about?" Mia smirked.

"Yeah, clue us in," Kenyon smiled as he plopped his tray down and slid in across from Jade.

"Nothing, really," Jade said while Noah took a big bite of his burger.

Mia rolled her eyes, "whatever, Mouse." She turned her gaze on Noah, "are you excited for the holidays?"

Noah smiled, thankful for the change in subject. He didn't want to embarrass Jade by continuing their conversation in front of their friends. There was something intimate about the way she spoke, which lead him to believe that she never shared those feelings with anyone else. "Yeah, I am. We normally don't do anything too major. Kenyon comes over on Christmas Eve and eats up all the food and then the rest of the night is spent drinking and playing referee between him and my brother."

"Hey, your brother and I are a great time," Kenyon laughed.

Noah snorted, "Yeah, okay. Maybe to y'all."

"It sounds like a great time," Jade smiled.

Noah had been trying to find a way to ask what her plans were for the holidays, but again, he didn't want to seem rude or like he was being too intrusive. This conversation gave him a great opening, though. He just hoped that she wasn't spending it with her mysterious husband. "What are you doing for the holidays?"

Jade's smile grew big and his heart dropped. He figured that smile and excitement would be reserved for her husband only. He wondered what their story was. She surprised him when she said, "Mimi and I are going to do a little shopping after work and then we are going to a hotel for a few days. Just me and her with a nice comfortable bed and oohhhh a TV!"

Noah's heart melted. She was genuinely excited about something so simple. It was so refreshing to him because most women that he dealt with were high maintenance. Not Jade, though. She really enjoyed the small luxuries in life, and that made Noah like her even more.

"Hey, why don't y'all come on over to Noah's house? No need to spend money on a hotel when this man has plenty of room. We can make a fun long weekend out of it," Kenyon smiled deviously.

It wasn't lost on Noah that this had been Kenyon's plan all along. He could tell by the way he was smiling and glancing at Mia who was grinning right back at us, but Noah wasn't mad at all. In fact, he was mad at himself for not thinking of it first.

"Oh, wow. That is so nice of you to offer!" Mia squealed. Everyone could tell that she was putting on a show.

"I don't know," Jade said smiling as another blush overtook her face. "I don't want to intrude."

Noah spoke up, "You wouldn't be intruding at all. Besides, I could use a friend while dealing with him and my brother."

Everyone laughed. But Jade still wasn't sure.

"Isn't it weird for us to stay at your place? I mean, you are our bosses," Jade asked.

"Girl, go on with all that. In case you haven't noticed, we see you two as more than just employee's. I don't know what it is about y'all, but you're cool as hell to be around. Even Mia's big-headed ass," Kenyon joked as he gently mushed Mia in the head.

She snatched his hand and held it in midair, "Boy, you better watch it. I know you don't know me too well yet, but trust me, you don't want these problems."

"Ohhhh I am so scared," Kenyon mimicked.

Once they were done arguing and Jade and Noah were finished laughing, all eyes turned on Jade and she sighed, "I suppose that's okay. As long as it's really okay with you, Noah."

Noah smiled, "It's really okay. I promise."

Jade smiled back at him, and she could have sworn her heart fluttered at the thought of staying the night under his roof.

"I CAN'T WAIT UNTIL YOU OPEN YOUR GIFT," MIA SQUEALED.

They were in the company car on the way to Noah's house and Jade was a bundle of nerves. The thought of being in Noah's personal space had her frazzled. On one hand, she couldn't wait to spend more time with him and be in a real home for the holidays, but on the other hand she was scared shitless because of the feelings she had for him.

She tried to calm down as she talked to Mia. "I hope you didn't go overboard."

Mia rolled her eyes, "I didn't, trust me. I still have plenty of money left over, and I even got Kenyon something."

"What did you get him?" Jade giggled because she could only imagine what kind of gift Mia would get Kenyon. Those two were something else when they were together, and they kept Noah and Jade laughing.

Mia winked, "you'll have to wait and see."

Noah let them get off work two hours early so they could get their Christmas shopping done before coming over to his place. After stopping at the bank and cashing their checks, they hit some stores in lower Manhattan. They steered clear of the high-end stores, but they found a few stores that were within their price range. Jade knew just what to get Mia, but she was lost on what to get Noah. Her plan had always been to get him a little something once her first check hit, but now that it was here she didn't know what the hell to do. She was about to give up when she walked passed a store with exactly what she needed in the window.

Now, it was almost nine o'clock and Jade was exhausted and cold. They pulled up to Noah's house after an hour drive all the way to the upper east side, and both Mia and Jade's mouths dropped at the huge house. It wasn't a mansion or anything, but it was the biggest house that either had been in for a very long time. Jade could immediately tell that this wasn't a house that Noah designed and built himself. As beautiful as it was, it paled in comparison to his architecture firm.

Either way, both ladies were excited to sleep in a normal bed that night with an actual comforter.

They hopped out of the car with all of their bags, once their driver, Tommy, opened the door for them.

"Thanks, Tommy. Have a good holiday," Jade said.

"You as well, Jade. You too, Mia," He said with a smile. Tommy was an older black man and very kind. The day he met Mia and Jade, he made sure that he stressed that they could call him anytime, day or night, if they needed anything.

"Bye, Tommy," Mia waved as he got back into the car and drove off.

They walked up the front stairs and knocked on the front door. A moment later Kenyon opened it, grinning down at the two women. "Ladies, so glad you could make it!"

He was dressed comfortably in some grey sweatpants and a white t-shirt. He bent over and grabbed the bags out of Mia's hand, leaving her with only her backpack.

Noah appeared behind Kenyon. "Man, move aside and let them in. It's cold as hell."

Jade's insides turned to jelly when she saw that Noah was dressed in grey sweatpants as well, along with a black long-sleeved shirt that showcased his muscular build. Unlike Kenyon, who wore the occasional pair of jeans to work, Jade had never seen Noah without a suit on. She wasn't sure which looked better on him; his suits or his casual gear.

Once they were inside, Noah grabbed Jade's bags from her hands as she bent to take off her shoes. He waited by her side, eager to show her his house.

"I didn't think shopping would take us so long. Sorry we're here so late. Your home is beautiful," Jade said.

"It's all good. We just got here a bit ago ourselves. We had some last-minute shopping to do as well. Did you get what you needed?" Noah asked as he looked Jade up and down. He could tell that she was cold by the redness of her skin and how she was hugging herself.

"Yeah, we did. Thanks again for letting us stay here. I love the decorations," Jade commented as she looked around. They were standing in a small hallway, lit with Christmas lights that were strung on the walls. She could see a large Christmas tree in the room at the end of the hall she assumed was the living room.

"Not a problem. Here, let me take your coats and I'll show you around," Noah said as he reached out for Jade. She allowed him to take her coat off of her and he gathered Mia's as well before tossing them to Kenyon. "Hang these up."

Kenyon sucked his teeth and rolled his eyes dramatically as the women giggled. They watched as he opened up the hall closet and hung them haphazardly on the hangers. Noah motioned for them to follow him, and he led them down the hall, pointing out different rooms. "There is a bathroom here, and this is the living room."

They stepped into a cozy living room with a huge sectional and a loveseat. The walls were painted a nice maroon color that gave the room a warm feel along with the glowing of the lights from the Christmas tree. The best part about the room was that it had a huge fireplace, and it was lit, warming Jade and making her smile. Hanging on the fireplace were stockings, and she wondered who they were for.

"Over here," Noah gestured to the right, "is the kitchen and dining room and down that hall," he said gesturing to the left, "is the laundry room and the stairs to the furnished basement. There is a guest room and a big TV down there."

Next, he led them up the stairs that were off to the side of the living room. "These two rooms are more guest rooms, and my office, and this is the bathroom."

There was only one more room on the second floor, and Jade assumed that it was his. He confirmed her suspicions when he pushed the door open just enough for them to see. "This one, is my room."

Inside, there was a king-sized bed with a black comforter that was neatly made. Off to the side there was a walk-in closet and a bathroom. There was a dresser and a few nightstands, but other than that the room was simple. He closed the door and turned to them.

"You guys can stay in either of those rooms," he pointed at the two guest rooms as he set Jade's bags in front of one of them. "Get settled and come back down to the kitchen. I'll make hot chocolate. Are you hungry?"

"You know I am," Mia laughed as she pushed open the door to one of the guest bedrooms and sat her backpack just inside it.

"Cool, I'll order some food, too. See you in a minute," he winked at Jade before disappearing back down the stairs.

"Now where the fuck did Kenyon's goofy ass go with my bags? He better not be peeking in them!" Mia fussed as she bolted down the stairs after Noah.

Jade giggled and then pushed the bedroom door open, dragging her bags inside. It was a decent-sized room with a queen-sized bed and a small closet. It may have been basic to others, but to Jade it was magnificent. It had been months since she slept in a comfortable bed, and that fluffy beige comforter and matching pillows were calling her name. She was exhausted from a long day of work and shopping. She hopped onto the bed and sighed contentedly as she sunk into the fluffy fabric that surrounded her.

She must have dozed off because the next thing she knew Mia was jumping on her bed yelling at her to wake up. "Girl, wake up! Noah made some bomb ass hot coco. From scratch, too. Not any of that nasty fake shit. Kenyon is working my nerves as usual. I caught his ass looking through my bags. Nosy ass. I cussed him out real good, too. Oh, and Noah ordered some Chinese food and girl he ordered enough to feed a damn army. I can't wait until it gets here. Get up! It feels nice being in a *home*, doesn't it? It feels so nice, Mouse. I'm happy we're here."

Mia was talking a mile a minute, and it took a minute for Jade to process what she said and realize that she asked her a question. Jade sat up and stretched as she said, "Yeah, girl. It's nice being here."

"Come on, let's get some hot chocolate," Mia said. She was acting like a little kid on Christmas, and her mood was infectious.

Jade giggled as Mia pulled her off the bed and down the stairs. The kitchen was warm and inviting with orange walls and red appliances. The granite island had three bar stools, Kenyon and Noah occupied two of them.

When the ladies entered the kitchen, Noah looked up and smiled. "I hope you like Chinese food, Jade. Mia said you ate just about anything."

Jade smiled and then stiffed a yawn. "She's right. I'm not picky."

Noah smiled back at her and realized she looked tired. He hoped that she would get a good nights sleep tonight. With a full stomach and a warm house, he was betting she would, and he was glad that he could make that happen for her. For a moment, the two were caught up in each other's eyes, while Kenyon and Mia looked at them and then at each other with knowing smiles. Mia winked at Kenyon before clearing her throat. Jade and Noah pried their eyes from each other, embarrassed, and turned their attention to Mia. "I hope you have some kind of booze to put up in this hot chocolate. Jade needs it. I found her ass upstairs sleeping!"

Jade nudged her best friend, "I'm tired and any kind of liquor will make me fall asleep even quicker."

"Not if you have enough of it. Trust me, I know how to get people turnt up," Mia grinned.

Jade giggled and shook her head, "Not tonight, Mimi. Tomorrow, I promise. I'm just so damn tired. All I want is to eat and go to bed."

Mia poked out her bottom lip and crossed her arms over her chest, "Fine, but tomorrow you owe me."

"Tomorrow I'm all yours, I promise," Jade said.

Noah got up to fix the women some hot chocolate. When he finished, he set them on the island. "No alcohol, but extra whipped cream for Jade and spiced rum for Mia. Come on, let's go sit by the fire while we wait for the food."

"Thank you," Jade said before taking a sip. "Oh, my gosh. This is so good."

The hot liquid traveled through her body and warmed her from the inside out. She never had hot chocolate as good as this before. It was like drinking heaven in a cup. Noah loved the look of pure delight on Jade's face, and he promised that over the next few days he would do anything in his power to keep that look on her face as much as possible. As long as she was under his roof, he would make sure she enjoyed herself. He had to admit that it excited him at the prospect of getting some alone time with her, too. He wanted the chance to get to know her a little better, but he didn't want to seem too forward. He couldn't gauge how she felt about him and if she was even interested in him the way he was in her. He was willing to be patient, though, because he understood that she was fragile.

The group got situated in the living room. Jade grabbed a fluffy brown throw blanket from the back of the couch and wrapped herself in it before sitting directly in front of the fireplace, smiling at the warmth it provided. Noah sat in the chair next to the fireplace, so close that if Jade leaned back only a fraction of an inch, she would touch his legs. Noah loved being this close to her, and Jade had to admit that it felt nice for her too. Kenyon and Mia curled up on opposite ends of the couch, arguing over who should get the other throw blanket that hung over the couch. They finally settled on sharing it, with Mia getting more of the blanket, while Kenyon only got his feet covered.

There was soft Christmas music playing through an unseen speaker, and Jade felt as though she were in heaven. She hadn't felt this peaceful in a long time. She sipped from her mug, oblivious to Noah watching her. He couldn't take his eyes off her as she drank her hot chocolate and watched the fire with a serene look on her face. He wanted to pull her closer so she could rest her head in his lap and he could stroke her hair. He didn't know where those feelings were coming from, but he wanted nothing more than to explore them.

It wasn't long before the doorbell rang, signifying the food's arrival. Noah stood up, careful not to bump into Jade, so it surprised him when she stood up as well. "I'll help you out. Mia made it sound like you ordered a lot."

"Thanks," Noah smiled, grateful for her kindness. Any other women he had dealt with in the past were entitled and refused to lift a manicured finger to do anything they didn't feel like doing. Jade was like a breath of fresh air, and he appreciated her genuine kindness more than she knew.

While they went to handle the food, Mia slyly turned to face Kenyon. "Our plan is working out perfectly."

"Yeah it is. Noah can't take his eyes off her," Kenyon laughed. "I ain't ever seen him so whipped over a female before. This shit is wild."

Mia nodded, "Yeah, your boy is definitely wide open for my girl. She ain't slick either, though. I see her sneaking glances at him, too. I think she likes him, but she doesn't feel like she can open up to him."

"Why not? My nigga is a catch," Kenyon joked.

Mia rolled her eyes, "Yeah, he is, but she's been through some shit. It really isn't for me to speak on, but it'll take a lot for her to see Noah as someone she could potentially be with."

"I guess we'll have to make sure they get plenty of time together then, huh?" Kenyon smiled.

"Guess so," Mia said.

"We make a good team," Kenyon grinned.

"Mostly because I'm the brains," Mia quipped, and that was all it took for them to begin bickering again.

In the front of the house, Noah opened the door and paid the delivery man and then handed Jade a bag of food while he took the remaining two. They brought the bags into the kitchen and Jade began taking the food out while Noah grabbed plates. Jade looked up and when she noticed that Noah had grabbed real glass plates.

"Why don't we just use these? Less clean up and less hassle," she said as she held up a small stack of paper plates and plastic silverware the restaurant packed along with the food.

Noah smiled. Another thing he liked about Jade. She didn't expect the finer things in life. Noah was willing to bet that she would have been okay with eating straight out of the containers, even sharing with everyone else. That would repulse other women, but not her.

"Cool, that works for me."

Together, they set all the food out, and it wasn't long before Kenyon and Mia joined them in the kitchen. Jade ate quickly, both famished and ready for bed. It disappointed Noah when she excused herself for bed once she was finished eating, but he reminded himself that he had a solid four days with her and that thought overshadowed his disappointment.

CHAPTER 7

Jade woke up more rested than she had been in years. Even while living in the lap of luxury with her rich husband, she hadn't slept as well as she had last night. Living with Elijah had kept a constant fear in her heart and sleeping in the same bed as him left her restless. Last night, she was warm and full and she felt safe inside of Noah's home, like nothing bad could touch her.

Noah made her feel safe in a way that she couldn't understand. Maybe it was his gentleness or his deep, but soft-spoken voice. He was always a gentleman when he was around her and he was the most kind man she had ever met, but Jade knew better than that. She had fallen victim to a man pretending to be something he wasn't before, and she promised that she would never allow it to happen again. As much as she wanted to like Noah, she forced herself to keep it friendly. It was better that way.

Jade rolled over and looked at the clock on the nightstand. It was almost eleven in the morning, and she couldn't believe that she had slept for over twelve hours. She felt good as hell, though, and she was more than ready to get up and start her day. She rolled out of bed and grabbed her backpack. Dressed in only a black tank top and a pair of black leggings, she pushed open the door to her room and ran right into Noah, who was just passing her door and on the way to the kitchen.

"Oh, sorry!" he said as he backed up a couple of steps. He was dressed in a pair of blue and black pajama pants and a white tank top. Muscles were bulging everywhere, and Jade had to force herself to tilt her head up and look into his eyes instead of staring at his chest.

"No, I'm sorry. I'm the one that walked into you," Jade responded shyly.

"I was just going to make some breakfast," Noah said. He couldn't help but notice that she wasn't wearing a bra and the shape of her full breasts were on display beneath the thin fabric of her tank top. Her nipples were poking through and it took everything in Noah to keep his eyes focused on hers and not reach out and brush his fingers across her nipples.

They stared at each other awkwardly for a moment before Jade broke the silence. "Is it okay if I use the shower?"

Noah broke out of his trance and smiled. "Of course. You are welcome to use whatever you need while you're here. There are towels in the linen closet."

"Thank you," Jade said excitedly. She couldn't remember the last time she had taken an actual shower. "When I'm finished, I would love to help with breakfast."

Noah smiled, "Great. Come on down when you're ready."

Jade returned his smile and nodded before stepping around him and opening the linen closet. Noah watched her as she grabbed a towel and then peeked her head into Mia's room.

"She's still asleep," Noah whispered. "Her and Kenyon stayed up until God knows what time, drinking. I went to bed at one this morning and they were still going strong."

Jade laughed, "I guess she won't be waking up any time soon, then."

"Nope," Noah chuckled softly.

She stepped into the hall bathroom and said, "I'll be down shortly."

Noah nodded and walked down the stairs, happy as hell that her face was the first one he saw this morning. He took the eggs and sausage out of the refrigerator and grabbed some potatoes off the counter. He decided to make more of his hot chocolate since Jade enjoyed it so much last night. Just as he was finishing it up, Jade came down the stairs smelling good as hell. She was dressed in his favorite outfit, the same one she wore on her first day of work. Leggings and a sweater dress. It showed off her thin frame and the curves that went along with it. Her braids were drawn back into a ponytail, and she looked happy as hell.

"That shower was amazing," she beamed. It suddenly struck Noah that the shelters she stayed at probably didn't have showers. His heart ached at the thought of her not being able to enjoy the small luxuries of everyday life. She held up her backpack, and her cheeks turned red. "Is it okay if I use your washer and dryer? I haven't had time to go to the laundromat and—"

"Yes and please don't feel embarrassed about asking me to use anything in this house. Seriously, what's mine is yours. Do you remember where it is?" Noah asked, cutting her off. He wanted her to feel comfortable in his home, and he really meant it when he said that she could use whatever she wanted. She didn't need his permission, either.

"Yes, thank you, Noah. Really," she replied.

"You don't have to keep thanking me, Jade. It's really my pleasure. Everything you need should be in there but let me know if you need anything."

"I will. Be right back," she said as she disappeared down the hall towards the laundry room.

Noah had just poured her a mug of hot chocolate when she came back into the kitchen. He set it down on the island and smiled, "Good morning, by the way."

Jade blushed, "Good morning, and thank you."

"No problem," Noah smiled.

She grabbed the mug and looked around the kitchen. "How can I help?"

"Don't tell me you know how to cook?" Noah smirked and raised an eyebrow at her.

"Boy, yes, I know how to cook! I love cooking," Jade giggled and Noah was once again, pleasantly surprised. It shouldn't come as a shock that Noah never had a woman cook for him aside from his mother. Most women wanted to be wined and dined and none of their asses could even boil water.

"Alright, do you want to finish up with these home fries while I make the waffle batter?" Noah asked.

"I'd love to," Jade said as she moved around the counter to grab the knife from his hands. Noah smiled down at her before grabbing a mixing bowl and the ingredients for his famous waffles.

He set everything down next to Jade and they worked in silence for a few moments. Wanting to take this opportunity to learn more about her, Noah asked, "Who taught you how to cook?"

Jade smiled. "My mother. She was the best cook ever. When I was little, she would let me pull a chair right up to the stove so I could watch what she was doing. I learned all my cooking skills from her. I wished I'd had more time to pick her brain for her red beans and rice recipe. She wrote it down for me, but no matter how many times I make it, I can never seem to get it right."

"What happened?" Noah asked.

Jade's smile faltered as she asked, "What do you mean?"

"You mentioned that they died yesterday at lunch. I was just wondering what happened, but if you don't want to talk about it, that's okay," Noah said in a rush. He didn't mean to ask so bluntly, he was genuinely curious about her. He hoped he hadn't made her uncomfortable.

Jade cleared her throat and replied, "They died about four years ago now."

Noah stopped pouring ingredients into the bowl and turned to Jade, "I am so sorry, Jade. That must have been so hard for you."

Jade nodded sadly, "It was. I'm an only child and we barely have any other family, so I was left all alone. Depression kicked in, but painting got me through it. That was when I discovered my real talent, and I submitted my work in art shows. That was how I met... my husband."

She glanced up at Noah, but she only saw kindness in his eyes, so she continued. "He bought out all my art from my first art show. Next thing I know, we're married eight months later."

"He sounds like a great guy," Noah hated to admit. "Where is he now?"

Jade scoffed, "Elijah Willis is anything but a great guy. I haven't seen him since I left and I really hope it stays that way."

She didn't want to go into full details about what happened between her and Elijah, but a huge part of her wanted Noah to know that although she was married, she wanted nothing to do with her husband.

"So...you're getting a divorce?" Noah asked. He was confused on the situation and he desperately wanted to know the details so he could know how to proceed with her. He'd known that she was married since the day she started working for him, but he sensed that her and her husband were separated. Still, not knowing the details was exactly what had been holding him back from making a move on her.

Jade let out an unamused laugh, "I wish it were that simple."

Noah boldly grabbed Jade's chin. He didn't think about what he was doing, but he wanted her to know that he was serious about what he had to say. She stopped cutting the potatoes and looked into his eyes, startled by his hand on her chin, but not upset by it.

Satisfied that he had her full attention, he said, "If you need anything, all you have to do is ask. If you don't want to be married to this man, then I can help you get a divorce attorney. I can help."

She stared deep into his eyes as tears filled her own. "He can't know where I am, Noah."

Noah recognized the look in her eyes. It was fear. Anger bubbled up in him as he pulled her close to his chest. He knew he was being extremely forward with her, but he didn't care in that moment and he only hoped that she wouldn't care, either. It felt so good to hold her, and he hoped that she felt safe in his embrace. Jade fought the tears that threatened to fall as she melted in his strong arms. She inhaled his scent and basked in the moment before stepping away. She wiped her eyes and focused back on cutting the potatoes. "He can never find out where I am. Filing divorce papers will only get closer to finding me.

Noah stood staring at her before asking quietly, "What did he do to you?"

Jade kept her eyes on the cutting board and said, "It's Christmas Eve. Let's just enjoy the day, please?"

Noah shook his head, "Let me help you."

Jade looked up at him, "You can't, Noah. You have already done above and beyond for me. More than you could ever even know. This is one aspect of my life you cannot fix."

Noah looked down into her sad eyes and sighed, "I'll tell you what. I won't press you on this matter, but please know that I'm here if you need me. Okay?"

Jade nodded and then smiled, erasing all of that pain from her face, just like that. "Do you have some onions and peppers?"

Noah smiled, although he really didn't feel right about dropping the conversation. He sensed something dark about her husband, and he wanted to know what exactly went down between them. Pushing the thoughts out of his head, he focused on the task at hand.

"Oh, so you're trying to show off?" Noah teased.

"Hell yeah! This is the way mama made home potatoes. I'm just trying to show you a thing or two," Jade giggled.

Noah laughed and got the rest of the ingredients for her. It only took them another twenty minutes to finish cooking, and when they finished, they had a feast spread out in front of them. Like clockwork, Mia came down the stairs, awakened by the smell of the food, and Kenyon came jogging up the stairs from the basement.

"Y'all ain't shit," Noah laughed.

"What I do?" Kenyon asked in a deep sleepy voice as he plopped down on a barstool. Mia plopped down next to him and rested her chin in her hands as she looked at Noah and Jade.

"You came up just when the food was finished after Jade and I just slaved over it," Noah laughed.

Mia waved him off, "I have a major hangover. I need some of that food to soak up this liquor that's in my system."

"Same," Kenyon said as he reached for a plate. Jade sat down next to Mia while Noah stood. They filled their plates up and proceeded to eat entirely too much.

"I don't think I'll have to eat for the rest of the day," Jade moaned as she held her stomach.

"That's too bad because for dinner I planned to make a crab boil," Noah said.

Jade perked up, "Oh my God. I haven't had crab in forever. How did you know that was my favorite food?"

Noah laughed, "I didn't. Come on, let's go down to the home theater and we can watch some movies. By dinner time you'll be hungry again."

"Sounds like a plan to me," Jade said, hopping off the barstool.

Kenyon and Mia got up and started following them down to the basement when Noah turned around and stopped them. "Nah, that kitchen isn't going to clean itself."

Jade giggled at the looks on their faces as she made her way down to the basement with Noah.

IT WAS LATE AFTERNOON AND *FRED CLAUSE* HAD JUST GOT DONE playing. All four of them had fallen asleep during the movie and were in a deep slumber. The home theater had a huge screen with a projector and a large sectional that was so plush anyone that sat in it immediately melted into the fabric. Kenyon had his legs spread across

Mia's tiny body, his feet damn near in her face while Jade had fallen asleep curled up next to Noah. It was completely innocent, but it felt so right to Noah. When the movie started, they were already sitting close, but once she had fallen asleep, she gravitated closer and closer to Noah until she was pressed right up against his side. He put his arm around her and watched her sleep. He paid more attention to her than the movie until he succumbed to sleep as well.

"AYEEE! The muthafuckin party is here!" A loud voice shouted, causing Jade to jump awake and cling to Noah. For a moment, she thought she was back with her husband and her heart raced. She was used to being yelled at to wake up, and she was just waiting for the pain that normally came with it.

When the pain didn't come, she slowly opened her eyes in time for Noah to shout, "Yo, man. Shut the hell up!"

"Yeah, asshole. Shit, I almost pissed myself just now," Kenyon grumbled as Mia was jostled awake and tried to move under Kenyon's legs.

"Kenyon! Get your funky ass feet off of me! Ewwwww!" she screeched as she tried to wriggle free. Kenyon simply laid back down, not bothering to move.

Jade blinked. She had been in such a deep sleep, she couldn't remember where she was for a few moments, but hearing Kenyon and Mia bicker brought her right on back to the present. Noah had noticed how startled she was, so he pulled her close and rubbed her back. Jade stiffened for a moment and then relaxed slightly before pulling away from him and giving him a tired smile.

"Yo, my bad, bro. I ain't know we had guests," a handsome man that could pass for Noah's twin grinned down at him.

"Yeah, man. I'm regretting giving you that key," Noah said through clenched teeth. "This is Jade, and that's Mia." He gestured to the women, then back to the man. "And this is my little brother, Roman."

"Don't get it twisted, ain't shit little about me," Roman grinned as Noah grunted at his brother's remark. Roman plopped down next to

Mia, who was still struggling under Kenyon's legs. Kenyon was putting extra weight on her on purpose, and Mia was getting frustrated.

"Kenyon, let my friend go," Jade said.

"Hell no. I'm comfortable," Kenyon stretched out even further so that his feet were touching Mia's face. She screamed and scooted closer to Roman so her head was in his lap.

Roman took pity on her, and effortlessly pushed Kenyon's legs off her. She smiled up at him and before sitting up. "Sorry about that. Your friend really has no manners. He's like, the complete opposite of Noah. I'm sure Noah would never put his stankin feet in a woman's face. No offense, Noah. My mom always told me to date men that *respect* me, which is exactly why I am not going near Kenyon with a ten-foot pole. Nasty ass. You're lucky I consider you a friend otherwise I would have bent your pinky toe back until it popped off."

"Yeah, yeah, whatever," Kenyon waved her off.

Roman laughed, "Damn, girl. I've never met a woman that could resist Kenyon's good looks. The shit is infuriating, actually."

"Ewww, no. I see past all that pretty hair and those mesmerizing eyes. Kenyon ain't shit," Mia scrunched her nose up.

"I second that," Roman laughed.

"I agree," Noah chimed in happily.

"Ha ha. So y'all just gonna talk about me like I'm not sitting right here?" Kenyon asked.

"Yup," They all said in unison and then laughed.

"Hilarious," Kenyon said as he got up and stretched. "That's why Jade is my favorite. She doesn't talk shit about me."

"I'm pretty sure Jade is everyone's favorite," Mia quipped.

"True," Noah smiled.

Jade blushed, but stayed quiet.

"No offense, shorty, but I don't think you're everyone's favorite," Roman glanced back at Jade with a smile and then focused back on Mia.

Mia blushed furiously, and then hastily got off the couch. "I'm going to go shower. I'm finally feeling better after last night and I'm ready to do it all over again. Jade, be ready to turn up tonight."

Jade sighed, "I promised I would."

"That's my girl," Mia beamed. She bumped Kenyon as she walked passed where he was still laying on the couch and he grabbed her and started poking her in her ribs and stomach, causing her to shriek with laughter. When he finally let her past, she playfully slapped him on the arm before jogging up the steps.

"I think I'm in love," Roman said as he stared at the stairs where Mia just was.

"This nigga," Kenyon laughed.

"Man, that girl is fine as hell, and she talks shit to you. This has to be love," Roman said as he placed a hand to his heart with a goofy smile on his face. He turned to Jade and asked, "Yo, Jade, was it? What's the deal with your girl?"

Jade was about to respond when Noah said, "Nah, fool. You aren't about to sit up in here and interrogate the guests."

"Whatchu mean? I am a guest," Roman argued.

"Nope. You're family. There's a difference," Noah laughed.

"Man, whatever," Roman said before looking at Jade again. "Are y'all hanging out for a while?"

Jade nodded, "We'll be spending the holidays here."

"Even better. I have plenty of time," he smiled mischievously.

"Ro, you better be nice to Mia. I don't have any claim on her, but on a serious tip, she's a good friend of mine and I know how you are. If you don't plan on coming to her correct, then don't come to her at all," Kenyon said and Jade didn't think she ever remembered Kenyon sounding so serious before.

"Yeah, yeah, I got you," Roman said nonchalantly.

"Nah, bro. I'm serious," Kenyon said.

"Okay, man. Damn! You sure nothing is going on between y'all? I don't want to step on anyone's toes," Roman eyed Kenyon.

"I'm positive. We're just friends. I don't look at her like that because I already know I don't have nothing for her but heartbreak, but like I said, she's a good friend and I don't want to see her hurt. She's been through too much to get her heart broken by anyone, especially you," Kenyon responded.

"Aight, bet." Roman nodded his head and looked at his brother and Jade. "So, what's the story with y'all? Noah hasn't brought a girl home in years. You must be special if you're spending the holidays here."

Jade blushed and said, "Oh, no. We aren't...I mean, uhm—"

"We aren't together," Noah helped her out.

"No?" Roman asked with a smile. "It sure looked like it when I walked in and y'all were all cuddled up."

Ignoring his brother, Noah stood up. "Okay, I'm going to get started on dinner."

Jade stood up with him, avoiding Roman's gaze. "I'll help."

Together, they walked up the stairs and Kenyon turned to Roman. "Damn, man. You sure know how to clear out a room."

"What I do?" Roman asked.

Kenyon stood up and laughed as he made his way towards the room he had been staying in so he could take a shower and get ready for dinner.

CHAPTER 8

"Gotdamn that food was goo"Gotdamn that food was good as fuck," Roman said as he leaned back in his chair and rubbed his belly. They were sitting in the dining room full as hell from the meal they'd just eaten. Jade and Mia had already cleaned up the kitchen and cleared the dishes so everyone was ready to unwind. Not that their day had been particularly exhausting.

"Yeah, Jade did her thang," Noah smiled over at her. Jade had taken over the kitchen that night and showed Noah what she was really working with in the kitchen. Not only did she do a crab leg boil, she had Mia and Kenyon go to the store to get her a few more ingredients. She made steaks, cheddar jalapeno, cornbread, cajun rice and creamed spinach. It was a true feast.

Noah had merely been her sous chef as she got in her zone and ordered him around. He didn't mind one bit. He was happy that he could give her an outlet to allow her creativity to flow. She was in her element as she chopped, seasoned, and cooked everything to perfection. He loved watching her work, and they talked the whole time. It was exactly what Noah hoped for when he asked her to stay the weekend at his house.

"I'm happy you all enjoyed it. It was the least I could do for letting Mia and I stay here for the holidays," Jade said shyly.

Ever since Roman insinuated that Jade and Noah were dating, Jade had gotten extremely shy around him. She didn't want to give Noah the wrong idea. She simply couldn't allow herself to have those kinds of feelings for him for many reasons. The main one being that he was her boss and the second reason being that she was married. Not that she loved her husband or even cared about him at this point, but what man would want her if she belonged to another? It wasn't fair to Noah, so she had to stay strong and fend off her whatever feelings she had for him.

Noah sensed her distance with him and decided to get everyone to loosen up a little. He got up and went into the kitchen while the others talked amongst themselves. When he came back out to the dining room, he plopped a big ass bottle of Hennessy on the table along with some plastic cups.

"Let's have a drink," he smiled.

"My nigga," Roman clapped his hands together, ready to get a little turned up. It wasn't often that he got to see his brother and Kenyon, so he was excited to spend a few days kickin' back with them. Their jobs kept them busy, and Roman being into illegal dealings, he didn't like bringing his family around too often for their own protection.

The ladies were a nice addition, Roman had to admit, and he couldn't wait to get next to Mia and get to know her on a personal level. She was good looking, but he also loved that she was sassy as hell and not afraid to cuss someone out. She was definitely his kind of woman, and he wanted to know her in the worst way.

"Aight, then," Kenyon smiled, "but you know Henny gets me to actin' a fool."

"As if you don't already," Mia rolled her eyes.

Noah looked to Jade, "You in?"

She sighed and then gave Mia a weak smile, "I said I would, but I have to warn you, I'm a complete lightweight. It's been forever since I've had any hard liquor so I will not be responsible for my actions."

"I'll take responsibility, Mouse," Mia grinned at her.

"Alright, then," Jade sighed and then smiled up at Noah who was already pouring shots into the cups.

He handed them out to everyone and then made a toast, "To spending the holidays with family and friends."

"Cheers!" Everyone said and then drank up.

Everyone took theirs like a pro, but Jade had a hard time getting the nasty ass liquid down. She made a face and her eyes watered after forcing it down. Noah saw her struggling and laughed. "Let me get you a Coke."

"Good idea," Jade choked out.

Noah disappeared back into the kitchen while Mia patted her on the back. "Don't worry. The first shot is always the worst shot."

Jade eyed her. "You're going to make me do that again?"

"Oh yeah. At least two more times," Mia winked at her and Jade groaned, already feeling warm from the shot she just took.

Noah came back into the room with a two liter of Coke in his hands. He poured a cup for Jade and handed it to her before saying, "Let's take this into the living room. We still have to do our Christmas Eve tradition."

"And what tradition is that?" Jade asked.

"Every year, we open up one present on Christmas eve. You get to choose which one," Roman said.

"We been doing this shit since we were little," Kenyon smiled.

"You spent the holidays with the Bennett's, Kenyon?" Mia asked.

"Yeah, our families are really close so we would switch off on who was hosting each year," Kenyon replied. "Our parents initially started the tradition because us three boys would whine and complain about not being able to open up presents, so to pacify us they started letting us choose one gift to open on Christmas Eve. The shit just carried on and it's still how we do it."

"Where are your parents this year?" Jade asked curiously.

"Once Ro turned twenty-one, our mom and Kenyon's mom do a holiday cruise every year. Since our pops passed away and then Kenyon's parents got divorced, Christmas wasn't really the same anymore, anyway." Noah said.

"They go live their best lives as single cougars," Kenyon laughed, "and us men get together and chill."

"That's sweet," Jade said sadly. The holidays were always a hard time of the year for her and she wished that she had some close family friends or siblings to help her get through the past years. All she had was her abusive husband who hated Christmas, and for a gift he would leave her with his shoe up her ass for wanting to put up a Christmas tree. She was happy that this year held some resemblance to a normal holiday for her. This time of year used to be her favorite, and she hoped she could get that magical feeling back.

"You don't have to tell me twice. Kenyon, what did you get me? I want to open that up right now," Mia giggled as she grabbed the bottle of Henny and raced towards the living room with Kenyon hot on her heels.

"How do you know I got your ass anything?" Kenyon shouted as they disappeared.

Roman followed them as he loudly apologized for not getting Mia something for Christmas, as if he'd known her more than two hours ago, and Jade laughed, feeling the effects from the liquor.

"They are a hot mess," she giggled.

"They really are," Noah chuckled and then held his hand out to her. "We'd better get in there so we can keep an eye on them."

Jade grabbed his hand and stood up, no longer feeling shy around him as warmth spread over her whole body. "I hate to break it to you, Noah, but I think you're on your own with that one. I told you I'm a lightweight and I am already feeling that liquor. It won't be too long before I'm acting just like them."

She giggled and walked towards the living room, pulling him along.

"Now that's a sight I want to see," he laughed as he said it. When they made it to the living room, Kenyon, Mia, and Roman were already tearing the paper off gifts excitedly like children.

"Y'all couldn't wait?" Jade asked. None of them answered. They were too focused on their gifts as Jade shook her head with a laugh and walked over to the tree. "Which one are you going to open?"

"Hmmm...I think I have my eye on this one," he picked up the gift that Jade bought for him. She was happy that she had the store wrap it for her because as much as she loved Christmas, she sucked at wrapping gifts.

"Good choice," Jade grinned. She peeked around the tree and saw a lot more gifts for herself than she expected. She saw one from Mia and a couple from Kenyon, but most of them were from Noah or from both Noah and Kenyon. "Wow, I wasn't expecting all of this, Noah."

She instantly felt bad, and she looked down at the one gift that Noah had in his hands from her. Noah saw the look on her face and knew what she was thinking.

"Hey, none of that." He lifted her chin up. "I'll admit that Kenyon and I went a little overboard, but we had fun shopping for y'all and we wanted to do it."

Jade nodded and picked out the biggest gift that was tagged for her from Noah. "If you're opening mine, I'll open one of yours."

"Sounds fair to me," he grinned at her and they sat down on the couch side by side. Everyone else was sitting on the floor looking over the gifts they opened. Kenyon got Mia a ton of clothes and she kept thanking him repeatedly. Kenyon was touched by the New York Knicks hoodie and sweatpants she had gotten him, especially knowing that she didn't have much money. He pulled her into a hug, while Roman thanked Noah for getting him a new virtual reality gaming system.

"No problem, bro. Maybe we can try it out here," Noah suggested.

"Hell yeah! I'll try to hook it up downstairs." Roman hopped up and headed for the stairs to the basement.

Noah turned to Jade. "Go ahead. Open it."

Jade looked down at the shiny wrapping paper that covered the oddly shaped gift. She carefully tore away at the wrapping paper, sensing Noah's eyes on her the whole time. She gasped when she realized what it was and quickly tore the rest of the paper away, discarding it on the floor. Unable to speak, she felt tears welling in her eyes as she stared at her gift.

"Awww, Jade. This is perfect for you. Noah, this was an amazing gift!" Mia cooed from the floor in front of them, but when she saw the emotion on her friend's face, she got to her feet and pulled Kenyon up, too. "We'll give you two a moment."

"But I wanted to see what she got for Noah," Kenyon protested as Mia pulled him out of the room.

"Boy, shut up!" she hissed as they disappeared from view.

Neither Jade nor Noah paid them any mind. Jade's gaze was fixed on her gift, and Noah's gaze was fixed on her. He was growing worried that she didn't like what he had gotten for her. "If you don't like it, I understand. I just thought—"

Jade cut him off by pulling him into a tight hug. She wrapped her arms around his neck and let the tears fall. "It's perfect."

Shocked by her sudden show of affection, he froze for a moment and then wrapped his arms around her small frame and buried his nose into the nape of her neck. She smelled like fresh laundry and body wash. He basked in the hug and let her cry on his shoulder as he stroked her braids. "I'm happy you like it, Jade."

"I love it. Thank you so much. This means the world to me," she whispered before pulling away from him. She wiped her tears and gazed over at the painting easel. She hadn't realized just how much she truly missed painting until she saw it sitting in front of her. She yearned to put it to use, and her heart leapt at the thought that she would be able to soon.

"You know, it's just us two up here. I won't tell anyone if you want to open up another one," Noah said as he got up and went over to the tree. He picked up another package that was wrapped in the same shiny red paper as the one she just opened.

She grinned up at him. "Okay, but you open yours first."

He sat down and wasted no time ripping open the wrapping paper to his own gift. His smile grew wide when he saw it. Jade felt the need to explain in case he thought it was silly, "I noticed that your other one broke last week. I know it isn't much, but when I saw it I thought of you."

"It's perfect," he grinned down at the black leather briefcase she had gotten him. One of the handles on his broke last week, and he hadn't had time to get a new one. It touched his heart that she had been so thoughtful and it looked like she spent a nice amount on it, which warmed his heart even more because he knew that she didn't have much to begin with.

"I'm glad you like it. I didn't know what to get a man that already has everything," Jade giggled.

Noah looked at her intensely, "I don't have everything."

Jade shuffled around in her seat and cleared her throat. "Are you sure you want me to open this now? I can wait."

"I'm sure. Open it."

She ripped the paper from the gift and smiled when she saw it was a couple of canvases, paints and paint brushes all sitting neatly in a gift box. She turned to Noah.

"Thank you, Noah. This is amazing, but I don't have anywhere to put all of these things." She said sadly.

"Keep them here. You're welcome to come any time and use them. I can put them in the basement for you and you can work on them in peace," Noah said. He'd thought about this already, and he wasn't ashamed to admit that he loved that this gift not only would make her happy, but gave her a chance to come to his home more often.

"How is that going to work when you're always at work?" Jade smiled coyly.

Noah shook his head and laughed along with her. She wasn't

wrong. He worked a lot, and that presented a problem. Suddenly, an idea popped in his head and without thinking it through he said, "I'll make you a key so you can come and go as you please."

Jade was taken aback by his suggestion and she wasn't sure how she should feel about it. On one hand, Noah's house has given her a great sense of security in the last twenty-four hours and she was secretly dreading her return to the cold streets of New York, but on the other hand, she was terrified of Noah. Not in the way that she was her husband, but because of the growing feelings she was gaining for him. Noticing her hesitation, Noah quickly added, "Think of it as an art studio."

Jade grinned and finally nodded her head, "Okay, but on one condition."

Noah cocked his head to the side, "What's that?"

"Any time I use that key then I have to cook you a meal," she smiled.

"I won't argue with that," Noah beamed.

Jade stood up and began picking up the wrapping paper off the floor. Noah got up to help and together they cleaned up the living room before making their way down to the basement to check in with the others.

CHAPTER 9

"NEVER HAVE I EVER...SLEPT OUTSIDE," ROMAN LAUGHED loudly and Noah roughly hit him upside the head. "Ow!"

"Nigga, that was a low blow and you know it," Noah said through clenched teeth. Jade and Mia giggled uncontrollably and took their shots back effortlessly. They didn't care that Roman was playing dirty, because they had something for his ass.

The five of them were sprawled out in the basement playing *Never Have I Ever*. Jade and Mia were sitting on the fluffy white carpet with blankets wrapped around them while the guys were spread out on the couch. They'd been playing the game for the last hour once they'd all had their turn with Roman's virtual reality game. The game allowed them all to get to know each other better, and by now, Roman knew all about Mia and Jade's living situation. In Roman's eyes, Mia's story only made her more sexy. He loved a woman that was down to earth and familiar with the streets. Mia was playing hard to get, though. She found Roman very attractive, but she had already dated a street nigga and he was the reason she was in the situation she was currently in. She could tell that Roman was about that street shit from the moment she laid eyes on him, which gave her pause. She refused to make the same mistake twice, so she would keep an eye on his sexy ass.

Jade giggled and said, "It's okay, Noah. The game isn't over yet."

She was drunk as hell at this point and really enjoying herself. It had been a long ass time since she could let her guard down and act a fool. Basically, she was able to act like a normal twenty-five-year-old and she was loving it. Noah shook his head, mad at his brother for letting that nonsense come out of his mouth, but too drunk to do anything about it. Then, a thought came to him and he smiled maliciously. "That means us three have to take a shot, too. Remember when our dads took us on that camping trip when we were little?"

Kenyon groaned and then hit Roman upside the head. "Stupid ass nigga."

"Y'all better stop putting yo hands on me," Roman gritted out before pouring himself another shot out of the almost empty bottle of Hennessy.

They took their shots, and Mia jumped in as soon as they were done, slurring her words. Homegirl was tore up. "Never have I ever... eaten pussy!"

Jade's whole face turned dark red as she covered it with her hands and shrieked with laughter. She stopped giggling long enough to lift her head up and see that Noah was taking his shot back with a smirk on his face while staring directly at her. Jade instantly stopped laughing as she stared into Noah's lust filled eyes. The Henny was doing something to her and giving her urges she'd suppressed long ago. Once she got married, it was clear that sex was for pain, and not pleasure, so she forced herself to forget about what sex was really like. She couldn't cheat because if Elijah found out, he would kill her. So, she masturbated from time to time to keep her urges from becoming too great. Otherwise, she forced her needs away and kept them locked in a small box in the back of her head.

Tonight, that box was nudging its way forward and begging to be freed. Those feelings she had for Noah that she was desperately trying to bury were fighting to be freed as well, and she wasn't doing much at the moment to stop any of it from happening. She licked her lips seductively while maintaining eye contact with him. Noah could feel his manhood hardening and he wanted nothing more than to bring Jade up to his room, but he forced himself to calm down. They were all drunk as hell, and he wouldn't take advantage of her like that. He couldn't.

"Oh, so y'all want to play nasty. Aight, then. Fuck this game. How about we get a game of truth or dare going?" Kenyon asked.

"What are you, in junior high?" Mia laughed.

"What, you scared, mami?" Kenyon asked with a grin.

"Never scared, boo. Let's do it," Mia grabbed the bottle of Henny and downed the rest of it.

"Okay, then, you're up first. Truth or dare?" Kenyon asked.

"Dare, papi," Mia said confidently.

"I dare you to lick my feet," Kenyon cracked up laughing at Mia's expression.

"Hell, no. I am not licking your crusty ass feet, Kenyon. You must have lost your damn mind."

"If you refuse to do the dare or speak your truth, then you have to strip off an article of clothing," Roman piped in as he grinned at Mia's sexy ass.

"You can't just make up new rules like that!" She protested.

"Sure he can," Kenyon chimed in.

Mia sighed and tried to focus her eyes on what she was wearing. She was drunk, and it wasn't as easy as it sounded. Once she could focus enough, she realized she didn't have anything simple on, like socks, so she opted to take off her bra with her shirt still on. She looped her arms through her shirt until she could unhook her bra. Her big breasts bounced free from under the tank top she was wearing. She had to be careful continuing on with this game, because all she had left were her black leggings and her tank top. She wasn't even wearing panties.

Mia turned her gaze on Jade, who was trying to act innocent and blend into the damn carpet.

"You aren't invisible, Mouse. I can see your ass," Mia giggled and Jade cracked a smile and rolled her eyes.

"What the hell do you want, Mimi?" Jade asked playfully.

"Truth or dare?" Mia asked.

Jade smiled at her while sticking her middle finger up. She hoped that she could stay quiet and skip out on playing this game, but Mia had other plans.

"Ohhh I like drunk Jade. Who would have ever thought you were so feisty?" Mia giggled.

Jade waved her off and said, "Truth."

"Okay, where is your soft spot?" Mia asked with a grin.

Jade blushed again and then glanced at Noah before focusing on her best friend. "My nipples."

"Ohhhh, mine too. That shit be feeling so good, especially when they suck on them lightly and then use a little bit of teeth. I swear I could cum from that alone," Mia rambled.

Jade was too drunk and too caught up in the moment to remember that she was surrounded by three men and it wasn't just her and her bestie in the room.

"Hell yeah, and then when they do that little flicking thingy with their tongue right on the nip—" Jade stopped talking and looked around the room. All three of the men were looking at them with their mouths open.

Noah shifted his erect dick around in his sweatpants discreetly while Roman licked his lips at Mia. Kenyon discreetly pulled out his phone as they were talking and began typing notes in it with his dumb ass.

Jade didn't even have it in her anymore to be embarrassed. This was her. This was how she used to be before she was married. A free spirit and a sexual being. She loved that she could be her old self again, even if it was just for a night. Her pussy was soaking wet just from that conversation, and she felt like she needed to masturbate soon before she exploded.

She cleared her throat and said, "uh, okay. Kenyon, truth or dare?"

"Truth," he answered after setting his phone back down.

"What's the most amount of women you've slept with in a twenty-four-hour period?" Jade asked.

"Ten," Kenyon said without hesitating.

"Gross!" Mia giggled and Jade just looked at him like he was crazy.

"What? There were a couple of threesomes thrown in there and...I don't know. Shit just happens," he grinned.

Noah shook his head as he laughed, "That shit is just nasty, bro."

"Man, anyway. Truth or dare, Noah?" Kenyon asked.

"Dare," Noah said, still fighting to get his dick under control.

"I dare you to suck on Jade's nipples," Kenyon could barely get his sentence out before falling out laughing. Mia and Roman burst into laughter, too, while Jade turned red again.

"Why y'all always messing with us?" Jade asked with a small giggle.

"Cause, y'all obviously like each other, so we're just trying to move the shit along," Kenyon said between laughs and Mia nodded her head happily.

"Man, I can't do that," Noah grinned as he took his shirt off exposing his solid chest and hidden tattoos.

Jade stared at him. He looked like a Greek God to her, with his sexy dark skin and toned body. She wanted to touch all over him, but she settled for staring at him. They kept stealing glances at each other as the game continued. At one point, Mia dared Jade to sit in Noah's lap for the rest of the game. Jade had already taken off most of her clothing when she passed on some crazy ass dares and the only thing she had left was her sweater dress. She was determined to keep that on and sitting on Noah's lap wasn't the worst thing she could think of.

She sat on him sideways like a baby and laid her head on his chest, her head spinning. She was so tiny compared to him and being on his lap and in his arms really made her feel secure. At some point,

Jade passed out, and when she woke up again, she was moving. Noah was carrying her up the stairs to the second level. She peered up at him and when he realized she was awake he said, "Hey, sleepyhead. I'm just taking you to your room."

Jade shook her head against the bare skin of his chest and whispered, "I don't want to be alone tonight. Can I sleep in your room?"

Noah stopped outside her room and stood there for a moment. He wasn't sure if he could sleep in the same bed as her and control himself, but he also knew that he couldn't have sex with her tonight. Against his better judgement, he nodded his head and carried her into his room. He laid her down on his king sized bed and she sunk into the plush comforter. "Do you need anything?"

Jade nodded sleepily, "Can I take a shower?"

He smiled, "Of course. Wait here."

She saw him moving around in the dark and a moment later there was a soft glow coming from the nightstand beside her. Another appeared, and then another, and in her drunken state, it took Jade a few moments to realize that he was lighting candles. When he was finished, she could see him clearly in the glowing light. He left out of the room and Jade was almost asleep again when he returned a few minutes later. He smiled down at her and asked, "Are you sure you want to take a shower now? It can wait until morning."

Jade nodded, "Yeah. I won't be long."

He helped her sit up and get out of bed. Her sweater dress rose up her thighs, and it took everything in him not to pull it up over her head and lay her back down in his bed. He shook his head to clear his drunken thoughts as he did his best to steady himself and her.

"I brought you a towel, and I grabbed your bag from your room in case you needed anything from it, but here, drink some of this first," he said, handing her a bottle of water.

She took the bottle gratefully and drank half of it before setting it on the nightstand. "Thank you."

"You don't have to continue thanking me, Jade," he said as he stared down at her.

She cocked her head to the side, "But that's what you say when someone does something nice for you."

He laughed, "That's true. The bathroom is right through that door. Feel free to grab one of my T-shirts in my dresser to wear to bed. I'm going to take a quick shower down the hall but let me know if you need anything."

"Oh, I will," Jade looked at him with a playful smile on her face as she walked backwards towards the bathroom, almost falling down backwards as she tripped over her feet. She righted herself quickly and said, "I'm okay!"

Noah laughed at her and made sure she got in the bedroom okay before gathering his things and heading down the hall so he could take a very cold shower.

Jade was finished with her shower first. She came out to the bedroom with a towel wrapped around her and feeling a little more sober than she had before. She walked into Noah's walk-in closet and rifled through his dresser drawers before finding the one that held all of his t-shirts. She selected a blue one from the top and slipped it over her head, loving that it smelled like him. Dropping the towel in the laundry basket, she walked back into the bedroom when Noah came through the door. They both froze when they made eye contact, sizing each other up.

That cold shower did nothing for Noah because as soon as he saw Jade standing in the middle of his room with his shirt on, his manhood stiffened up again. Her nipples were poking straight through his shirt and he wanted to drop to his knees and take them into his mouth, one by one.

Jade couldn't take her eyes off Noah, who only had a towel wrapped around his waist. She could see his dick imprint and her pussy got wet all over again.

Ignoring how turned on she was, she made her way over to the bed and got under the comforter. His bed was ten times more comfortable than the one in the guest room, and she knew she would sleep well tonight. It didn't hurt that the smell of him was everywhere. She sighed in satisfaction as Noah went into his closet so he could but some pajama pants on, opting to leave his chest bare.

Jade felt the bed dip as Noah got in, and she turned over so she was facing him. He laid down close to her and stared her in the eyes. She was so beautiful to him. Her sleepy eyes bore into his, and in that moment, everything seemed right in the world. He wanted to kiss her and he threw caution to the wind as he lifted his hand to caress her face.

Jade flinched when she saw his large hand coming towards her, and she scooted away from him. Confused, Noah asked, "What's wrong?"

Jade's heart was racing as tears welled in her eyes from embarrassment. She wasn't used to someone being gentle with her, so she assumed that he was going to slap her when she saw his hand coming towards her face.

"I-I'm s-sorry," Jade stammered as she tried to get her heartbeat under control.

Just like that, her husband ruined the peaceful feeling that was residing inside of her all day. That was enough to reduce her to tears. The liquor didn't help, of course. She let the tears fall and an alarmed Noah didn't know what to do. He wasn't sure what he had done wrong, but he wanted to figure it out so he didn't do it again. "Jade, I'm so sorry, I didn't mean to—"

"It's not you. You're perfect, Noah," she said in between cries.

"Then...what's the matter?" He asked. Jade tried to calm herself down, but she couldn't as she thought about all the shit she had been through. She hadn't really allowed herself to cry about her situation, but in this moment it all seemed to come out. Noah watched helplessly as Jade sobbed into his pillow.

"Can I hold you?" he asked hesitantly. Jade nodded her head, and Noah wasted no time pulling her against his body. He rubbed her back in small circles and said, "please, tell me what's wrong?"

It took a moment for her to speak, and when she did, it broke Noah's heart. "He used to beat me. My husband. H-he's such a big guy, and I'm so small. There was nothing I could do to fight back. Even if I could, I'm terrified of him. If I ever fought back, he would kill me. He almost *did* kill me, Noah. That's why I ran. It's why I'm poor and homeless. I was in the hospital after a particularly bad beating, and I decided that enough was enough. I decided to love myself for once, so I ran and left everything behind."

The more Jade talked, the angrier Noah became. The thought of a grown ass man putting his hands on Jade was enough to drive him to insanity. She was the most sweet woman he had ever met, and she was so fucking small. He couldn't imagine how much abuse her little body could handle, but it wasn't long before he found out.

"He wasn't like that when we were dating...you know? As soon as we got married, it was like a switch flipped. It started out as a few slaps here and there. That turned into full-blown punches, but never on my face. Once he started actually breaking bones, it was as if he no longer cared about me at all. He started fucking up my face, too. I got really good at covering that shit up. Don't even get me started on the sexual abuse. He would stick just about anything inside of me for his own amusement. Broom handles, hammers, wrenches...anything that he thought would give me the maximum amount of pain. He shoved those things everywhere, too." Jade shivered as she thought about all those foreign objects entering her body and Noah held her tighter.

As she cried in his arms he said, "I'm sorry that happened to you, Jade. I wish there was something I could do to take your pain away."

She sniffled. "You already have in so many ways. You don't understand how much you've helped me in these last few weeks. You've done more for me than anyone has in a very long time... possibly ever."

Noah's jaw ticked as he fought to keep his anger under control. He couldn't help it. Thinking of Jade battered and broken had his nerves completely shot. It made sense to him now why she wanted to use her maiden name on her work documents and why she was insistent that she didn't want to be found. "I'm happy I could help you, Jade, but it doesn't feel like enough."

Jade looked up into his eyes as she wiped her own. "Believe me when I say that it is more than enough, Noah."

Her words were slurred, and Noah wondered if she would even remember this conversation tomorrow. She'd had a lot to drink tonight, and he wondered if she would have ever shared this part of her life with him had she been sober. He sighed heavily as his own thoughts swirled around in his mind. He'd had a great deal to drink tonight, too, but he was trying his hardest to keep a sober mind. "Get some rest, Jade. It's been a long night."

Jade wasn't paying what he was saying any mind, though. Instead, she stared at his full lips as he talked. His handsome features pulling at her heartstrings. She didn't know what it was about Noah that had her so open, but it scared her and enticed her all at the same time. That throb in her pussy was back and being this close to Noah made her reason fly out of the window. She grabbed his face with her small hands and brought her lips to his. She kissed him softly and sensually. Despite wanting to keep a sober mind and refrain from doing anything that Jade might regret in the morning, Noah kissed her back. He couldn't resist the feel of her soft lips on his own. Her heavenly scent caused him to moan into her mouth as he parted his lips. Their tongues danced together as they explored each other. The soft glow from the candles provided such a sensual vibe throughout the room and Jade couldn't stop the heat that was rising within her, pulsating through her womanhood.

Without breaking the kiss, she shifted and climbed on top of Noah so she was straddling him. Noah lifted the blanket, so it fell over her and created a cocoon for the two of them. Jade settled into Noah so that her bare pussy was directly on top of his hard dick. She moaned when she felt how thick it was. Jade ground down into him, causing them both to moan out in ecstasy.

Noah's mind was racing as he palmed her ass and started kissing her neck. He didn't know what the hell Jade was doing to him, but he'd never craved a woman so badly in his life. He felt like he was spiraling out of control as he thumbed her nipples through his shirt she was wearing. Her moans intensified as she rocked into him, the thin fabric of his pajama pants the only thing between them.

Noah grunted and flipped Jade onto her back, both of their heads spinning as he settled in between her legs. He lifted her t-shirt off and tossed it to the side. Leaning back, he took a moment to take in how beautiful she was. As small as she was, she had curves that dipped and swerved in the exact right places. Her flat stomach gave way to curvy hips and a nice ass. Not too big, but perfect for her tiny frame. Her breasts were a full C cup and her nipples pointed straight up at him. He wasted no more time as he pulled one into his mouth and sucked slowly.

Jade squirmed beneath him as her pussy got wetter. She needed relief...*bad*. She clawed at Noah's back and moaned loudly, loving the sensation that his mouth was giving her. As he went to work on her nipples, Noah scooted to the side so he could trace his finger down her body. It traveled down her stomach and dipped at her belly button until it rested at her womanhood. He traced it over her wet folds, never breaking his rhythm with his mouth on her nipples, rotating between the two. Jade cried out as Noah found her clit and began sliding his finger over it, back and forth slowly.

Without warning, he dipped his finger inside of her gently and the walls in her pussy clenched around him tightly. He groaned out loud with her when he felt how tight she was. His fingers were in a sanctuary right now, and he wanted to make sure that Jade understood that. He took his time with her and slid his thick finger in and out of her slowly. She gasped when his thumb found her clit and rubbed it in slow circles. His pointer finger curved in and hit her g-spot. It was game over after that. Her hips thrusted up to meet his finger. Her body shook as an orgasm built from her stomach and traveled down to her pussy.

Juices flowed out of her as she moaned loudly. Noah didn't slow his pace or stop until her body stopped shaking and she went limp. He took his mouth off her nipple and kissed up her body until he reached her lips. Jade kissed him feverishly, pulling him into her. She tried pulling down his pants, ready to feel him inside of her, but he pulled back. "Nah, baby. I can't do that. Not tonight."

Jade stared at him, "What? Why?"

It took every bit of strength for Noah not to give in and give Jade exactly what she wanted, but she deserved more than that. He wanted not only her body, but he wanted her mind and heart, too. "Jade, when we have sex, there won't be any turning back. I already like you a lot, and sex will only intensify that. There will be no turning back after that, and I want you to be sober and completely ready for that. Tonight isn't the night, baby. I want you to be sure you're ready for everything I'll give you."

Jade was speechless as she stared into his eyes. He rolled off of her and adjusted his stiff dick, wishing like hell he could get just a little taste of Jade's sweetness, but knowing that it wouldn't be right. She thought about it for a moment and couldn't find anything wrong with giving in to Noah, but she also knew that he wouldn't believe her if she said it out loud in that moment. She was drunk as hell and any promises she agreed to tonight might not be held up tomorrow. She sighed loudly and curled up next to him, trying to calm the heat that was raging between her legs. Instead of telling him she was sure that she was ready for every delicious thing he wanted to give her, she said, "For the record, I really like you, too."

Noah smiled and pulled her in closer. Eventually, the rhythm of Jade's breathing slowed as she drifted off into a blissful sleep. Noah, on the other hand, stayed up until the wee hours of the morning, thinking about Jade and how he could make her his.

CHAPTER 10

A POUNDING HEAD WOKE JADE UP LATE ON CHRISTMAS afternoon. She squinted her eyes at the clock on the nightstand and saw that it was almost one in the afternoon. She shook her head, trying to get some fuzziness to clear up when she remembered whose bed she was in. She smiled shyly and rolled over to find Noah missing. She continued to smile to herself as the memories of last night slowly came back to her. She was happy that she remembered with as much as she had drank. Her aching head reminded her of just how much alcohol she consumed and her smile faltered a bit. She felt like complete shit.

She glanced back at the nightstand and saw that there was a cold bottle of water and a couple Advil laying there. *He's always thinking of me,* she thought with a smile as she sat up slowly. She grabbed the bottle of water and chugged half of it before taking the pills and chugging the other half. Knowing that it would take a bit of time for her headache to go away, she decided to take a shower and get dressed so she could get something to eat down in the kitchen.

"Maybe that will settle my stomach," she muttered as she slowly got out of bed. The room started spinning as she stood up, so she grabbed onto the nightstand to steady herself. Once she felt as though she could walk, she made her way into the bathroom and took a long steamy shower.

She opted to wear a pair of loose fitting jeans and a black long-sleeved shirt. It wasn't the cutest outfit, but the jeans were comfortable and the shirt made her breasts look huge and it had a dip in the front so it showed cleavage. Opting to leave her hair down, she pulled opened the bedroom door and grinned when she saw Mia sneaking out of her room.

Mia made eye contact with her and froze.

"What the hell are you doing in *there*?" Mia whispered playfully.

Jade shushed Mia as she rushed towards her and grabbed her hand, pulling her into the guest room that she'd stayed in a few nights ago. Jade closed the door and then sat on the bed, grinning at her friend. "Nuh uh. You first. Why were you creeping around like a thief in the night?"

Mia waved her off, "Because Roman was still asleep."

Jade Shrieked, "I knew it!"

Mia grinned at her, "The dick was bomb, too. I can't even lie. It was like biiiig and—"

Jade held up her hand. She knew that Mia would ramble on and on and Jade really didn't want to hear her freaky details knowing that she didn't get to even see what Noah was working with last night. "I don't need details, Mimi."

"Girl, whatever. What I want to know is why your ass was coming out of Noah's room," Mia beamed, ready to hear all the juicy details.

Jade blushed. "Not much to tell. We slept together, and that's really it."

She didn't want to give any details about what went on last night. It was such an intimate moment, and she wanted to keep it between her and Noah.

"Uh, huh. Let me find out you let Noah beat the kitty up," Mia giggled.

Jade playfully shoved her and said, "No, but for real, we had a deep conversation. I told him about Elijah. He was so sweet about it all, too."

"Mouse, that man is wide open for you. I'm happy y'all are finally giving it a chance," Mia grinned.

"I'm not exactly sure what we're doing, but I will say that it feels right," Jade blushed again.

Mia had never seen her friend so happy, and it overjoyed her. Jade deserved the best that life offered, and Mia fully believed that Noah would be the one to give that to her. She just hoped that Jade would be open to it. "Listen, I was just going to use the bathroom before I woke Roman up again. I need a little more time with him, if you know what I mean. He does this thing with his tongue—"

"AHT! I don't need to know," Jade giggled. "Go ahead, girl. Get your groove on! You deserve it."

Mia got off the bed and winked at Jade, then started twerking her ass, "Damn right I do! We'll be down in a while. I'm ready to open up my presents."

Jade giggled and said, "Bye girl," before walking out of the room behind Mia.

She made her way down the stairs and through the hall, peeping into each room, looking for Noah. She found him in the kitchen warming up some leftovers from last night. When he saw her in the doorway, his breath caught. She was so fuckin gorgeous without even trying. Her brown eyes bore into his as they smiled at each other.

"Good morning," she smiled shyly at him.

"Good morning, beautiful," he grinned at her. "I was just warming up some leftovers from last night. Do you want some?"

She giggled, "No breakfast?"

"I didn't have it in me to cook anything. Besides, it's more like lunchtime," he said, glancing at the clock on the stove.

"True," she laughed. "Yeah, I'll have some leftovers."

"Here, you can have my plate," he said as the microwave beeped. He took the plate out of the microwave and sat it on the island.

"It's okay, I can make my own plate. Go ahead and eat, Noah," she said as she walked over to the refrigerator so she could pull the food back out, but he stopped her by putting his arms around her.

Her back was to him as he massaged her hips and bent down to whisper in her ear. "You're a guest here, baby. Let me cater to you."

Jade's legs turned to jelly as she turned around in his arms so she was facing him. She tried to play cool as she asked, "What if I want to cater to you?"

Noah smirked at her, and without warning he lifted her effort-lessly and sat her on the counter. Her legs automatically wrapped around his middle as he set his large hands on her small waist. He leaned in close to her and said, "then I'd say let's take turns, but today is my day."

She smiled, their lips almost touching. "Oh yeah?"

"Yeah," he said before kissing her. Jade cupped his cheeks as they kissed, tongues intertwining and dancing together. She instantly got wet as she replayed in her mind how good he'd made her feel last night with only his fingers.

She pulled away from him and looked into his eyes. "I want you."

He smirked down at her. "Do you remember what I said last night?"

Jade gulped, but nodded her head. Noah chuckled and said, "Patience, baby."

Before she could protest, he kissed her again, and she melted against him. Someone cleared their throat from behind them and Noah groaned and without looking asked, "What, Kenyon?"

Kenyon walked into the kitchen, grinning. "Oh, nothing. Nice to see you two getting along so well."

Jade's whole face flushed red as she buried her head in Noah's chest, embarrassed that Kenyon had caught them in such a heated moment. Noah chuckled, and rubbed Jade's back. "Man, what do you want?"

"In case you haven't noticed, this is the kitchen, not your bedroom. I'm hungry. Ohh, look! Leftovers." Kenyon picked up the plate of hot food on the island counter.

Noah snatched it out of Kenyon's hands. "This is Jade's food. Get your own."

Kenyon laughed, "Fine."

Kenyon busied himself with grabbing food out of the refrigerator while Noah pried Jade's face out of his chest. She looked up at him and let out an embarrassed giggle. He loved how shy she was around people, but he was happy that she wasn't like that with him anymore. "Here. Eat. It'll help you feel a little better."

He set the food next to her on the counter and she made a move to jump down. Noah stopped her and shook his head as he bent down so he could whisper in her ear. "Stay here. You look so sexy sitting up there like that."

Jade blushed again, but stayed where she was. She grabbed her plate and began eating the steak, potatoes and cornbread that were left over from last night. When Noah was finished warming his food up, he lifted Jade off of the counter and sat her down on a stool, taking a seat next to her. Kenyon watched them with a mouthful of food, grinning at them happily. "Aren't you too just the cutest things ever?"

"Shut up, man," Noah grumbled while Jade covered up her mouth with a napkin and giggled.

It wasn't long before Mia and Roman joined them in the kitchen looking a hot mess. Mia's hair was all over her head and Roman's pajama pants were on backwards.

"Ewww, not y'all, too!" Kenyon shouted. Mia swatted at him and told him to shut up. Everyone laughed and Kenyon said, "damn, how did I become the fifth wheel? Fuck all that. I'm inviting someone over tonight."

"Nobody wants to be around one of your whores on Christmas," Mia chuckled.

Kenyon thought about it for a moment and said, "You're probably right. I wouldn't want to give them the wrong idea, anyway. Spending the holiday with them and all."

Mia giggled, "You ain't shit."

"I know," Kenyon grinned.

"Anyway," Noah stood up and grabbed his and Jade's plates before putting them in the sink. "We'll be in the living room. Come join us when you're done so we can open presents."

Noah grabbed Jade's hand and led her out of the kitchen. There was a collective *awwww* behind them, and Jade's cheeks burned in embarrassment. She wasn't used to all the attention. Her husband normally treated her as though she were invisible. Sometimes, she really felt as though she were. She felt a pang in her heart when she realized the situation she was in. It wasn't fair to Noah at all that she was still married. How could she truly have something with him if she had a husband?

She sat down on the couch next to Noah, deep in thought. He pulled her close to him and asked, "Penny for your thoughts?"

"I meant what I said last night, Noah. I really do like you."

He smiled and kissed her forehead. "That's great, because I really like you, too."

Jade bit her lip in worry and stared at the Christmas tree. Noah pulled her chin towards him so she was looking him in the eye. "Hey, what's on your mind?"

"I'm married," she said with tears brimming in her eyes. "And it isn't fair. I'll always be married to him. How is that fair to you?"

"What if I helped you get a divorce? I can protect you, Jade. You don't have to stay married to that bitch made nigga," Noah seethed.

Jade had never heard such venom in Noah's voice. Her heart leapt because she knew he only wanted her to be happy and safe, but Noah really didn't know who he was dealing with. Elijah was a dangerous man, and if he ever found her, he would kill her. She shook her head, "He's a powerful lawyer. He's defended some of the most dangerous criminals in New York, and they all owe him favors. I couldn't ask you to get in the middle of that, Noah. We would both end up dead."

Noah's jaw ticked in anger. He took a moment to calm down before kissing her on the forehead and saying, "It's Christmas. Let's not talk about it today, okay? I don't want you thinking about it, either. Let's just enjoy the day and worry about the other bullshit tomorrow."

Jade sighed somberly before nodding her head. "Okay."

"Hey, I don't want to see anything but a smile on your face today. Think you can manage that?" Noah asked.

Jade gave him a small smile. "I can try."

"Good," Noah grinned. He wanted to make this Christmas a good one, and allowing thoughts of her punk ass husband wasn't on his agenda today. He knew that he would figure out a way to get rid of that nigga for good, but today wasn't the day. He wanted Jade to have the best Christmas she had ever had. In Noah's mind, she deserved it more than anyone, especially since he had found out more about her past.

Noah got off the couch and put some wood into the fireplace. He remembered how much she loved sitting in front of it the other night, and he hoped that it would bring a smile to her face today. As he stacked the wood in the fireplace and then lit the fire, his mind wandered to visions of him and Jade making love in front of the fireplace on top of a fluffy blanket. He had to stop himself from delving too far into that dream because his dick was rising and now was not the time. Last night had been incredible for him, and it was only PG-13 in his eyes. He craved more, but he knew he needed to be patient.

When the fire was lit, he went to the linen closet and found a plush comforter that he kept for guests and threw it on the ground in front of the fireplace and right next to the tree. Noah sat down and leaned his back against the couch and then looked at Jade. "Come sit with me."

She smiled and got off the couch with a brown throw blanket in her hands. She sat between his legs and leaned back into his chest before putting the blanket over them. His arms wrapped around her and Jade felt so safe and happy in this moment. Thoughts of her husband tried to creep their way in, but she pushed them away and focused on the warmth of the fireplace and the heat between her and

Noah. They didn't speak, they just watched the fire crackling and got lost in their own happy thoughts. It wasn't long before Kenyon, Mia, and Roman made their way into the living room. The three of them stopped when they saw Jade and Noah cuddled up together. Mia spoke first, "Aww don't you two look comfy?"

Jade's head snapped towards the doorway of the living room, and her cheeks burned red. She had practically forgotten that she and Noah weren't the only two people in the house. She tried to pull away from Noah out of shyness, but he held her in place so she relaxed back into him and just smiled sheepishly at her friend.

"That's nothing. You should have seen what I walked in on them doing in the kitchen," Kenyon grinned.

"Man, shut up," Noah said as he grabbed a pillow off the couch and threw it at Kenyon, who ducked just in time for the pillow to miss him. It landed with a soft thud behind him as Kenyon continued to grin at Noah.

Mia quirked her eyebrow at Jade and Noah with a wide smile on her face, but she didn't say anything. Instead, she walked over to the tree and started grabbing gifts. "I'm ready to open some presents."

"You're like a little kid," Jade laughed.

Mia shrugged, "Christmas is my favorite holiday."

Roman helped Mia pass out presents and before long everyone was tearing into packages and chatting excitedly amongst themselves. Jade, who was now sitting across from Noah on the floor, opened up a huge box from Kenyon and Noah full of clothes and shoes. Her eyes watered at the site of all the clothes. She thanked them both and put the box aside after promising Noah that she would model each outfit for him later. Mia screamed and then jumped on Jade when she opened her gift from her. Jade had gotten Mia and herself a cellphone with a combined plan. Jade laughed as Mia hugged her, "You're welcome, Mimi. I got one, too. I figured we can split the bill each month. It's not the unlimited plan, so make sure you're mindful and—"

"Okayyyy, mom," Mia giggled as she rolled her eyes in mock

annoyance. "Seriously, thank you. I love it. I can finally get back on social media!"

Jade laughed as her friend became fixated on setting up her new phone, ignoring the rest of her gifts. She opened up her gift from Mia, who had gotten her a huge MAC makeup bundle that had everything she needed to beat her whole face to perfection. At this rate, Jade couldn't wait to go back to work so she could wear a new outfit and makeup and feel like a new woman.

Kenyon and Mia began arguing loudly over the fact that Mia had gotten him a large box of condoms. Mia was laughing her ass off while calling Kenyon all types of hoes and Kenyon was acting offended like he wouldn't use the whole box up in a week. Everyone ignored them as they bickered and continued opening gifts.

By the time Jade finished opening her gifts, she had so much shit, she really didn't know what she would do with it all. She had clothes, shoes, makeup, all kinds of body sprays and body washes, perfumes, and gift cards to different department stores and restaurants. Kenyon and Noah really spoiled her and Mia. They went crazy and bought them both everything in order to live a semi-normal life. They had all only known each other for a few weeks, but they'd formed such a tight bond and Jade had a sense of family for the first time in years. She felt loved, safe, and she had a full belly. Life was so good in this moment, and she wanted to hold on to it forever.

Jaded peeped Roman whispering something in Mia's ear. She giggled and nodded her head. They stood up and left the room without telling anyone where they were going. Kenyon grimaced and said, "Nasty asses."

Jade giggled. She knew exactly where her friend and Roman were going, but she couldn't even be mad.

Kenyon stood up, too, and said, "I have to make a call to one of my shortys."

He started to walk out of the room and when he was at the doorway, he turned and grinned at Jade and Noah, "Y'all be good."

Jade buried her head in her hands and giggled while Noah said, "Get lost."

Kenyon chuckled and left the room, and Jade peeked out from behind her hands before lowering them to her sides. Noah watched her for a moment and asked, "What do you want to do now?"

Jade thought about it for a moment. She honestly wouldn't mind getting back in bed and taking a nap since her head was still hurting, but she didn't want to sleep the day away. She looked at Noah and shrugged her shoulders, "I don't know. I wouldn't mind a nap, but I also don't want to sleep the day away and I already slept so late."

"Would you like to paint? I can get you set up in the basement," Noah asked.

Jade smiled but shook her head, "No, my head is hurting too bad right now."

Noah stood up and reached for her hand. He pulled her up from the floor and started pulling her out of the room. She looked back at the mess they'd left behind and said, "Don't you want to clean all this up first?"

"Nah, I'll get it later," Noah said, so she followed him out of the room and down the hall. He led her down the steps of the basement and said, "Let's watch movies. What's Christmas without watching a ton of movies and eating cookies all day?"

Jade laughed, "But we don't have any cookies."

"True, and I have to admit that I'm not much of a baker, but would you settle for other forms of junk food?" He grinned.

Jade sat down on the huge couch and nodded. Noah disappeared up the stairs and came back a few moments later with his arms full of junk food. He had candy, chips, popcorn, and even ice cream. He laid it all out on the automan that sat in front of the couch before grabbing the remotes and settling them next to Jade.

For the rest of the day, they watched movies and laughed together, only getting up from their spots to use the bathroom or to grab more snacks. The others were in and out of the basement as well, joining them for a movie here and there. It was another lazy day, and Jade loved it. She dozed in and out of sleep, never leaving Noah's arms. Some movies they paid attention to, while others they talked over and slept through.

Noah had ordered catered food for dinner so that nobody had to cook, and when it came, they set everything up in the basement and had a casual dinner down there. Noah loved how low-key Jade was and how she didn't mind lying around all day doing nothing. He was learning a lot about her this way, and he loved every moment. Once everyone was full, they cleaned up the basement and put away the leftovers before settling in for more movies.

Noah and Jade finally fell asleep right on the couch, her head on his chest and his arms around her waist, both of them happy as hell to be sleeping next to one another for the second night in a row.

CHAPTER 11

"GIRL, I CANNOT BELIEVE WE'RE BACK AT WORK. THIS IS SOME bullshit," Mia complained. It was now Monday, and the two women were back in their office trying to focus on work. It was always hard coming back to work after a holiday, and today was no exception. The nice part was that they only had to make it through Wednesday and they were off Thursday and Friday again for New Years.

"I agree," Jade yawned as she stared at her computer blankly. They were both wore the fuck out from the weekend. It had been the most relaxing weekend that either of them had in a long time, but they had gotten used to the late nights and the long naps during the days. Their sleep schedule was way off and they were currently paying for it.

Jade, never one to complain, was just happy that she was sleepy because of those reasons and not because she had spent the night sleeping outside in the freezing cold. She was eternally grateful towards Noah. Their friendship continued to bud over the weekend. They basked in each other's company and got to know each other on a deeper level, both mentally and physically. No, they hadn't had sex, but Jade was in Noah's arms every chance she could get, and they kissed so much that it became a part of their normal routine.

Noah opened up more about his life and past relationships while Jade told him more about her parents and her husband. They bonded over their grief at losing parents, and they even shed a few tears together as they had a deep conversation that included several bottles of wine. They hadn't talked about the fact that she was still married again. Neither of them wanting to ruin the happiness they'd felt all weekend. Instead, they danced around that topic and treated Elijah as though he were an ex of hers. They both knew that it was something they would need to talk about soon, though. The way things were heating up between them, it would have to be sooner rather than later.

When Sunday finally rolled around, Roman and Kenyon went home leaving Mia holed up in her room on her phone while Jade and Noah stayed curled up on the couch pouting that their long weekend was ending. It was then that Noah convinced Jade to stay with him until she and Mia could get into their own place. Jade was reluctant at first because she didn't want to be a burden and she definitely didn't want to be seen as a charity case, but Noah reassured her that neither of those things were true. Jade told herself that she finally relented because she knew Mia would probably punch her in the throat if she turned down Noah's comfortable home for the cold streets. Truthfully, Jade had been dreading going back to her normal life of shelters and the trench. Noah had been dreading it as well, and he would not take no for an answer from her. He would never be okay with her or Mia going back to the streets. They'd become friends to him, and he would do whatever he could to keep them safe and comfortable.

Mia was excited as hell that her time living on the streets had ended. Both she and Jade had been expecting to shelter hop for the next couple of weeks until they got their next checks, but being able to put that behind them lifted a huge weight off their shoulders. They finally had a normal routine going and a safe place to lay their heads at night, and that was all they could ask for. Gone were the cold nights and the curfews. They finally felt as though things were looking up for them and they had Noah to thank for it.

Like clockwork, at noon Noah and Kenyon came into the girls' office and told them to get ready for lunch.

"Okay, but we're going out to lunch today. On us," Mia said as she grabbed her purse. Jade nodded and grabbed her coat. Noah noticed her putting it on and ran over to help her. Both Kenyon and Mia chuckled at him. Noah was like a puppy dog whenever he was around Jade, and both Kenyon and Mia teased him mercilessly about it. That nigga was wide open for her, and Jade couldn't even see how deep it ran.

"Damn, Kenyon. You aren't going to help me with my jacket?" Mia pouted.

"What the fuck for?" Kenyon grinned, knowing it would piss Mia off.

"Kenyon—" Mia started, but Kenyon held his hands up in mock surrender.

"I'm just joking, geeze."

Jade giggled at their bickering while Noah zipped her coat up for her.

"We can go out, but y'all aren't paying," Noah said once Jade had her coat on.

"Yes we are," she smiled up at him in a playful manner. "Let us do this for y'all. After everything you've done this weekend, it's literally the very least we could do."

Noah sighed. He felt bad for allowing Jade to spend her hard earned money on him, but he knew that she had her mind made up and that it wasn't worth the fight. "Fine."

"Shiiit, you don't have to tell me twice. I'm getting the most expensive thing on that muthafuckin menu," Kenyon beamed, and Mia smacked him on the arm.

"Boy, shut up," she giggled.

Kenyon rubbed his arm, "Think I'm playing?"

"I know you aren't," Mia rolled her eyes.

"I bet if I was Roman you wouldn't mind," Kenyon winked and Mia blushed fiercely.

"Like I said, shut up!" She stammered and then walked out of the office.

"What's the matter, Mimi? You can tease me and Noah, but we can't tease you about Roman?" Jade giggled as she walked out behind her friend. She didn't realize that Yolanda was listening in on them, and her jaw dropped when she heard what Jade had said.

She whipped around in her chair at the front desk as her eyes followed Jade and Mia to the elevator. Noah and Kenyon went to their offices and grabbed their jackets and were back talking to the ladies within seconds as they waited for the elevator.

"It's not like that," Mia was saying. "Roman and I aren't all googly eyed at each other like you and Noah. It's different."

"I don't know...you guys seemed to spend an awful lot of time together this past weekend," Jade teased.

"Yeah, I barely saw y'all around the house. Remind me to throw that whole bed away once y'all leave," Noah cracked.

Jade's whole face turned red, "Y'all are so damn nosey."

"Oh, I'm nosey? Don't think I don't know that you and Kenyon orchestrated the whole weekend from the get-go. I'm not dumb," Jade laughed.

Noah joined in. "I'm glad I wasn't the only one that peeped that. You two fools aren't slick at all."

"Aye, it worked though, didn't it? Or do I have to remind you what I caught y'all in the kitchen doing—" Kenyon said, but Noah interrupted.

"Shut up, fool."

"That's what I thought," Kenyon winked, and the elevator chimed, signaling its arrival.

They piled on the elevator and went down to the first floor so they could grab lunch, leaving a fuming Yolanda at the receptionist's desk. She had become like the damn wallpaper to them as of late, and she was not happy about it at all. They'd all come into the office together this morning, but she thought nothing of it. Never in her wildest dreams would she have thought while she was at home by her damn self during the holiday, masturbating to Noah's picture and thinking about him nonstop, that he and that whore were together. She was even more upset because Jade had come in with brand new clothes and makeup all over her face, looking way cuter than normal, and Yolanda knew it was only to impress Noah. The bitch was really working her nerves and impeding on her territory.

Yolanda was fuming as she stared at the closed elevator, wishing that it would drop and kill everyone inside of it. In her mind, Noah was hers and if she couldn't have him after all the work she'd put in to be the woman he wanted, then nobody should have him. She wanted to make sure that any woman that tried to get close to him disappeared, leaving him lonely.

"I have got to get rid of this bitch," Yolanda mumbled to herself as she got to work on her computer. "I'm about to dig up dirt on this bitch so he can see she ain't the woman for him."

LATER THAT DAY, WHEN WAS TIME FOR JADE AND MIA TO GO home, Jade poked her head in Noah's office while Mia went to bug Kenyon in his. "Hey, we're off. Do you want us to wait up for you or should we call Tommy?"

Noah looked up from his blueprints and smiled. He motioned for her to come in and said, "Close the door."

She did as she was told and smiled as she walked over to him. She was looking extra good today in her black skinny jeans and red blouse. She had on a pair of black high-heeled boots and her makeup was natural but highlighted her beautiful face. Noah couldn't get enough of her, and most of the day he'd found reasons to be around her. From going over some of his sketches to taking pointless meeting minutes for meetings with clients, he had her by his side most of the day. He was ready to move her damn desk into his office just so he could stare at her all day, but he knew that he wouldn't get shit done if he did that.

When she was close enough to him, he reached out for her and pulled her down onto his lap by her waist so she was straddling him. She giggled and looked into his eyes. "What can I do for you, boss?"

"Nothing. I just wanted to hold you for a minute," Noah whispered as he hugged her close and buried his face in her neck, inhaling her sweet scent. He pulled back again and without wasting any more time, he kissed her.

They'd kept it professional all day, but Noah couldn't stand it. He loved the feel of her lips on his and he could feel his dick rising in his pants. Jade slowly ground into him as she felt her juices soak her panties. They had quite a few steamy moments in the past few days, but Noah never allowed it to go as far as he had on Christmas Eve. He knew that if any part of him got to feel her wet, tight pussy again, he wouldn't be able to stop himself, so, just like every other time, he broke the kiss before it got too heated and moved his hand to adjust himself beneath her. He grazed the fabric of her pants where her pussy sat, and she moaned in his ear.

Jade sighed and then pulled back, responding to what he said a moment ago, "I'm sure you've realized this already, but I sort of live with you for now, so you can hold me all you want once we get back to your place."

Noah laughed, "This is very true, but I won't be home until late. I need to get some things done since I'll be taking a half day tomorrow and I'll be off the rest of the week."

Jade looked confused. "Why is that?"

"Because, a little birdie told me it's someone's birthday tomorrow," Noah smiled.

Jade looked confused again until she realized what he meant. "Oh, wow. I completely forgot that my birthday was tomorrow."

Noah smiled, "I've known since the day you started, but Mia may have brought it up to me as well. So, as your boss, I'm demanding that you take the rest of the week off with me."

Jade shook her head, "Noah, I can't do that. I just started here and I need to put in just as much work as everyone else. What will everyone think of me taking time off so soon and—"

Noah put his finger up to her lips, "shh...don't worry about it, Jade. I have everything covered. I just want to show you a good time for your birthday."

"But you've already—"

"I'm not taking no for an answer. Now, get out of here and don't wait up for me. I'll be late," Noah said as Jade got off his lap, giggling.

"I don't think I could stay up even if I wanted to. I'm so sleepy," she yawned.

"Get some sleep and don't you even think about sleeping in that guest room. I want to hold you when I get home," Noah grinned.

Jade's heart fluttered. She hoped that they weren't moving too fast, too soon. She was still married and Noah was well aware, but he acted like that didn't matter. Jade knew that it had to bother him, even if it was just a little, but she decided to just go with the flow. Things felt right with Noah and although they were happening fast, she was happy for the first time in a very long time and that had to count for something.

Jade put her small hand on Noah's cheek before kissing him on the forehead. "I got you."

Noah smiled as he watched her walk out of his office. He was falling fast for Mrs. Jade Lawrence and he was one hundred percent okay with that.

CHAPTER 12

THE SUNLIGHT FILTERING IN THROUGH THE WINDOW WOKE JADE early the next morning. She rolled over to find Noah's side empty. She vaguely remembered him coming in late last night and pulling her close to him, but she had immediately fallen right back to sleep. She noticed a small card laying on his pillow, and she smiled. She tore open the envelope and read the card.

To the most beautiful woman in the world,
Today is your day, Jade. I want you to enjoy it to the fullest.
Enjoy breakfast downstairs.
Love, Noah

She smiled and rolled out of bed. The last time she celebrated her birthday had been when her parents were still alive. Back before everything changed. She was excited to celebrate this year with the people closest to her. She grabbed the new purse that she bought from one of the gift cards Kenyon and Noah had gotten her for Christmas and put the card inside. Then she quickly dressed in a sweatsuit she had gotten for Christmas. Not bothering to brush her hair, she walked into the bathroom and went pee before brushing her teeth.

When she walked into the kitchen, it surprised her to see it flooded with flowers. They were everywhere. On the table and the counters, there were even a few tall vases standing on the floor. The only places that were flower-free were the island, where there was a ton of food, and the barstools, one of which Mia was occupying.

"I didn't know you were off today, too!" Jade squealed as she threw her arms around Mia's neck.

"Girl, Noah swore me to secrecy. He has a bomb ass day for you planned. My ex used to shit like this for me, but he would have his homies plan it all out, you know? He wasn't really into actually putting in effort and shit. Noah really planned every detail of your day, though. He is so sweet, Mouse. He really likes you, girl. Happy birthday, by the way," Mia rambled on as she hugged Jade back.

Jade sat down on the stool next to her and her stomach growled at the site of all the food. "Did you cook all this?"

Mia scrunched her face up, "Hell no! I love you, and that is exactly why I will never cook for you. I don't want to give you food poisoning, Chica. Noah catered all this shit in. I just had to let the people in so they could set everything up. The flowers arrived early this morning, too. He must have dropped a small fortune because flowers are not cheap."

"I can't believe he did all of this for me," Jade said.

"You really don't pay attention then. That man loves him some Jade," Mia giggled when Jade looked at her with a wide-eyed expression.

"Love? He doesn't love me, Mia. We're just getting to know each other. Besides, I'm still married."

Mia waved her off, "Girl, in case you haven't noticed, that gilipollas doesn't matter to any of us. In our eyes, you have no husband and besides, it only takes seconds to fall in love. Trust me when I say, no man would do anything like this for a woman unless he had some serious feelings for her and this is only the beginning of your day."

Jade felt like everything she had woken up to was more than enough to make this an amazing day. She couldn't fathom what else Noah could do for her that he hasn't done already. She suddenly felt bad for Noah. He was always giving, and all she had to offer him was a friendship. She couldn't buy him anything nice, and she had a husband for goodness' sake. In her eyes, Noah deserved so much more than she had to give.

"Mia...what am I doing with Noah? I mean, really. I can't fully commit to him because I'm married and that is so unfair to him. I can't plan fancy dates or give lavish gifts. I just don't see how I'm benefitting him in any way," Jade said with her head held down, looking at the empty plate that sat in front of her.

Mia dropped her fork and took Jade's face in her hands, forcing her to look in her eyes. "You have to stop all that shit right now. I know your situation is tough, Jade, but that doesn't give you any right to feel worthless. Noah likes you for you, not what you can do for him. As far as your no-good husband...that's something you two really need to talk about if you want to continue seeing him. Noah knows what he's getting himself into by falling for you. Now you just need to decide if he is worth it or not. Personally, I think that man is worth it and I think you need to say fuck your husband and do something that makes you happy for once."

"I want to keep seeing him, Mimi. He's so good to me and not because of the material things. He's the most thoughtful and kind man I have ever met. He listens to me when I talk and we have a great time together. I just don't see how I can ever take things to the next level with him. Not with what I have going on. It just wouldn't be fair to him."

Mia sighed and dropped her hands. "Let me ask you this...is Noah worth standing up to Elijah and getting a divorce?"

Jade didn't know how to answer, and Mia saw her hesitate. She held her hand up and said, "You don't have to answer me...just think about it, Mouse. Elijah is dragging you down, and I just want you to be happy. I understand why you're scared of him, but maybe facing your fears will open up a whole new life for you that you never thought you could have. Just think about it."

Jade was speechless, so she simply nodded and piled some food on her plate. As she ate, she thought about what her friend said, and she knew that she would ponder it for the rest of the day. *Was Noah worth it?*

When they finished eating, Mia rushed Jade out of the door, not allowing her to shower or put a different outfit on. "Trust me, you'll have plenty of time for that later."

Tommy was outside the house waiting for the ladies. Jade smiled and waved at him before Mia pushed her into the car. Tommy chuckled, "Happy birthday, Jade. Good morning, Mia."

"Thank you," Jade giggled. Tommy closed the door and got into the driver's seat.

"You know where to go, Tommy," Mia grinned.

"Are you sure I'm dressed okay? I have no idea what we're even doing," Jade looked down at her clothes and then back at Mia, who was dressed in a cute top and skinny jeans.

Mia waved her off, "You're fine. Trust me on this."

They chatted happily during the ride and about twenty minutes later they pulled into a shopping district. Mia pushed Jade out of the car and then turned to Tommy, "I'll call you when we're done. It'll probably be a few hours at least."

Tommy nodded and then waved after Mia slammed the door closed. She turned around with a smile and looped her arm through Jade's before walking her towards a cute building that that had a huge sign that said *Red's*. The women stepped inside and Jade instantly got excited. The decor was red and white and judging by the salon chairs and the smell of hair products wafting through the air, Jade could tell she was in for some pampering. She turned to Mia and grinned. "I'm getting my hair done?"

Mia grinned. "Not just your hair. This place does everything, and when Noah told me to pamper you for a day, I knew this was the place. The owner of this spot is this girl, Ryder, and she's hood famous in LA. She's like a legend and shit. She has a couple of salons out that way, but this one just opened and they been booked up for months. I don't know how Noah got us in for a full day, but he did, girl, and I plan on enjoying this shit. I'm talking hair, nails, makeup, waxing, lash extensions...you name it, and that isn't counting the hot stone massages. I heard that Ryder chick hand selects the best of the best and only the elite work for her. This shit is about to be off the chain."

Mia was overly excited, and she barely took a breath as she spoke. Jade laughed, and she couldn't seem to wipe the smile off her face the entire time they were in the salon. They didn't have to wait more than five minutes until they were called back to start their pampering. They were seated in the hair wing first and offered drinks. Mia ordered them both champagne, and they sat back sipping, giddy about their makeovers.

A beautiful black woman with coffee-colored skin named Tosha was handling Jade's hair while Latrice was taking care of Mia. Latrice was short and curvy and gorgeous as hell. She and Mia got to talking about what she wanted to do with her hair while Tosha welcomed Jade with a warm smile. "Alright, Jade. What were you thinking today? I'll be taking your braids out and deep conditioning your hair. Did you want more braids or something completely different?"

Jade thought about it for a moment and concluded that she definitely wanted to do something different. She always had some kind of long fake braids in because Elijah liked them. She liked them just fine at first, too, but she soon figured out why Elijah liked them so much. It was so he could drag her around by them, or hold on to them roughly while he was having sex with her. He pulled out so many of her braids, that it surprised her that she wasn't permanently bald in some spots on her head. She'd grown to hate them over the years, and there was something so freeing about finally being able to get rid of them. There was no reason to keep them, so she smiled politely to

Tosha in the mirror and said, "No...no more braids. I want to rock my natural hair. It'll definitely need a trim, but I just want my natural curls to shine."

Tosha smiled, "You got it, girl."

Tosha got to work and Jade sat back and relaxed, thinking about Noah and how she couldn't wait to see him.

IT TOOK HOURS, BUT THE WOMEN WERE FINALLY FINISHED AT the salon. Jade felt fantastic as she stepped back out into the cold streets of New York. They did her nails and toes in matching gold polish. Her nails had glitter and stones glued on them. They were coffin-shaped and long. She loved them. Elijah liked her to keep her nails short and in a French manicure and Jade was sure that was so she wouldn't get any ideas about scratching him. She loved her new bedazzled nails and couldn't stop staring at them. It surprised Mia at how long Jade's natural hair was. She let Tosha put some honey brown highlights in her dark brown hair and her curls were touching the top of her bra strap.

Mia talked her into getting lash extensions, and it surprised Jade at how much she actually liked them. They framed her pretty brown eyes and made them pop. Her perfectly arched eyebrows complimented her makeup really well. They did it to perfection, and she even picked up a few tricks from the makeup artist, and she couldn't wait to try them out on her own.

Mia had also talked her into getting her first Brazilian wax, and once the pain subsided, she loved the feeling of having no hair down there. She felt cleaner somehow, and she knew it was a routine that she would keep up. She had always gotten her eyebrows waxed, but there was something liberating about having her womanhood bare as well. To top everything off, she was extremely relaxed after her hot stone massage.

Although they did absolutely nothing all day aside from get

pampered, both women were exhausted and they collapsed inside the car once Tommy picked them up. Jade admired Mia's long blown out hair and her natural makeup. Mia was going on a date with Roman later to dinner and the movies, so she opted for a more subtle look, but Jade was looking like she was about to step on a runway. All she was missing was a bomb ass dress. It made her wonder what exactly Noah had planned for the night.

"Tommy, can you stop at a Starbucks, please? We're going to need some coffee if we are going to make it through the rest of the day," Mia said as she stifled a yawn.

"Sure thing, Mia. There's one coming up here," Tommy smiled in the rearview mirror.

Jade was happy that Mia thought to stop for coffee because the way she was feeling, she could fall asleep right now and stay asleep for the rest of the evening. They ordered their drinks when they got to the drive thru, and by the time they got back to Noah's house, they felt a little more energized.

Mia disappeared in her room without giving Jade any more information or instructions on what she was supposed to do, so she went into the kitchen to finish her coffee and find a snack. She was surprised to see Noah sitting on a barstool tapping away on his laptop amongst all the flowers.

He turned when he heard footsteps coming his way, and he was rendered speechless. Jade blushed at the way he was looking at her and said, "Hey, you."

He stared at her, silently wondering how she could possibly be so beautiful. She was breathtaking and looked like a brand new woman. He barely even recognized her with her makeup and hair like that, and she smelled wonderful from all the lotions and hair products. Realizing that she had spoken to him, he looked into her eyes and said, "Happy birthday."

She smiled and walked over to him. He welcomed her with open arms. She hugged him around his neck as she stood between his legs while he sat on the barstool and hugged her waist. "Thanks, Noah."

"Have you enjoyed your day so far?" he asked as he pulled away. He kept his hands on her waist, and she looked up in his eyes.

"Yes, and I don't know how to thank you. This has been above and beyond anything I could have imagined. Seriously, thank you."

Noah smiled. He loved the peaceful look on her face, and that smile was infectious. "You're welcome, Jade. I just thought you'd had a rough year...shit, a rough couple of years, and I want this year to be different for you. I wanted it to start off right."

Jade felt her eyes misting over and she cleared her throat. "It means the world to me, Noah. Really."

Seeing the emotion in Jade's eyes, Noah massaged her hips before standing up and holding his hand out to her. "Come on. Your birthday isn't over yet."

Jade giggled as Noah pulled her through the house and up the stairs. He led her into his bedroom, where more surprises awaited. Jade gasped when she took in the room. There were rose petals everywhere...on the floor, the bed, and leading into the bathroom. There were also fancy unlit candles in all shades of red scattered around the room. Upon further inspection, Jade noticed that they were customized with her name and birthdate. There were gold balloons scattered above them, touching the ceiling, and gifts were piled on the bed. Noah turned to see her reaction. It had worried him all day that he overdid everything. He didn't want to scare her away, but he wanted her to feel special on her birthday. Jade had a huge smile on her face as she looked around the room, and his heart leapt. Her eyes finally fell on his and she jumped into his arms, burying her head into his neck as he held her tightly.

She was overwhelmed with happiness as she hugged him. Never in her life had she met a more thoughtful man, and she couldn't believe that he would do all of this for her. She had only known Noah for about a month now, but she knew that she was falling in love with him and it terrified her. Swallowing her fears, she pulled back and kissed Noah. Their tongues met as Jade wrapped her legs around Noah's waist. He backed her against the wall and palmed her ass as their bodies yearned to come together as one. Like he always did, Noah pulled away before things went too far and set her back down on her feet.

Playfully, Jade growled and then pouted. She had been so horny constantly being around Noah and she'd been masturbating in the shower every day just to keep her temptations at bay. Noah chuckled when he saw her pouting and said, "Fix your face, girl, and go open your presents."

Jade grinned, "Noah, I can't accept anything else from you. You have done—"

Noah grabbed her chin and tilted it up so she was looking at him. "It's your birthday. Let me spoil you a little."

"You spoil me every day," Jade grinned.

"That's my right. Let me do it," he grinned back at her.

Jade sighed, "Fine, but I promise that I'm going to start spoiling you, too."

Noah shrugged as he smiled down at her. He would worry about that later. All he wanted was her time and to be in her presence. He didn't need anything else from her. Jade walked over to the bed and sat down in the middle of it. Noah followed her and got comfortable next to her. There were four gifts for Jade to open, so she started with the biggest box.

She carefully unwrapped it and lifted the top off a gold box. Inside was a beautiful gold designer dress with a bodice top and a sweeping skirt. Jade jumped off the bed and held the dress out in front of her excitedly as she admired the way the stones on the top of the dress sparkled and glimmered under the light. "Noah, this dress is gorgeous!"

He chuckled, happy to see her so excited over the dress he picked out. Mia helped him with her sizes, but he picked the dress out himself and he was happy that she liked it so much. He grinned at her, "Open the rest."

She went back to the bed and laid the dress out on the bed so it wouldn't get wrinkled, and then she grabbed another gift. This one contained a pair of Louboutin heels that matched the dress perfectly. Jade squealed in delight, and Noah didn't think he had ever seen her so happy. He knew that she didn't particularly care for high-end shit, but what woman didn't like a pretty dress and a bomb ass pair of shoes? His heart swelled because he knew that he was the one to put that beautiful smile on her face. She looked over at him and said, "Noah, these are beautiful, but I literally have nowhere to wear these things. All I do is go to work and hang out around here."

Noah scrunched his face up. "You didn't think we were staying here all night, did you?"

Jade beamed at him, "Where are we going?"

"If I told you, then it wouldn't be a surprise," Noah grinned.

She playfully threw a wad of wrapping paper at him and opened the next gift, which held a silky pink pajama shorts set. Jade ran her hands down the fabric and loved how soft it was.

"Are these so I don't wear your shirts to bed anymore?" she giggled.

Noah laughed, "Nah, I love when you wear my shirts. I just thought you might want some pajamas of your own."

"Thank you," she smiled down at them before grabbing the last gift, which was the smallest of them all. She ripped at the packaging and her heart skipped a beat when she saw that it was a jewelry box. She lifted the lid and gasped when the sight of all those diamonds stared back at her.

Set neatly in the box was a simple gold necklace with a jade stone at the middle surrounded by small diamonds and a bracelet and earrings that matched the same pattern. She had never owned anything with her namesake stone on it, and it touched her at the thoughtfulness of the gift. Judging by the diamonds, it was all real, too, which meant it cost a pretty penny. Elijah would buy her expensive shit to wear all the time, but it was all for show. It never really felt like hers. He would buy her things he liked and never did he put any real thought behind any of the things he gave her. All he cared about was dressing her up like a barbie doll and showing her off at dinner parties.

As she stared at the jewelry, she couldn't stop the tears from falling as she buried her head in her hands. Noah scooted over to her and wrapped his arms around her. He knew that this reaction was coming. He'd learned that Jade was extremely sensitive. She cried when she was happy, sad or mad, and he hoped that these were tears of joy.

"What's wrong?" he asked as he rocked her back and forth.

"I don't deserve any of this," she cried.

Noah's face scrunched up when she said that, and he pulled back so he could look at her. Nothing could have prepared him for her to say that. Her hands were still covering her face, so he pulled them away and stared into her tear-filled eyes. "Why would you say that?"

Jade shrugged as the tears continued to fall, looking everywhere but at Noah's handsome face. He shook his head and said, "Look at me, Jade."

She did what she was told and looked into his brown eyes. Once he was satisfied that he had her attention, he said, "Don't let that bitch made nigga get in your head. You spent years in an abusive relationship and up under that nigga's foot, but I'm here to show you how you should be treated, whether it's me or any other buster out here. You deserve nothing less than the best, beautiful. Please, just trust me on this one. Don't you ever again in your life feel less than worthy of the good things that come your way."

Jade cried harder at his words, trying her best to dab away the tears so she wouldn't ruin her makeup. Deep down, she knew that what he was saying was right, but she also knew that it would take her some time to believe his words. Elijah had torn her down and now she was in the season of building herself back up and loving herself again. The shit was hard, but she had to admit that Noah was doing a good job of helping her. He was a great example of how a man should treat a woman, and she suddenly realized that she didn't want any other woman to experience what Noah had to offer. For the first time in years, she wanted to be selfish about something, and that something was Noah. She knew how she could pay him back for everything that he'd done for her in the short amount of time that she'd known him.

Suddenly, she smiled through her tears, and she hugged Noah around his neck. "Thank you, Noah."

He hugged her back, happy to see the smile return to her face. "No problem, sweetheart."

She blushed at the pet name and pulled away. He wiped the last of her tears from her face and then got off the bed, pulling her off with him. She giggled when he picked her up, "Where are you taking me now?"

He set her down on her feet in the bathroom and she saw that a bubble bath was drawn with rose petals in the water. "Go ahead and relax. I know you've had a long day. I want you to put that dress and those shoes on when you're done. Be ready by five."

He walked out of the bathroom and Jade checked her phone and realized that she had a full two hours before she had to be ready. She walked back into the bedroom and grabbed her coffee cup before slipping out of her clothes and pulling her hair up so it didn't get wet. She checked her makeup in the mirror and was relieved that it still looked perfect. After dabbing the rest of her tears away, she moved towards the tub. She sighed contentedly as she slipped into the water and thought about the gift she would give Noah at dinner tonight. Nervous jitters fluttered in her stomach, but she smiled anyway, excited that she would be able to put a smile on Noah's face that reflected her own.

CHAPTER 13

"I'M SORRY, I JUST CAN'T STOP STARING AT YOU," NOAH SMILED as he took in Jade's beauty. The dress fit her to perfection and it showed off the roundness of her breasts and how slim her waist was before swooping out into a long skirt. Her curly hair was free and beautiful, with the honey brown highlights contrasting her natural dark brown hair. Her makeup was still flawless and the jewelry that Noah got her complimented her look perfectly.

Jade's cheeks warmed at all the attention she was getting. They were in a limo on their way to a secret location, and she was excited to see what the night brought. "You're looking good yourself, Noah."

And he really was. He had on one of his custom suits that fit him to perfection. It was a taupe color and his button up underneath it was black. His hair was freshly cut and his goatee was lining his big lips perfectly. Jade wanted to kiss him so badly, but she didn't want Noah to think she was some kind of sex fiend because she wasn't. It had just been so long since she'd had enjoyable sex, and Noah was constantly looking good enough to eat. It was a constant struggle for her to keep her urges at bay, especially since she felt Noah should make the first move. She was married, after all, and she didn't want to assume that he wanted her in that way.

Noah grabbed Jade's hand, and they sat in silence for the rest of the ride, both lost in their own thoughts. Before long, they pulled up to a beautiful building. The driver double parked on the busy streets and rushed to open the door for the couple. Noah stepped out first before grabbing Jade's hand and helping her out of the limo. Noah tipped the driver and let him know that he would call when they were ready to be picked up before pulling Jade towards the buildings entryway.

Jade marveled at the beauty of the building as they entered through the glass doors. Although it wasn't furnished, Jade admired the tall ceilings and the vast windows. The chandeliers seemed to glitter with each step she took, and the staircases were made from a thick glass. In the middle of the lobby was a giant fountain, and the lights within the water made it appear as though it were changing colors.

"This place is beautiful," Jade whispered as she looked around.

Noah grinned, "Thanks."

She spun around to look at him, "Is this place yours?"

He shook his head, "No, but I designed it. It's brand new and the interior designer just started her work on the place so it isn't open to the public yet. It'll be a hotel."

"Wow, Noah. Seriously, this is beautiful. You have serious talent."

Noah's cheeks warmed at her compliment, "Thanks, sweetheart, but this isn't what I wanted to show you. The owner owed me a favor and said we could have the place to ourselves tonight. Come on."

He held out his hand and waited for her to take it before walking towards the elevators. They rode the elevator up to the top floor and when they got off, Noah led her to a staircase. They walked up it and when Noah pushed open the door, Jade's breath caught in her throat.

They were on the rooftop, and the view was magnificent. She could see all of New York from where she stood, and it was captivating. She noticed that there were outdoor heaters, so it wasn't cold at all. In fact, she was a bit warm in her jacket. There were more rose petals scattered on the floor, and in the middle of the rooftop were a ton of pillows and blankets. Off to the side there was a table filled with food and there were what seemed like hundreds of the same candles lit that Noah had customized for her back at his house. There was soft R&B music playing and the whole thing was unbelievably romantic. A lump formed in her throat as she turned to look at Noah. "This is all so beautiful."

"I'm happy you like it. It's one of the best views in the city and I wanted to share it with you," he said as he caressed her cheek.

She caught his hand with her own and squeezed it. Her stomach chose that moment to growl loudly, and Noah laughed, "let's get you some food."

Jade nodded her head, embarrassed. "I guess I haven't eaten since breakfast this morning. Thank you for that, by the way."

Noah nodded his head with a smile and led her over to the table where there was a mini feast. There was Jade's favorite food, crab legs, with all the fixings, and a small fruit and cheese plate along with a mini chocolate fondue fountain.

"This all looks so amazing," she said as they piled their plates and brought it over to the area with the blankets and pillows.

They set their plates down and Noah helped her get out of her jacket before they settled in. As they ate, Jade giggled and said, "I feel a bit overdressed."

Noah smiled, "I wanted to give you a chance to dress up and feel like a princess, but I selfishly wanted to keep you to myself. I hope you don't mind."

Jade shook her head quickly, "Not at all. This is perfect."

Noah smiled, and they continued eating and making small talk. They drank a couple glasses of champagne and Jade was feeling really nice by the time dinner was over. When they finished, they went inside to wash their hands after tearing up those crab legs before making their way outside again. Noah held his hand out to her and asked, "May I please have this dance?"

Jade giggled and nodded her head shyly. He led her near the

pillows and blankets before pulling her close and swaying to the beat. Jade rested her head on his chest and basked in the moment. Her life was absolutely perfect. It didn't take a lot to make her happy, and her heart was bursting open with joy and a huge reason was because of Noah. He made her happy in ways she never thought possible. She didn't feel worthy of his kindness and attention, but he reminded her daily that she deserved all the good things that were happening to her. Noah deserved something special in return, so she took a deep breath and leaned back so she could look up at him. "I really don't know how to repay you for all of this, Noah."

He stubbornly shook his head and opened his mouth to speak, but Jade stopped him. "No, let me finish."

Noah stared down at her and nodded his head with a small smile, "As you wish."

"I just mean that...you have made me so happy in these last few weeks. It's because of you that I'm coming out of my shell and learning to trust again. You have given me everything that I need to survive. Not only material things, but emotionally and mentally, too. I don't think you will ever fully understand how you have impacted my life."

"I understand, Jade," Noah responded. "It's the same way you've impacted mine. Before I met you I was so engrossed in work and never thought about women in the way I do you. Now, I'm actually taking days off work and I don't even bring work home with me. You've taught me how to live again and not waste my life away."

Jade shook her head, "I don't doubt that I've impacted your life, and I'm happy that I've taken you mind off work, but what I mean is different. You have literally given me food when I hadn't eaten for days. You've given me clothes just when I was sure I would get frostbite or die from the cold. You've given me a job, shelter and means of transportation. You're helping me to learn my worth and helping me to love myself again. I may have impacted your life on the surface, but you completely flipped my life upside down and made it one hundred percent better. I know we haven't known each other long, but you mean so much to me. I..."

Jade stopped for a moment and swallowed the lump in her throat before continuing. She didn't want to lose her courage. "I want to divorce Elijah so I can be free to be with you, Noah. I want to face my fears...for you."

Noah blinked down at her, and then a smile nearly broke his face in half. He picked Jade up off the ground and swung her around in a circle. She squealed and giggled as he planted kisses all over her face. Finally, he set her back on the ground and looked down at her. "I promise I will keep you safe. I'll hire the best lawyer, one that doesn't work with him. I'll make sure he never has to lay eyes on you if you don't want him to, baby. I'll protect you."

Noah was over the moon about what she just said. He never wanted to push her to this conclusion, and he was willing to wait it out for as long as she wanted. Never in his wildest dreams did he expect for her to come around so soon, but he was happy as hell about it. He could finally open himself up to the possibility to a future with Jade. He had never cared so much about a woman, and he knew that he wouldn't let her go anytime soon, if ever. He would make sure she was safe and happy every single day.

Jade beamed up at him, elated that she could make Noah so happy. She was happy as hell, too and excited for her future. She just had to get over the hump of divorcing Elijah, but she would worry about that another time. Right now it was about her and Noah. She grabbed his face in her hands and looked directly in his eyes. "I trust you, Noah. I won't lie and say that I'm not afraid, but I know that this is necessary. I just want to be free and I want to live my life with no worry."

Noah pulled her closer and said, "I'll make sure you get everything you desire. You deserve that, Jade, and I won't let anyone hurt you. You have my word. That nigga doesn't even matter. In my eyes, you're mine already."

Jade smiled and leaned in to kiss him. Noah bowed his head so he could meet her lips. Jade parted her mouth, and their kiss deepened. The champagne had went straight to her head, but she was still sober enough to know what she was doing. The alcohol only amplified her feelings for Noah, and she was more than ready to show him just how much he meant to her.

Noah walked them backwards and lifted Jade up before lowering her down on the blankets and pillows. There were so many of them it felt as though they were laying on a plush bed. The sky was dark, and the moon was high. The candles made the rooftop glow with soft lighting and the flowers were fragrant, adding to the sexy ambience.

They continued kissing each other hungrily for a few moments before Noah pulled away. Jade thought he was repeating his same routine and was about to protest when she saw that he was removing his suit jacket and taking off his tie. She helped him unbutton his shirt, so he only had on a black muscle shirt and his boxers and pants. Noah lifted Jade up slightly so he could unzip the back of her dress. "You won't be too cold, will you?"

Jade shook her head and giggled, "I'm used to the cold, baby."

Noah didn't find that comment funny at all since she was referring to her time living on the streets. Instead of responding to her, he pulled a blanket over himself and then slid her dress up over her head before immediately covering her again with his body and the blanket.

"I promise to always keep you warm," he whispered in her ear before kissing down her jawline to her neck. Jade sucked in a sharp breath as he kissed and sucked at her neck and then down to her breasts. Her dress didn't allow for a bra, so the only article of clothing she had on were her panties, which were soaked with her juices.

Noah sucked on her left nipple while his thumb played with her right one. Jade's head fell back into the pillows as she moaned loudly. His tongue flicked across her sensitive flesh, leaving her panting for more. He took his time with her as he caressed, sucked and licked her soft spot, relishing in the sounds she was making. His dick was getting hard as hell, but he forced himself to take it slow with Jade. This was about her pleasure. His own could wait.

While he sucked on her nipples, he worked on lowering her panties down over her knees and past her ankles until they were off. As soon as he flung them aside, he rose up and took off his muscle shirt and pants, leaving only his boxers. Jade was curious as hell to see what he was working with, but Noah's face dove straight into her pussy, leaving her to forget all about what was going on in his boxers and focusing on what his mouth was doing. She had never felt anything like this before. When she married Elijah, she had only been with a couple other men in her life and none of them had done oral sex. Elijah never did when they were dating, either, but when they got married, he would chomp on her pussy until it was raw and sometimes bleeding. She'd been to the doctor for it a couple of times which was humiliating as hell, but since she wasn't pressing charges the doctors couldn't do anything but patch her up and give her some medication to take the swelling and pain away.

What Noah was doing to her was something entirely different, though. His tongue worked its way around her slippery mound as he wiggled it back and forth on her clit. He kissed, sucked and swirled his tongue around like it was the best ice cream cone he had ever eaten. "Fuck, Jade. You taste so damn good."

All Jade could do was moan his name as her knees shook uncontrollably. A stirring started in her navel and shot straight down to her womanhood as Noah continued his assault on her folds. Jade trembled as her juices flowed out of her and then tried to squirm away as Noah licked up every last drop, holding her in place. "Ahhh...Noah, please..."

He kissed up her body and whispered, "I ain't done with you yet."

Jade quivered beneath him as she anticipated him filling her up and making love to her. She yearned for more of him and she knew that he was about to rock her world, judging by the things he just did to her with his mouth. Noah laid down beside her and took off his boxers, revealing his long, hard dick. It stunned jade into silence for a moment as she stared at it. She knew he was working with something big based on all the times she'd copped a feel during their heavy make-out sessions, but she hadn't been expecting *this*. Not only was it long as hell, it was thick. She wasn't used to men this size, and she was a little worried that he might hurt her.

Noah noticed her hesitance and pulled her close to him so that his girth was resting against her bellybutton. "We don't have to do anything you don't want to do, baby."

Jade looked into his eyes and instantly relaxed. Noah would never hurt her, and she knew it. He wasn't like Elijah. She took a deep breath and smiled at him before whispering the three words that kicked Noah's desire into overdrive. "I want you."

Noah kissed her as he simultaneously rolled on top of her, nestling in between her legs. He dipped his finger in between her thighs and was glad that she was still wet as hell. He wanted this to feel just as good to her as it would for him, which meant she needed to be slick as hell down there. Slowly, he inserted the tip of his dick inside of her and she gasped at how wide it stretched her. Noah cursed under his breath as he felt how tight she was, willing himself to not get too excited and cum too quick.

"Damn, baby. You feel so fuckin good," he breathed as he rocked into her a little more once she was adjusted to his size.

Jade could only respond with a moan as he filled her up, inch by inch. It hurt her, but it was a different kind of pain. This pain was borderline orgasmic. She knew that once her body adjusted to his size completely, it would be game over. This connection was what she had been craving for years. This gentleness, this pleasure...this *love*. Noah took care of her with an ease she had never experienced before, and she couldn't get enough.

Once Noah had completely filled her, he stayed still for a moment, giving her time to adjust. Jade wasn't having none of that, though. Breathing heavily, she moved against him, and Noah took that as his queue. He began rocking into her slowly, her pussy making sounds like he was stirring mac and cheese. Jade grabbed onto his back and dug her nails in as she moaned into his ear. "No—Noah, you feel ssoooo good."

Hearing that Jade felt as good as he did turned Noah on even more. He kissed her feverishly as their bodies moved together before flipping them both over so that Jade was on top of him. She was so small that he could handle her body with ease and he loved it. Jade froze for a moment, suddenly shy and not sure what to do. She hadn't rode a dick in a very long time and even then; it wasn't with someone as big as Noah.

Noah pulled her forward and sucked one of her nipples in his mouth, and that was all Jade needed as a shudder took over her body. She eased down on his length and began rotating her hips up and down, then back and forth. She found that when she sat all the way down on him and ground slowly, his dick hit something inside of her that caused sparks to shoot through her pussy and it stimulated her clit as well. She ground into him faster and Noah moaned along with her, loving the feeling of her warm walls restricting around him.

Seeing that she was almost at her peak once again, Noah grabbed her hips and ground into her, causing a loud moan to escape her lips. He loved seeing her in this way. Hair bouncing, skin damp, face contorted with pleasure. Just looking at her was enough to make him cum inside of her, but again, he refrained.

Jade's body shook violently as she came on his dick, "Ahhh Noah...Oh—Oh my God."

Her climax lasted several seconds before she went limp. Noah gently turned her over on her back and kissed her passionately as he slid back inside of her. She gasped and held onto his back as he lifted her leg onto his shoulder. It was his turn now, and he wanted to pick up the pace.

With one leg wrapped around his back and one on his shoulder, Jade couldn't possibly understand how he had more to give her. She had never in her life cum more than once in a night, and here he was about to give her round three. Jade swore that his dick was hitting her esophagus as he slammed into her repeatedly. She moaned loudly every time he put all eleven inches up in her guts, and he grunted as he picked up the pace even more. He was pounding her out, and they rocked into each other recklessly, desperately needing a release. Noah pulled up to his knees, never breaking his pace, and pulled her bottom half up with him.

Jade held onto her breasts and played with her nipples while Noah wrapped his arm around her waist and under her back to support her. He then took his other hand and began playing with Jade's clit. That was all it took for Jade to reach her third orgasm. Her body jerked, and her pussy walls constricted, causing Noah's nut to explode. He pulled out of her and came all over her stomach while still playing with her clit so she could get the last of her orgasm.

Once they were both finished, Noah collapsed beside Jade and they both lay there breathing heavily with faint smiles on their faces. Once he caught his breath, Noah got up and grabbed a towel that was lying on one of the chairs nearby. Jade admired his body as he walked back towards her, cleaning himself off. He smirked down at her, "Like what you see?"

Jade licked her lips and blushed slightly, "A little too much."

Noah chuckled, and then kneeled down so he could wipe off Jade's stomach. He looked at her in concern as he cleaned her off and asked, "Are you okay? Did I hurt you at all?"

Jade giggled, "No, you didn't hurt me, but I am sore."

She couldn't lie, her lady parts were sore as hell from being stretched so wide, but she was not complaining. This wasn't the pain that had her crying in a heap of blood and sweat. This soreness she was feeling left her relaxed and satisfied.

"Baby, I am so sorry I didn't—"

Jade shushed him, "Noah, it's okay. Really. I might be sore, but I feel good. Nobody has ever made me feel like that before, and I mean that in the best possible way. That was amazing."

Noah relaxed slightly, but he still looked concerned. "Okay, but still...let me get you home. I'll run us a bath and give you a massage."

Although Jade wanted nothing more than to curl up right where she was laying and fall asleep, she smiled up at Noah and allowed him to help her get dressed again. Then, he picked her up and carried her back through the building and to the waiting car, never allowing her feet to touch the ground, even when she insisted that she could walk. Noah didn't want her out of his arms for one second. She had made him the happiest man in the world tonight, and she deserved to be carried around like a princess.

Later, when they were snuggled up in bed after another mind blowing session of lovemaking, Jade dozed off with a smile on her face, excited that she and Noah had the next few days off to get acquainted physically and plan for their future.

CHAPTER 14

"Why are you always wearing sunglasses inside?" Jade asked with a giggle as she swayed to the beat.

She reached out and snatched the glasses from Noah's face and placed them on her own before Mia took a picture of her.

"Ohhh, Mouse. This look is fierce on you!" Mia giggled as she snapped pictures of her friend.

"I can't even be mad," Noah grinned. "They look better on you."

"Aw, man. It must be love if you're letting her wear your shades," Kenyon laughed and Roman nodded his head in agreement as he pulled Mia against his body.

It was New Years Eve, and they were chillin at a lounge eating, drinking, and smoking hookah. Their table was near the dance floor where they were currently dancing to *No Guidance* by Chris Brown featuring Drake. The vibe within the club was filled with excitement, and it was infectious. It was almost midnight, and everyone was drunk and feeling good. The music was loud, the food was good as hell, and the company was even better. It had been a hard year for Jade...shit, a hard five years, and she was ready to put it all behind her and start the new decade out with a clean slate.

Noah was excited as hell for the coming year, and he had been working overtime to make sure that Jade got her freedom, just like he'd promised. He hired a lawyer and the divorce documents were ready to be served. They were complete with a statement from Jade about the abuse she'd endured and records from the hospital as well as a statement from her nurse the night that she'd run away from Elijah. Noah was confident that not only would Jade easily get a divorce, but that Elijah would go to jail for the abuse that Jade had endured. The first thing his lawyer advised him to do was to have Jade file a restraining order on Elijah, which they would do tomorrow. They would have the papers served after the new year. For now, they just wanted to enjoy the last bit of the holiday season.

Noah pulled Jade close and kissed her softly on the cheek.

"Something like that," he said in response to Kenyon's remark before he started singing the words to the song in Jade's ear. *"You got it, girl, you got it."*

Jade blushed and turned in his arms. She stretched up and kissed him on the lips while the rest of the group whooped and hollered at their affectionate display. Mia was snapping pictures with her phone, intent on documenting the night. She was glad that Noah and Jade had finally gotten together. Jade insisted that they weren't officially boyfriend and girlfriend yet, but Mia knew better. They could call it what they wanted, but they were together and Mia was happy for her best friend. Noah pulled away before they got too hot and heavy, knowing that once they really got started, they wouldn't be able to stop.

They'd been holed up in his house for the past two days, barely leaving his room. They'd had sex at least five times each day, and it never seemed like enough. Jade's sexual appetite had been awakened after her birthday night, and now it was insatiable. She wanted it all the time, and Noah was happy to give it to her.

Jade pouted when Noah pulled away and he laughed as he put an arm around her shoulders, looking her up and down and loving how good she looked. Her curls were wild all over her head as they hung down her back. Her makeup was perfect with a hot red lip and glittery eyeshadow. She was wearing a pair of denim high waisted short shorts and a black bralette with some black knee-high heeled boots. She and Mia went shopping last night once they heard that they would be going out for New Years Eve and Noah was loving how sexy Jade was looking. He bent down so he could whisper in her ear and said, "Stop pouting. I have something for you later, baby."

Jade's frown instantly melted into a smile as she licked her lips sexily up at Noah. He was wearing the hell out of an all white suit, and she'd decided that white was her favorite color on him. It complimented his dark complexion well. Noah grinned down at her and willed himself not to get hard. The littlest things about Jade turned his wood into a brick and it drove him crazy. He pulled her over to their table and poured her another drink from one of the bottles they purchased. He passed it to her and then poured himself a drink before he made a toast, "To 2019 for bringing me the most beautiful woman I have ever laid eyes on and to 2020 and our bright futures."

"I'll drink to that," Jade smiled and clinked her glass with Noah's. Just as they finished downing their drinks, Kenyon made his way over to the table with some random girl, followed by Roman and Mia. Looking gorgeous as hell, Mia had her long hair slicked back into a tight ponytail at the top of her head. Her makeup was smoked out, and she had dark red lipstick making her pouty lips seem even fuller. Her sparkly grey dress was barely covering her ass, and her heels were silver and tall as hell. She strutted around confidently in them and she looked as though she were back in her element.

"Damn, y'all drinking without us?" Kenyon slurred. He was wearing black denim pants and a black sweater with some blacked out Timbs. He'd been talking to every woman in the lounge since they walked through the door, and it looked as though he'd finally settled on one to bring home.

Jade giggled while Noah asked, "Who is your friend?"

"Her name is Irene," Kenyon grinned confidently.

The girl sucked her teeth, "My name is Kelsey."

Mia burst into laughter while the girl mean mugged Kenyon. She was cute with a curvaceous body, short curly hair and pretty brown skin, but the rest of the group already knew that Kenyon was only talking to her for one thing. Sex. Which was why he didn't care what the poor girl's name was.

"My bad, shorty," Kenyon grinned at her, showcasing his dimples. Kelsey melted under his gaze and smiled back at him.

"It's all good," she said as she twirled a strand of her short hair around her finger. Kenyon's good looks enamoured Kelsey, and she really didn't care what he called her, as long as she got to go home with him and show him a good time. She hoped that if she put it on him good enough, he would come crawling back to her in no time. Sadly, the girl was wrong. Kenyon never double dipped and tonight would be her only chance to get in his bed, so she'd better enjoy it while it lasted.

Mia stifled a laugh as she eyed the girl sympathetically, feeling bad for how Kenyon was probably about to give her some bomb ass dick and then leave her alone like she didn't mean shit. Roman shook his head with a grin and said, "Come on, y'all. Let's take a shot. It's almost midnight!"

"Hell yeah!" Mia said as she grabbed a fresh glass from their table. "I'm trying to get turnt the fuck up. Fuck everything else. It's 2020, bitches!"

"Okay, no more drinks for you after this," Roman chuckled as he kissed Mia on the cheek. She sucked her teeth and then began dancing in place. Home girl was definitely feeling all the liquor she had consumed.

Roman got busy filling up shot glasses and passing them out while Noah poured the champagne they ordered for when the clock hit midnight. When everyone had a drink in each hand, Roman made a toast. "Let's take this shot as the final drink of 2019! It was one hell of a year, but we made it and now we can lay it to rest!"

"I'll drink to that," Jade shouted as she did a little dance before taking the shot back.

Noah took his and then leaned over to whisper in Jade's ear. "You've had a lot to drink tonight, baby. You good?"

Jade swayed into him and giggled, "I'm phen-nenomal."

Noah laughed, "Okay, sweetheart. Maybe you should take it easy on the drinks, too. You and Mia are already a handful."

Noah tried to pull Jade's champagne glass out of her hands, but she slapped his hand away playfully. He shrugged and made a mental note not to drink any more himself and to keep an eye on her. He had never seen her drink as much as she had tonight, and there were way too many thirsty niggas eying her in this place. Pulling her closer, he tried to clear his mind and sober up as the countdown began. Jade was standing in front of him, and he had his arms wrapped around her small waist. She was wiggling around as she counted down the new year and was oblivious to the fact that she was rubbing all over Noah's dick. He groaned softly and began massaging her hips sensually as he pulled her closer into him. Jade felt him behind her and forgot all about the countdown as she turned around and wrapped her arms around his neck, still holding onto her champagne glass. She pulled his head down and they kissed just as everyone around them screamed, "Happy New Year!"

Balloons dropped from the ceiling as people cheered around them, but Jade and Noah felt as though they had the room to themselves. Noah palmed her ass and picked her up as he deepened the kiss. She wrapped her short legs around his waist and kissed him passionately. After a few moments, Noah pulled away with a sigh and said, "Happy new year, baby."

Dizzy from the electrifying kiss, Jade smiled drunkenly and said, "Happy new year, Noah."

He set her back down on her feet and kept his large hand on her waist as she downed her champagne. She set her glass on the table and was about to say something to Mia when a woman stepped in front of her. Noah took one look at the woman and immediately pushed Jade behind him as he looked down at the woman. She was a few inches taller than Jade and much curvier. Her body was out of this world and stacked just right. Her ass stuck out so far, Jade was sure she could set a couple of her empty shot glasses on it. Her breasts were bulging out of her sequins crop top and she had long ass wavy hair. Jade could tell it was real, too. She had a chocolate complexion, and she was really cute in the face.

Jade looked up at Noah who was clenching his jaw, his arm holding her in place behind him. She idly wondered who the pretty woman was as she watched them stare each other down. Mia was suddenly at Jade's side whispering in her ear. "You okay?"

Jade looked at her confused. "Why wouldn't I be?"

"Roman just told me that chick is Noah's ex, Alana. Apparently the bitch is loca," Mia said as she twirled her finger around her ear.

Jade peeked around Noah again with more interest this time. Alana now had her hands on Noah's chest and Jade's temper flared. Normally, she would have let Noah handle the situation, but the liquor in Jade's system was causing her to act out on all of her emotions. She tried pushing forward, but Noah's strong arm blocked her while his other hand gently pushed Alana away from him. Alana laughed and said something, but Jade couldn't hear her so she tried pushing forward again and this time Noah pulled her next to him and held her tightly by his side.

"This is your new bitch?" Alana smirked at Jade.

Noah gritted his teeth, "Watch your mouth."

Alana shrugged and threw her long hair over her shoulder confidently before looking squarely at Jade. "Enjoy your time with him, bitch. Eventually he'll kick you to the curb just like he did me. Shit, he'll probably remember how good he had it with me and come crawling back. Either way, enjoy it while it lasts."

It shocked jade that the girl was so disrespectful, and she was momentarily speechless. Luckily, Mia wasn't, and she wasn't being held back by Noah, either. Before anyone could comprehend what was happening, Mia had Alana on the floor as she wailed punch after punch at her. She was taking all of her anger out on the girl and wouldn't let up. Roman finally lifted Mia off the floor and started walking towards the exit at the same time Noah picked Jade up and followed right behind his brother while Kenyon and his random girl followed.

Once they were outside on the busy streets, Mia shouted, "Ro, put me down!"

"Are you going to continue to act a fool?" he chuckled as she beat her little fists into his muscular back.

"Depends," she screeched.

Roman shook his head with a smile and let her down. Noah let Jade down, too, and they stood out on the street looking at each other before they all burst into laughter.

"Yoooo, Mia. I didn't know you were a certified boxer," Kenyon laughed as Kelsey covered her mouth and giggled.

"Did y'all see Alana's face, though? She was genuinely scared. I doubt that anyone has ever laid a finger on her." Roman chuckled while Noah cracked a smile and nodded in agreement.

"She had it coming! She called my best friend a bitch one too many times. Stupid ass hoe. Who the fuck does she think she is, anyway?" Mia asked to nobody in particular.

"That's Alana. She's delusional and thinks the world revolves around her, but Roman is right. If we ever see her again, she will probably steer clear of us. I'm sure she has never been beat up before in her life," Noah chuckled.

Mia waved him off, "What did you see in that disrespectful puta, anyway?"

Noah shrugged, "I wish I could tell you."

"Don't be like that, bro. It was her body. Shiiiit...I would have made the same mistake had I met her ass first," Kenyon chuckled.

Uncomfortable with the conversation and noting that Jade had been silent the whole time, Noah said, "aight, man. We're out. I'll talk to y'all tomorrow."

Jade looked at Mia and spoke up for the first time since they left the lounge. "Are you coming home with us?"

"Nah, she's coming with me. I'll drop her off sometime tomorrow," Roman answered for her.

Jade nodded, walked over to her friend and threw her arms around her. "Thank you, Mimi. I love you, girl."

"You know I always got you, Mouse. I love you too." Mia hugged Jade back tightly before letting go. "I'll see you tomorrow."

Jade waved goodbye to Roman and Kenyon before taking Noah's outstretched hand and allowing him to lead the way to the waiting car where Tommy had been patiently waiting. She felt unsteady in her heels as the alcohol took ahold of her body. She clung to Noah's arm and allowed him to help her into the car.

On the ride home, Jade was quiet even as Noah took her legs into his lap and took off her heels for her. She stayed silent and stared out the window, thinking about Noah's ex girlfriend and wondering if what she had said was true. What she and Noah had seemed real, but she had been dead wrong about relationships before and she couldn't discern how this time was different. She couldn't get her thoughts to slow down and her mind to clear up as she tried sorting out her emotions.

Noah knew that what Alana said had gotten into Jade's head, and he was trying to figure out how to approach the conversation. Before he knew it, they were pulling up to his home and when Jade reached for her shoes, he held them away and got out of the car. She looked at him inquisitively, but didn't speak. He smiled down at her and poked his head back in the car, holding his arms out to her. Jade scooted towards the door and Noah scooped her up into his arms and walked her into the house.

He was drunk as well, although not on the level Jade was on, but he stumbled a bit as he walked up the stairs. Jade squealed and clung to his neck. As he steadied himself, he held her tighter and said, "I got you, baby."

Jade relaxed in his arms as he unlocked the door and pushed it open. Noah still didn't put her down once they were inside. Instead, he locked the door and made his way through the dark house and up the stairs. He sat Jade down once they were in his room. She swayed a bit once she was back on her feet, but Noah didn't let go of her until he was sure she was steady. He looked down at her and caressed her face. "Do you need anything?"

Jade nodded her head once. "Water, please? And get one for yourself, too."

"I got you," he said before disappearing out of the room.

Jade immediately took her shorts and underwear off before walking into the bathroom and relieving herself. She had been peeing all night long, but that was what liquor did. She felt like she had to pee every five minutes and every time she did; it felt like a whole gallon of liquid came out of her. When she finished, she washed her hands and then took off her bra and top, discarding them on the bathroom floor. She was crawling in bed butt ass naked when Noah came back in the room.

"Here, baby. Sit up and drink this," Noah said as he sat down next to her in the bed.

Jade sighed and then pulled herself up into the sitting position. She mumbled *thank you* to Noah and drank half the bottle of water before clumsily trying to put the cap back on. Noah saw her struggling and grabbed it from her, securing the lid and putting it on the nightstand. Jade laid back down and stared up at Noah, trying her hardest to keep her eyes open. He caressed her face and asked, "Are you feeling okay?"

Jade nodded her head and then changed her mind and shook it as if she were saying no. Noah looked at her with a confused expression and she gave him a sad, drunken smile. "The room is spinning and you're going to go back to your ex girlfriend, but I've been through worse. I'll be okay."

Noah's heart ached that she even thought that was a possibility. He gathered Jade in his arms just as she cried and his heart broke that he was causing her any kind of pain. He knew that the liquor that she'd consumed wasn't helping and he also knew that because she was so drunk, now was not the time to have a conversation about it.

Instead, he held her close and simply said, "I promise you I am not going anywhere."

Jade sniffled and continued to cry for a few minutes until she passed out. Noah sighed as he carefully positioned her out of his lap and onto the pillows. He wiped her tears from her eyes and pulled the blanket over her before kissing her on the cheek. Quickly, he undressed and used the bathroom before getting into bed and cuddling up to Jade. Noah passed out just as quickly as Jade had, and they both slept a dreamlessly.

<hr>

"UGH, HOW MUCH DID I DRINK LAST NIGHT?" JADE MOANED AS she laid back down in bed. She had a rude awakening when vomit was fighting its way up her throat. She had to run into the bathroom and barely made it before it spewed out of her mouth.

Noah woke up from hearing her retching into the toilet and he was instantly by her side, holding her hair back and rubbing her back in small circles. He held her steady as she brushed her teeth, and then he pulled her hair back into a ponytail for her in case she had to throw up again before helping her back into the room.

"A lot," Noah responded as he tucked her back in bed. His own head was pounding and his stomach wasn't feeling too well, either. "I'm going to get us a few things from the kitchen. Do you need anything specifically?"

Jade shook her head and closed her eyes. Noah moved her hair out of her face before getting off the bed and ambling down to the kitchen. He hadn't been this hungover in years, and he made a mental note not to get that drunk ever again. He could handle his liquor just fine, so being drunk wasn't the problem. It was the hangover that was a bitch.

Once he was in the kitchen, he grabbed a loaf of bread and made some toast. He grabbed a whole jug of orange juice, not bothering to pour it into glasses, and then he grabbed two bottles of Smart Water before bringing everything back up to Jade, only stopping in the bathroom to grab a bottle of Tylenol.

Noah discarded the items on the bed and then crawled back in so he could be next to Jade. She peeked through one eye at the things Noah brought and then closed it again before saying, "I feel like I've been hit by a truck."

Noah chuckled, "I don't feel much better."

"I guess that means we had a good night?" Jade said, still with her eyes closed as she snuggled up to a pillow.

"Do you remember anything about last night?" Noah asked, hoping that she did. He knew they needed to talk about Alana, and it would be so much more awkward if he had to explain to her what happened.

Jade thought about it for a moment and then groaned as she popped her eyes open, "Your ex...Elaine."

Noah relaxed and smiled, "Alana, yes."

Jade rolled her eyes, "Whatever. I remember that she was feeling all over you and then she said some shitty things to me before Mia dragged her ass."

Jade giggled and Noah reached for the jug of orange juice. "Yeah, that about sums it up."

Noah took a long drink from the jug and then passed to to Jade who asked, "No cups?"

"Didn't feel like creating extra work," Noah grinned over at her. Jade shrugged and tilted her head back so she could take a drink. When she finished, Noah said, "I think we should talk about what she said to you."

"I know I was trippin when we got home, Noah, but it was the liquor talking. I'm okay, I promise," Jade smiled over at him.

Noah was relieved, but he still wanted to put to rest any doubt she might have, "Still, I just want you to know that Alana means nothing to me. She's delusional as hell and I'm even contemplating on having a restraining order put on her. What she said to you was completely untrue. I hope you can trust me when I say that."

Jade was happy to hear him say that. She nodded her head and scooted over to him before laying on his chest. "I believe you."

"Are you sure? Because last night—"

"I know I was a mess last night and I'm sorry. I've been hurt before and there's still a part of me that believes I'll be hurt again. Just be patient with me, please? I'm trying to do better."

Noah kissed the top of Jade's head, "No need to apologize, sweetheart. I'll be as patient as you need me to be."

Jade smiled, "good. Now, about today...I hope you know I don't plan on leaving this bed."

Noah chuckled, "I didn't plan on allowing you to leave this bed, either. Glad we are on the same page."

Jade giggled and relaxed into him, glad that they had the chance to rest and recover today because last night was sure enough epic. All she wanted was to cuddle up and watch movies with Noah and get rid of her headache and nausea.

CHAPTER 15

"Do you have to go?" Noah asked Jade with big sad puppy dog eyes. He'd been moping around all week in preparation for today.

Jade giggled, "Yes, Noah. I can't live here forever."

"Says who?" Noah asked seriously, causing Jade to giggle again as she kneeled down to move a box out of her way. Noah raced over to help her. They were in his bedroom and there was a stack of boxes piled in the room's corner.

"Seriously," Noah argued. "You could save money by staying here. You and Mia."

Jade whirled around to look at him. "Noah Bennett. I can't just live off of you because we're sleeping together. I need to be independent for once and take care of myself."

Noah's face fell, "I didn't mean that I wanted you to stay because we are sleeping together...I just enjoy having you around and—"

Jade put her hand on Noah's chest and looked up into his eyes, "I know what you meant and I hope you know how much I appreciate you, but I don't think us living together so soon is healthy. I'll never be able to repay you or thank you enough for everything you have done for Mia and I, but it's time for us to get back on our *own* two feet."

Noah sighed and nodded his head as he embraced Jade. It was now creeping towards the end of January, and Mia and Jade had finally signed a lease on an apartment for the two of them. Noah was happy for them. Seeing how far they'd come compared to when he first laid eyes on them made him extremely proud, but he was would be lying if he said he wasn't sad to see Jade go, although, he respected her so much more for standing her ground. Other women that he had dealt with would have been elated to stay with him and leech off of his success, but not Jade. She wanted to stand on her own two feet, and Noah knew he needed to be supportive of that. It would be an adjustment for them both, though. For the past month they'd slept in the same bed and seen each other every day. He would miss her, but he knew that this was for the best for Jade.

He kissed Jade on the forehead and said, "Okay, I understand that, sweetheart. I'll just miss you is all."

Jade giggled, "I'll still see you at work every day and nobody is stopping me from coming over here and spending the night."

Noah perked up at that, "And I can stay over at your place, too."

"Let's hold off on that until we get proper furniture," Jade scrunched up her face.

"I wish you would let me help with that," Noah mumbled.

Jade pulled out of his arms and went back to moving boxes around, checking to make sure they were labeled correctly. Granted, her and Mia didn't have much to move, but labeling everything would make their day run more smoothly.

"Don't start with that again," Jade said.

"What?" Noah asked, exasperated. "I'm just saying, I can have everything you need delivered to your place today."

"No," Jade said firmly. "What's the point of getting a fresh start if I'm not going to do it on my own?"

Noah shook his head, "I just want to make sure you're comfortable."

Jade stopped what she was doing and walked over to the bed. She sat down and then patted a spot right next to her. Noah sighed, knowing that he was about to get a lecture, and slowly made his way over to her. Once he was sitting next to her, Jade hopped up and stood in between his legs so they were eye-level. "I promise that I will be comfortable, Noah. Don't lose sleep over me, okay? I will be fine. Mia's bed is being delivered today. Her and I will share that bed until we get paid again and I can order one for myself. We've shared beds before, babe. Then, we will get a couch and then a table and so on. We got this."

Noah was trying hard to see things her way, and he knew that she was being smart about her money, but he still didn't like the thought of her not having a bed for herself. "I just wish you had bought a bed for yourself, too."

Jade laughed, "I would have, but we needed food for our apartment and other basic necessities, like toilet paper, laundry detergent, and towels. We are starting completely over so I had to spend most of my money on things like that."

Noah's jaw clenched, and Jade caressed the side of his face until he relaxed.

"Your stubbornness will be the death of me," Noah finally said as he gave Jade a weak smile.

"Get used to it," Jade giggled. She knew that her moving situation wasn't ideal and that their apartment would basically be bare for the next few months, but she didn't care. She and Mia were ecstatic to have a place they called their own. It surprised jade that Mia was so down for it since she loved Noah's home and all the perks that came along with it, but Mia wanted her own space just as much as Jade. They both wanted to walk around in their underwear and play loud music. They wanted to cook their own food and own their own pots and pans. Both of the women wanted to get back to a sense of independence in their lives.

Noah grabbed Jade and trapped her in his arms as he kissed her all over her face. Jade squealed with laughter, and Noah's heart swelled. The sound of her laughter made his days twenty times better. He couldn't get enough of her. He finally pulled back to see a wide grin on her face. He smiled back at her as he held her hips. "You're still coming over on Sunday to meet my mom, right?"

Jade's grin faltered a bit as she said, "Only if you're sure that you want me to meet her. You don't feel like it's too soon? Maybe we should wait until after the divorce so—"

"Hey, stop that. I'm sure. Roman's already ran his big ass mouth to her about you, anyway, and she's curious about you. I haven't dated anyone in a long time and she's eager for some grandchildren." Noah grinned at the look of bewilderment on Jade's face and decided to tease her. "What? You don't want to have my babies?"

"That's not—I mean...I don't. I-I didn't—" Jade fumbled over her words as she tried to process Noah's words.

"I'm just kidding, sweetheart. I know. It's too early to even think about something like that, but I guarantee you that my mother will bring it up on Sunday," Noah chuckled.

Jade's cheeks warmed, "I still don't understand why Mia can't come. Her and your brother have been fooling around just as long as you and I."

"Yeah, but let them both tell it, they're just sleeping together. No strings attached."

Jade shook her head, "I don't believe that. They like each other more than they are willing to admit."

"I agree," Noah nodded, "but my mother doesn't care to meet any more of the women in Roman's life. Don't get me wrong, he isn't as bad as Kenyon, but let's just say that he has brought around one too many women for mama's taste. She told him not to bring another one around unless he's going to marry her."

Jade groaned, "I've never really been good with parents. I suppose I've only ever had to deal with my in-laws, but still...they hated me."

"And why is that?" Noah asked, "You never talk about them. Did they know how their son was treating you?"

Jade nodded her head, "Yeah...they knew, and they really didn't care. It's easy to see how Elijah got so fucked up in the head. They basically encouraged anything that he did and if he did something wrong, which was more often than not, they would blame anything or anyone else, but never him."

Noah shook his head incredulously as Jade continued, "I remember one time Elijah made me go over to their house for dinner after he beat my ass real good. I was looking real bad and his parents didn't even say a word to me. They all carried on like I wasn't even there. I have never in my life met a group of human beings that were as cruel as them."

Noah cleared his throat as he tried to control his anger. He was happy as hell that they had the divorce papers served. It was no surprise that Elijah decided to represent himself. It was also no surprise that he wanted to take it to court, but Jade didn't want to face him unless she absolutely had to. Her lawyer and Elijah had been back and forth on that for the past week, and both Jade and Noah were ready for the whole ordeal to be done with.

He grabbed Jade's hands and looked her in the eye. "I promise you won't have to worry about that with my mom. Darlene Bennett can be a bit of a handful, but you two will bond over that."

Jade playfully scoffed and hit him in the shoulder before he continued, "Nah, I'm serious, though. She is very blunt and says what's on her mind, but she is also the most kind woman I have ever met...right alongside you. She will love you."

Jade was still nervous, but she decided to worry about meeting his mother another time. For now, she wanted to load up Noah's truck so her and Mia could go get the keys to their new place. Jade pecked Noah on the lips and said, "I'll try not to be nervous. I can't wait to meet her."

"Good. Now let's get this stuff downstairs. Where is Mia's lazy behind at, anyway?"

Jade giggled, "Don't call my friend lazy! Only I can call her that."

"Yeah, whatever," Noah chuckled as he waved her off.

"She's in her room waiting on Roman to get here. Actually, he should be here right now. We should get going. We have to meet the landlord in an hour."

Noah sighed, "Alright. Let's get this over with."

Jade giggled, "Perk up, buttercup. I'll tell you what. I'll spend the night with you on Sunday after I meet your mom. Deal?"

"But that's two whole days away," Noah complained.

"Hey, take it or leave it," Jade giggled as she held out her hand for him to shake.

"Deal," Noah grinned, already counting down the hours to having Jade back in his bed again.

"Oh goodness," Mia groaned as she flopped down on the soft carpet next to the bed in her room. "I am so happy we are all moved in. How the hell did it take so damn long and we barely had shit to move? Can you imagine if we actually had shit? Remind me to never move again. This is it for me. I am so damn tired. My feet hurt and I think I have a bruise on my elbow from when I hit it on the counter earlier. Fuck this shit."

Jade only half listened as she grabbed a brand new purple fuzzy towel and threw it at Mia. "Here, take a shower first. We don't want to dirty up your new bed on the first night and stop complaining about having shit to move. Two months ago this wasn't even possible."

"Can you bathe me?" Mia whined, ignoring the last part of Jade's statement.

Jade laughed loudly, "No, Mimi. You're a big girl. Go handle that and hurry because I'm tired as hell, too."

Mia pulled herself off the floor and exited the bedroom at a snail's pace so she could take her shower. Jade shook her head at her theatrics, and then stifled a yawn. She was more than ready to climb into Mia's queen sized bed, too. It had been a long ass day of moving boxes, unpacking and running back and forth to the store for stuff they didn't think to get. Thankfully, Roman and Noah put Mia's bed together for them and they even made it up with the new purple and black bedspread that Jade bought for her.

That was the beauty about Mia and Jade's friendship. They were never greedy about their money, and they shared everything. They worked well together in that manner. Jade knew that Mia had spent almost her whole check on this new bed, so she bought her a bedspread and pillows along with everything else they would need for their new home. She also gave Mia one hundred dollars for spending money for the next couple of weeks. Jade knew that when they got paid again, Mia would extend her the same favor when it was time for her to buy her own bed.

Rent would be split evenly between the two of them, and they divided up the other bills as well. They were lucky enough to find a two-bedroom apartment that fit within their budget and was fairly close to work. Money would be tight for them, and they wouldn't be going on any shopping sprees anytime soon, but they could survive and that was all either of them wanted to do.

Jade took a moment to walk through the small apartment as she smiled to herself. The kitchen was small, but she was able stock it full of food as well as silverware, plates, glasses, and pots and pans. The living room was right next to the kitchen, and it was a decent size, but it was completely bare. They would get a couch and a television soon, but for now they could go without it. Those weren't on the top of their list, but Roman was nice enough to get them a bluetooth speaker which sat on the floor up against the wall. Jade knew her and Mia would put that to use tomorrow when they cooked their first meal in their home.

The bathroom was at the end of the short hall with both of the girls' bedrooms on either side and everything in the home was girly. The pots and pans were purple, the plates were white with pink flowers, and the bathroom was pink and baby blue. It was definitely a bachelorette pad, and Jade was happy to call it her own.

She stepped into her bedroom, which was bare, aside from the small closet where her clothes hung on pink hangers. The few pairs of shoes she owned were sitting up against the wall. Jade closed her eyes and imagined a queen-sized bed with a pink comforter on top of it. She smiled as she opened her eyes.

"I think I'll hang some lights in here, too," she said out loud. Whatever she did with the apartment, she was happy that the only person she needed permission from was her best friend. She felt as though she were free...now, if only Elijah would sign the damn divorce papers. Then she would throw a fuckin' party.

CHAPTER 16

"You look beautiful, baby. Stop stressing," Noah said as he walked up behind Jade who was standing in front of the mirror in the bathroom fussing over her hair.

"My stupid hair won't lay flat. Ugh! I should just go wash it so that it's curly. This is so dumb," Jade threw the comb in the sink.

Noah turned Jade around and held her face in his hands, "You are beautiful, Jade. It doesn't matter if your hair is curly or straight or the clothes you wear. You are beautiful inside and out."

Jade let out a deep breath and leaned into Noah. His mom would be there in a few minutes, and she was getting more and more nervous as the minutes ticked by. She did her best to relax in Noah's embrace as she said, "I'm sorry. I know I'm acting crazy right now. This is just a big step and...well...what if she asks where we met or if I've ever been married before?"

Noah thought about it for a moment, "We only have to tell her as much as you want. How about we just wait to see if she even asks those questions and we can worry about it then?"

"That doesn't help," Jade whined.

Noah rubbed her back in slow circles, "Jade take a deep breath. She will love you."

Jade did what she was told and then nodded her head just as the doorbell rang. Noah grabbed her hand, and they made their way down to the front door. When Noah opened it, his mother flew into his arms, "It has been too damn long, son."

She was a short woman and very fit for her age. Her skin was a couple shared lighter than Noah's, but they had the same brown eyes. Other than that, Noah and Roman looked exactly like their dad.

Noah chuckled as he wrapped his arms around his mother, "That isn't my fault, ma. You and Aunt Anita extended your holiday trip."

Noah was referring to Kenyon's mom, Anita. She and Darlene had been best friends since high school, and they were thick as thieves. They had only just gotten back from their holiday trip and they were coming up on the end of January. Retirement was treating the ladies really well for them to have been able to take a month trip without notice.

"Boy, hush. I got back last week and I haven't heard diddly squat from either of you." Darlene's eyes landed on Jade, who was nervously standing slightly behind Noah. "And this must be the reason why. You must be Jade?"

"Yes, Ma'am. It's nice to meet you," Jade said shyly.

She stuck her hand out for Darlene to shake but she waved her off, "I'm more of a hugger."

Jade smiled and stepped into Darlene's open embrace. Noah stood back and grinned as he watched the two most important women in his life hug. Jade had tried on at least five different outfits before settling on some leggings and a green tunic top. She had straightened her hair, so it fell down to the small of her back, and she decided not to wear any makeup. She was beautiful as hell to Noah, and as usual, he couldn't keep his eyes off her.

Jade seemed to relax some as his mother hugged her, and he was glad. She was worried for no reason. Noah had never allowed a woman to meet his mother, not even Alana. His mom knew that Jade had to be something special and based on that alone she won major points and she didn't even know it.

When the two women separated, Noah said, "Come on, ma. Jade cooked for us and I don't know about you, but I'm starving."

Darlene looked at Jade impressed, "You know how to cook, dear?"

Jade smiled, "I'm no master chef, but I can get around the kitchen."

Noah grabbed Jade's hand and pulled her into him. He kissed the top of her head and then smiled at his mom. "She's being modest. She is an amazing cook."

Jade blushed, and Darlene beamed at the two of them. As a mother, Darlene was happy to see her son in a loving relationship. They genuinely looked happy around each other, and she knew what young love had looked like. Her and Noah's father had it many years ago. They'd met in college, and it was like love at first sight. Murphy Bennett had been the most kind man that she had ever met. He always put other people's feelings ahead of his own, and he was a helpless romantic. He swept Darlene off her feet, and it was a whirl-wind romance that resulted in two children and twenty-seven years of marriage. The day he died was the day that Darlene threw all of her love and attention into her boys. Some might think she was over-bearing, but what else was Darlene supposed to do once her husband died and she had an excess amount of love to give? Certainly she wasn't expected to pour it out into another man. No, she'd already met her soulmate, and she was content to live the rest of her life a widow. Her boys meant everything to her, and as long as they were happy, then she was happy. A few grandchildren wouldn't hurt, either, but Darlene would get around to that later.

Noah reached out for his mom with his free hand. Once she grabbed it, he happily led the women into the dinning room. Jade had set the table, and it looked beautiful with flowers for a centerpiece and all the mouth watering food.

"Wow, this looks great," Darlene commented as she took her seat.

"Jade did it all. I just sat back and watched," Noah grinned as he sat across from his mother. Jade sat down next to him and smiled.

"And why didn't you help, son? I know I raised you better than that," Darlene scolded.

Noah put his hands up in mock surrender. "There is no helping Jade when she's in her zone."

Jade giggled, "It's true. I all but banned him from the kitchen. He was only getting in my way."

A burst of laughter erupted from Darlene. "I used to do the same thing to Noah's father. The only difference was that fool couldn't boil water. He sure tried to help out, though. Just so he could spend time with me."

Noah chuckled, "Remember that time dad insisted on making Thanksgiving dinner?"

"Do I remember? He damn near burned the whole kitchen down," Darlene laughed.

"He sounds like a character," Jade giggled.

"Oh, he was. He sure was," Darlene smiled sadly.

Noah cleared his throat and said, "Let me say grace so we can eat. I don't want the food to get cold."

Everyone bowed their heads as Noah prayed over the food. When he finished, they began dishing food onto their plates. In a nervous fit, Jade had outdone herself. Since it was still early afternoon, she opted for a brunch menu. She made entirely too much food, and she knew she would be asking Noah to drive her to a shelter to drop the leftovers off later. There were homemade caramel rolls, fried chicken and waffles, crab cake benedicts, grits, cheesy eggs, hash browns, bacon, salad and rolls.

"This is quite a spread, Jade," Darlene said as she put butter on a roll.

"I didn't know what you liked, so I thought I would make a bit of everything," Jade responded a bit embarrassed at how much she made. "I guess I went a little overboard."

"Nonsense. I might even take some of this home for later," she smiled.

Jade relaxed and bit into a caramel roll. The sweetness from it immediately invaded her taste buds, and she almost groaned out loud in satisfaction. SHe hadn't realized how hungry she was until that moment. She made a mental note to have Mia stop by later to grab a plate. Jade knew she would never hear the end of it if she caught wind that Jade had cooked this big feast and hadn't saved her any.

After a few moments of everyone sampling everything on their plates, Darlene broke the silence. "Tell me about your friend Mia, Jade. I hear she's dating my other son and he doesn't have the best trek record with women."

Jade suppressed a giggle as she covered her mouth with a napkin so she could finish chewing her food. "I might be biased, but Mia is a great woman. She's my best friend, and she was there for me when I was at my lowest. We've really been there for each other. She's the type to give someone the shirt of her back."

"She also talks a lot," Noah butted in and Jade playfully slapped him on his arm.

"Yes, she talks a lot, but she has a good heart. I know that she got out of a bad relationship a few months ago, so I'm not too sure how serious her and Roman are. I do think they like each other a lot more than they've admitted to each other or even themselves," Jade grinned.

Noah nodded, "I got that feeling, too, but they're going at their own pace and there isn't anything wrong with that."

Noah grabbed Jade's hand that was resting on top of the table and lifted it up to his mouth. He planted a soft kiss on it and smiled at her. Jade blushed and smiled back. Darlene zeroed in on them from across the table and smiled, "Speaking of going at your own pace...seems like you two are falling for each other pretty fast."

Jade was sipping on her orange juice and sputtered when she heard Darlene's observation. She set her glass down as Noah patted her on the back. He chuckled and said, "Ma, don't—"

"Oh, hush boy. I'm allowed to ask questions," Darlene waved him off. Noah knew better, so he backed off and let the inevitable happen. His mother was sweet as she wanted to be, but she was also feisty and although he towered over her five foot six inch frame, she was the only woman he was afraid of.

"Tell me, when did you guys meet?" Darlene asked with a smile.

Jade's face grew a deep shade of red. She knew where the conversation was heading and she tried to relax as Noah responded. "Last month."

"Don't be shy. What's the story there?" Darlene looked between the two of them with her big brown eyes.

Noah looked down at Jade, wishing that he had taken her more seriously earlier when she was fretting over how to answer these questions. Jade looked into Noah's brown eyes that looked so much like his mothers and sighed. She took a deep breath and then looked over at Darlene. "Mrs. Bennett, I want to be completely honest with you."

Darlene's eyebrows rose as she waited for Jade to continue. Jade looked back up at Noah with tears in her eyes. She kept her eyes on him as she spoke. "My marriage was built on lies and I don't want what we have to be tainted by them as well."

"You don't have to share anything you don't want to, sweetheart," Noah said as he rubbed her back. His heart ached for her because he knew that she didn't open up to people easily.

"It's okay," Jade said before looking back at Darlene. "Noah and I met in a women's homeless shelter. That's where he met both Mia and I, actually. His company does a charity dinner for the shelter every year and I was there to...uhm...to eat."

Jade risked a glance up at Darlene and saw that she had a look of concern on her face. Jade swallowed the lump in her throat and said, "A couple of months ago, my husband beat me. It wasn't the first time, but it was the last. It was bad enough that I had to be put in the hospital. I was able to escape, but that meant leaving everything I had behind. I didn't have money, food, a cellphone or even proper clothing to keep me warm. I'd met Mia not too long after that, and we sort of clicked right off the bat. We stuck together and took care of each other. She was the one that dragged me to the charity dinner and we met Noah. Mrs. Bennett, your son is the most kind man I have ever met. He has helped Mia and I out more than he will ever understand. He's given us food and clothing along with shelter, transportation and jobs. With those jobs, we could finally move into our own apartment this past Friday. I really care about Noah and not because of the money he has spent on me, but because he has been the first person to make me feel safe and secure since my parents died. He is my best friend before anything else, and I really don't know what I would do without him."

One tear slipped out of Jade's eye, and she felt so embarrassed to have spewed all that out to Noah's mother. Now, on top of that, she was crying. As always, Noah was there for her when she needed him most. He wiped the lone tear from her face with his thumb and then leaned in to give Jade a kiss before looking at his mother. "I really wasn't expecting Jade to share all of that with you today...but I feel the same way about her. She is my best friend before anything else. We are taking things slow and sorting her divorce out. We'll go from there once everything is finalized."

Darlene chuckled as she finally responded, "Child, there is nothing slow paced about you two. Y'all are in love. I know it when I see it and you two have it. Y'all can pretend to be best friends or whatever, but remember, mama always knows best, and Jade, honey, I'm sorry if I made you uncomfortable with my questions. Thank you for being honest and sharing that with me. I want you to know that I am not judging your situation. As long as you are honest with my son and treat him right then I'm happy. He's smart and I trust that he knows what he is doing."

Jade relaxed a little, happy that Darlene didn't seem upset. Jade wouldn't have blamed her if she was, though. Hearing that her son was dating a homeless woman that was still married to an abusive husband was grounds for Darlene to hate Jade, but she didn't. On the contrary, Darlene actually liked Jade. She prided herself on being able to sniff out a person's true intentions at first glance, and Jade was nothing but genuine around Noah.

Darlene looked at Jade and added, "I can't imagine how hard it was for you to talk about those things, but just know that there is no judgment on my behalf."

"Thank you, that means a lot. I just want to make sure that I do right by Noah and that means being honest about myself around the people he loves," Jade responded sincerely.

Darlene looked impressed and then turned to Noah, "I like her, son. Don't let her get away."

Noah laughed, "I don't plan on it."

The rest of brunch went by quickly. Jade packed Darlene a couple of plates to bring home, and Darlene embraced her when she was leaving. "It was good to meet you, Jade."

"Likewise," Jade beamed at her as she pulled away.

Noah engulfed his mother in a hug and said his goodbyes before closing the door behind her. He turned to face Jade with a huge grin on his face. "What did I tell you?"

Jade giggled and backed away from him as he moved towards her. She feigned ignorance, "I don't know what you're talking about."

"Uh uh...none of that. Come on, let me hear it." Noah said as he tackled her in a hug and began planting kisses all over her face.

Jade tried to wiggle out of his grasp, but Noah held on tightly.

"Okay, Okay!" Jade sputtered between laughs. "You were right. I was nervous for nothing."

Noah stopped his assault and smiled down at her. "I just can't wait for you to realize that your past does not define you as a woman. "

Jade thought about what he said and she didn't know how to respond. Noah was right, but her past did make her who she was. It was an everlasting conflict within herself but it was something that she was working on coming to terms with. Instead of responding to the ever-wise Noah, she stepped up onto her tiptoes and kissed him on his lips. Noah pulled her closer and leaned into her, deepening the kiss before pulling away. "Do we have to go to work tomorrow?"

Jade giggled, "I don't know. You tell me, boss."

His smile widened. "In that case, let's play hookey and lay in bed all day. I've missed you."

"I've missed you too and speaking of work," Jade looked up at him with a cautious smile.

Noah's eyebrows raised as he looked down at her. "What?"

Jade cleared her throat and stepped out of his embrace. She wrung her hands nervously and looked everywhere but at him. "Well...you know I've been painting again?"

Noah nodded. "Yeah, and you're great at it, baby. I love watching you work."

Jade smiled, "Thank you...and thank you for letting me keep my painting supplies here. There really won't be any room for that stuff once we get more furniture."

"You know I don't mind. It ensures that I'll see you more often," Noah grinned.

"I knew you had ulterior motives," Jade teased and then she became serious. "Noah, you know that I really appreciate everything that you have done for me and I know that I have only worked with you for a little over a month now, but...I'm putting in my official two week's notice."

She said that last part quickly, cringing as she waited for his response. It surprised Noah that she was quitting and his shock quickly turned into concern, "What are you going to do for money, Jade?"

She didn't want Noah to think that he didn't appreciate him and everything that he'd done for her, but she had made a promise to herself at the beginning of the year that she would start living for *her*. She straightened her shoulders and looked at Noah, "A few weeks back I submitted photos of a couple of my pieces to this art show. It was on a whim and I really didn't even think it was my best work or that anything would come of it...but yesterday somebody got back to me and let me know that they wanted my pieces in their upcoming show. It's next weekend, and they priced my paintings really high,

Noah. If I only sell one painting, I won't have to worry about my half of the rent for two months."

Noah was silent for a moment before he broke out in a wide smile and picked Jade up. He spun her around in a circle and she giggled uncontrollably until he sat her back down on her feet. She peeked up at him through her thick lashes and asked, "You aren't mad?"

"Why would I be mad? This is amazing news, Jade. Architecture is my love, not yours. You deserve to work in a field that makes you happy. I would never hold you back from that, although, I will miss seeing you every day. First you move out and now you're quitting on me," Noah placed his hand to his heart and acted as though he was in pain. "I don't know how much more my heart can take."

"Oh, stop it," Jade laughed. "Your heart will be just fine. Besides, I'll be over here more often creating new masterpieces."

"And there's that silver lining," Noah grinned at her.

"I figured you would like that part," Jade replied with a small smile.

"And since I am technically still your boss, I'm ordering you to only work through Wednesday this week."

"But—"

Noah held his hand up, "Use your remaining PTO to cover the rest of the two weeks. You're going to need the time to prep for the art show and to create more pieces."

Jade rested her hand on Noah's cheek and sighed happily, "Always the hero."

Noah grabbed Jade's hand and planted a kiss on it before responding, "Always."

CHAPTER 17

THE WEEK WAS FLYING BY IN A BLUR, AND WEDNESDAY WAS already here. Jade, Mia, Kenyon and Noah had an intimate farewell lunch for Jade yesterday and today they were having an office party during the lunch hour. Noah went all out and had food catered in and they decorated the office in purple with farewell banners and balloons. He knew it was one of Jade's favorite colors and he wanted to make it special for her.

"Can your man ever just be normal? He is so damn extra." Mia rolled her eyes when she peeped the caterers coming in and setting up lunch. The two women were sitting in their office with the door opened and only pretending to work. Jade was packing up her things and emailing all of her clients over to Yolanda while Mia was scrolling on her phone. Mia consistently had a lot less work than Jade because Kenyon did the bare minimum. He only had two clients at a time, tops while Noah had between seven to ten at a time. Kenyon really could get by without an assistant, but he wasn't complaining that he had Jade to do most of his work for him. All he really had to do was design, which he didn't mind at all. Mia could handle the interaction with the clients on his behalf.

Jade laughed, "first of all, he isn't my man—"

"Yet—" Mia interjected.

"—and he's just being nice. I'm sure he does this for all the employee's."

"Nah, Mouse. I talked to that girl Sheri in accounting and she said that the company has never had a going away party like this. Face it. That man goes above and beyond for you and only you," Mia smirked.

Jade waved her off as she slipped her favorite pens into her back-pack. She had been a little down all day about leaving the company. She would miss her daily lunches with her best friend, Noah and Kenyon. She would definitely miss Kenyon and Mia's constant bick-ering, and she had to admit that she would miss being in Noah's pres-ence every day. Despite her sadness, Jade was excited to dive headfirst into her paintings. She'd completed a couple of pieces since Christmas, but she needed to get her ass in gear and create more if she wanted to make a decent living. She still had a few contacts she could track down that had bought from her before and she planned to do that tomorrow so she could invite them to her art exhibit this weekend. Overall, she was nervous, but she knew that with hard work she could thrive in the art industry, even more so than she had before. Elijah always held her back and restricted her, but now, she was free and she would not waste that freedom on her own fears.

"You know, I'm going to miss your ass around here," Mia said before pursing her lips for the selfie she was taking.

Jade watched her best friend take picture after picture of herself and laughed, "We live together, Mia."

"I know, damn...but still. We got this job together when we liter-ally had nothing. We've done everything together since the moment we met. It's a little bittersweet," Mia pouted and Jade completely understood where she was coming from. "Plus, you're leaving me here to deal with Kenyon's ass all on my own, and you know how he works my nerves."

Jade giggled, "Yup, I know. I just hope y'all don't kill each other without me there to keep the peace."

"Shit...we just might," Mia laughed along with Jade. "And don't get me started on Yolanda's ass. I can't believe you're leaving me here with her."

"You're a big girl, Mia. You can handle her skinny ass," Jade shrugged.

"Yeah, and if she keeps talking reckless, I'm really going to handle her ass," Mia spat and Jade didn't blame her. Yolanda had been cold towards them since day one, but lately she had been a straight up bitch. She would make nasty comments to Mia and Jade about their clothing whenever they walked by her desk. She even started slacking on her work so that Jade had more of a workload. Jade didn't mind that part too much because it allowed her more time with Noah, but she knew that Yolanda was trying to get under her skin. What she didn't understand was why. Both Jade and Mia had been nothing but nice to Yolanda from the start, but they figured that she was just one of those bitter bitches.

They hadn't brought up her behavior to Noah or Kenyon, yet. They didn't think it was that serious, but Jade wanted to make sure her girl was alright when she left. "Mia, make sure you tell Noah or Kenyon if she gets out of hand. I know that most of her comments have been harmless, but make sure you say something if it gets to be too much and don't lose your job over that girl. She isn't worth it."

"Yeah, yeah, whatever. She just needs to stay in her lane and everything will be all good," Mia mumbled just as Noah poked his head into the office.

"Hey, ladies. Lunch is ready and I'm requesting that the guest of honor go through the food line first," he smiled.

"I should go first since I'm the one that is the most depressed about her leaving," Mia pouted.

"No, Mia. I think that I am the most depressed," Noah argued.

Mia scoffed, "Nah, fuck that. No disrespect, but you'll still see Mia a lot since y'all are fucking and her painting studio is at your crib."

Jade gasped in embarrassment. *"Mia!"*

Mia shrugged, "What? It's true."

"That may or may not be true, but you live with her so by default that means you'll see her more," Noah grinned.

"Okay, you two, that's enough," Jade let out an exasperated laugh.

"Awww, Jade, I was just getting started," Mia whined playfully.

"Enough, please," Jade giggled as she got up from her desk chair.

Noah walked fully into the office and stole a quick kiss from Jade. Mia made a face and said, "Eww, you two. Get a room."

"I thought we were in a room," Noah quipped as his mouth turned up in a smirk.

"Ugh, I'm out of here," Mia pushed past the couple and out into the main office area.

Jade giggled and followed her friend while Noah trailed behind her, mesmerized by the way her hips were swaying. Jade was a small woman, but she still had some curves and the knee-length skirt she was wearing showed off each and every one of them. Noah could feel himself hardening, so he focused on the other faces that were congregating in the reception area so that his lower half could settle down.

Kenyon came out of his office yawning and Noah laughed, "How was your morning nap?"

Kenyon smiled, "Nigga, don't act like you know me! But, man, it was great. Thanks for asking."

Noah shook his head at his friends laziness and then clapped his hands together before speaking to his staff, "Alright, everyone. Thanks for coming to Jade's going away party. She hasn't been here long, but I think we can all agree that she has been a great asset to the team. I know that she has personally helped me a lot and I think Yolanda was thankful for her help as well."

Jade was standing next to Noah, and she smiled up at him before glancing over at Yolanda, who looked like she just ate a mouthful of shit. She scowled at Jade, but Jade shook it off and listened to what Noah was saying. "Now that Jade is leaving and realizing that having two assistants was extremely beneficial, I would like to announce that I am promoting Mia Reyes to a dual assistant position. She will now take on Jade's workload and still assist Kenyon in his work."

Mia was surprised, but honored. Truth be told, her days could get kind of boring because Kenyon didn't have much work to be done, so she was excited to have something more to do to make her days go by quicker.

"Does this promotion come with a raise?" Mia wiggled her eyebrows up at him.

Noah chuckled, "See me later and we will talk about it."

"Perfect," Mia chirped happily.

Jade clapped excitedly along with the rest of the staff, "Congrats, Mimi!"

"Thanks, Mouse," Mia beamed.

"Yeah, yeah. Just make sure you're still available for me," Kenyon said.

Mia waved him off, "Don't worry, Kenyon. I'll still do all your work for you."

"Jade, do you want to say anything?" Noah asked before Kenyon could start an argument with Mia.

Jade shifted uncomfortably by the attention, but she cleared her throat and looked out at everyone. "I really just want to thank everyone. Most of you have been kind to me and it was easy asking for help when I needed it, so thank you. I especially wanted to thank Noah for hiring me and showing me the ropes. You have been an amazing boss and I will forever be grateful to your kindness."

She smiled up at Noah and then quickly looked back at everyone else, not wanting to be too obvious. "Most of you don't know this, but I am an artist at heart and I am having my first art exhibit since taking a hiatus. It's this weekend and I would love for you all to come."

There were cheers and murmurs from all the staff as they discussed the art exhibit. Any of the staff that interacted with Jade had grown to like her. She was always kind and polite, and most of them were sad to see her go. Yolanda, on the other hand, couldn't stand that she was getting all this attention. She watched as Jade grabbed a plate from the beginning of the line and her eyes followed her as she got her food and then sat at one of the tables that had been set up for the day. One by one Kenyon, Mia and Noah made their way over to the table and Yolanda's anger skyrocketed. *What is so special about this raggedy bitch?* Yolanda wondered as she watched how everyone interacted with her. Damn near every employee stopped by her table to wish her well, and Noah looked at her as if she was shitting diamonds. Yolanda got up and stomped over to the food line, budging in front of several people as she grabbed a plate and began filling it, not really paying attention to what she was adding to it.

Yolanda hated to see another bitch getting all the attention, which was why she didn't have any female friends. Her father was a very rich man. He had a huge stock in Google since its birth, and it had made him a millionaire when Yolanda was very young. She was the only child so her parents spoiled her rotten and she never learned those core values like being kind and working hard. The only reason she kept this job was because of Noah. Hell, he was the reason she applied for the job in the first place because God knew that she didn't need to work. Her father paid all her bills, rent included, and he gave her a hefty weekly allowance. She wanted for nothing, well, except for Noah Bennett.

When she first laid eyes on him at an upscale restaurant, she swore that it was love at first sight. He was on a date with some other woman, and Yolanda was dining alone. She could tell that Noah wasn't really into his date and she knew that she could easily take that broads place. She also knew that in order to be dining at that specific restaurant, he had to have money. Only the elite dined there, and that made her even more curious. She waited until the couple left before briskly walking over to his table and snatching his receipt off the table. It was how she first learned his name. She went straight home and got to digging. She was an expert at finding people. The internet and social media made sure of that. It wasn't long before she found out that he owned an architecture company, and upon further investigation she saw that he was looking for an assistant.

It was as if fate was on her side and she just knew that this was the best way to get close to a man like him. She paid someone to create a flawless resume for her, and the following evening she submitted it. It came as no shock that she got a callback, and that was the first time she heard his voice. It was so deep and sexy. Believe it or not, she masturbated right there on the phone with him and he was none the wiser. Her in person interview went perfectly, and he hired her on the spot.

Since then, Yolanda had been fixated on Noah. She was in love with that man and in her heart; she knew that he had feelings for her, too. She wasn't dumb enough to think he loved her, but she knew that he liked her. She had been doing everything in her power to win Noah over and to show him he could open up to her. She even thought she was making progress before Jade came along. Now, Noah barely spoke to her, and she knew that bitch had everything to do with it. It was okay, though. Yolanda knew that soon, Jade would be out of the picture and Noah would be back to relying on her. Jade was not the one for him, and Yolanda knew just how to prove it.

Once Jade finished eating, she stood to throw her plate away and Yolanda quickly formed a devious plan to knock her her down a few pegs. She quickly got up and grabbed her plate that was still full of pasta and salad, as well as her plastic cup filled with punch, and she intercepted Jade as she was on the way to the trash can. In one swift motion Yolanda bumped into Jade and sent her plate and cup tumbling down Jade's outfit. Jade shrieked and backed away as she looked down at her clothes and then back up at Yolanda, who had a sinister smirk on her face.

"Whoops, next time watch where you're going, bitch," Yolanda murmured just low enough for Jade to hear. Then, when she saw Noah making his way over to them, she said, "Oh, my goodness. Jade, sweetie, I am so sorry! I am so clumsy."

Jade was fuming by the time Noah reached her. He looked down at her and asked, "Are you okay?"

Jade didn't speak, she only stood there and slit her eyes at Yolanda. Noah grabbed Jade by the elbow and ushered her into his office. He closed the door and locked it before turning to her. "What happened, sweetheart?"

Jade was shaking she was so upset, "That bitch, Yolanda, has been nothing but rude and conniving towards Mia and I since day one."

Jade was nearly shouting and Noah went over to her, careful not to touch her spoiled outfit, and he grabbed her face in his hands, "Quiet down, baby. Shhh...take a few deep breaths."

Once he was convinced that she calmed down, he asked, "What do you mean? Why haven't you told me?"

"Because, it wasn't anything I couldn't handle. Just a few comments about the way Mia and I dressed here and there, but today she crossed the line. She did this shit on purpose, and I have no idea why she hates me so much. I haven't done shit to her," Jade seethed.

Noah had never seen Jade this upset before, but he knew just how to get her back to smiling. He grinned down at her and she balled her face up even further as she asked, "Why the hell are you smiling, Noah? Do you see what she just did to me?"

Noah's grin spread across his face, "Yes, I do, and after I write her ass up, I'm going to thank her for this opportunity that she has presented."

Jade glanced up at him confused, "What are you talking about?"

Noah didn't respond. Instead, he grabbed her hand and led her over to the sofa that was sitting in the corner of his office. Jade sat down carefully so that the pasta sauce and punch wouldn't drip all over, and Noah bent down to take off her shoes. He took them off one by one and then pulled off her soaked pants. Jade now understood where he was going with this, and a smile graced her face. Noah noticed her smile and said, "This might be the last chance we get to make love in my office. We haven't done that yet, so why don't we just go ahead and check that off our list?"

Jade giggled, "I didn't know we had a list."

"Oh, yes. We definitely have a list. My office, a limo, at Kenyon's house—"

Jade's laugh interrupted him, "Why Kenyon's house?"

Noah shrugged, "Why not?"

Jade continued to giggle as he carefully slipped her blouse over her head and then he discarded it on the floor. He unsnapped her bra and ripped off her panties, "Sorry, I'll buy you more."

Turned on, Jade said, "Don't even worry about it," before leaning forward and kissing him feverishly.

While they were kissing, Noah took off his shirt and his undershirt. He broke the kiss so he could stand and he quickly discarded his pants and boxers, leaving them both naked and breathing hard. Noah's hard dick was right in Jade's face, so she licked her lips and then grabbed it, urging him closer so she could put him in her mouth. They both moaned when her wet mouth made contact with his pulsating dick. She circled her tongue around the tip and Noah's eyes rolled to the back of his head. He moaned quietly in satisfaction when she wrapped her lips around him and began moving back and forth over his length.

Jade cupped his balls and gently rolled them in her hands while she slobbered all over his manhood. After a few moments, she could feel Noah expand in her mouth, and that was when he pulled away. Without speaking, he lifted her off the couch and walked her over to his desk. In one swift motion, he swiped all of his papers to the floor and laid Jade down on top of his desk. The cold wood met Jade's back, and she gasped but didn't have time to move before Noah's tongue was gliding across her clit.

Jade bit her knuckles to stop herself from moaning too loudly as Noah inserted a finger inside of her and sucked her clit lightly. With one hand, she reached down and pushed Noah's head further into her pussy and with the other hand she squeezed her nipple. Her body convulsed as Noah worked his tongue faster and before she could catch her breath, she was coming.

Noah let her ride the wave of pleasure before he stood up and pushed into her. Jade gasped when he entered her, and her walls contracted against him. Noah cursed quietly and said, "I will never get enough of you, baby."

Jade bit her lip sexily as she stared into his eyes. Her heart swelled and she couldn't help but think for a brief second that Darlene had been right about them being in love. She would do anything to keep Noah happy and she never wanted to to live a life without him. She had never been in love before, not really, but she was sure that this was what it felt like.

She didn't have the chance to think on it long, though, because in the next moment, Noah grasped her legs and cocked them open. He held them there and began stroking in and out of her. They'd never done this position before, and the way his dick was hitting her g-spot was driving her wild. She wanted to scream, but she didn't want the whole office to hear them, so she stuffed her fist back in her mouth and moaned quietly. Noah smirked as he saw her struggling not to make a noise. Truth be told, in that moment he didn't care if the whole office heard him. In his mind, Jade was his woman, and he wanted everybody to know it.

"You like that, baby?" he asked as he stroked her slowly. He let go of one of her legs and began playing with her clit.

Jade couldn't answer. He was making her feel so damn good that she couldn't speak. Noah cocked his head to the side and then stopped everything he was doing. Jade's eyes bucked as she said, "No...why did you stop?"

"I asked you a question," Noah said sexily.

"Yes, daddy. Yes, I like it. Please, don't stop," she murmured as she looked into his eyes.

It drove him wild when she called him daddy and he wasted no time picking up where he left off, only at a faster pace. He slammed into her, and Jade yelped. Noah reached down and covered her mouth with his hand as he slammed into her again, "Shit, Jade. You feel so fuckin good, baby."

Jade convulsed again, and Noah could feel her walls contracting against him repeatedly. He kept his same rhythm as he said, "Cum for daddy."

Jade didn't have to be told twice. She came all over his dick, her juices wetting him up. Noah wasn't far behind her. He came and just barely remembered to pull out at the last second. Once they caught their breath, Jade asked, "Now who is going to clean all this up?"

Noah chuckled before kissing her on her forehead.

"I will while you take a shower," he said, gesturing to the restroom that connected to his office.

Jade nodded, looking like she was about to fall asleep right there on Noah's desk. Noah tapped her thigh and said, "After that, you can go home if you want. I doubt you will actually get any work done after that."

Jade laughed as she sat up, "You're probably right. A nap sounds wonderful. Text Mia and have her bring my backpack in here. Some habits die hard and after being homeless I still tend to carry around things I may need...just in case."

Hearing Jade say that broke Noah's heart. She didn't fully finish her sentence, but he knew that she meant just in case she had to run again. Now wasn't the time to delve into that topic, so he simply nodded his head and grabbed his wrinkled suit off the floor while Jade hopped off the desk and walked into the bathroom.

Outside of the office, Yolanda was discreetly listening, and she had heard everything. Her blood was boiling at what had just transpired. She quickly moved away from Noah's office before Mia's happy ass came around with Jade's backpack and caught her lurking. She made it to her desk and pulled out her phone.

She tapped out a simple text before putting her phone away.

Yolanda: *Let's do it this Saturday. I'll call you with the details later.*

A quick response came back, but Yolanda was too busy daydreaming about Noah to realize it.

718-565-9090: *Can't wait.*

CHAPTER 18

THERE WAS BEAUTIFUL ARTWORK DISPLAYED THROUGHOUT THE industrial building. Paintings that were as high as the ceilings or as small as the palm of someone's hand and everything in between were being showcased. Sculptures made from various materials were scattered through the exhibit, and the people mingling looked just as gorgeous. It was a black-tie event, so ladies were wearing their prettiest dresses while the gentlemen were rocking tailored suits.

Jade was wearing the dress that Noah got her for her birthday. He wanted to buy her something new, but she refused. The dress he had already bought her was gorgeous, and she wanted the excuse to wear it again. It also brought back fond memories for her, and she was excited to wear it tonight.

Jade had been a ball of nerves all day as she prepared for this event. She had managed to paint three more paintings that she felt were good enough to be showcased and sold in the silent auction, so that made it a total of five of her pieces that were included in the exhibit. Personally, she felt as though her work was rushed and not her best, but she knew that she had to start somewhere and she was proud of herself. She knew that she wouldn't do another exhibit for a few months so she could have time to create true masterpieces, but she was surprised at all the positive feedback she had been getting.

As shy as she was, she knew that exhibits were about getting her name out there and schmoozing with art collectors, so that was exactly what she did. So far, everyone really loved her work, which consisted of one abstract portrait of a naked woman, two landscape paintings with a great amount of detail and two experiment paintings that turned out really well. They were painted with spray paint and instead of a paintbrush to get the detail she wanted; she used newspaper, which gave it a blotchy effect. They actually turned out really well, and she was excited to make more pieces like that.

"And why did you choose black and blue for this one?" A man asked Jade as she explained her pieces to him.

"I'd actually like to get your take on it before I give you my answer," Jade mused. She'd picked up this trick long ago when talking to art snobs. They loved giving their own interpretation of art, and most of the time Jade let them be right. If they thought they were correct in their interpretations, it gave them the illusion that the piece was speaking to them in ways that it really wasn't, but that was the beauty of art. It could mean whatever a person wanted it to mean. If they believed they were right, they were more inclined to put in a bid for it.

The man smiled, causing his wrinkles to become more defined on his pale skin. "Well, my dear, I think the woman is in pain. The colors black and blue can mean anything when separate, but together they give a sad and eerie feel. If we want to be literal, black and blue can signify physical pain through bruising and whatnot. I see that there is also a hint of red near her eyes...as if she was crying or maybe it's blood."

It surprised jade that this man was actually dead on in his assessment. This piece had been the first one she painted just after christmas. It was simple, but to her it signified a lot and this man picked up on it. She smiled at him, "You are exactly right. Let's just say that this was a therapeutic piece for me to create."

The man smiled warmly at her and clasped one of her hands in both of his. "I would love to bypass the auction and buy this one from you personally, but only if you paint two more to go with it. I'll pay five thousand for the three. Up front and right now."

Jade's jaw dropped, and tears instantly flooded her eyes. She cleared her throat to get rid of the lump that was forming before saying, "Sir, thank you. Really, this means a lot. I took a hiatus from painting and to be welcomed back like this is a huge blessing."

The man waived her off, "You deserve it. Through the few pieces you have here tonight, I see so much potential. You have gained a loyal customer. Keep channelling those emotions of yours into you work. It's a beautiful thing."

Jade nodded her head and swiped away a tear, "Yes, sir. I will. I can have those other two paintings done for you in a couple of months."

"That's perfect. I will have my assistant write the check out for you and hand it in to the foundation so you can collect it at the end of the night along with your other earnings. I'll have her leave my contact information as well. I look forward to seeing you again, my dear."

With that, the old man was off and talking to the next artist. Jade couldn't believe that she had made a sale outside of the auction. That was rare at events like this, and she was beaming when she felt a hand slip around her waist. "Hey, baby."

Jade whirled around and jumped into Noah's arms. He'd been off checking out the other artists work through the exhibit. They'd come together along with Mia and Roman, who were off somewhere doing God knows what. Jade had also run into a few of her coworkers. They'd all gushed over her work, and a few even promised to bid for her pieces. She was over the moon with happiness and giddy at how well the night was going.

"Guess what?" Jade asked Noah.

"What?" He asked, noticing her smile.

"A man just bought this piece outright and wants me to paint three more to go with it! He gave me a lot of money for all three pieces," Jade practically sang the words out.

"That's what I'm talking about! That's my girl," Noah embraced her and then kissed her on the cheek. Sometimes, he would watch her paint and it amazed him at how talented she was. He would have gladly bought all of her artwork from her if he didn't think she would get offended. Noah knew that Jade was stubborn, and she wanted to do everything on her own, so if he purchased all of her work it would piss her off. In her eyes, she would probably think he was saying she wasn't good enough for anyone else to buy her art. That was something her husband would do, but not him. He wanted her to be as free as she wanted to be, and he knew that her work would sell. She was like a creative genius in his eyes.

Jade pulled away from him and smiled, "I'm just really excited to be back on my own two feet and doing what I love. I owe it all to you, you know?"

Noah shook his head, "I didn't do anything aside from help out here and there. This is all you, baby."

Jade opened her mouth to respond, but Mia appeared from out of nowhere with Roman beside her. Mia flashed a big ass cheesy grin towards Jade as she grabbed Roman's hand. Noah shook his head and smiled at them. "Where y'all been?"

"None of your damn business," Roman cheesed.

"Y'all are so nasty," Jade giggled.

Mia stuck her middle finger up at Jade and said, "We weren't doing nothing that you and Noah weren't doing the other day in his office."

Jade blushed profusely as Noah chuckled, "anyway, I think the silent auction is about to finish."

"How does that work, anyway?" Roman asked.

"Every exhibit does it differently, but for this one they numbered all the pieces are for sale," Jade explained as she pointed at the numbers that sat beside her own pieces. "Anyone that wants to take part in the auction writes down the corresponding numbers to the pieces they want to buy and when they are finished walking through the exhibit, they make their offer at the table over there." She pointed to where volunteers were now sorting the papers and tallying the ballads.

"Then how do you get paid?" Mia asked.

"Since it's silent, the volunteers send out text messages to the people that won and need to pay for their pieces. Anyone that took part is told to check their phones periodically. Artists check in at the desk once the event is over to collect their earnings. This one is pretty seamless, but I have been to a few exhibits that were a hot mess and the artists didn't get paid until days later."

"Oh, hell no," Mia smacked her teeth.

Jade giggled, "Right? Best believe I took my pieces home with me in those situations and didn't give them back until I got my money. The good thing is that they always paid out, eventually."

"That's good, at least," Roman chimed in.

"Looks like they're about to make an announcement," Noah nodded towards the stage.

A group was forming around the stage that was set up in a corner of the warehouse, so it wasn't in the art's way. The host of the event, Allen Arlington, stepped up to the microphone and gave everyone a smile. He was a handsome white man in his mid-forties with white blonde hair and a chiseled jaw. Jade had looked him up prior to the event, and through her research she found out he was born into a family of art critiques. Being a part of one of his exhibits was a true honor because his family's name carried a lot of weight in the art industry. Only the elite art snobs attended his events, and artists around the world wanted to partake in one of the family's events. Jade hadn't heard of the Arlington family until she submitted her pieces last month, but she knew of other families like them that dominated the art scene. It was always good to be associated with at least one of the families. She was truly honored.

"Good evening, everyone," Allen spoke into the microphone. "Thank you so much for attending tonight's show. Our volunteers are currently sorting out the auction, and they will notify anyone that took part in it within a few minutes. Until then, please have one last drink and make your final rounds before the event closes."

People clapped politely, and then everyone began dispersing. Jade turned to her friends and said, "You guys don't have to stay. I know everyone from work already left. Kenyon even found some girl to go home with."

Jade giggled, and Mia rolled her eyes while both Roman and Noah smirked.

"Girl, hush. We are going to stay until you're done," Mia said before turning to Noah. "Besides, we can take Jade home since I have to stop at the apartment to grab a couple of things before going over to Romans for the weekend."

Roman curled his arm around Mia's waist and kissed her cheek. Mia smiled and leaned back into him and Jade couldn't help but ask, "Are y'all together or what? Because you should be."

Mia rolled her eyes and said, "If you must know, we made it official the other day."

Jade's smile grew. "And you couldn't tell me?"

Mia shrugged, "I figured y'all already thought we were together, anyway."

Noah and Jade glanced at each other and then laughed before saying, "Yeah," in unison.

"I'm happy for y'all. Wait until I tell mom. She's going to want to meet you, Mia," Noah said as he clapped his brother on the back.

Mia smiled, "Fine. I'm great with parents."

"Darlene is really nice, Mia. You'll love her," Jade chimed it. "I'm happy for you two, but Roman you better not hurt her or you'll have to deal with me."

Roman smiled, showcasing his dimples, "I got you, Jade."

They laughed together before Noah turned to Jade and asked, "Are you sure you don't want to come over tonight? Or I can come to your place."

Jade wanted to end the night wrapped up in Noah's arms, but she hadn't been home as much as she should have been in preparation for the art show, and she felt like a night alone would be good for her. Her life had been a whirlwind for the past couple of months, and she had rarely had a moment alone. She smiled sweetly up at Noah and said, "How about you come over for dinner tomorrow? I'll cook and you can help me put together the new bed I'm going to buy."

Noah thought about it and said, "Only if we can test said bed out together."

Jade giggled as a blush spread across her cheeks. Mia sucked her teeth, and Roman shook his head with a smile. Jade opted not to answer him, but she did give him a wink when Roman and Mia weren't looking. He chuckled and grinned at her, hoping that the following night came quickly.

As the night came to a close, Jade collected her earnings. It surprised her to see that she had sold four out of her five pieces. The two spray painted ones sold for five hundred dollars each and one of her landscape paintings, which was the largest of them all, sold for twelve hundred dollars. She was so proud of herself and tonight gave her hope that she could make a decent living off her paintings. The options were endless as her brain whirred with ideas.

Roman had already brought her last painting that didn't sell out to his car. He and Mia were waiting for her while she finished up inside. Once she was finished talking to Allen Arlington, Noah appeared from out of nowhere and offered her his arm. "Are you ready to go?"

Jade giggled, "Yes, I am. Allen wants me to be a part of another exhibit in a few months. Can you believe it, Noah?"

They walked through the building and towards the exit, neither of them realizing they were being followed. Noah grinned down at her. "Yes, Jade. I can believe it. I am so proud of you, baby."

She blushed. "Thank you for coming tonight and for supporting me. You really are amazing."

She rested her head on Noah's arm as they walked. Before they walked out of the doors, Noah wrapped her up in his arms and kissed her deeply. Jade's knees became weak, and she was ready to forget about her night alone and hop into Noah's car so he could take care of the craving that was developing between her legs. Noah finally pulled back and moved Jade's long silky hair out of her face. "Are you sure you don't want to come home with me?"

Jade sighed and then looked up at him through her full lashes with a smile. "Noah Bennett, you know exactly what you're doing."

He chuckled, "I might have hoped that a kiss would change your mind."

"You almost got me, but I'm sure. I want a night alone to just unwind and process the last few months of my life. I promise that tomorrow I'll be all yours."

Noah pressed his head against hers and sighed. "Fine, but I want you to be naked when you answer the door tomorrow."

Jade giggled, "I'm not going to—"

Noah pulled back with a smile. "Either you answer the door naked or I'll take your clothes off for you. Either way, you will be naked and I plan to do very naughty things to you."

Jade's cheeks flushed as her breaths came out in quick spurts. "O —okay."

"Good girl," Noah grinned. "Make sure you call me when you get home. Don't forget, okay? Or I'll come over to make sure you're alright."

Jade nodded and swallowed as she tried her best to get her breathing under control. "Okay, Noah."

He kissed her on the forehead and then wrapped his arm around her shoulders as he led her out to the waiting car. As they kissed one last time, Yolanda, who was watching from the shadows, typed out a quick text. She dropped her phone back into her purse and smiled. Come Monday, Noah would be all hers again and she couldn't wait.

CHAPTER 19

"ARE YOU SURE YOU HAVE EVERYTHING?" JADE ASKED AS MIA pulled her backpack over her shoulder. "You know you always forget—"

"Yes, mom. I have everything." Mia rolled her eyes.

Jade laughed, "I was just making sure, Mimi."

Mia smiled at her, "I know. I love you, girl. Have a good weekend and I'll see you Monday after work."

"I love you too, Mia," Jade said. "Oh, and I'm sending you some money."

Mia waived her off, "I'm cool. You know Ro's got me."

"I know, Mia, but it's always a good idea to have your own just in case."

"Fine, if it will make you feel better," Mia smiled.

"It would. I know you don't get paid until Friday. I got you, babe," Jade smiled.

"That's why you're my best friend," Mia chirped before kissing Jade on the cheek and walking out of the room. Jade followed behind her and waved goodbye to her friend as she closed and locked the door behind her.

Jade smiled because she finally had the apartment to herself. She loved rooming with Mia and she had to admit that it would be weird as hell to have the bed to herself for the night, but she was excited to play some R&B and take a bubble bath with a cold glass of sweet wine. She absent-mindedly went to her room, tapping on her phone so she could cashapp Mia two hundred dollars. She deposited her check from the art show through the mobile app, and they had already made two-hundred of it available. She had everything she needed at home, so she had no problem sending everything in her account to her best friend. She hit send and then opened her texts so she could let Noah know that she was home safe. She opened her bedroom door and flipped on the light.

When she looked up, she let out a high pitched screamed as she dropped her phone on the floor. It skidded across the carpet and landed at the feet of the one person who instilled fear into Jade's heart. Her eyes traveled up his long legs and chiseled torso until they rested on the handsome face of her husband.

"Elijah," Jade breathed out in fear.

"In the flesh, Doll Baby," Elijah smiled sinisterly at her.

Jade's skin crawled at the nickname. He had given it to her after they got married, stating that she was his doll to do whatever he pleased with. Tears formed in her eyes as she took Elijah in. He looked the same with his dark skin and eyes so dark that they looked black. The features in his face were sharp and angular, making him look like he was carved from stone. His muscles bulged and flexed as he open and closed his hands. Jade stared at him in fear, stuck in place as she wondered if this was how she would die.

Her mind flashed to Noah and Mia, and even to Kenyon, Roman and Darlene. Tears spilled out of her eyes and down her cheeks as she realized that her best friend would be the one to find her body. She shuddered at the thought, and suddenly, her phone rang, startling her. Her eyes flitted down to her vibrating phone and then back up to Elijah, whose sinister smile grew. He bent down and picked the phone up. In one swift motion he threw it at the wall and it shattered into a thousand pieces as Jade shrieked, surprised at his sudden aggression.

"What's the matter, Doll Baby? Aren't you happy to see me?" Elijah asked as he advanced on Jade. She backed away as he continued to talk. "Imagine my surprise when my wife disappears from the hospital and then off the face of the god-damned earth. I looked for you. Every fucking day, and I wasn't going to stop until I found you."

"H—how, did you find me?" Jade asked. She was still slowly backing out of the room and down the hall, visibly shaking in fear and wondering if she could be fast enough to get out the front door.

"Divine intervention," he said as he took a big step forward. Jade stumbled backwards but caught herself just as they made it into the living room. "I got a call from a woman that worked with you. Does Yolanda Jenkins ring a bell?"

Jade's eyes widened in shock. She knew that Yolanda hated her, but she never knew it ran this deep. "Elijah, Please—"

He waived Jade off, "I think we've done enough talking."

In one swift motion, he yanked Jade up by the neck. She struggled to breathe as he pulled her off her feet so she was eye level with him. Jade scratched at his hands as he spoke, "Bitch, I own you. If you think you can divorce me and live your life, you have another thing coming. I will kill you and that nigga you been fuckin. You didn't think I knew about him, did you?"

Elijah spit in Jade's face before releasing her. She twisted her ankle as she collapsed to the floor, gasping for air. No matter how deep she breathed, there just wasn't enough air in her apartment to take in. Elijah didn't give her time to recover. He bent over and punched her in the face, busting her nose wide open and simultaneously swelling her right eye. Jade saw stars as Elijah climbed on top of her. He punched her again, this time in the chest, and she heard a rib crack. Jade yelped in pain and tried to turn to her side so she could curl into a ball, but Elijah held her on her back. He grabbed her neck and slammed her head into the floor repeatedly until Jade stopped fighting. She was still conscious, but her arms and legs felt numb. She couldn't move as her focus shifted in and out.

The next thing she knew, her pants were being yanked down and Elijah pulled a gun out of his jacket pocket. Jade's good eye widened in fear as he roughly spread her legs apart and inserted the gun inside of her. A strangled scream tore from her sore throat as he shoved the whole thing inside of her repeatedly.

"Bitch, shut your ass up before someone comes up in here," Elijah punched her in the mouth and her lips instantly split open. Blood seeped into her mouth and she tried to spit it out, but Elijah began choking her again with one hand while his other hand worked the gun in and out of her roughly.

"Don't worry, Doll Baby. It'll be over soon and then you'll be reunited with your parents," Elijah spoke through gritted teeth.

He was working up a sweat as he continued to rape and beat her. He switched off between putting the gun inside of her and penetrating her with his hard dick. What felt like five hours had really only been about fifteen minutes. Jade's whole body felt broken as she fought to stay conscious. Elijah finally stopped his assault, and he stood up to admire Jade's battered body. He was breathing heavily as sweat dripped down his face.

"I have to admit, Doll Baby, that I'm upset that this is the last time we get to do this." Elijah snapped his fingers together as a thought hit him. "I'll take a picture. That way, I have something to remember you by."

Jade's eyes fluttered closed as Elijah pulled his phone out of his pocket. She knew that this would be her final moments on Earth, and she didn't want to waste them looking at Elijah. Instead, she thought about Noah and the love she had for him. Tears spilled out her swollen eyes as the salty tears stung the cuts all over her face. She silently chastised herself for not telling Noah how she really felt about him. She allowed Elijah to hinder her happiness until the very end, and she hated herself for it.

Jade's eyes popped open when she heard a key in the front door.

She couldn't see much because her eyes were almost swollen completely shut, but she saw Elijah freeze as he looked at the door, panic on his face. Panic set in for Jade, too. She swiveled her head around, searching for the gun. It was sitting on the floor a couple feet away from her and she tried to reach out for it, but she couldn't move. She knew she had some broken bones, and she cried harder as she willed her hands to move.

Mia opened the door and said, "Okay, you were right. I forgot my—"

Mia gasped as she took in the scene before her. She took a couple of steps back when she saw Elijah, but Jade's still body lying on the floor caused her to drop to her knees.

"Babe, what are you doing? Move out of the way so I can use the bath—" Roman stopped dead in his tracks when he saw Elijah standing in his girls living room. His eyes moved over to Jade and he became enraged. "You bitch ass nigga."

Elijah looked around for the gun. He wasn't there for anyone except for Jade, so he didn't have time to deal with this nigga and his bitch. He already planned on committing one murder tonight and he didn't mind committing two more as long as he could get rid of any evidence that he was ever there. He worked enough cases in court to know exactly how to get away with murder. He would make it look like a home invasion and be on his way. Jade drove him to the point of no return, and in Elijah's mind, her death was her own fault.

When she left, he went crazy looking for her. He became enraged that she would even be bold enough to leave him and everything he provided for her. Sure, he hit on her from time to time, but any woman would be happy to be in her position and he intended on reminding her of that tonight. Now, he was even more pissed that he was interrupted. He originally had a night full of torture prepared for Jade, but now he realized that he needed to get out sooner rather than later.

Elijah spotted the gun next to Jade and just as he was about to dive for it, Roman punched him in his head. Dazed, Elijah staggered back and tried to block Roman's next blow, but he was too slow. Elijah fell to the ground next to Jade as Roman began kicking him and beating him, just as he had done to Jade only a few minutes ago.

While Roman was trying to beat Elijah's face in, Mia crawled over to her friend, "Jade, wake up. Jade!"

Mia sobbed as she gingerly pulled her best friend away from the fighting men, fearing that they would roll over her and hurt her even more. Jade cried out in pain and Mia smiled through her tears. "You're alive."

Jade did her best to nod her head up and down. She kept her eyes closed, because it hurt too much to open them, as Mia dragged her over to the corner of the living room, away from the chaos. Mia put Jade's head in her lap and rocked her back and forth as she whispered that it would be okay repeatedly as she kept an eye on Roman. Elijah managed to get a punch or two in and Mia noticed that Roman's nose was bleeding. Both men were now standing and throwing wild punches. There was blood everywhere, and the living room was completely trashed. Fresh tears pooled in Mia's eyes as she helplessly looked around for something to help her man.

Jade made a gurgling noise and Mia looked down at her, trying to figure out what she was saying. Mia watched as Jade lifted a bloody finger and pointed towards an object on the floor. Mia's eyes widened in surprise when she realized it was a gun. She quickly, but gently, laid Jade's head on the floor and was about to dive for the gun when her phone rang, startling her. She quickly pulled her phone out of her pocket and answered as she moved towards the gun.

"Hello?"

"Mia? Did you drop Jade off already? Her phone keeps going to voicemail and—" Noah was cut off by a scream on the other end of the phone and a loud *BANG!* His car swerved into the next lane, and he fought to regain control.

He'd already been on his way to Jade's house after making it home and not being able to get ahold of her. He was going to play-fully remind her that her safety was everything to him, and he meant it when he asked her to check in with him. After not being able to get ahold of his brother, he got a little worried and called Mia. Now, in a full on panic, he screamed into the phone, "Mia? Hello! What the hell is going on?"

Noah strained to hear what was happening on the other end of the phone as he pressed on the gas. He was still about fifteen minutes from their apartment, and he was ready to cut that down to five. He noted that there wasn't anymore screaming, only soft crying. The line suddenly went dead, and Noah cursed loudly as he punched the steering wheel. He quickly called 911 and gave them Jade's address as he sped down the highway, silently thanking God that the traffic was light.

He made it to the apartment in record time, not caring that he'd broken several laws to make it there. Not wanting to wait for the elevator, Noah took the stairs two at a time and pushed open the door to the apartment. He zeroed in on the man that was ripping the clothes off a bloodied body that lay on the floor. His heart dropped when he realized that it was Jade. Anger consumed him as he charged at the man, knocking him off balance. He fell to the floor, and Noah didn't give him the chance to defend himself. He hammered his fists into the man relentlessly.

"Fight back, bitch!" Noah shouted. "You can beat on my woman, but you can't fight me?"

He had never been more livid in his life. He wasn't sure how long he'd been beating him, but when his mind snapped back to reality, the man was no longer moving.

Noah stumbled off of him and made a beeline towards Jade. His heart hammered in his chest as he examined her still body. Tears filled his eyes as he spoke, "Baby...no, no...please be alive."

Noah took her bloody hand in his own and put his ear gently to her bruised chest. He let out a sob when he heard her take in a soft breath. She was barely breathing, but she was alive.

"Where the fuck are the police?" He shouted. He jumped when he heard a movement behind him. He whirled around and noticed that Mia was lying on the ground with blood running down her head. "Mia! Are you okay?"

Her eyes popped open when she heard Noah's voice and she sobbed as she rolled over and got to her knees, holding her head in her hands.

"Ro-Roman!" she cried as she crawled over to yet another body that was lying on the floor.

Noah's eyes grew big as he took in the site of his brother. He'd completely missed him when he walked in, and now, he wanted nothing more than to be by his side. Noah's heart broke at the sight of his brother laying in a pool of blood.

"Roman! Yo, man, wake up, bro!" Noah shouted. He was torn. He didn't want to leave Jade's side, but his brother needed him, too. Luckily, he didn't have to decide because two police officers came rushing into the room.

One was a short black woman with short hair and the other was a short latino man with a buzz cut. One glance was all they needed before they spoke into their radios that rested on their uniforms. "We need backup, now! Multiple people down!"

"Help them! They need help!" Mia screamed as she frantically tried scooping Roman's blood back into his body.

The male officer pulled his gun out of the holster and aimed it out and down towards the ground as the female officer did the same. "Everyone put your hands up where I can see them!"

"Are you fucking kidding me?" Noah roared.

"Sir, please. We need to make sure you all don't have weapons on you." The lady cop said patiently.

Mia put her hands up as she cried over Roman's body while Noah took his time putting his hands up. He didn't want to let go of Jade's hand, but he knew he wouldn't be any help to her if he was dead.

"Keep your hands up while we search the room," the male officer said.

Mia kept her hands raised but pointed one finger at Elijah, "The only weapon in here is over by that man. He's the one that did this to us."

Quickly, the female officer went over to Elijah and kicked the gun further into the corner. She knelt down next to him and checked for a pulse. Growing agitated, Noah said, "Fuck him! He did this shit to them! Did you not hear her? Help my brother and my girl, please!"

"Sir, what is your name?" The lady officer asked as she pulled her handcuffs out of their holster.

Noah bit the side of his cheek to keep from lashing out. He hung his head with his hands still up and said, "Noah Bennett."

She quickly snapped the handcuffs around Elijah's wrists before moving over to Jade. She looked at Noah and said, "I'm officer Gabby. Is it okay if I call you Noah?"

"Yeah," Noah's voice cracked as he watched her gently check Jade's pulse.

"Good, Noah. I know you've been through a lot tonight but we are here to help. What is her name?"

"Jade," He murmured.

"Jade is still alive, Noah, but barely. I called in the medics and they will be here very soon."

Noah only half listened to officer Gabby as he looked behind him to check on his brother. Mia was covered in blood. She sat with her knees up to her chest as she rocked back and forth. Noah watched as the officer performed CPR on his brother. Tears fell from Noah's eyes as he watched helplessly. His heart constricted, and he felt like the walls were closing in on him as he watched two of the most important people in his life fight for their own lives.

Just when Noah was sure that he couldn't take any more of the madness that was going on around him, a group of medics burst through the doorway and the two officers began barking stats to the team.

"These two are alive but unresponsive and that man is unresponsive with no pulse."

They pushed Noah out of the way as they began working on

Jade, Roman and Elijah. Within minutes, they hauled all three of them onto stretchers and carried out of the apartment. Officer Gabby kneeled down, so she was eye-level with Noah. "Have you been hurt, Noah?"

Noah shook his head and stood up suddenly, "I have to get to the hospital."

Mia appeared at his side, "I'm coming with you."

"No, miss. You have to get checked out by the paramedics. Your head—"

"I'm fine! I need to see about my boyfriend and my best friend!" she screeched, cutting the officer off.

Noah threw an arm around her shoulders and pulled her close. Mia collapsed against him and began sobbing again while officer Gabby said, "It's okay, Luis. Let them go. We'll make sure she gets checked out once we're there."

Officer Luis eyed Noah and Mia and said, "You two go ahead to the hospital. We need to stay here and wait for the rest of the team to get here, but we will be at the hospital later to get a statement from both of you. Understand?"

Noah didn't even bother to respond as he pulled Mia out of the room and down the stairs. He tucked her in the passenger seat of the car and then took off towards the hospital, praying that Roman and Jade would be alive when they got there.

CHAPTER 20

NOAH KNEW IT WAS TIME TO CALL HIS MOM. HE'D HELD OFF for as long as he could, but he knew that if he waited any longer, she would kick his ass. This wasn't something that he wanted to burden his mother with. She had already lost so much, but she deserved to know what was going on with her son. He glanced over at Mia whose eyes were puffy and red and asked, "Have you talked to Kenyon?"

Mia shook her head and her eyes grew wide, "I didn't even think —I...I don't—"

Noah nodded and then put his hand on top of hers. They had been sitting in the waiting room at a small ass uncomfortable table for two hours while Jade and Roman underwent surgery. Jade had internal bleeding, and the bullet that Roman took was extremely close to his heart. They were able to revive him on the way to the hospital, but they were worried about his brain function after literally being dead for over twenty minutes. That was all Noah and Mia knew, and it had them on pins and needles.

Mia felt as though she were falling apart. She hadn't known Roman or Jade very long, but they had become her family when her own family disowned her. She'd tried contacting her parents a couple of times since she'd been back on her feet to let them know that she was no longer with her ex, but they'd blocked her. It hurt her more than she let on that her family wanted nothing to do with her, but it comforted her that she had formed a new family so quickly. It didn't take away from the fact that her parents hated her, but it helped. Now, her boyfriend and her best friend were fighting for their lives and she didn't know how she could move on in life if they died.

"It's okay. I'll call him," Noah finally said, jerking Mia from her grim thoughts.

"Yes, please. Call him," Mia said as she stared at the wall in a daze.

Noah pulled out his cellphone and pinched the bridge of his nose before dialing Kenyon first. He hadn't even paid attention to the time and when Kenyon answered in a deep sleepy voice; he realized that it had to be well after midnight. "Noah, man. Someone better be dying."

Fresh tears escaped Noah's eyes and after a moment in a cracked voice he whispered, "Kenyon."

Now fully awake, Kenyon jolted out of bed and asked, "What's wrong, bro? What is it?"

Noah broke down, and panic set in for Kenyon. Mia watched the whole thing unfold, and she knew she needed to be strong for them. She pulled the phone out of Noah's hands and patted him on the back as he cried. She knew that this would be a rough few days for all of them, especially Kenyon and Noah, who had known Roman the longest. She tried her best to clear the lump out of her throat before she put the phone up to her ear and said, "Kenyon, it's Mia."

Kenyon could hear Mia sniffling on the other end, and his heart ached. "Mia, what the fuck is going on? Where are you?"

"We're at Lenox Hill Hospital. It's Roman and Jade," Mia sniffled as she fought back tears.

Kenyon was already halfway dressed, "I'm on my way. What floor are you on?"

"Third," Mia choked out.

"I'll be there soon, Mia. I'm on my way."

The line went dead and Mia slid the phone back over to Noah, who was trying to collect himself. He grabbed his phone and said, "I have to call my mom."

Mia instantly stood up, not having the heart to witness that conversation. "I'll give you some privacy. Kenyon is on his way."

Noah nodded once and dialed his mom's number as Mia left the room.

KENYON LOOKED AT MIA IN HORROR AS HE TOOK IN HER BLOOD-stained clothes. She was standing by the vending machines getting some water bottles for her and Noah when Kenyon came flying down the hall. "Yo, what the fuck, Mia! Are you hurt?"

He ran to her and wrapped her small frame up in his arms. Mia collapsed against him and let out a cry that caused more panic to set into his heart. He pulled back and grabbed Mia by the shoulders. He took inventory of her body and although she was covered in blood; she didn't seem hurt aside from the bruise on her forehead. Kenyon looked into her bloodshot eyes and asked, "What happened?"

A sob tore through Mia's throat, but she pushed through it so she could fill Kenyon in. "Jade's husband...he—"

"Wait...her husband? Jade is married?" Kenyon asked, perplexed.

Mia nodded, realizing that he had never been told that bit of information. "He used to beat her so she left. It was why she was on the streets in the first place. She was trying to run away from him."

Kenyon nodded and then ran his hand down his face in anger. Not at Jade, but the son of a bitch that would put his hands on a woman. Mia had never seen Kenyon so serious or angry before. This was a whole new side of him, and it put her on edge a little. She eyed him wryly as she continued, "He showed up to our apartment. I left Jade there...I left her there, and he got in somehow and attacked her. I —I forgot my phone charger and Roman...he had to use the bathroom so we doubled back and we found Elijah—"

"Elijah is her husband?" Kenyon asked, trying to keep the story straight.

Mia nodded and continued. "Elijah was standing over her...I thought she was dead, Kenyon. Roman and Elijah started fighting and everything happened so fast...One minute I was on the phone with Noah and then next minute Elijah shot Roman and then knocked me unconscious. They're both in surgery now, but it doesn't look good."

Kenyon's jaw ticked as he listened to Mia talk. Tears spilled out of her eyes at a rapid pace, and he knew that she was just barely keeping it together. He needed to be strong for both her and Noah, even though his own heart was breaking. Jade was a good friend, and he hated that this happened to her, and then there was Roman who was like a little brother to him. They'd grown up together and even though Noah was his best friend, they were all family and this shit would not be easy for him at all. He took a deep breath and asked, "Where is Noah?"

"Just around the corner in the waiting room. He's waiting for you and his mom. Go ahead in. I'm just going to grab a couple more bottles of water," Mia sniffled and then turned back to the vending machine.

Kenyon gently turned her around and said, "As soon as we get an update on those two, you need to get your head checked out. You might have a concussion. Then, we need to get you some fresh clothes."

Mia nodded numbly, "Sure."

Kenyon reached over and gave her shoulder a squeeze before turning on his heels in search of Noah. He rounded the corner and went into the only room that was in the hallway. The room was small, with a TV hanging from the wall and a couch sitting up against the wall. Noah was sitting at the table in the middle of the room with his head in his hands. Kenyon cleared his throat and said, "Hey, man."

Noah looked up and then stood. The two men embraced and

patted each other on the back before sitting down at the table across from each other. "Everything is all fucked up, Kenyon."

"I saw Mia in the hallway and she filled me in. Bro, why didn't you tell me that Jade was married to a psychopath? I could have helped you keep an eye on her or—"

Noah shook his head. "It wasn't my place to tell. She had a hard enough time telling me, and I couldn't betray her trust by telling others. Besides, we didn't think he would find her. When we filed her divorce papers, the lawyer kept her address private. We even filed a restraining order on the bastard."

Kenyon shook his head, but stayed silent. A moment later, Mia entered the room and sat four water bottles on the table and then sat down next to Kenyon, who reached up and touched the spot on her head where the angry red and blue bruise was.

"Ouch!" Mia winced when his fingers made contact.

Kenyon's jaw ticked as he turned to look at Noah, "Did you get hurt, bro?"

"Nah," Noah said.

"Liar. Your knuckles are split wide the fuck open," Mia grumbled as she crossed her hands over her chest.

Noah looked down, and his eyes widened in surprise. He hadn't noticed that his knuckles were raw and bleeding, but before his jumbled mind could react to it, his mother entered the room. She took in the blood covering Mia and Noah and let out a scream. Noah was up and at her side within seconds. "Mama, it's okay. It's going to be okay."

"My baby...my poor baby," Darlene wept as Noah guided her over to the small couch, trying to keep his own tears at bay. Noah had filled his mom in on the phone while she was getting dressed. He sent Tommy over to pick her up, because he didn't want his mother driving while she was panicking.

While Noah was consoling his mother, a doctor walked in looking tired. Mia shot up from her seat at the table and was standing right in front of the doctor within seconds. He was old with grey hair and sad eyes. Noah's heart dropped as Mia asked, "How are they?"

The doctor eyed Mia and then glanced up at everyone else. "Are you all the family of Jade Willis?"

Noah cringed at the use of Jade's married name as he stood up and walked over to stand next to Mia. He looked the doctor in the eye and said, "I'm her...boyfriend, and this is her best friend. We're the only family she has."

The doctor nodded. "I'm Dr. Landry. Jade had extensive internal bleeding along with a few broken bones. She has three broken ribs, a few broken fingers, and a sprained ankle. Luckily, we were able to repair everything. Her broken bones are set and in casts and we were able to stop the internal bleeding. She isn't out of the woods yet, I'm afraid. During surgery she was touch and go. She's lost a lot of blood and we will be monitoring her for the next few days."

"Is she awake? Can I see her?" Noah asked. It relieved him that Jade was alive, and he needed to see her. He needed to be by her side. The guilt he'd been trying to fend off crept in, and he desperately tried to push it away. He promised Jade that he would always protect her and that nobody, especially Elijah, would ever hurt her again. He'd failed her, and he prayed that she didn't hate him because of it.

"She's asleep. We can only let one person in at a time for now. We don't want to overwhelm her room with too many people. She has to rest as much as possible right now. She's in room 308," Dr. Landry said before turning to leave.

"Wait! Doctor?" Darlene said loudly just as he was about to leave. "Please...do you know anything about my son? Roman Bennett? He was brought in with Jade."

Dr. Landry looked down at the iPad that was clutched in his hands and tapped on the screen. A moment later he said, "I see that there were two men brought in with Jade...ah, yes. Roman Bennett. It looks like he is still in surgery. I'll have one of his doctors come out and update you all."

"Thank you," Darlene whispered with tears in her eyes.

Dr. Landry nodded and exited the room. Mia looked over at Noah and said, "Go ahead and go see Jade. I'll go in after you."

Noah was grateful that Mia was letting him go first. He felt as though his heart would break in two if he waited any longer to see her. He knew that she needed his comfort right now, but he also needed hers. He exited the waiting room and glanced around the halls. He turned to the right and walked a short distance to room 308. A nurse opened the door and came out of the room just as he grabbed the door handle to push inside.

"Oh! Sorry, I didn't mean to bump into you," she said apologetically.

"It's okay," Noah murmured as he tried looking past the short woman. Her silky blonde hair was piled up at the top of her head and her big blue eyes stared up at him thoughtfully.

"Are you Jade's husband?" she asked in a cheerful voice.

Noah hesitated before answering. The truth was, after this incident he wanted nothing more than to be Jade's husband, but he wasn't. Elijah was, and that thought made his blood boil in anger. He clenched his aching fists together and said, "No. I'm her...I'm her boyfriend. The man who did this to her is her husband."

The nurse looked perplexed at his statement, but Noah didn't care. Their situation wasn't for anyone else to understand. He was more focused on the fact that he had called himself Jade's boyfriend twice in the last five minutes. He knew that once Jade was better, they would have to have a conversation about their relationship because there was no way that he could continue on being nothing less than her man. Not after almost losing her.

"Oh...right...okay," the nurse stammered before clearing her throat. "She's pretty banged up. I just wanted to warn you. She should heal completely, but it'll take quite some time. We have her on a sedative so she's sleeping now and will be in and out of sleep for the next twenty-four hours while she's in the ICU. As long as she does well, we will move her in a day or so to a normal room. My name is

Nancy and I'll be right over there at the nurse's station if you need me."

She pointed to a desk that was down the hall, and Noah nodded before turning and bracing himself as he walked in the room. He had already seen Jade back at her apartment, but that didn't make entering her hospital room any easier. His breath caught when he saw her laying in the hospital bed. There was an IV running through her arm and a handful of different medicines were connected to it, slowly making their way through her veins. Noah inched closer to her, taking in her appearance. They'd cleaned all the blood off her, but somehow she looked worse than when they were at the apartment.

Angry bruises varying in colors covered every inch of her body. Her face was swollen to the point that Noah wouldn't have recognized her if the nurse hadn't used her name when he was coming in. They wrapped her head in white material, and there were several bandages covering her face and collarbone. Her ankle and both of hands had fingers wrapped in casts, and the rest of her body was covered with a thin blanket.

Noah gingerly sat down in the chair next to Jade's bed and gently took her small hand in his own. He couldn't make much skin contact because three of her fingers were set in casts, but he managed to gently rub her ring finger as he stared at her. She was always someone that he treated delicately because of her past and the fact that she was such a small woman, but in this moment she was downright fragile. Noah felt as though she would break if he breathed on her too hard and he fought back tears as he looked at his baby laying up in that hospital bed.

"I'm so sorry, baby. I wasn't there to protect you," Noah said as the tears he'd been holding back sprang out of his eyes.

He bent his head and let the tears fall as he thought about what Jade had gone through in that apartment. Rage began boiling within him as he allowed Elijah to enter his thoughts. Noah typically wasn't a violent man. He left that trait to Roman, who hung out with thugs and criminals. That shit was in his brother's blood. Since they were young, Roman was always getting into trouble and dragging Kenyon and Noah into it with him. Roman loved fighting, and he loved partaking in illegal activities. As Roman got older, Noah stopped trying to set his brother on the right side of the law and simply started urging his brother to be safe. Noah never questioned Roman on how he could afford the multiple cars or the mini mansion. All Noah card about was the safety of his brother.

His heart twisted at the thought of his brother laying on some sterile table somewhere in this hospital, but before he could ride the new wave of emotion that was wrestling to overtake him, he felt Jade's fingers move slightly. Noah's head shot up and he saw Jade's swollen eyes barely open and looking into his. Tears started gushing out of her eyes, and Noah gently rubbed her hand. "Shh, baby. It's okay. I'm here."

"What happened?" Jade squeaked.

Noah shook his head and responded, "Don't talk, baby. Just rest. You're okay. I promise I'll explain everything later."

Jade looked like she wanted to protest, but her eyes fluttered shut and she drifted back to sleep. Noah bent down and kissed her on the hand and then again on her arm. Just as he lifted his head up, he saw Kenyon standing in the doorway with tears running down his face. Noah's heart dropped and sped up all at once as he waited for Kenyon to speak. When he did, his voice cracked and so did Noah's heart.

"Bro, it's Roman."

CHAPTER 21

It was an unusually warm day for early February. The sun was shining brightly, and there wasn't a cloud in sight. Church bells were ringing as a sleek black limo pulled up to Grace Baptist Church and parked in front of the entrance where people dressed in black were walking in.

Jade winced as she reached over and took Noah's hand. He helped her out of the limo and she leaned on him as she limped towards the entrance of the church while noticing how good her man looked. Noah was wearing his signature sunglasses and suit combo, today in all black. Jade opted to wear a pair of oversized shades as well hoping they would hide most of her bruising.

It had been two weeks since the incident and a week since they had released her from the hospital. Her bones still ached and her bruises had turned to an ugly blueish green color. Since she'd been released from the hospital, she'd been staying with Noah. In fact, Mia had been staying there as well, and it appeared both Noah and Mia had busied themselves with taking care of Jade so they wouldn't have to think about the fact that Roman was dead.

Tears burned at Jade's eyes as guilt weighed on her shoulders. Roman was dead because of her. It was something her and Noah had yet to talk about. Shit, she and Mia hadn't even talked about it, and it was driving Jade crazy. Both of them tiptoed around her like she was made of glass, barely raising their voices above a whisper around her. Meanwhile, Jade was grieving over Roman, a man she had barely known, and yet, she was responsible for his death.

Noah gingerly helped Jade sit in the front pew before sitting down next to her. "Are you okay? Do you want me to find a pillow for you to sit on? These pews are so hard and—"

Jade held her hand up and said, "Noah, please stop it. Today is about Roman and better yet, it's about your mom, you, Mia and Kenyon. I am the absolute last person you need to be worried about... especially today."

Noah looked at her in concern. "It's the first time you've been out since—"

"Hey," Jade said, cutting him off again and reaching up to caress his face, "I'm okay. I promise. I should be the one asking you if you're okay?"

She said the last part as more of a question. Noah inhaled deeply and cleared his throat before responding. "This shit ain't right. My baby brother is laid up in that room," he pointed towards a small room off the side of the church where Roman's casket was, "because I wasn't there to protect him. Or you."

Jade swallowed the lump in her throat and said, "Noah, none of what happened that night was your fault, okay?"

Noah cleared his throat again and shifted in his seat so he was looking straight ahead at the large photo of his brother that was surrounded by flowers. He opted not to respond to Jade. At least, not in that moment, because he knew her. He knew that she was carrying the guilt of Roman's death and he made a mental note to have that conversation later, when they were home and in private.

Unable to look at Roman's smiling face on the oversized photo, Jade turned slightly, grimacing when she bumped her broken pinky finger on the back of the pew. She saw Mia and Kenyon were walking down the aisle, Kenyon's arm thrown around Mia's shoulder. They were supposed to ride in the limo with Noah and Jade, but Mia had an emotional breakdown just as they were about to leave. Kenyon offered to stay behind with her, leaving Noah and Jade the big ass limo to themselves since Darlene opted to ride separately.

Mia's hair was pulled back into a curly ponytail and her beautiful face was void of makeup. Her eyes were puffy and her nose was red from blowing it so much. Kenyon was sporting some shades as well, along with a black suit. He guided Mia into the pew next to Jade and then took a seat next to her, leaving the spot next to Noah open for Darlene.

Mia sniffled and then leaned over and asked, "How are you feeling?"

Jade rolled her eyes and said, "I'm going to tell you like I told Noah, don't ask me that today. I'm good and I'll be good all day long. Let me worry about y'all today."

Mia rolled her eyes, "Fine. It just that it's the first time you've—"

Jade held her hand up, "Doesn't matter."

Mia gave Jade a weak smile, "I love you."

Jade's heart twisted at the sadness in her friend's voice and said, "I love you too, Mimi. Are you okay?"

Mia nodded her head once and said, "I'm just ready for this to be over with so I can go home and curl up in bed."

Jade nodded and placed her bandaged hand on top of her friends. "Whatever you need today, I'm here, okay?"

"Okay," Mia said.

Jade felt Noah get up from beside her, and she turned to see Darlene walking into the church. Noah rushed up the aisle and hugged his mother before ushering her to the pew. Darlene had tears streaming down her face and her knees buckled when she saw the photo of her son at the front of the church. Noah held her tightly and guided her into the pew before taking his seat in between her and Jade.

Jade felt her own tears splash down her cheeks as she watched Noah comfort his mother. Flashbacks of her parent's funeral flitted through her mind, and she forced them away with a quickness. Today wasn't the day to reminisce about her dead parents. She needed to remain strong for everyone else. She pushed the unwanted thoughts away and focused on Darlene and Noah.

Darlene collected herself and looked passed Noah to Jade. She smiled weakly at her and asked, "How are you, baby? Are you feeling okay?"

Jade clenched her mouth shut and smiled at the woman, not wanting to disrespect her. Truthfully, she was sick of everyone fussing over her, or rather, she wasn't used to people fussing over her. When Elijah used to beat her, she had nobody to turn to for help, so everyone checking in on her was a lot to adjust to. It wasn't that she disliked it, but it was embarrassing for her. She'd been raped and beaten in front of her friends, and it was awkward as hell for her.

Even Darlene had been fussing over her, coming over in the evenings with home-made meals and home remedies to ease the pain in Jade's aching bones. It surprised Jade because she was certain that the woman would blame her for the death of her son, but she hadn't. In fact, she acted as though she were happy that Jade was there for Noah during this time. Jade was extremely thankful for Darlene because the home-cooked meals and the Epsom salt and oatmeal baths had become the highlight of her day. Still, it troubled Jade that she seemed to be the only one blaming herself for the events that had occurred that night. She couldn't understand how they weren't blaming her.

Pushing the war going on within herself aside, Jade smiled at Darlene and said, "I'm fine. Are you okay? Do you need me to get you anything?"

Darlene blew her nose and then dabbed at her eyes before responding, "No, baby. You rest. I'll be fine."

Jade was about to insist on getting her a glass of water from the entryway where she had seen refreshments set up when the pastor took the podium and spoke into the microphone. "Thank you all for being here today. Service is about to begin, but we wanted to give the family a moment alone in the viewing room before we get started."

Darlene let out a little cry, and Noah rubbed her back. He stood and held his arm out for his mother. When she was securely in his arms, he turned to Jade and offered her his arm. Jade shook her head and said, "Go ahead, baby. I'll be here when you get back."

"Are you sure?" He asked.

"Positive," Jade smiled up at him. Truthfully, she didn't do well with viewing dead bodies. It brought back horrible memories from her parent's funeral, and she opted to remember people as they were when they were living. Noah reached out and caressed her face before leading his mom back up the aisle.

Mia patted Jade on the thigh and said, "We'll be back," before taking Kenyon's hand and trailing behind Noah and Darlene.

Jade turned and watched them enter the room with a heaviness weighing on her heart. She took a deep breath and prepared herself to be strong for the people she loved for the rest of the day. Her own emotions could wait until she was in bed later that night.

Darlene slowed a little when she got to the room where her youngest son was. Noah looked down at his mother with pain in his eyes. He cleared his throat and gestured for Kenyon and Mia to go ahead to them. "Y'all go ahead. We need a minute."

Mia nodded absent mindedly, but stayed right where she was. It felt as though her legs were frozen in place. Kenyon gently coaxed her forward before Darlene stopped him. She stepped over to Mia and grabbed her hands. Tears spilled onto Mia's cheeks as she took in Darlene's appearance. She and Roman shared the same eyes. They were dark brown, and with small flecks of light brown mixed in. They shared the same thick, long lashes, too. Mia stood transfixed as she stared into the woman's eyes.

"I can see that you cared about my son very much," Darlene said the young girl. Darlene and Mia hadn't formerly met, but they had talked in passing over the last few weeks and Darlene could see that Mia was a good person. She only wished Roman were alive. He would have loved to see his mother finally approve of someone he was dating. Mia was polite, and she obviously cared for Roman and wasn't only with him for his money. She dressed respectively, unlike the other hoochie's her son dated. Not to mention, she was gorgeous. Darlene stared at the girl and let the tears fall as she thought about the fact that she would never see her son get married or have children.

Mis sniffled, "Yes, ma'am. We only recently started dating, but he was a good man. You should be proud of the men you raised. Roman...he stood up for what was right up until the very end. I only wish I could have protected him—"

Mia's words caught in her throat as she thought about those last moments Roman had been alive. Seeing Mia getting emotiona again, Kenyon pulled her into him and held her tightly. He shed a few tears as he thought about how awful it must have been to watch Roman die.

Darlene smiled, though. She reached out and patted Mia on the shoulder and said, "Roman was a lot like his father in that way. They were so good that they died trying to help others. Lord knows I just want my baby back, but if he had to go, I'm happy that he was protecting the people that he and his brother loved. I'm sure that you probably wish you weren't there that night, but I'm happy he had someone there that cared about him."

Mia's face was wet with tears as she nodded her head. Kenyon dipped down and asked, "Are you ready?"

Mia nodded her head, and they stepped into the room, Kenyon trailing behind Mia. Roman was dressed in a black suit. His coffin was marble white and both Kenyon and Mia smiled when they saw the crisp Jordan's on his feet. Mia's eyes traveled from his feet, up his legs and past his torso to his face. She gasped at how different he looked and her knees buckled. Kenyon was next to her in an instant, holding her up. His heart ached as he looked at his friend laying up in that casket, and it hurt even more to see Mia break down again.

Back at the house earlier she had a complete breakdown and

Kenyon was able to calm her down after an hour of her sobbing uncontrollably. He knew that she cared about Roman. They all did, but he personally thought she was also traumatized from the events that happened that night. After the funeral was over and she had time to process that Roman was gone, he hoped that he could convince Mia to go to therapy. After her family disowning her, her ex kicking her out, living on the streets and then Jade almost being beaten to death and Roman dying, Kenyon wanted to make sure that Mia would heal properly.

He supported her weight while she cried over Roman's casket. She reached her hand out and straightened his tie before smoothing down his suit jacket and uttering a few simple words.

"Ro, I'll miss you, baby. Rest in roses, king," Mia kissed the tips of her index fingers and middle finger before pressing it to Roman's cool lips. "Until we meet again."

Kenyon kept quiet as she spoke to Roman, holding in tears of his own. When she finished, she stepped back and grasped Kenyon's hand. He looked down at her and asked, "You good?"

Mia shook her head sadly, and Kenyon squeezed her hand. "I'll help you get through this, Mia."

Mia shook her head again, "You're hurting just as much, if not more than me. You knew Roman longer than I did...I can't imagine what you and Noah must be feeling right now. I can take care of myself. It isn't your job to help me through this, Kenyon."

"True, but you knew Roman in a more intimate way. Just because we knew him longer doesn't mean our pain is more important or bigger than yours," Kenyon responded.

Mia nodded, and in that moment she appreciated Kenyon for being so serious and comforting. Normally the two of them were at each other's throats, in a playful way, but in the last week Kenyon had been there for her in ways she never thought he was capable of.

Kenyon tore his gaze away from Mia and stared down into the coffin at the man he considered a little brother. He was glad he had sunglasses on so that people couldn't see the grief in his eyes. His pain was heart wrenching, but he was trying to stay strong for Noah and Darlene. Mia too.

He cleared his throat, trying to get rid of the growing lump, and spoke, "Damn, bro. This wasn't in the plan. Don't worry, I'll hold the family down, Ro. I love you, man. I didn't tell you that enough when you were here with us...I regret that shit."

Kenyon laughed, and then cleared his throat again before continuing. "If our moms could hear me right now, they would beat my ass for cursing in church. If you were here, you would be right along with me. This ain't right, bro. Rest easy, man."

Kenyon turned on his heels and grabbed Mia's hand, pulling her out of the room, unable to see his friend like that any longer. Mia nodded sadly at Noah, and Darlene as she passed, and Noah braced himself. He took his mother's arm and together they entered the small room.

Darlene stopped short when she saw her baby boy. A sob wrecked out of her throat and she cried out, "Why, God?"

Noah's own tears spilled out of his eyes, and it was the first time since his brother died that he couldn't comfort anyone else. He was stuck as he stared at his brother resting in the casket. Roman looked peaceful, but the scene in front of him was somehow all wrong. Roman's naturally cocky smile was replaced with a slight frown. His smooth dark skin was ashen, and his brown eyes were forever closed.

Noah looked down at his mother who was on her knees sobbing into her hands. It was then that he realized that he and his mom were the only two Bennett's left. Only half of his family remained, and that tore his heart apart. He reached down and helped his mother stand up. "Shh, ma...it's okay. I'm here, mama."

"I know, baby," Darlene's voice cracked. "I know you're here, but Roman isn't. Murphy isn't. What has happened to our family?"

Noah didn't have an answer, so instead he said, "Daddy and Roman have each other, ma. Just like you and I have each other."

As he was saying it, Noah realized that gave him a great deal of comfort. He knew that his father and brother were looking down on him, and a sense of peace washed over him. Darlene processed Noah's statement and although a huge part of her heart was missing, she knew that what her son said was true. She took in a deep breath and straightened up before approaching the casket. She peered down into it and held back more tears as she spoke.

"My baby boy, I love you so much. I would do anything to trade places with you. Tell your daddy I said hi and give him a big hug for me. I will always love you, son. Rest now, my prince."

Noah's tears continued to fall as he listened to his mother. His heart ached for her. No parent should ever have to outlive their children. He put his arm around his mom's shoulder and looked down at his brother. He didn't know how to say goodbye, so he decided to just speak from his heart.

"What's up, baby bro?" Noah whispered softly and then took a moment to gather himself before continuing. "You remember when we were younger and you would always get me into trouble? I used to get so mad at you, but it never stopped me from going along with you to do some stupid stuff. You're my baby brother and I always had to make sure you were good. I'm sorry I wasn't there for you the one time you truly needed me. I just hope you forgive me because I don't know if I'll ever forgive myself. You've been my best friend since the day you were born, man. I promise I'll hold you down, even in death. I love you, Ro. I always will."

Noah took one final look at his brothers face before turning around and walking out of the room with his mom. When they made it back to the pews, he noticed that Anita, Kenyon's mom, was sitting next to Kenyon, speaking softly with Mia and her son. Mia had tears running down her face as Anita, and Kenyon comforted her.

When Anita glanced up, she saw her best friend approaching, and she shot out of her seat and embraced Darlene while Noah took his seat next to Jade. Jade noticed that Noah had been crying, and her heart ached as she placed her hand on his thigh. He gently placed his hand over her bandaged fingers and gave her a tired smile. Jade opened her mouth to speak, but the pastor invited everyone to take their seats so the service could get started. Jade shifted uncomfortably in her seat, the wooden pews digging into her aching backside, but she gritted her teeth and suffered through the service. She felt as though it was the least she could do for Roman.

EVERYONE WAS EXHAUSTED AS THEY FILED INTO NOAH'S HOUSE later that night. The funeral had been emotional as hell, and the repass wasn't much better. Mia was in the worst shape. Her eyes were swollen and red and her head hurt from crying so much. She didn't want to go to bed because her dreams were plagued of the horrific night that Roman died, so Kenyon suggested they watch a movie. Noah noticed Jade was exhausted, so he declined Kenyon's invite for a movie and carried Jade up to bed.

"You know I can walk, right?" Jade asked softly.

Noah sat her down gently on his bed and gave her a tired smile, "I know. I also know that it hurts you to climb up those steps. I'm only trying to help."

Jade quickly backtracked and said, "I know and I appreciate you. I just wish you wouldn't fuss over me so much."

Without responding, Noah reached around and unzipped Jade's black fitted dress. Jade didn't protest as she watched him undress her. A yearning stirred in her stomach, but she quickly pushed it away. They hadn't had sex since before everything went down and Jade wasn't sure she was ready. Her womanhood still ached from being brutally raped, and flashbacks of that night continued to inhabit her mind.

She shivered involuntarily, and Noah looked up at her, concern radiating in his eyes. "Are you okay?"

Jade nodded her head as she looked down at her bare legs. They were covered in bruises, and some spots were heavily bandaged where she had to get stitches. Noah sighed and stood up with Jade's dress in his hands. "Do you want me to run you a bath?"

"No, that's okay," Jade responded before slightly lifting herself off the bed so she could take her panties off. "Would you mind getting my medicine, though? I left it in the bathroom."

Noah nodded and disappeared in the bathroom while Jade reached back and unsnapped her bra with a grimace. It felt as though every single one of her bones ached and she wasn't able to move around freely like she was used to. Exhausted from the day's events and the constant pain in her body, Jade laid back on the pillows and watched as Noah emerged from the bathroom and handed her a glass of water along with her various pill bottles. Jade accepted them and sat up slightly so she could get her newfound nightly routine out of the way.

While she took her pills, Noah undressed with a heaviness in his heart. The fact that he would never see his brother again was a hard pill to swallow. He choked back tears as he got in bed. Jade finished with her pills and put them on the nightstand before turning to see Noah wiping away a tear. A lump formed in her throat as she sighed and said, "I'm sorry."

Noah turned to look at her with his brows furrowed, "Why are you sorry, baby?"

"Because...this is my fault. Elijah—"

"Elijah is the only person at fault for this mess," Noah gritted out, becoming enraged. "Is that what you think? Do you really think I blame you for everything that happened?"

Jade had never seen Noah so angry before. She scooted back on the bed as tears fell from her eyes. Unable to verbally respond, she nodded her head and Noah's head snapped back like someone had punched him. He roughly got out of the bed and in a voice that was barely below shouting said, "This shit is not your fault, Jade. Elijah did this shit. He ruined my family, man! He ripped my brother off the face of the earth and had I been a minute later, he would have killed you, too. That nigga deserves nothing short of death!"

Jade winced at his loud tone and scooted even further away from Noah, who was now pacing back and forth. They hadn't talked about any of this since it had happened. Not about their feelings or the details of that gruesome night. Noah looked over at Jade who looked terrified of him and his heart ached. His eyes softened, and he stopped pacing. Getting back in bed, Noah put his head down to his chest and let the tears fall freely. He hated that he reacted that way towards Jade, especially after everything she had been through. His mind was so clouded, and his thoughts were tossed all over the place. He just wanted to go back to when things were less painful.

Jade noticed his tears, and she tentatively crawled over to him, ignoring the pain shooting through her body. When she reached Noah, she placed her small hand on his shoulder and whispered, "I'm sorry."

Noah shook his head and said, "You have nothing to be sorry about. If anything, I'm sorry. I told you I would keep you safe, and I failed you. I failed you and my brother."

"You didn't fail me, Noah. I'm alive, and that's a miracle and a blessing. I know that Roman wouldn't blame you, either. This isn't your fault."

Noah lifted his head and wiped his tears before looking into Jade's eyes. "This isn't either of our faults and the sooner we accept that, the sooner we can move on."

Jade peered into his eyes and realized that what he was saying was true. She needed to place the blame with Elijah, and Elijah alone. It was hard, though. She couldn't comprehend why nobody was blaming her for the awful things that happened, and that was only frustrating her.

Noah wrapped his arms around Jade and pulled her back so she was lying on his chest. The medication was making her sleepy and Noah knew it would only be a matter of minutes before she fell asleep and he was welcoming the rest as well. They both had a long day, and he was more than ready to put it behind him.

CHAPTER 22

"It's not fair that he gets to walk around breathing while Roman is dead," Jade said in frustration.

"Jade, I know that shit. I think about it every fucking day, but we have to stop letting that run our lives. Just remember that Elijah can't hurt you again. He can't hurt any of us," Mia said.

Jade scoffed as she loaded another dish into the dishwasher. "At what price, though? I would rather Roman be alive and deal with a few beatings from time to time than the shitty hand we've been dealt."

Mia shot off of her stool and was in Jade's face within seconds. "Do you hear yourself, Jade? It doesn't help you to think of *what if* scenarios. As fucked up as it is, this is the situation we have to deal with. Now, I've allowed you to walk around with your shitty ass attitude for the past week, but I'm sick of it. I don't know how many times any of us have to tell you that this isn't your fault for you to get it. Roman is dead because of Elijah, who is currently rotting in a jail cell, I might add. At least look at the positives that came with all of this. My mother always used to say that there is a bright side to every situation, no matter what it is. Elijah being in jail and being forced to divorce you is the good in all of this. Not to mention Yolanda's dumb ass sitting right up in there with him! If that doesn't cheer you up, then I don't know what the fuck to tell you aside from suck it the fuck up and deal with it!"

Mia was seething when she finished up her rant, and Jade couldn't blame her. Since she and Noah had that talk the night of Roman's funeral, Jade had tried her hardest to place the blame with Elijah, but it was hard. Every time she saw Mia staring off in the distance or Noah wiping a tear away, she couldn't help but feel like it was her fault. In return, she'd developed a terrible attitude. She and Noah were bickering, something they had never done before, and now Mia was yelling at her. Jade hated the person she was becoming, and she knew she needed to do better. Besides, Mia was right. She was now divorced and Elijah would most likely spend the rest of his life in jail, but if she was being honest, it upset her that Elijah survived the beating that both Roman and Noah put on him. He'd spent two weeks in the hospital and then was transferred straight to jail. He was being held on one count of murder and three counts of attempted murder along with smaller charges like breaking and entering.

Upon further investigation, the police recovered hundreds of text messages between Yolanda and Elijah. Nobody, besides the police, knew exactly what they said, but Yolanda was being held for an accomplice to murder. Jade remembered Elijah mentioning Yolanda that night, but she still didn't understand why she was involved. She knew the woman hated her, but to want her dead was unfathomable to Jade. It shocked everyone else when they found out that Yolanda had somehow been involved in everything that went down, and nobody could understand how she was connected.

Their trials would start next week, and in the meantime, the judged granted Jade approval to go back to her old home and gather her belongings. Jade blew out a deep breath and then looked at her best friend before saying, "I'm sorry, Mimi. I know I've been impossible to be around lately...there's no excuse for my behavior."

Mia sighed and then hugged her friend, forgetting about her

anger. "You have all the excuses in the world to behave like you are, but I'm here to tell you when enough is enough. I know that you're still in pain from all of your injuries. I also know that Elijah's upcoming trial has been taking a toll on you. I'm sure there is a lot of trauma lingering from being married to Elijah...not to mention him trying to kill you, but you have to start coping, Mouse. We are your family and you shouldn't be taking your anger and frustrations out on us."

Jade allowed one tear to fall before swiping the rest away. "You're right and I really am sorry. I guess...I'm still scared. I'm scared that he will somehow be found innocent and he will come back to finish what he started and if I'm being honest, I'm nervous about going back to the home Elijah and I shared. There are a few things that I want to get from there, but it will be hard stepping back into the place that felt like a prison for me."

"We'll be there every step of the way," Mia smiled and Jade was happy that Mia had called her out on her attitude. She'd hated the way she had been acting, but it was as if she couldn't help it. She would lash out at the people she loved for the smallest things, and she knew she needed to get a grip and do better. None of this was their fault, and they were all still grieving for Roman.

Jade grimaced when she thought about how rude she'd been acting when everyone was still trying to deal with Roman's death. She grabbed Mia's hands and leaned back against the sink before asking, "How are you? I mean, really...how are you dealing with everything?"

Mia shifted from foot to foot and gazed in her friend's eyes. "Some days are better than others. I know it's crazy grieving so hard over someone I had only just started dating, but we had a connection, you know? I could talk to him about anything and never feel judged. He was a straight thug that turned to mush whenever I was around," Mia giggled as her eyes glossed over. "I miss him, but it's more than that because I know I can never talk to him or kiss him again, if that makes sense."

Jade nodded her head. She knew exactly what her friend was feeling because she still felt that way about her parents. It was a void that would never be filled. She squeezed Mia's hands and said, "I'm sorry I haven't been there for you."

"You get a pass," Mia smiled. "Besides, Kenyon has been extremely helpful."

Jade suggestively raised her eyebrows at Mia and asked, "What's up with you two, anyway?"

Mia's eyes widened as she stared at her friend. "Nothing! Absolutely nothing. Gross, Jade. You know me better than that. Kenyon and I have always been friends. Have you forgotten that he's slept with half of Manhattan?"

"I know...but if I'm being honest, I always thought you two might become a thing before Roman came into the picture," Jade shrugged.

"Yuck, no way. He literally has a different woman in his bed every day of the week."

"According to his mama, so did Roman," Jade pointed out.

Mia scoffed, "That's different."

"Right," Jade grinned and then shook her head.

At that moment, Noah came walking into the kitchen. He saw Jade and Mia and froze awkwardly in the doorway. Noah and Jade had an argument earlier that morning, and he wasn't sure what to expect when he saw her. He'd been holed up in his den working on some designs, but he was getting hungry. Jade spotted Noah and exhaled. She looked at Mia and said, "Can you give us a minute?"

"Of course," Mia rubbed her friend's shoulders. "Remember what I said. Do better, Mouse."

Jade nodded sadly and watched Mia leave the kitchen before turning to Noah. She wrung her hands nervously and said, "Do you want me to make you something to eat?"

Noah shook his head and advanced towards the refrigerator, "Nah. I'm just going to make a sandwich."

Jade rushed over to the refrigerator and yanked it open before Noah could reach it. "Let me do it. Have a seat."

Noah eyed her cautiously before taking a seat at the island. The two remained quite as Jade fixed Noah two ham sandwiches with cheese, mayo, dijon mustard, lettuce and tomato on thick sliced white bread. Jade was thinking about how rude she'd been to Noah earlier. When they woke up, Noah simply asked her what time she wanted to go over to her old home and Jade, feeling overwhelmed, lashed out at him. She cringed as she added some potato chips to the plate before sitting it in front of him.

"Thanks," Noah said.

Jade sat down on the stool next to him and took a deep breath before saying, "I'm sorry."

Noah grunted and continued eating. Jade nodded her head, accepting that she deserved that response from him. Noah had been amazing to her, like always, and she hadn't been the easiest to be around.

"I know I've been a complete bitch lately," Jade tried again. "You didn't deserve the things I said to you this morning, and you haven't deserved the way I've been acting, either. I mean...calling you over-bearing when you were only trying to help was wrong. I apologize."

"Don't forget you said you wanted to move out just so you could get away from me," Noah mumbled sadly and Jade's eyes filled with tears.

She looked down at her hands and said, "I didn't mean that, Noah. Truth is, I don't know what I would have done without you these last couple of weeks. I really do apologize for how I've been acting. I've had so many feelings taking residence in my heart that I've been lashing out and that isn't fair to any of you...especially since you guys are dealing with Roman's death."

Noah nodded slowly as he continued to eat. "Yeah, I have been dealing with the death of my brother and it would have been nice for you to support me more. Do you know that while you were in the hospital, I called you my girlfriend to the doctor and nurses?"

Noah laughed sadly while Jade softly responded, "No."

"Yeah, man. As shitty as I felt, calling you my girlfriend made me feel good as hell, but I don't know anymore. You've turned into someone I don't even know. It's like you're trying to push us all away and that shit hurts, Jade."

Once again, Jade felt like lashing out at his assessment of her, even though it was true. Instead, she reeled her anger and hurt in and said, "I don't know how to explain what's been going on with me, but I can try if you'd like?"

Noah stopped eating and pushed his plate away before turning to Jade and giving her his full attention. "I'm all ears."

"Mostly, I've been embarrassed," Jade started. "It was already embarrassing enough to tell you guys that Elijah used to beat me, but for you guys to actually witness it was mortifying. None of you should have witnessed that. Mia and Roman walked in when I was... when Elijah was...raping me, and God knows what condition I was in when you came into our apartment."

Tears freely fell from Jade's eyes. Noah opened his mouth to say something, but Jade stopped him. "Let me get this out. I think it might help me to talk about it, and it might help you understand my feelings a little more. I'm not trying to be selfish, I know you have your own feelings and I want to talk about you, too, but I don't know if I'll have the courage to say this if I wait."

Noah nodded and said, "Okay. I'm listening, baby."

"Thank you," Jade said before taking a calming breath and continuing. "I thought I would die and all I could think about was you. It terrified me that I would never get to see you again and tell you how much you mean to me. Then, Elijah...he raped me and I knew that if you found out you wouldn't want me anymore, anyway. Then, Mia was there, and things blacked out from there. I thought for sure I was dead until I woke up in the hospital and you were there. I kept thanking God repeatedly that I was alive and had been given a second chance. When I learned that Roman died trying to save me...I felt so guilty"

Noah opened his mouth to say something, but Jade held her hand up to silence him before continuing. "I'm trying to understand that none of this was my fault. Really, I am, but it's hard when all of it was my mess to begin with. Your brother died because I was being attacked. He died trying to save me and I keep waiting for everyone around me to realize that it was my fault. Instead, you have all been so supportive and caring towards me, which only makes me feel worse. I'm carrying this guilt and embarrassment around, and it's causing me to lash out. I don't know how to fix any of this, Noah."

Noah sat quietly for a moment, and when he spoke, it threw Jade off guard by the change in subject. "What time do you have to be at your house...or I mean, Elijah's house?"

Jade's mind spun as she cleared the lump out of her throat that had formed as she was spilling her heart out to Noah. "I can go at any time. The house won't officially go on the market until after the trial."

Since the house was in Elijah's name only, if he ended up getting life in prison like they were all hoping, the house would go on the market and be sold. For now, it would sit empty and probably go into foreclosure since the mortgage wouldn't be paid. It was a mess, and Jade was happy that she didn't have to deal with any of it. As much as she hated the house not being in her name before, she was thankful for it now. It made everything so much easier on her.

Noah stood up, his lunch forgotten, and reached his hand out to Jade. "I want to take you somewhere."

Jade's glossy eyes peered up at him through her long lashes in confusion. "Noah, we were in the middle of talking. I don't think—"

"Trust me. This has everything to do with our conversation," Noah breathed.

Still confused, Jade nodded, deciding to trust Noah. He led her out of the kitchen and into the hall, where he helped her put her shoes and coat on. She was still sore, and she had just had her stitches from her surgery taken out so her wounds were tender. Luckily, her bruises were healing and instead of the hideous black and blue they had been previously, they were fading into an ugly yellow color that blended in more with her skin tone. Her broken bones were still in casts and would be for the next couple of months, but Jade never complained about her injuries. In fact, she welcomed the pain because it meant she was alive.

Once they were ready to go out into the cold weather, Noah helped Jade out of the house and down the icy driveway to his car. He helped Jade in and when he tried to buckle her seatbelt for her, Jade almost lashed out at him again. Instead, she took a deep breath and said, "I got it, Noah. Thank you."

Noah smiled down at her, and Jade's heart fluttered. It was the first smile she had seen from him in weeks, and that was all the motivation she needed to get her attitude and emotions under control. Things had been pretty stale between them, but it was time for that to change and Jade wanted to try hard to put her own feelings aside and attend to Noah just as he had been doing for her. Once their seatbelts were on, Noah pulled out of the driveway. They fell into a comfortable silence as Noah drove, and Jade wondered where they were going.

Thirty minutes later, they were pulling up to a modest neighborhood in Queens. Jade looked around at the apartment complexes towering around her. They were nice, and they reminded her of her, and Mia's place. A shiver ran down her spine as she thought about the place that she was once so proud of. Neither her nor Mia had been back. Kenyon and Noah collected their things and put them in a storage unit for them, and the landlord was currently in jail for giving Elijah the keys to their apartment in exchange for money. The judge granted that their lease be voided and once again, Mia and Jade were living with Noah. Not that they wanted to go back to their place, anyway. They hadn't even talked about getting a new place, but Jade didn't think they were ready for that yet, anyway. Despite what she had said to Noah earlier, she wasn't sure she could sleep at night without him around. A part of her would always be nervous to be on her own for as long as she lived.

Jade snapped out of her thoughts when she realized that Noah was opening the car door for her. He leaned in and asked, "You okay? You zoned out for a minute there."

Jade nodded, "Yeah, sorry. Where are we?"

"We're visiting a friend of the family. Come on," Noah said as he reached out for her hand.

Jade hesitated as she looked down at her grungy clothes and thought about the ugly yellow bruising on her face. "Noah, I look terrible. Why—"

"You're beautiful. Come on. I'm hoping she can help," Noah responded as he reached over and unbuckled her seatbelt before pulling her out of the car.

Jade looked up at him as he closed the car door with her eyebrow quirked up. "She?"

Laughing, Noah shook his head and said, "Nothing like that," as they turned away from the car.

He matched her slow pace as they walked up the walkway to the nearest apartment building. Although they were moving sedately, Noah was happy with how much progress Jade had made since last week. At the funeral, she could barely stand up by herself. He guided her to the front door and then pressed the buzzer, hoping that someone would answer since he didn't call ahead. It was a Saturday, though, so he knew there was a good chance she would be home.

A moment later, there was a crackle through the worn out speaker and a feminine voice said, "Hello?"

"Cassy, it's Noah," Noah grinned at the buzzer.

"Noah, baby? Come on in," the woman said as a loud buzzer sounded in the entryway.

Jade quirked her eyebrow up at Noah as she walked through the buzzing door. Noah shook his head and grinned down at her as he led her down the long hall of the apartment complex. The grey carpeted floors were clean, and it smelled like fresh linen as they passed the laundry room. There was a lot of space between the doors lining the hallway which meant thick walls in between each apartment. Jade made a mental note to keep these apartments in mind for when she and Mia were ready to be out on their own again.

Noah stopped at the last door in the hallway on the right and knocked. A moment later, a tall boy in his teens answered the door with a smirk on his face. He was lanky and already about Noah's height, even though he couldn't be more than fourteen years old.

"Whussup, Noah," the boy said in a surprisingly deep voice as he slapped hands with Noah. Jade smiled at the cool confidence the boy exuded.

"Man, look at you. You get taller and taller every time I visit," Noah said proudly.

"The ladies love it," he responded, and before Noah could respond, a tall woman in her mid-forties stepped into the doorway.

"Kai! Get your butt in your room and finish doing your homework, and I better not hear you talking about *the ladies* again. You're too young for all that."

"Awww, mom! I was just kidding around—"

"Aht! Go finish your homework and get out of the way so our guests can come in," the lady snapped. Kai lifted his hand and waved at Noah before disappearing down the hall.

"Sorry about that. I don't know how to deal with being a mother of a teenage boy, sometimes. Noah, honey, how are you?" she asked as she looked into Noah's eyes before reaching in for a hug. She acted motherly towards Noah, and Jade wondered if she was a family friend or an aunt she had never met.

"It's been rough," Noah responded as he hugged her back. He released her and then turned and reached out a hand for Jade. "Cassy, this is my...uh, friend, Jade."

Jade grimaced as he introduced her as his friend, but now wasn't the time for her to have that conversation with him. She knew that they needed to talk about the state of their relationship, sooner rather than later, though. Jade reached out and clasped Cassy's warm hand. Her fingers were long and narrow, and her grip was firm. She smiled down at Jade, noting the bruises on her face, and said, "It is so nice to meet you, Jade. Please, come in."

Cassy moved to the side, and Noah led Jade down the short hall into the modest living room. The couch and chairs were matching brown leather and there was a big TV set in front of them. To the right of the TV was a large bookshelf crammed with books that looked like they had been read more than a few times.

Noah sat down on the couch and Jade gingerly sat next to him. Cassy stopped short just inside the living room and asked, "Are you thirsty or hungry? I can make us all a late lunch if you'd like."

"No, thank you," Jade said kindly, and Noah shook his head with a smile.

"Come and sit, Cassy. I'm hoping that you can help me out with something," Noah said.

Cassy moved into the room and sat down in the recliner opposite Noah and Jade. She looked at Noah and said, "First, I want to say how sorry I am about Roman. You know I loved him as if he were my own. I reached out to your mama a few times and I swear that woman is stronger than I will ever be. If you all need anything at all, you'll let me know?"

A lump formed in Noah's throat as he nodded his head. "Thank you, Cassy. I will."

"Good. Lord knows that your family has been through enough grief," Cassy said as she wiped at her glossy eyes.

Jade shifted uncomfortably, wondering why Noah had brought her here. So far, she only felt worse seeing yet another person grieving over Roman. Jade cleared her throat and spoke up. "Excuse me, but how do you two know each other?"

Cassy's eyes snapped over to Noah as she asked, "You didn't tell her who I was?"

Noah shifted uncomfortably, "No...this was kind of a spur-of-the-moment visit. I hoped that you could tell her your story and how we came to meet because...well...Jade was—"

Noah stopped speaking and then looked down at Jade, who was sitting stiffly next to him. "Do you mind if I share that night with her? I promise that it will make sense in a moment."

Jade knew exactly what night he was referring to, and her first instinct was to cuss him out for bringing her here to display her life story for a woman she had never met. Then, she remembered the promise she made to herself on the way here, and blew out a deep breath before nodding her head, deciding to trust Noah.

Noah grabbed one of her hands that was sitting in her lap and squeezed it gently, careful not to hurt her broken bones, before turning his attention back to Cassy. "The night Roman was killed, Jade's ex husband broke into her home and tried killing her. He beat her pretty badly and Roman walked in..."

Noah knew he didn't have to finish. Cassy would understand. So, he let his sentence fall off and watched as tears brimmed her eyes before closing them slowly and nodding her head once. When she opened them, she whispered, "He saved you."

Cassy was now looking directly into Jade's eyes. Jade nodded, and she wasn't sure why, but she felt an unexplainable connection to Cassy. She didn't feel the usual shame that normally consumed her when she told someone about Elijah, nor did she feel the need to explain herself. The look on Cassy's face was understanding, and it was so much of a relief to Jade that she could have hugged the woman right then and there.

Cassy cleared her throat and began speaking. "Now I see what this impromptu visit is all about, although, Noah could have told you who I was before coming here."

She speared Noah with a venomous look, but both Noah and Jade could tell that she didn't mean it. Her eyes held too much love for Noah, and Jade understood that she wasn't truly upset with him.

"I was once in your shoes," Cassy continued as she looked directly at Jade. "Kai's father, Terry, used to beat me, even when I was pregnant. I was so sure that Kai wouldn't make it out of my womb. I was barely three months in my pregnancy, and I wasn't even showing when Terry lost his damn mind and tried to stomp Kai out of me in public for everyone to see. It's New York, though, right? So barely anyone looked my way, and those that did weren't brave enough to stand up to Terry. Except for Murphy."

Jade gasped and whirled around to face Noah whose head was

hung down to his chest. Tears were running down his cheeks as he listened to Cassy speak. Jade immediately put her hand on his back and rubbed it slowly, but she didn't know what to say. She couldn't imagine losing a sibling and then having to relive his father's death.

"I understand now," Jade spoke up finally. "You don't have to contin—"

"No, you don't understand, Jade. Please, let her finish. I'm alright," Noah said in a low voice as he stared at the ground.

Jade glanced over at Cassy who had tears streaming down her own face as she continued. "He got Terry off of me. He saved me and Kai, but Terry beat him to death. By the time the police got to us, Murphy was dead, but I was alive. I hated myself for it. In my mind, I had gotten this sweet man murdered all because I said something smart to my crazy ass boyfriend, which caused him to snap. Luckily he was arrested on the spot and sent to jail for life, but that did nothing to ease my pain.

"It made matters worse when I found out Murphy had a wife and two sons. I swear, I wanted to die. The only reason I didn't take my own life was because of Kai. The guilt that I carried was suffocating, but one day, right after they released me from the hospital, Darlene came by my house along with Noah and Roman. I was so sure they were there to tell me how much they hated me, and I was happy to sit there and let them. To my surprise, they brought me a gift basket, and Darlene paid my hospital bills. They were grieving, but they were still caring for me...the person who had gotten their husband and father killed. It only made me realize that Murphy's kindness and bravery didn't stop at him, but it overflowed into his family. We became like family over the years and I'm honored to call Darlene one of my best friends."

Jade was crying now, and she wished that she could have met Noah's dad. Then, she remembered that Roman was exactly like Murphy and so was Noah. She already knew his kind heart through his sons and his wife. Jade smiled through her tears and leaned into Noah, who was holding his arms out for her. Cassy smiled at the couple and said, "Jade, sweetie...whatever you are feeling, I promise that it will pass. The guilt will fade, the embarrassment will fade, and even the anger will fade. Eventually, you will be left with an overwhelming sense of gratitude and love. Take it from me, you do not want to push the people closest to you away right now, because when everything else fades, you won't have anyone around to give your newfound gratitude to. That comes from having a second chance. Don't waste it, baby.

"Above anything else, remind yourself every second of every day that none of what happened was your fault. It is an uphill battle, but it gets easier. Roman was so much like his father, and he will be missed, but you are still here. Make the most of it."

Jade nodded as tears splashed off her cheeks and into her lap while Noah pressed his tear-stained face into her hair. His heart was heavy, but hearing Cassy's words made him believe that Jade would be okay and that she would get through this. She was stronger than anyone he knew, and Noah was sure that she would come out on the other side even better than she was before. He only hoped that Cassy's words would help speed up the process.

CHAPTER 23

"Are you okay?" Noah asked as looked down at Jade. She had been frozen in place for the past five minutes, and Noah was beginning to worry. Once they left Cassy's house, the two went straight to Elijah's so they could get it of the way. They were already emotionally drained from their visit with Cassy, but Jade didn't want to put this off any longer.

"Come on, baby. It's cold out," Noah urged her forward, and she finally snapped out of her daze and looked up at him.

"I'm sorry...I just...I never thought I would be back here," Jade admitted. "For years this place was like a prison to me and I really don't want to go back inside. What if he destroyed all my stuff?"

Noah shook his head. "There's only one way to find out, sweetheart."

Nodding her head, Jade took a step closer to the front door of the mini mansion and pulled the key out of her pocket. Her lawyer had given it to her a few days ago with strict instructions to get it back to him by today. The judge was being extremely lenient with Jade because of the circumstances, and the lawyer wanted to make sure they abided by her rules to remain in her favor.

She slipped the key into the lock and turned it. As soon as she pushed the door open, a chill ran up her spine. The clean pine needle smell struck her nostrils and flung her mind straight into the terrible memories this house possessed. She quickly tuned everything out and made a beeline for the stairs. Noah followed behind her as he took in the vast house. It wasn't very cozy. Everything was stark white, save the artwork hanging on the walls. The tiled floors were shiny white, along with the walls and the banister on the staircase. The vaulted ceilings were high, and there was a crystal chandelier hanging in the middle of the foyer. Overall, it looked like a piece of art and not a home where a husband and wife lived.

Jade rushed down the long hall on the second floor with various rooms on either side, finally stopping at the last door on the right. Grasping the doorknob, she took a deep breath and pushed it open just as Noah reached her. He wanted to make sure she was okay, but Jade seemed like she was on a mission and he had no intentions of slowing her down. If she wanted to do this quickly, he wouldn't stop her.

Inside the room it was cold and bright white like the rest of the house. The large bed was neatly made with a satin white comforter, and there was a fluffy white rug that sat underneath the bed. The floors were the same shiny white tile and other than the connecting master bathroom and walk-in closet; the room was bare. Jade went straight into the closet and Noah gave her a moment. He stood just inside the room waiting patiently, not wanting to invade in her privacy. He knew this couldn't be easy for her, and he was right. Having Noah there was comforting for Jade, but it was also as if her two worlds were colliding and she couldn't handle that. Noah was a part of her new, happy life while this house belonged to Elijah and the hell she had come from. She wanted this over as quickly as possible and luckily; she knew exactly where the things she wanted most were kept.

She flicked the light on in the large closet and let out a sigh of relief when she saw all of her designer clothes still neatly hanging inside. She wasn't concerned about the clothes, but what they were hiding. She crouched down and moved the longer dresses and shoes aside until she found two specific boxes sitting in the back where she had left them. One of them was a bigger brown box and the other one was a shoe box. A smile spread across her face as she lifted them out of the closet and peeked inside. Everything was there and for the first time in a few weeks her eyes glistened with tears that were of pure joy.

She stepped out of the closet with her items, not bothering to turn off the light, and Noah rushed over to her and grabbed the boxes. "Which room is next?"

Jade shook her head and replied, "This is it. This is all I wanted to get."

Noah's brows furrowed as he asked, "Are you sure?"

"I'm positive. Let's get out of here."

Noah shrugged and followed Jade out of the house and to the car, ready to get home and unwind after this emotionally exhausting day.

***

THE HOUSE WAS QUIET AS EVERYONE STAYED COOPED UP IN their own rooms. Mia was in her guest bedroom, Jade was in Noah's room and Noah was in his office. Even Kenyon was over, but he was in the basement watching a movie by himself. This had become the norm for them, and Jade realized that she needed to do something to lift everyone's spirits. She had been in a major funk the past couple of weeks, but Cassy's words from earlier echoed in her head, *Roman was so much like his father, and he will be missed, but you are still here. Make the most of it.*

She knew she needed to take strides to be happy again, and that started with the people she loved. Flinging the covers off herself, she rolled out of bed and walked into the bathroom. She checked her appearance in the mirror and decided she looked fine. Her mass of curls were sitting wildly at the top of her head and her face was void of any makeup. After getting home, she had jumped in the shower and put on a pair of black leggings and one of Noah's white t-shirts that hung down to her knees. Despite how dressed down she was, Jade realized that she looked pretty, even with the fading bruises covering her body.

The woman in the reflection staring back at her had a kind heart, was shy and loving. She was gorgeous, inside and out, and for the first time in years, she truly believed that about herself. Her pouty lips spread into a smile as she gazed at herself. She took one last long look before going back into the bedroom and grabbing the boxes she discarded on her nightstand from earlier.

Noah was hunched over his desk, drawing in his sketch pad when Jade walked in. Startled by her presence, he immediately closed the pad and looked up at her. "Is everything okay?"

Jade smiled at him shyly and uttered a quick, "Yes," before setting the boxes on his desk and taking a step back.

"What's this?" Noah asked in confusion.

"The boxes I got from Elijah's house," Jade said nervously.

"I know that, but—"

"I wanted to open them...together," Jaded interrupted. She didn't know why she was being so shy suddenly, but this was kind of a big deal for her. It suddenly hit her that she was finally divorced and what that meant for her and Noah. She could open up to him in ways that she never thought possible, and that was why this moment was making her so nervous. She was about to share with him some things that were extremely precious to her.

Noah smiled up at her and leaned back in his chair. "Come over here."

Jade did as she was told and made small steps towards him until she was standing in between his legs. Noah pulled her down onto his lap and kissed her on the cheek before saying, "Show me."

Jade smiled and then, with a shaking hand, lifted the lid on the bigger box. Tears instantly came to her eyes as she saw the items inside. Her smile grew as she reached out and grasped the baby blanket. She pulled it towards her face and inhaled deeply as the smell of her childhood home filled her nostrils.

"My baby blanket," Jade smiled as she shifted to the side so that Noah could get a better view.

He smiled at her and reached out to touch the soft pink fabric. He didn't say anything. Instead, he watched with pure joy in his heart. She seemed to be so happy in this moment, and in return, that made him happy. He wished he could capture this moment forever, and he realized that she was showing him a piece of her life that had been happier for her. He watched intently as she set the blanket aside and pulled out a jewelry box.

"My parents' wedding rings," she smiled as she looked at the glittering diamonds on her mother's wedding bands.

"They weren't buried with them?" Noah asked, hoping he didn't sound too insensitive.

To his relief, Jade simply shook her head and said, "No. At the last minute, I decided I wanted them. I just wanted something tangible that they wore every day, you know?"

Noah nodded, "I completely understand."

She handed the ring box to him and Noah examined the beautiful rings while Jade took out an assortment of her baby clothes, her first paintings, birth certificate, and a couple of VHS's that held her baby videos.

"We definitely have to watch those," Noah remarked.

Jade playfully grimaced and said, "Maybe one day."

The bigger box was now empty, so Jade took great care placing everything back inside and then slid the smaller box over. She lifted the lid and this time, tears sprung out of her eyes as she smiled down at the two books that lay inside. One was her mother's recipe book that she passed to Noah, and the other was a photo album. Jade flipped the album open as Noah sat the recipe book down and leaned in.

"Those are my parents," Jade whispered with a smile as her tears splashed on the laminated sleeves the photos sat in.

Noah imagined many tears hit those laminated photos over the past few years as Jade longed for her parents. He leaned in to get a better look and smiled as he instantly realized that Jade looked exactly like her mother. In the photo, her mother's wild curly hair reminded Noah of Jade when she wore it down. She was a petite woman, as well. She had her mother's eyes and skin tone, but her father smile. His smile was wide and his lips were full, just like Jade's. He towered over his wife and had a hand wrapped securely around her waist. His dark skin complimenting her light skin perfectly. There was no doubt that the two had been in love. Anyone could see it from the way they were laughing together in the photo. Their body language exuded love.

"They were a beautiful couple," Noah said.

Jade nodded her head, "They were the best. This was taken on their honeymoon in Jamaica."

She flipped the page and there were wedding photos of her parents, followed by pregnancy pictures of her mother. About halfway through the album, Jade's baby pictures appeared. Noah laughed in delight when he saw baby Jade smiling at the camera with chubby cheeks. "It's official. You are the cutest person I have ever met."

Jade giggled at his silliness and said, "God, these are embarrassing. I don't know if I thought this through all the way."

"Oh no, don't stop now. Are there any pictures of you as a teenager?" Noah grinned.

Jade laughed and flipped the page, "I'm afraid so."

Noah let out a hearty laugh when he saw Jade as a pre-teen and then photos from her high school days. "What were you wearing?"

Jade smacked her lips, "Boy, don't get too comfortable. I will call your mom right now and have her bring over your baby pictures. I bet she has some good ones."

Noah thought about it and then said, "Okay, you're right. My bad."

"That's what I thought," Jade giggled.

They finished looking at the photo album and Jade put it back in the box and leaned back into Noah. They were quiet for a moment before Noah spoke up. "Thank you for sharing all of that with me."

Jade turned so she could see Noah's face and sighed. "I never thought I would get these things back. Thank you for coming with me to get them, and Noah?"

"Yeah?" He asked.

"Thank you for everything. I know I tell you this all the time, but you are an amazing man. I'm sorry that I lost sight of that these past few weeks and I apologize that I haven't been there for you. I'll never forgive myself for that, but I hope that you'll forgive me."

"Of course, I forgive you," Noah said.

Jade closed her eyes and savored his words before opening them again and saying, "Good, because I want to make it up to you as well as Mia and Kenyon tonight."

Noah quirked his eyebrow up at her and asked, "How do you plan on doing that?"

Jade grinned and snatched her mother's recipe book up and responded, "I bet you've never had shrimp and grits with homemade butter biscuits as good as my mama's."

"Damn, was she from the south or something?" Noah laughed as his stomach grumbled.

"Nope, but my daddy was. She learned to perfect all of his favorite dishes and they're all in here," Jade tapped the recipe book and slowly got off Noah's lap, careful not to irritate any of her injuries.

She turned around just as she got to the door and said, "Oh, and Noah?"

"Yeah?" Noah asked.

"Never introduce me as *a friend* again."

Without waiting for a response, Jade turned on her heels and walked out of Noah's office slowly. Noah chuckled and shook his head as he yelled after her, "Glad we had that talk!"

"How the hell did you even make a meal this damn good with all those broken fingers?" Kenyon asked as he smacked his lips together like he had no sense.

Mia and Noah froze at Kenyon's ignorance and Kenyon asked, "What? Too soon?"

Jade laughed and said, "It's okay. It's the first joke I heard you crack in a long time. I can't even be mad at it."

"Well I can," Noah reached over and smacked Kenyon on the head.

Kenyon yelped and rubbed his head. He frowned at Noah while Mia started cussing him out in both Spanish and English. Jade sat back and smiled as she looked around the table, happy that everyone was getting back to normal. All it took was a little push from her and a good ass meal to get them there.

"How about some shots?" Jade asked loudly over everyone arguing.

Mia stopped cursing Kenyon out mid-sentence and eyed her friend from across the dining room table. "Did you just say you wanted to take some shots?"

"Why not?" Jade asked with a smile.

"The Jade I know normally has to be begged to take shots," Mia said, still eying Jade.

"I hate to say this, but Mia's right," Kenyon said.

Mia gave Kenyon a withering look as Jade said, "I think we could all spare a night to let loose and have some fun. It's not like any of us have to work tomorrow, so why not?"

"Turn up!" Kenyon exclaimed as he hopped up went over to the liquor cabinet.

"Are you sure you can drink while you're on your medications?" Mia asked Jade.

"I'm not on any meds anymore. They only gave me them for the first week for pain and to make sure my incisions didn't get infected," Jade replied.

Mia grinned, "I'm about to get you so fucked up."

"Hey, now, take it easy on my girl," Noah chuckled.

"Your girl, huh?" Mia quirked an eyebrow up at Noah and then turned towards Jade, who blushed and turned away.

"Mia, stop acting so damn surprised. This was our plan all along," Kenyon joked as he sat a bottle of tequila on the table.

"True," Mia laughed obnoxiously and slapped hands with Kenyon.

Jade shook her head incredulously at her friends while Noah got up to grab Jade a chaser. He came back a few moments later with orange juice in his hands along with a bag of chips, some cookies, and four shot glasses. The table was still littered with their dinner plates, so he moved a few of them to the side to make room for the snacks before sitting down next to Jade. Kenyon snatched the shot glasses up and began pouring a hefty amount of tequila in each one.

"Damn, Kenyon," Noah chuckled as Kenyon passed the glasses out to everyone.

"What, man? This first one is for Ro," Kenyon said somberly.

Everyone fell quiet as they each raised their glasses and clinked them together in remembrance for Roman. Even Jade didn't complain about the burn of the liquor once she had taken the whole thing back. They remained quiet for a moment, lost in their own thoughts, but Mia broke the silence. "As much as I miss Roman, I just want one night where I'm not sad."

"Same," Jade agreed sadly.

"Okay, then. For the rest of the night all we're going to do is laugh," Kenyon grinned. He hopped up from the table and darted out of the room. A moment later he came back into the dining room carrying *Twister*.

"Who wants to get their ass beat in drunk Twister?" Kenyon asked cockily.

"Aww, shit," Mia exclaimed excitedly before downing another drink. "You're on!"

The two of them rushed out of the room to find a spot to set the game up, leaving Noah and Jade behind.

"Looks like we're in for a long night," Jade grinned.

"Guess so. I'd better take another drink if I'm going to put up with those two arguing over that game all night," Noah groaned as he poured another shot.

Jade slide her glass over to him and said, "Pour me one, too."

They took their shots together and then Noah made a move to get up, but Jade stopped him by reaching over and placing a hand on his knee. She slowly stood up and walked in between his legs. Bending over, she kissed him deeply on the lips. Noah's hands automatically went to her waist as he pulled her down to his lap. They hadn't kissed like this in days, and Jade felt good to be close to him like this again.

Not wanting to get too carried away, Jade pulled away from him and smiled. "I've missed that."

"Shit, me too," Noah grinned.

He helped Jade move off his lap and kept his hands on her waist as they walked out into the living room where Kenyon and Mia were already arguing over the game.

CHAPTER 24

"HE WAS IN MY ROOM," JADE SPOKE INTO THE MICROPHONE with tears running down her face. "I was so scared when I saw him. My mind was racing...I can't even remember if he said anything. All I remember was backing away from him—"

"It's okay, Jade. Take your time," her lawyer, Samuel Langston, soothed. "Did Elijah mention Yolanda?"

Jade shivered as she thought about what Elijah had said to her before he started beating her. She lifted her head and looked around the courtroom at all the people, and it felt as though a heavyweight had been placed on her chest. Elijah was sitting directly ahead of her with a murderous look in his eyes. Jade knew he was beyond pissed because he could barely get a good lawyer since he murdered Roman. None of his hotshot lawyer friends wanted anything to do with him and all the criminals he had won cases for turned their backs on him. Nobody wanted to be brought down just because he lost his mind and murder someone.

Yolanda was sitting at the same table as Elijah, separated only by a gang of lawyers. She had her head buried in her hands and her shoulders were shaking from the sobs that wrecked her whole body.

Jade didn't feel bad for her ass, though. Yolanda tried to get her killed, so sympathy wouldn't be found on Jade's end.

Behind them, Elijah's parents were glaring at her and they were a reminder that Elijah got away with everything. Next to them were two people who looked so similar to Yolanda, she was sure they were her parents. They were eying her with disdain in their eyes and Jade quickly looked away from them and focused on her own family, Darlene, Mia, Kenyon, and Noah were sitting. Even Kenyon's mom and Cassy were there. Jade caught Noah's eye, and he nodded to her encouragingly. He knew that today would be hard for them all. They'd each taken their turns testifying as witnesses to the horrendous night and Jade was the final one to take the stand. Mia had already explained what happened when Elijah shot Roman and Noah described the condition that his brother, Jade and Mia were in when he entered the apartment. Jade testifying was to give the jury a full picture of the kind of man Elijah was. She had already covered the kind of husband he had been while they were married, and now she had to talk about the last time she saw him. Jade drew in a breath and nodded her head slightly at Noah and then focused back on her lawyer.

"Yes," she said confidently.

"Do you remember what he said?" Samuel asked.

"I asked him how he found me and he said that Yolanda called him," Jade revealed.

"And what happened next?" Samuel prompted.

"Then...he started choking me and beating me. He had a gun... he...raped me and then he inserted the gun inside of me and I thought he was going to kill me..." A sob tore out of Jade as she thought about the traumatic events.

Samuel stepped in and helped Jade out. He knew that his client wouldn't last long on the stand, and she still needed to get through cross-examination. "Ms. Lawrence, at what point did Mia and Roman enter the apartment?"

Jade got herself together and answered, "It wasn't long after he raped me with the gun. I was in so much pain and I think I blacked out not too long after...the next thing I remember is waking up in the hospital."

Samuel had been pacing in front of the stand, listening to her intently, but when she finished, he stopped and slowly turned towards her and said, "I only have one last question for you, Jade. Think hard about this one. Do you remember anything else that Elijah said to you? Did he mention Yolanda anymore or maybe what his intentions were that night?"

Jade closed her eyes and breathed deeply as she thought back to that night. Her eyes snapped open when she remembered something, and she quickly spoke into the mic. "He said that he would kill me and then Noah. He said that if he couldn't have me, then nobody could."

There was a hush that fell over the courtroom as everyone processed what Jade said. It didn't last long, though. Elijah sprung out of his chair and started shouting, "This is all your fault! You were a shitty wife and you damn sure better believe you and your punk ass nigga were supposed to be dead that night!"

At the same time, Yolanda broke out into thunderous cries as she lunged towards Elijah, "You weren't supposed to kill Noah, that wasn't the deal! Jade was the one we were after. You son of a bitch! Noah was supposed to be mine!"

Jade was stunned as she watched multiple police officers gain control of the situation by handcuffing Yolanda and Elijah and dragging them out of the room. The judged called order to the courtroom and after several moments, everyone calmed down. The judge sighed and asked, "Does the defense want to question the witness?"

Both lawyers shook their heads. There wasn't much they could say after their clients confessed to everything in front of the jury. Jade looked at her lawyer, who had a smug smile on his face, and she relaxed slightly. Samuel motioned for her to get off the stand, and she did as the room cleared.

Court was now in recess for deliberations and Samuel explained that they could break for lunch and hang around close to the court-house because he had a feeling that it wouldn't take long.

Once they were outside, Noah pulled Jade in for a hug and asked, "Are you okay?"

Jade was dazed by what had just happened, but she nodded slightly and said, "I just can't wait for this to be over."

Noah knew what she meant and said, "Me too. Let's go get you something to eat."

Together, they joined their friends and started the agonizing wait of the verdict of Elijah Willis and Yolanda Jenkins.

"WE, THE JURY, FIND THE DEFENDANTS GUILTY ON ALL charges," the man stated loudly into the microphone. The judge clanged his gravel, and court was adjourned. Jade sat still as everyone moved around her. Mia cried tears of joy along with Darlene and Anita. Noah and Kenyon clapped hands and gave each other a broth-erly hug.

Seeing that Jade was still sitting, Noah bent down and pulled her up into him. "It's finally over, baby."

Jade heard what he was saying, but she couldn't really process it. She was able to peek over Noah's shoulders and catch a glimpse of Elijah's parents, who were stomping out of the room, while Elijah glared menacingly at her and Noah as an officer handcuffed him. Jade pressed into Noah, taking comfort in his arms as Elijah stared her down. He better get used to those cuffs because he was going to prison for life without parole. Yolanda, on the other hand, had twenty years with the possibility of parole, but that was something Jade would worry about later. Much later, because for now, she was finally free. She never thought she would see the day that she was free from Elijah and no longer his wife, but it had come and it stunned her into silence from the invisible weight that was lifted off her shoulders.

Noah pulled back and looked Jade in the eyes, trying to gauge how she was feeling. "Are you okay?"

Jade nodded numbly and then staggered backwards as Mia pushed Noah aside and leapt into her friend's arms. Luckily, Jade's ankle was completely healed, and she had been feeling a lot more like herself the past few days. She could move around easier and those nasty bruises were finally gone. Of course, she still carried some scars that would never fully go away, but she was alive and thankful for that.

"That motherfucker will never see the light of day, Mouse. He's gone for good and he's going to die in that shitty ass prison. I hope that he gets raped every fucking night by the biggest man in there and I hope someone cuts off his—"

Kenyon interrupted Mia's tirade and said, "Okay, killer. Simmer down."

Jade chuckled at that, and then she was laughing uncontrollably. She finally felt as though she could breathe again, and she hadn't realized how much Elijah had been holding her back. She didn't have to hide anymore or constantly watch her back. She didn't have to worry about falling in love or never being able to be in a happy marriage. She could truly live freely now and that made her so fucking happy that she could only laugh. She looked up at Noah, who was smiling hesitantly at her, unsure if she was truly happy or having a mental breakdown.

She controlled her laughter enough to ask, "I'm free?"

Noah's smile grew as he nodded his head and gathered her in his arms again. "You're free, and tomorrow night I want to take you out on our first official date as boyfriend and girlfriend."

Jade was giddy as remembered that tomorrow was Valentine's Day. She knew that it would be a special occasion and there were no words to describe the excitement she felt at finally being able to give Noah her all and put Elijah behind them. She planted a kiss on Noah's lips right there in front of everyone. When she pulled back, she said, "It's a date."

The lights were dimmed, and candles sat in the middle of the table. Jade appreciated that Noah opted to sit next to her versus at the head of the other side of the table. She wanted to be near him so she could hold his hand or caress his cheek.

In typical Noah fashion, he had showered her with gifts from the moment that she woke up. From a large teddy bear that was bigger than her, to flowers and chocolate, he had done it all for her. Jade surprised him with a large painting of the two of them. She had started it before the attack and was happy that she could finish it in time, even with her broken fingers. It was a beautiful rendition of the date he took her on for her birthday. They were gazing into each other's eyes with the gorgeous sunset behind them. Noah got teary eyed when he saw it and wasted no time hanging it up above the fireplace in the living room.

Luckily, it was the weekend and Noah didn't have to work, so they had the whole day to spend together. Not that he had been at work much lately, anyway. Both he and Mia had been working from home since the incident, and Monday would be their first days back on the job. The only reason they were even going back on Monday was because they had interviews for another assistant. Without Yolanda there to pick up some slack, the job was much for Mia, especially since she still assisted Kenyon occasionally. Noah was also aware that Mia desperately wanted to be transferred over to the accounting team, so he wanted to get more people hired so he could make that happen for her.

Kenyon had been slacking off hard over the past month, but Noah made it clear that he needed to get back on his regular schedule starting Monday as well. Everyone suspected that the reason Kenyon didn't put up too much of a fight about that was because Mia would be going back to work, too. Those two had always been close, but over the past month they were inseparable. Both of them insisted that they were only friends, but Noah and Jade suspected that there was more to the story. Mia and Kenyon were currently spending their Valentine's Day together at the movies, and Jade teased Mia about it mercilessly all day until Mia threatened to stay home. That shut Jade up real quick because she knew that Noah wanted them to have the house to themselves tonight.

"I hope you don't mind staying in tonight. I tried making reservations elsewhere, but every damn restaurant in the state was booked," Noah said as he looked up from his plate of chocolate cake.

He had insisted that he cook dinner for Jade tonight since he couldn't take her out on a proper date. Their seafood feast had been amazing, and he'd baked a cake for dessert, even though he wasn't much of a baker. The cake turned out great, and it was moist and rich. The perfect way to top off their meal. Jade had already devoured her slice. She was full as hell and couldn't wipe the smile off her face.

Although they were still in the house, Jade still dressed up for the occasion. She wore some skintight black pants and a red silk top that showed off her cleavage. Her thigh-high boots completed the look, and Noah couldn't stop staring at her. She felt the same about him. He wasn't wearing one of his suits, but he was still dressed nicely in some black pants and a red button up.

Jade covered his hand with her bandaged one and said, "I don't mind. I'm just thankful to be with you. After everything...I just want us to be happy...together."

Jade blushed fiercely, suddenly shy. She felt as though she were treading into new territory. Noah was her man, and she could finally start talking about the future with him. It was surreal, but she welcomed the feeling.

Noah chuckled at her bashfulness and lifted her hand to his lips and kissed it. Jade made a face and said, "I can't wait until these casts are off. They aren't very sexy."

"On the contrary. I think you're are the most sexy woman I have ever met," Noah grinned.

Jade smiled back at him, and the love in heart overflowed. She owed this man everything. Hell, he was her everything and she couldn't keep it in any longer. She stared into his eyes and suddenly got emotional as she said, "Noah, I love you. I love you so much. I should have said it a long time ago, but my past was holding me back. I've loved you for a long time, now and I regret not saying it sooner."

Noah's heart swelled, and he couldn't keep the smile off his face. He'd planned on saying those very words to her tonight, but she beat him to it. His heart felt as though it was tap dancing against his ribcage as he said, "I love you too, Jade. Since the first time I saw you I knew I was a goner."

They chuckled, and Jade was so relieved that he felt the same way. She had known all along that Noah loved her, but it was something else completely to hear him say the words out loud. She couldn't keep the smile off her face as she reached up and caressed his face. Noah made a move to cover her hand with his, but Jade stood up quickly and said, "I have a surprise for you."

Taken aback by the change in subject, he responded, "Okay—"

"It's in your room, but give me five minutes to get it ready before coming up," Jade said before turning on her heels and heading for the stairs.

Noah sat back and shook his head with a grin as he watched her leave. He wasn't sure what was so urgent that couldn't wait until they were done professing their love for each other, but judging by the sparkle in her eye, Noah knew it would be worth it.

He finished his cake and cleared the dishes from the table before making his way up the stairs. In the hall he could hear soft music playing, causing him to become curious. He pushed the bedroom door open and his jaw damn near hit the floor. The lights were dimmed, and the same customized candles Noah got for Jade's birthday were lit through the room. There were rose petals on the bed and Jade was laying in the middle with a red, skimpy bra and panty set.

Noah's dick immediately stiffened, but he ignored it as he

cautiously walked over to the bed and asked, "Sweetheart, are you sure you're ready—"

"Yes," Jade responded before he could finish his sentence. The truth was, she had been ready for a while now. As terrible as it was, she was used to Elijah sexually abusing her. She had been cleared of any infections or STDs, so there wasn't anything holding them back from making love. Jade knew that Noah was nothing like Elijah, and she had been craving Noah's gentleness. She wanted to feel connected to him in that way again. She needed to feel his love physically and mentally. Noah made her feel things she had never experienced before, and she was ready to take it to the next level with him.

Noah still looked concerned as he gazed down at Jade. She was beautiful, and her lingerie left very little to the imagination. *Damn, I love her,* Noah thought as he fought to control his urges. Jade could see that Noah was hesitating, so she took matters into her own hands. She raised up on her knees and pulled Noah close to her before kissing him passionately. Jade ran her hands down his chest and then began unbuttoning his shirt. Noah pulled back slightly and Jade looked up into his eyes and said, "Noah Bennett, if you don't make love to me right now then I'll take my painting back and throw it in the fireplace."

Noah's eyes got wide as he chuckled at her statement. "You wouldn't dare."

Jade quirked an eyebrow up at him challengingly, and Noah smirked as he gave into his desires. He tore his shirt off, not bothering to undo the last few buttons, which skidded across the floor. Jade threw her arms around his neck and ignored the pain it caused from the sudden movement. She was too horny to let her slight aches stop her now. Noah pulled her shirt over head and then unsnapped her bra while she kissed his neck. He groaned in pleasure as he unzipped her pants and then gently pushed her back onto the bed, pulling them off.

All that was left were her panties, and he had special plans for those. Quickly pulling his undershirt, pants, and socks off, Noah discarded them on the floor and climbed on top of Jade, who was shivering with excitement. Noah kissed her sensually before looking in her eyes and saying, "Tell me again."

Jade smiled, knowing exactly what her man wanted. She licked her lips and said, "I love you."

Noah groaned and kissed her lightly on the lips before saying, "Again."

"Noah Bennett, I love you," Jade giggled.

Noah kissed her on the cheek and then moved to her neck where he sucked lightly, leaving a passion mark. He moved lower to her nipples, knowing that he was about to make her juices flow like the Nile River. He sucked one into his mouth, and Jade gasped loudly at the sensation. She rubbed the back of his head as he gently sucked and nibbled on her soft spot. She was so damn wet and ready to feel him inside of her, but Noah was taking his time. He wanted to savor her body and to explore every inch of it. He kept his hands on her chest and played with her nipples as he kissed his way down to her pussy. It was soaking through her panties, and Noah's mouth watered.

He gently kissed her clit through her panties, and it drove Jade wild. "Please, baby. Please!"

Noah heard her pleas and ignored them as he stuck his tongue out and let it rest on her clit through the panties. The warmth that his mouth created and the sensation of her nipples being rubbed in slow circles caused Jade to scratch at his arms. Noah smirked and knew he was torturing her, so to put her out of her misery, he took her thong in between his teeth and pulled down on it. Jade quickly lifted her bottom off the bed and Noah pulled her panties off before diving headfirst back into her pussy. Jade moaned loudly as her legs shook just from his first lick.

"Shit, Noah. I'm already doing to cum," she panted.

Noah slid his finger into her slick slit and said, "Cum for daddy."

Jade gripped the sheets and convulsed as the pent up juices ricocheted out of her womanhood. Holding her firmly in place, Noah didn't stop his assault until her body went limp. He quickly tugged off his boxers and slid into Jade, needed to feel the inside of her tight walls. They moaned together as Noah slowly rocked into her. Jade wrapped her short legs around his torso, giving him room to go deeper as she clung onto him. Tears welled up in her eyes and slid down her cheeks as she felt the love emanating from his body.

Never in her life had she been made love to so sweetly before, and it caused her emotions to overflow. Noah kissed away her tears and said, "I love you so much, Jade. I love you, baby."

"I—I love you too, Noah," Jade stammered as he hit her g-spot.

Jade could feel Noah's dick expanding inside of her as her own body quaked again. She held onto him tightly and professed her love to him repeatedly as they came together, Noah's seed spilling into her already slick pussy.

Once they came down from their orgasmic high, Noah went to the bathroom to get them towels to clean up with. When he returned, he smirked at Jade, who was dozing off. He gently cleaned her off and then crawled into bed before pulling her into his chest.

"I hope you know that you only have about twenty minutes to catch your nap before I'm inside of you again," Noah said arrogantly as he rubbed small circles in Jade's back.

Jade sleepily grinned into his chest with her eyes closed before saying, "Shut up, then, so I can get some energy back."

Noah chuckled and pulled her closer, silently thanking God for his second chance with Jade.

CHAPTER 25

"Ah, Jade. You made a killing tonight, hun," The volunteer smiled as Jade approached her table.

Jade grinned and grabbed her check excitedly and hastily said, "Thank you," before rushing off to find Mia who was standing by the doors.

"How'd you do, Chica?" Mia asked as Jade approached.

"Sold completely out," Jade smiled weakly at Mia.

"I knew you would," Mia replied as she patted Jade on the back. "Let's get you home. You're starting to look green again."

Jade simply nodded and headed out to the car where Tommy was waiting, thankful that she sold out so they didn't have to haul her paintings back to the car. She was exhausted, and she hadn't been feeling well all week. She almost cancelled her show today because she felt like she had the flu, but Mia convinced her to go. It was her first exhibit since the night of the attack, and it was time for her to get back to work. It was April now, so she had the past few months to get her collection up and it was time she started making money off all her hard work.

"I'm fine. I just want to get home and in bed," Jade said before having a coughing fit.

"Damn, Mouse. Keep that shit over there," Mia said as she scooted closer to the window and further away from Jade. "I can't wait until Noah gets back tonight."

"You and me both," Jade sighed as she leaned her head against the window.

Kenyon and Noah went to California a few days ago for an architect convention, so Mia and Jade had the house to themselves. Jade pretty much stayed cooped up in Noah's room while Mia would periodically check on her and bring her soup, which she couldn't keep down, and cold medicine that didn't seem to help. All Jade wanted to do was sleep, and that was exactly what she had been doing. It was a miracle that she had made it through her exhibit, but Mia was right by her side the whole time, making sure that she stayed hydrated and had everything she needed in order to make the event successful.

"Thanks for helping me out today," Jade said. "I really appreciate you. You're the best friend, ever."

Mia rolled her eyes playfully and replied, "Yeah, I know."

The two of them giggled and then settled in for the ride home. Jade ended up dozing off, and when Mia woke her, they were sitting in Noah's driveway and Darlene was sitting in her car parked next to them. Jade's head was pounding as she focused her eyes on Noah's mother and she smiled slightly. "I wonder what she's doing here?"

"I don't know," Mia said as she opened the door, "but let's get you inside."

"Thanks, Tommy," Jade said tiredly as she slowly got out of the car. She had completely healed from Elijah's assault, but this past week her body had been aching and she felt like she was reliving those injuries all over again.

By the time she made it to the front door, Darlene and Mia were patiently waiting for her to unlock it as they chatted happily. Darlene was holding a few bags in her hands and she was dressed down in some leggings and a long dress t-shirt. For an older woman, she was very stylish and fit for her age.

"Hey, Darlene. What brings you here this afternoon?" Jade asked as she unlocked the door.

"Hey, baby," Darlene smiled as she leaned in and gave Jade a hug. "Noah told me you were sick, and I thought I'd better come and check up on you."

"That's so sweet of you," Jade said as they stepped into the house and removed their jackets. "I'm afraid I probably won't be much company, though. All I want to do is crawl into bed and sleep."

"That's okay, baby. I'm going to make you some soup and I have some of my homemade tea here I'll heat up for you. I'll wake you up when it's ready. You need to try to eat something," Darlene chided.

Jade's stomach flopped at the mention of having to eat something, but she smiled anyway and thanked the older woman. "I'm going to head up to bed, but come in any time. Thanks again."

"Yeah, thank you, because I've been working like a slave taking care of her," Mia said dramatically.

Darlene snickered and said, "Don't mention it," as she made her way towards the kitchen with Mia following close behind.

Jade went up to Noah's room and opted to turn on the TV that was in there so that she could try to stay awake. She didn't want to have to wake up once she went to sleep, so she turned on the new Tyler Perry movie that was on Netflix called *A Fall from Grace* and got comfortable. Luckily, the movie was interesting, and she was so into it that she didn't dare fall asleep. Darlene walked in right at the plot twist and smiled at Jade, who was engrossed in the TV.

"You're still up?" Darlene asked as she sat a tray of food and drinks on the nightstand.

Jade paused the movie and looked at the older woman with a soft smile and said, "Yeah. I'll probably be asleep for the night once I finally fall asleep, so I wanted to try to stay awake for you. I really appreciate all this."

Darlene waved her off as she busied herself with the tray of food. "It's nothing, child. Forgive me if I'm being too forward, but the thought of your mother not being here to do these things for you upsets me and...well...I have some space in my life for another child to take care of."

A lump instantly formed in Jade's throat, and she caught Darlene's hand to stop her from lifting the lid off the soup. Jade cleared her throat and said, "Please, sit for a second."

Darlene obliged and perched herself on the edge of the bed. Jade blinked away her tears, trying to plan what she would say to Darlene. She had been so kind to her ever since they'd met, and Jade found it hard to believe at times. She realized that living with Elijah for so long and being isolated from society had skewed her outlook on social interaction, and like Noah, Darlene showed Jade what good hearted human beings are like. She wasn't used to it, but she was grateful. Darlene had become the only mother figure she had in her life, and the love she felt for the woman was unmatched. She wasn't sure how to convey her gratitude, so she took a deep breath and started talking, letting her heart lead the way.

"For a little while I blamed myself for what happened to Roman—"

"No," Darlene interrupted sternly. "None of that was your fault. If I had known you were blaming yourself, I would have talked to you about it. The people that are responsible are behind bars."

Jade nodded and waited until Darlene finished before she continued. "I know that now, although there are still some days where that guilty feeling tries to creep its way back in, but I know that it wasn't my fault. I blamed myself for a while, though. I was so sure that you would hate me, but you never did. I just want you to know that your good heart and kindness have gotten me through the most rough times of my life. Mostly by extension of Noah. Your good nature passed on to him, Darlene. He is the most selfless man I have ever met, and it's because you and his father raised him right. I love him so much. He has given me a sense of purpose again, and he has given me a family. That's something I never thought I would experience again, but because of him I have Kenyon, the brother I never wanted."

Both women giggled at that and Jade continued, "and for a short time I had Roman and I've also gained you. I guess what I'm trying to say is that I have space in my life for a mother to love."

Darlene allowed her tears to spill over as she regarded Jade before pulling her into a hug. Jade rested her head on Darlene's shoulder and gave into her comforting spirit. It wasn't long before Jade fell into a coughing fit, and the two separated. Darlene clucked her tongue and stood quickly to grab the tray. Jade laid back and allowed Darlene to fuss over her for the next hour. As Jade suspected, the soup didn't stay down, and she barely made it to the bathroom before vomit was spewing out of her mouth. Darlene helped her get back in bed, and it wasn't long before sleep claimed Jade.

***

When she woke again, sun was flitting through the blinds. Jade squinted against the light and groaned as she rolled over. Her body was covered in sweat, and she somehow felt worse than she had yesterday. Her eyes widened when she saw Noah staring down at her in concern with his head propped on his arm. Jade smiled up at him, despite her pounding head and upset stomach.

"I would ask you for a kiss, but I don't want you to catch this flu," Jade whispered hoarsely.

Noah reached over and put the back of his hand to her forehead and his brows furrowed even further. "I'm taking you to urgent care."

Jade giggled lightly and said, "I've missed you, too."

"I'm sorry, Sweetheart. I've missed you. I just didn't realize how sick you were," Noah responded lovingly.

"It's just the flu, baby. I'll be fine," Jade said before having a coughing fit.

"That may be the case, but I'm still taking you to urgent care," Noah chided as he got out of bed.

He walked around and pulled the blankets off Jade and then lifted her out of bed. She giggled softly and said, "I can walk, you know?"

"Hush," Noah said as he carried her to the bathroom. "I'll run you a bath when we get home, but for now get in the shower and get dressed. I'll go get you some orange juice and toast."

Jade grimaced, "No toast."

"You have to eat—"

"It'll only come right back up," Jade warned.

Noah sighed and said, "Fine," before heading out of the bathroom.

Jade stopped him by putting her hand on his arm and asking, "You aren't going to shower?"

Noah turned and said, "My flight was delayed last night, so I only got in a couple hours ago. I showered before I got in the bed, but I will take a bath with you later."

He winked and then left the room, leaving Jade to her own devices. She peeled off her damp shirt and discarded it into the hamper before turning on the shower and adjusting the temperature. Just as she was going to step in, a wave of nausea hit her and she bent over to toilet and heaved. There was nothing in her stomach, so she only dry heaved for a few moments before the nausea passed. She sighed and begrudgingly got in the shower, hoping that she would start feeling better soon so she could get back to living her life like a normal person. She hated being confined to Noah's room and lying around in bed all day.

Once she finished with her shower, she brushed her teeth and redid her messy bun so she looked more presentable before going back into the bedroom and getting dressed in some sweatpants and a hoodie. She felt like death, and she knew she looked just as bad. Walking down to the kitchen, she realized that she had eaten nothing in four days. Suddenly, she was happy Noah was making her go to urgent care. She needed to make sure that nothing more serious was at hand.

Noah turned in his chair when he saw her enter the kitchen. He had made himself some eggs and toast and his mouth was full when he asked, "You ready?"

Jade nodded, noticing that Noah had dressed similar to her in sweatpants and a hoodie. He rarely dressed down like this, but Jade loved when he did. Despite feeling like shit, Jade licked her lips at Noah and smiled before responding, "Yeah, but take your time and eat."

Noah nodded and shoveled more food into his mouth. Jade's stomach flopped at the smell of the food, but she sat next to him, anyway. "Damn, when was the last time you ate, baby?"

"That airport food was shit," Noah responded in between mouthfuls of food. "And by the time I was hungry enough to eat it anyway, it was too late and everything was closed."

Jade giggled, "Awww, poor baby."

Noah grunted and took a large bite of some eggs, and Jade's stomach roiled. She scooted away from him a bit with a grimace on her face as she tried to keep her stomach at ease. She covered her nose with her hand and asked, "Where are Mia and Kenyon?"

"Downstairs asleep. They're on the couch all cuddled up together," Noah chuckled. "They must have fallen asleep watching a movie."

Jade's eyes got big, and she was thankful for the excuse to get away from the kitchen. She stood up from her chair and said, "I have to see this."

Noah nodded once, too engrossed in his food to notice that Jade had left the room in a hurry. She felt she could finally breathe once she was out of the kitchen and couldn't smell his eggs or slightly burnt toast. She would never understand why he enjoyed eating his toast like that, but it was one of those quirks she loved about him.

Jade quietly walked down the stairs to the basement and squinted as her eyes adjusted to the dim room. On the couch, Kenyon was lying on his back using his arm as a pillow while the other one was wrapped securely around Mia's waist. Mia's hair was splayed wildly over Kenyon's chest and draped over his arm. She was lying on her stomach with one of her arms resting on his chest and the other one holding onto his bicep. Their legs were intertwined, and they both had pajamas on.

Jade smirked at the site and knew that she would tease Mia about it mercilessly later on. Both Mia and Kenyon swore up and down that they were only friends, but Noah and Jade knew better. Just like Kenyon and Mia knew that Noah and Jade had a thing for one another when they first met. Kenyon hadn't been bringing any girls around anymore, and his phone didn't go off every five minutes with a different chick each time, either. Noah told Jade that the three of them didn't even go to lunch together anymore. Somehow, Mia and Kenyon had started going to lunch together, just the two of them, leaving him out. They'd stopped bickering so much, and their interactions were becoming more flirty by the day. It was cute, in Jade's opinion. She was sure that they were so adamant about only being friends because they didn't want to disrespect Roman in any way, and Jade knew that she would have to have a talk about that with her best friend really soon.

Jade grabbed a large throw blanket from the guest room and put it over them. It was cold in the basement and although they had each other to keep warm, she saw the goosebumps on Mia's arms. When she was finished, she made her way back upstairs and waited patiently in the living room for Noah to finish his breakfast. It didn't take long. Only a few minutes later he strolled into the living room and said, "Okay, baby. I'm ready."

Jade nodded and then sighed as she stood up from her comfortable position on the couch. She was so damn tired and she honestly could have gone back to bed if she didn't have to go to the doctor. Noah helped her out of the house and opened the car door for her. Jade was used to him worrying over her by now. Since she had come home from the hospital, he took extra care to make sure she was okay at all times. Jade found it overbearing at first, but she realized that Noah had probably been just as traumatized that night as her. Especially seeing Jade beaten so badly and witnessing his brother lying in a pool of blood. She knew that being overprotective of her was his love language and she reminded herself of that daily.

Noah took off towards the nearest urgent care office as soon as they were buckled in. He watched out of the corner of his eyes as Jade dozed off again and his worry heightened. He knew what the flu looked like, and although she was exhibiting symptoms of the illness, it seemed to be getting worse and not better. The flu normally only lasted a week at most, and Jade was at about five days since she started feeling sick with no sign of getting better.

Traffic was shitty, as usual, so it took him about forty-five minutes to get to the clinic. He unbuckled his seatbelt before getting out of the car and running to Jade's side to wake her up. He opened the door and kissed her forehead, alarmed by how warm she was. "Hey, baby. Wake up. We're here."

Jade's eyes fluttered open as focused on Noah. His eyes were brimming with concern, and she smiled weakly up at him. "Stop worrying. I'm fine."

"You don't look fine, sweetheart," Noah said as he unbuckled her seatbelt and helped her out of the car.

Jade's whole body ached, and she walked slower than normal as they made their way inside the clinic. To Noah's relief, it was close to empty, and it looked like they would be seen right away. Jade checked herself in and just as they were about to sit down in the waiting area, a nurse came out and said, "Jade?"

Jade smiled and followed the nurse to the back, with Noah following closely behind.

"How are you today, Jade?" The cheery nurse asked. She was a pretty woman with thick black hair piled on top of her head and striking green eyes.

"I could be better," Jade responded as they rounded a corner.

"I'm sorry you aren't feeling well, hun. I'll just grab your height, and weight before getting you settled in a room. I'm Laura, by the way."

They stopped at a weighing station and Laura instructed Jade to step against the wall so she could take her height. Next, she took her weight and Jade belatedly realized that she was down to one hundred and fifteen pounds. Her normal weight was consistently around one hundred and twenty pounds, so she knew that the past few days had caused the decrease. There was literally nothing left in her stomach. It had all come out of one end or the other and she felt hollow on the inside.

"Okay, Jade. We will be right in here. Is this your husband?" Laura asked as she sat her clipboard on the desk next to the chairs where Noah and Jade were getting situated.

Jade blushed and said, "Oh, no. He's my boyfriend."

"For now," Noah said happily. Jade's blush grew as she grinned up at him before laying her head against his arm. She just couldn't get rid of the sleepiness.

"Alright, then," Laura smiled brightly at the lovebirds. "Jade, tell me about your symptoms."

It took Jade a moment to tell Laura how she had been feeling the few days. Laura listened intently and tapped away on her keyboard as she entered notes into the computer before she asked Jade the standard questions for patients that visited the clinic. Once they were finished, Laura took Jade's blood pressure and temperature.

"Wow, one hundred and three degrees," Laura tsked. "You're definitely sick, hun. I'll have the doctor come in and he will run some tests to make sure it's nothing more than the flu."

"Thank you," Jade said weakly.

"No worries, hun. Feel better soon," Laura said as she stood up and left the room.

Noah put his arm around Jade who was still resting on him and pulled her closer. "Poor baby."

Jade snuggled up to him and relished in the comfort of his body. She loved being in his arms, and it somehow made her feel ten times better. She was about to tell him as much when there was a knock at the door followed by an older Asian man walking in the room.

"Hello, I'm Dr. Wong," he said as he shook each of their hands.

"Nice to meet you," Jade said. "I'm Jade and this is my boyfriend, Noah."

"Nice to meet you both. Jade, I hear you aren't feeling too well?"

Jade shook her head and Noah said, "She's been sick for about five days now and hasn't been able to keep any food down for four of them."

"Alright. I'll just do some blood tests and we'll see if there is anything more going on that a common cold or the flu, okay?"

"Sounds good," Jade said.

"Great," Dr. Wong said as he went to the cabinets and pulled out the supplies he needed to draw Jade's blood.

Jade hated needles, so she snuggled closer into Noah and stuck her arm out for Dr. Wong. He gently cleaned the area where her vein was sticking out before inserting a needle and filling up a few vials.

"Alright, Jade. All finished. I will get these to the lab, and it shouldn't take long for the results. We're a bit slow today so I should be back in here shortly," Dr. Wong smiled warmly at the couple.

"Thank you," Jade said as she watched him leave the office.

Jade stayed with her head buried in Noah's chest and before long, his rhythmic breathing lulled her to sleep. She woke up again when Dr. Wong knocked on the door and entered the room. Again, he smiled warmly at the couple before sitting down in the chair next to Jade.

"It seems that you do have a bad case of the flu, but there's more."

Worried, Jade sat up straight in her seat and Noah shifted in his seat beside her and asked, "What's wrong with her?"

"She's pregnant," Dr. Wong replied kindly.

Noah and Jade both blinked at him, trying to comprehend what he had just said. It was Jade who spoke first. In a dazed voice she asked, "I'm pregnant?"

"Yes, you are," Dr. Wong said. "We won't know how far along you are until you go in for an ultrasound, but judging by the blood work it appears you are around eight weeks."

Jade was in shock, but Noah finally comprehended what was being said and let out a loud gleeful laugh. "I'm going to be a daddy!"

A slow smile appeared on Jade's face as she turned to look at Noah, who was practically bouncing in his seat. Tears brimmed Jade's eyes and Noah quickly pulled her in for a hug. "Those better be happy tears."

Jade laughed as the tears fell and said, "They are."

"Good," Noah said, relieved.

Dr. Wong's voice interrupted their moment as he said, "I'll send you two home with some parenting brochures and we can make your appointment for your ultrasound now. As for your flu, I need you to stop taking cold medications because they can be harmful to the baby. I'll prescribe some anti-nausea medication that should help. Be sure to drink plenty of liquids and try to eat when you can. I know it's hard, but your body will work the sickness out. It just might take a little longer without the help of cold medication."

Jade took his words in and despite how she was feeling, she felt on top of the world. She and Noah had talked about kids plenty of times, and they both wanted them. They hadn't planned for a pregnancy now, but that didn't sway their happiness. Noah accepted the pamphlets from Dr. Wong and they made an appointment for an ultrasound for two weeks out and they were on their way. Neither of them could keep the smiles off their face as they drove home, in awe of the sudden turn of events.

CHAPTER 26

Noah coughed loudly before blowing his nose while Jade looked on with puppy dog eyes. They had just gotten back from the ultrasound appointment and Noah was in bed resting. The appointment had gone really well and Jade couldn't believe how fast the last couple of weeks went. The days kind of blurred together as her, and Noah had spent most of them in bed. Jade was finally over the flu and now she only got random bouts of nausea because of the pregnancy, but she had unfortunately passed the flu on to Noah. Luckily, the baby was healthy, and they confirmed that she was eleven weeks pregnant and already almost out of her first trimester. She wasn't showing at all, but the doctor assured her that was normal and that in her second trimester she would start to see a difference in her body.

She got set up with regular check-ups leading up to the birth of their baby. Her due date was November sixteenth, and it was already May, but Jade felt like there was so much to do to prepare. Noah told her not to worry about it and that he had everything under control, but Jade wanted everything to be perfect for their baby. They needed to get a nursery together and buy a crib, stroller, car seat, and clothes. That wasn't even touching on the other little things they needed to buy. She felt overwhelmed, and Noah worked daily to keep her mind at ease and stress free.

Jade climbed in bed and rubbed his back slowly as she smiled down at him. "Is there anything I can get you?"

"No, but you can get out of here so you don't get sick again," Noah grumbled.

Jade laughed. "We are constantly around each other. It doesn't matter at this point. If I'm going to get sick again, there isn't much we can do to stop it unless you want me to move out—"

"No," Noah blurted out.

"That's what I thought. Now, get some rest. I'll be right here if you need me," Jade whispered.

"Thank you, my love," Noah said sincerely.

"Of course. Are you sure you don't want me to cancel the plans tonight?"

"I'm sure. I'm honestly feeling a lot better. I can actually keep food down now. It's just this damn cough that won't go away," Noah grimaced.

"Okay...if you're sure," Jade replied apprehensively as she sifted through the mail that she grabbed on their way in.

A letter caught her eye and her breath caught in her throat. In a shaky voice, she called Noah's name. Hearing her tone, Noah turned over quickly and looked at Jade in alarm. She was gripping an envelope in her hands and they were shaking slightly as she slowly handed it to him. Noah sat up and grabbed the envelope from her, and his stomach dropped at the name scrawled across the envelope. It was from Yolanda.

"I'm not opening this shit," Noah said angrily, getting ready to rip the letter to pieces.

Jade placed a hand over his to stop him and said, "Wait. Maybe we should see what it says? I have been curious about why she did what she did...maybe this can give us some sense of closure?"

"Jade, the woman is a psychopath just like Elijah. There will be nothing in this letter that will give us closure."

"Maybe, but maybe she can give us some answers…I don't know," Jade whispered. That night was such a sore topic for the both of them, and rightfully so. They had dealt with the events that occurred, but there would always be lingering questions that nobody could answer, really. Why did it happen, or why did Roman have to die? Still, Jade was curious to know why Yolanda hated her so much that she wanted to have her killed.

Noah sighed and said, "Fine, but I'm calling our lawyer and making sure that she can't send us anything else. We were so damn focused on making sure Elijah couldn't have any contact that we let Yolanda slither by."

Jade nodded, acknowledging what he said as she ripped open the envelope and handed Noah the letter. He scooted over closer to Jade, and they silently read the short letter.

My Beloved Noah,

It has taken me some time to work up the courage to write this letter to you. I keep imagining how livid you must be with me and I wanted to explain myself. I have been in love with you since the first time I laid eyes on you, and that wasn't when I interviewed to be your assistant, either. I can get into that another time, if you'd like. What I'm trying to say is that I love you, Noah. I always have, and I know that we have a connection. I patiently waited for you to give me some indication that you were ready to be in a relationship. I was too scared to make the first move because I knew all about your rule of not dating employee's, but I knew you would eventually come around. Then that bitch Jade showed up looking like a homeless whore and I don't know how she trapped you, but she did. I knew I needed to save you from her, so I did some digging and found out the slut was married. There were so many times I wanted to tell you that she was a married woman, but I wanted to get you proof, so I contacted Elijah myself. He convinced me that he could get rid of Jade and that you would be all mine once everything was said and done. I had no idea I was dealing with a psychopath, Noah. You have to believe me. Your brother was never supposed to die.

Hell, Mia was never even supposed to be hurt. Jade was the only one
that was supposed to die a slow and painful death. Elijah tricked me,
Noah. You have to believe me. I would never do anything to hurt you,
and I only wanted to set you free from Jade's grasp. Can't you see that
she was only using you? What kind of woman would have a husband
at home and string a loving man like you along? She isn't the one for
you. I am. It's always been me. I know I'm in here for a long time, but
with good behavior they could release me early. I only hope that you
will write back and come see me from time to time. Knowing that I
have you waiting for me when I get out will get me through this hellish
nightmare. Please, Noah. Forgive me.
Love Always,
Yolanda

Noah and Jade stared at the letter in complete silence long after
they read it. Neither of them had any idea how delusional Yolanda
was prior to reading this letter. Jade opened her mouth to ask if there
was any reason Yolanda would feel the way she did, when Noah
shook his head. He knew what she was going to ask before she even
asked it, and it was because he was asking himself the same thing.

"No. There was nothing that I said or did to that woman to make
her believe that I was into her. I'm sure of it. Until you came along, I
had a very strict rule about dating employees, and I had even fired a
handful of them because they tried it. I was very upfront with
Yolanda about her place in the office and my place as her boss. No
lines were crossed. Ever."

Jade nodded her head and relaxed back into the pillows. "Well, I
guess that answers that. Make sure you call Samuel and make the
same arrangements with her as we did with Elijah."

Noah grabbed his cellphone from the nightstand and started
tapping away. "Already on it."

When he finished, he placed his phone back on the nightstand
and gathered Jade in his arms. "I love you, baby."

Jade smiled. "I love you, too."

"I promise to alway make you and our baby happy," he grinned.

"You already do that and so much more. You will be an amazing father," Jade smiled into his chest as she breathed in his scent.

"And you will be an amazing mother," Noah said as he rubbed her flat stomach.

"Get some rest, babe. We have a big night ahead of us," Jade smiled anxiously.

"That we do. Wake me up in two hours so we can get to the restaurant on time," Noah said, and then he kissed Jade on the forehead and rolled over to catch a nap.

Jade sifted through the rest of the mail, glad that her forwarding address was finally working. She and Noah had officially moved in together a month ago, but her mail was still being sent to her old apartment. It was finally coming to Noah's place, and it was one less thing Jade had to worry about. Setting Noah's mail aside, she grabbed her phone and went on Pinterest, her new favorite app. She browsed for two full hours looking at pregnancy announcements, baby room ideas, and even first birthday decorations. She was obsessed with the little human taking up residence inside of her, and thoughts of meeting her baby constantly ran through her mind. She couldn't wait to meet her child, but first, she had to wake their daddy up so they could get ready to tell their family and friends the good news.

THE RESTAURANT WAS FANCY AS HELL, AND JADE WONDERED why Noah had picked this specific one. When she asked him, he let her know that it was his mother's favorite place to eat. "Don't worry. It's fancy as hell but the food is delicious."

He didn't have to say any more than that. Jade was starving and couldn't wait to eat. Her appetite was weird as hell these days. She was either nauseous and throwing up, or she was starving. There was no in between. Noah led her over to the table where Darlene, Kenyon, and Mia were already seated.

"Hey, everyone," Jade smiled. "Sorry we're late. Noah didn't want to get up."

She grumbled that last part and rolled her eyes as she sat down. Noah laughed and said, "Don't mind her. She's just hungry."

Mia, who was sitting across from Jade and next to Kenyon, picked up a warm dinner roll from the basket in the middle of the table and threw it on Jade's plate. "I know how you get when you're hangry and I don't got time for that tonight."

Jade happily took the roll and buttered it, ignoring Mia completely. Everyone else chuckled at their antics as the waitress approached their table.

"Good evening, can I get you two anything to drink?" she asked politely.

"I'm fine with water," Jade said around a mouthful of bread.

"I'll have an iced tea with lemon, please," Noah responded.

The waitress quickly walked away to grab their drinks. Darlene turned to look at her son beside her and asked, "How are you feeling?"

"I'm better, mom. This cough just won't go away," Noah responded.

"I'm happy to hear you're doing better, but you could have stayed home, son. We could have rescheduled," Darlene said in concern.

"That's what I said," Jade piped in as she started in on her second dinner roll.

Noah nudged her and said, "No, mama. It's okay. Besides, Jade and I have some news."

"Oh! Are we doing this now?" Jade asked as she stuffed the rest of her roll in her mouth.

"Doing what?" Kenyon asked in confusion, and Mia's eyes lit up.

"Oh my God! You're getting married! Oh, my God! I knew it! I can't wait to plan your wedding. We have to set up an appointment for dress shopping and I know the perfect venue and—"

"Mia!" Jade interrupted what was sure to be a long rant.

"What?" Mia asked, startled.

"We aren't getting married," Jade blushed, embarrassed.

"Oh, God. I'm sorry, Mouse. I just thought..." Mia sagged back in her seat as color rose into her own cheeks.

"It's fine, Mia. It'll happen eventually," Noah chuckled as he winked at Mia.

Mia's eyes lit up again, and she rested her elbows on the table and leaned forward again. Everyone focused on Noah and Jade as Noah tried to find the right words to say. Jade knew he was over thinking it and she rolled her eyes impatiently before blurting out, "I'm pregnant!"

There was a stunned silence before everyone started talking at once.

"Oh my fucking God!"

"Yo, bro! Congrats!"

"I'm going to be a grandma!"

Jade laughed as everyone congratulated them. Mia had tears in her eyes as she stood up and walked around the table. She reached down and hugged her best friend. They hadn't even known each other a year, but the two had been through so much together and their bond was unmatched. Mia marveled at how Jade was thriving after only a few short months ago being homeless. There were nights when they didn't even think they would survive the cold, and here they were living their lives the best they knew how. She was elated for her friend, and the tears that fell from her eyes were of pure joy.

"I'm so happy for you," Mia whispered in her ear.

"Thanks, Mimi. I hope you're ready to be an auntie."

Mia pulled back and gazed into Jade's eyes with a smile. "You bet your ass I am. I hope you're okay with having a spoiled child."

Jade laughed, "Oh, lord."

"Oh, lord is right!" Mia giggled as she sauntered back to her seat.

"Jade, honey. How have you been feeling?" Darlene asked as she wiped her eyes with a napkin. It overjoyed her that her son was starting a family and Jade was already like family to her. This was the best news she heard all year and she couldn't wait to spoil her grandbaby rotten. She only wished her husband and Roman were here to join in on the celebration.

"Since I got over the flu I've been feeling a lot better," Jade responded. "I'm nauseous a lot of the time but I found these anti-nausea suckers that work wonders."

"Good, baby. Good. Y'all make sure you take care of each other, you hear me? This baby will change your lives and you will need to support each other through parenthood."

"Yes ma'am," Jade said while Noah grabbed his mother's hand and squeezed it.

"You don't have to worry about that, mama," Noah said.

Darlene smiled up at her son and nodded her head. As many storms as she and her son had been through, the blessings that were coming their way almost made it all worth it. Noah and Jade's children would carry on the Bennett bloodline, and that made Darlene proud. She knew that Murphy was looking down with a big smile on his face, too. Their legacy would live on, and Darlene couldn't be more proud of her son in this moment.

They spent the rest of the night talking about the baby. Mia and Kenyon shared their favorite baby names and when Noah and Jade vetoed them, insisted they would call the baby that regardless of what they said. Mia volunteered to plan the baby shower and Darlene said that she would go shipping the very next day for the baby. Both Noah and Jade were grateful to everyone, and by the time they got home, Jade felt as though a weight had been lifted from her shoulders. As she finally laid down in Noah's arms for the night, she realized that the relief she was feeling was because of everyone's willingness to help out. The saying was true...it takes a village to raise a baby.

CHAPTER 27

THE SUMMER WAS IN FULL SWING AND JADE WAS HOT ALL THE damn time. Her doctor wasn't lying when she said that Jade would start showing soon. Now, she was nearing the end of her second trimester and heading into her third, and she felt like she was bigger than a whale. Most people found her protruding stomach on her small frame adorable, but Jade felt uncomfortable all the time and she was ready to meet the tiny human that was holding her body hostage so she could start feeling like herself again.

The morning sickness hadn't went away and Jade felt like she had been sleeping her life away for the past several months. Pregnancy hadn't been very kind to her and it wasn't glamorous, either, but Jade wouldn't trade it for anything. Every time she felt her baby kick, it reminded her of the blessing that lived inside of her. She never thought she would be a mother, and she was in awe every day that her deepest desire was coming true. In three short months she would meet her baby and it was still surreal to her.

Noah spent most of his time working from home so he could take care of Jade. When he couldn't, he would make sure that Mia was there. He made sure that his woman was comfortable at all times and he tried to make sure she wasn't stressing, but that wasn't an easy task. She became more and more anxious every day because they still hadn't gotten the nursery together and there was so much they needed to do to prepare for the baby. Noah assured her that he had it all under control, but Jade wasn't sure he was taking it as seriously as he should have been.

The upstairs guest room across from Mia's bedroom would serve as the baby's room, and it still looked the same as it did when Jade slept in there over Christmas. She was getting frustrated that Noah was being so nonchalant about making a comfortable space for their baby, but for today, she would put that aside and have fun. They were finally finding out the gender of their stubborn baby today, and nothing could steal Jade's happiness.

They should have found out months ago, but every time they went into an ultrasound, the baby had their legs crossed tight. As soon as they would leave the appointment, disappointed as hell, Jade could feel the baby stretch out. It always caused Noah to laugh, but Jade's pregnancy hormones didn't find the humor in the situation. When they went in for their checkup a few days ago, the nurse did a surprise ultrasound and could see the baby's gender. She wrote it down on a piece of paper and Noah gave it over to Mia so she could do a gender reveal for them, much to Jade's dismay. This pregnancy made her emotional, irritable, and impatient as hell as she didn't want to wait until the party, but Mia insisted.

Today was finally the day, and Jade could barely sit still, she was so excited. She finished putting the final touches on her makeup in the bathroom and smiled in the mirror. It had been months since she did her makeup and got dressed up, and she felt good. She had went back to Red's salon and got her hair blown out so it reached the middle of her back. It bounced every time she moved her head, and she loved running her fingers through it.

Since she was constantly so hot, she opted to wear a purple halter top sundress that Noah bought her. It showcased her baby bump and since it was all about her baby today; she was happy to do just that, even though she knew people were about to drive her crazy touching her stomach all afternoon.

Jade went into the bedroom and sat on the bed. Noah walked in the room just as Jade was trying to put her sandals on and smiled. "Let me help you with those."

"I can't wait to get my body back," Jade grumbled as she gave up trying to put her sandal on around her huge stomach. "How do I still have three more months of this? My stomach can't grow anymore."

Noah chuckled and grabbed her sandals off the floor before bending down to put them on her swollen feet. "Three months will go by quickly and in no time you'll be missing your baby bump."

"I doubt it," Jade said as she scrunched up her nose.

Suddenly, her baby kicked her in the ribcage, and she winced before looking down at her belly. "Really? You're gonna kick your mommy where it hurts most, huh?"

Noah laughed as he finished putting her shoes on. He stood up and palmed her stomach, and the baby instantly calmed down. Jade's brows furrowed as she talked to her belly. "Traitor."

"Hey, leave my baby alone. She's a daddy's girl, that's all," Noah said proudly.

Jade arched her brow at him and asked, "Girl, huh?"

Noah nodded. "Yeah, I always wanted a little girl."

Jade held her hands up to him and Noah grabbed them and pulled her up from the bed before pulling her in for a kiss. Jade melted in his embrace and kissed Noah back passionately. He always knew how to calm her down when she was getting too crabby or if she was in a pregnancy funk. He had this way with her that nobody else could master, but what Jade didn't comprehend was that Noah loved her so much, he would do anything to keep her happy. In his mind, he had to learn the ins and outs of her mind to master her heart. He had done exactly that, and the two grew more in love as each day passed.

Noah pulled away and smiled down at Jade, who had a peaceful look on her face. He smirked, knowing that he accomplished exactly what he set out to do...calm his pregnant girlfriend down.

The doorbell rang and Jade smiled up at Noah when she heard Mia yelling in the halls for them to get downstairs. Luckily, the party was being held at their house and the only people coming were Darlene and Kenyon. Mia was already there, and she had decorated the whole living room in pink and blue, complete with a cake and food.

When Noah and Jade made it downstairs, Darlene and Kenyon were in the living room chatting with Mia. Everyone turned as they entered and there was a collective *awww* as they took in Jade's appearance. They had gotten used to her dressing in leggings and sweatpants paired with Noah's baggy shirts and her hair in a messy bun at the top of her head. Today, she was glowing. Mia was the first one to run over and palm her stomach, talking to it in baby voices like she did every day. Jade's eyes lifted towards the sky as Mia continued on for several moments before Kenyon nudged her out of the way.

"Cut that shit out, Mimi," He laughed.

"Thanks, Kenyon," Jade grinned at him.

"Any time, sis," he replied as he hugged her.

"Y'all are not going to keep me from talking to my niece or nephew," Mia scoffed.

Noah intervened before the three of them got to arguing. He angled himself towards Mia and said, "Mia, let's not get Jade in one of her moods."

Noah looked at her pointedly and Mia sighed, "You're right."

"You know I can hear you two, right?" Jade grumbled from behind them.

"And?" Mia asked playfully.

Darlene stepped up to Jade and wrapped her arms around her protectively and said, "Alright, now. Y'all leave my baby alone."

Everyone did what they were told and dispersed around the room. Kenyon went straight for the food while Mia started taking pictures of everyone on her phone. Darlene and Jade sat on the couch and Noah joined Kenyon at the food table to make his girl a plate.

Jade was too eager to eat, so when Noah handed her a plate she looked at Mia and asked, "When can we cut the cake?"

"Damn," Mia rolled her eyes to the ceiling. "You're so impatient these days. If it'll make you happy, we can cut it now."

Jade's eyes lit up, and she grinned. "Really?"

"Yes. Really," Mia mimicked Jade's tone and Jade laughed gleefully.

Noah sat the plate he was making down and watched as Mia waddled over to the pink and blue frosting covered cake. He joined her and held her waist while she grabbed the knife, and everyone crowded around them.

"Wait!" Mia yelled as Jade made a move to cut the cake that would reveal the gender of their baby. "Don't cut it yet! Let me get a few more pictures."

Jade groaned as Mia made her and Noah pose for some pictures. Noah grinned through it all, enjoying the celebration, but after a while, he knew Jade was about to combust from irritation so he said, "Alright, Mia. Can we cut the cake, now?"

"Okay, okay. Go ahead!" She squealed.

Jade wasted no time. She lifted the knife and cut a perfect piece of the cake and lifted it out onto the plate that Noah was holding. Everyone clapped at the blue frosting that was perfectly piped inside the cake.

"It's a boy!" Jade squealed as she jumped in Noah's arms, causing him to drop cake on the floor. He didn't care. In that moment, all that mattered was that he was having a son with the most precious person he had ever met. Tears welled in his eyes and he tried to keep them at bay as he hugged Jade tightly.

Jade pulled back and kissed him on the lips, overwhelmed with joy. Her life was absolutely perfect in this moment, and she couldn't wait to meet her baby boy.

Mia wrapped Jade up in a hug, followed by Kenyon and Darlene, each of them making it clear that now that they knew the sex of the baby they were going to go wild at the baby stores.

"Your baby shower is going to be off the chain," Mia grinned. "I already have plans for it and—"

"Can we focus on one event at a time, Mimi? I'm tired just thinking about it," Jade whined.

"Girl, shut up. You know you won't have to plan a damn thing. I got you, Mouse."

Jade grinned. "I know you do, Mia. Thanks for everything."

"Don't mention it, babe," Mia winked at her and then went for the food table, ready to relax and enjoy the fruits of all of hard work. Jade was ready to dig into her plate now, but Noah had other plans for her. Just as she made a move to grab her plate, Noah stopped her.

"I have a surprise for you," Noah whispered in her ear.

"A surprise?" Jade smiled, wondering what Noah was up to.

"Yup, but we have to leave here. Grab your plate and let's go," Noah grinned.

Caught off guard by his statement, Jade eyed him curiously, but did what she was told. Noah grabbed her hand and then told everyone they would be back shortly. Jade thought it was strange that nobody even looked up from what they were doing to acknowledge that the guests of honor were leaving the party, but she didn't care. She had her plate of food, and that was all that mattered to her in that moment. After all, she needed to feed her son.

JADE HAS JUST FINISHED LICKING HER FINGERS AFTER FINISHING her barbecue wings and then cleaning them off when they pulled up to a massive house. Noah cut the engine to the car and then looked over at Jade with a lopsided grin. She finally looked up from her empty plate and took in her surroundings. Her eyes got big as she took in the breathtaking house.

"Wow, baby. This is beautiful! Is this one of your designs? Is that a fucking skyway?" Jade asked.

Noah laughed and said, "It sure is and yes, I designed it. I wanted to show it to you to see what you thought."

"Are you sure it's okay? It looks completely done. Your clients aren't moved in?" Jade asked. She didn't want to be rude walking through someone's home just because Noah wanted to show it to her. She also couldn't figure out why he had to do it in the middle of their gender reveal party, but he seemed excited about it so she went with the flow.

"Yeah, baby. I'm sure," Noah said before getting out of the car and running around her side to help her out.

Hand in hand, they walked up the beautiful winding driveway and up the stairs that led to a large wrap-around porch. Jade took the glorious house in and smiled brightly, "I love this color, Noah. Did you choose it?"

"Yup. I had free range with this project to pretty much do as I pleased," Noah said proudly.

"What made you choose baby blue?" Jade asked.

"It just seemed to fit. It's a family home, and it felt soft and inviting," Noah replied with a grin.

"It's perfect," Jade said in awe. "And this wrap-around porch is *everything*. It's perfect for summer days. They could put a table right over here for meals. This is awesome, babe."

"Wait until you see the inside," Noah grinned as he unlocked the house and pushed open the white double doors. Jade waddled in behind him and her jaw dropped. The house was completely void of any kind of decorations or furniture, but it was almost as if it didn't even need any of that. It was like art all on its own, and adding things would only enhance the beauty of it. The floors were white marble and shiny as hell. Jade was afraid to scuff it so she asked, "Should I take my shoes off?"

"Sure," Noah said as he removed his own. "I wouldn't want to mess the floors up."

Jade nodded and then looked around for somewhere to sit. Realizing what Jade was doing, Noah chuckled and walked over to her. "Hold on to my shoulders."

Jade did and balanced herself as Noah removed her sandals. Expecting the floors to be icy cold, it surprised Jade when she realized the floors were heated. "Wow, I've never seen heated floors before."

"Nice touch, huh?" Noah asked.

"Yeah, it is. Especially in the winter. Is there a way to control the heat levels?" Jade asked curiously.

"Yeah, there is. It's built right in on the thermostats," Noah responded as he grabbed her hand and walked her to the right of the massive foyer. "Over here is the living room and laundry room."

The floor plan was open, so Jade could see the large living room with floor to ceiling windows and electric fireplace. It was magnificent, and she knew that the family moving in would have a ton of room to make the space comfortable. Maybe a plush rug and a few couches or something. The marble floors made the space look so elegant, and she could definitely see a baby grand piano in the room, too. The laundry room right next to the living room was large and had a nice washer and dryer inside. Other than that, it was empty, but some shelving would work nicely in the room and Jade thought this would be a good room for the cleaning supplies, too.

"Come on, let me show you the kitchen," Noah said.

"Is there food in there?" Jade giggled.

Noah shook his head. "You just ate."

"Your son is hungry," Jade said as she took Noah's hand and allowed him to lead her through the living room and into the dining room area. There wasn't much to see in there, but it was just as nice as the rest of the house. A large table would fit perfectly and there was a bar area tucked in a corner.

Noah rounded a corner, and they walked directly into a large open kitchen just as Jade said, "I can't help that your son is always hungry."

Noah stopped short and turned to face Jade. "Damn. I can't believe we're having a boy."

"Are you disappointed," Jade cocked her head at him.

"Not in the least," Noah grinned. "My boy. I'll teach him to protect his mama."

Jade blushed. "You're sweet, Noah Bennett. You know that?"

Noah laughed. "I try, baby."

Jade looked around the kitchen and nodded in appreciation. "Noah, this house is beautiful. Could you imagine how much damage we could do in here? Look at all this counter space? And those double ovens...wow. This is amazing."

"Let me show you the backyard," Noah grinned. He walked over to the glass doors that stood at the end of the kitchen and pushed them open.

Jade's jaw dropped as she stepped into the backyard. It was the best part of the house, hands down, and she hadn't even seen it all. There was a pool with a waterfall and a jacuzzi, but the best part was the outside kitchen covered by a fancy tent. There was a top of the line grill, an oven and stove as well as a brick oven. The green grass looked so healthy, and there was a cobblestone path to the pool and kitchen area. Flowers lined the path, and it looked like something out of a storybook.

"Noah...did you design all of this?" Jade asked.

"Are you surprised?" Noah asked as he pretended to be offended.

"No, not at all. I just didn't know you got this detailed in your drawings. I always thought the owners kind of added their own stuff when it was time to move in."

"Yeah, that's normally what happens," Noah vaguely replied. "Come on, I'll show you the rest."

He walked Jade through the rest of the house and it just kept getting better and better. The main floor had a huge man cave, complete with a bar, as well as a large bathroom, a large office big enough for two desks, a room that could be transformed into anything and a workout room that had a whole wall of mirrors. Downstairs in the basement was a full theater. There were sixteen recliner seats that heated. There was another built-in bar along with a popcorn machine. The projector reflected off a special kind of wall that made the images almost look 3D.

Finally, Noah lead Jade up to the top floor of the house. They opened a door to the left of the staircase and it led into a vast space with more doors. Straight ahead was the master bedroom, which had huge windows and a fireplace. There was a gigantic bathroom with a jacuzzi, a waterfall shower, and his and hers sinks. The other two rooms were closets the size of the guest rooms at Noah's house. They had perfect shelving and built-in drawers for clothing, shoes and accessories. There were large mirrors in each, and Jade knew that any woman would be happy to fill those closets up. It reminded her of a Barbie Dream House closet.

"You went all out for this house, Noah, but I hope we are almost done. My feet hurt from all this walking," Jade whined. The baby was moving around like crazy and she was ready to head home and get another plate of food and prop her feet up.

"Almost done, my love. There are four other rooms on the other side, but there is only one I wanted to show you."

Jade nodded and let Noah lead the way to their final stop. They crossed the mini skyway and Jade stopped for a moment to glance down through the glass floors at the pool below her. The skyway was completely made of glass and it had the perfect view of the backyard.

"This is so cool," she commented as she took one final look and then joined Noah on the other side of the skyway.

Noah grabbed her hand and led her to the closest door on the left. He pushed it open, and it took a moment for Jade to process why this room was so different from the others. She stepped further in the room and realized that it was because this one was fully decorated. There was carpet in this room, and it was a soft white color. The walls were painted blue with a brown stripe going around the whole room. There was a brown rocking chair in the corner next to the closet and a changing table to the right of that. A diaper genie sat next to the changing table and there was a small brown bookshelf filled with baby books in the other corner. A brown crib sat up against the far wall, and it was made up with blue and brown sheets and a fluffy baby blanket. Next to the crib there was a giant stuffed bear and in the center of the room there was a car seat and stroller with a red ribbon tied around each of them.

Confused, Jade turned and asked, "Are the owners of this place expecting a baby..."

Her voice trailed off as she realized that Noah was kneeling behind her with a smile on his face. He pulled a small box out of his back pocket and opened it for Jade to see. Inside was a large teardrop shaped diamond ring.

"Noah...what are you doing?" Jade asked as a lump formed in her throat. She placed a hand over her stomach to calm her son, who seemed to be doing a dance routine to cheer his father on.

"Do you like the house?" Noah asked.

"Of course I do," Jade cried as tears fell from her eyes. Her heart beat uncontrollably as her mind raced. She was having a hard time processing the obvious events that were taking place, and all she could do was cry and listen to what Noah was saying to her.

"I'm happy you do, baby," Noah smiled as he tried to keep his voice steady. "I designed it when I was in high school, you know? Kenyon and I had this ongoing competition through junior high and high school on who could draw up the best house. We agreed that I won right before we graduated. I put a lot of thought into this house and I promised myself that I would build it one day. It never seemed like the right time...until I met you. I started having it built back in January and then when I found out you were pregnant, I had my men working overtime to get it finished as soon as possible. I wanted you to have a home, Jade. You haven't had one in for so long, and what kind of man would I be if I allowed that to continue any longer?"

"Baby," Jade said through her tears. "My home is wherever you are. I don't need all of this...you know that. God, Noah...I love you so much."

Jade knew she was blabbering, but she couldn't get her thoughts together. She couldn't wrap her mind around the fact that this was her home. It was magnificent. It was a sanctuary. It was everything that she wanted, and she couldn't believe that less than a year ago she had been homeless. Now, she was living in a mansion with the man of her dreams and their son on the way. It was a lot for her to process, and she hadn't even thought about that ring that Noah was holding.

"I know, baby and that's what I appreciate about you the most," Noah said as he wiped a lone tear away. "You don't need all this fancy shit. You are happy with the bare minimum, and that's why there is no woman more deserving of this house. Let this be my gift to you for coming into my life. You deserve so much more than this, but I figure this is a good place to start. I love you, Jade. I've loved you from day one, and I've been wanting to ask you this since the first day we met. Please, baby, do me the honor of becoming my wife?"

A sob tore out of Jade's chest as she nodded her head happily. "Yes, Noah. I'll marry you!"

Noah slid the ring on Jade's ring finger and then stood to his feet so he could give his fiance a kiss. Jade closed her eyes tightly as she felt Noah's lips on hers and prayed that she wasn't dreaming. Noah pulled away and wiped her tears and said, "You have made me the happiest man on earth."

"No," Jade shook her head. "You...there is nothing for me to say in this moment that will convey my feelings. You have completely changed my life, Noah. I love you more than anything and I promise to be the best wife to you."

Noah caressed her cheek and pressed his forehead to hers. "I know you will, baby."

They hugged for a few more moments and Noah pulled away and gave her a crooked smile. "I really don't want to leave here, but I have just one more surprise for you."

"Baby, no. I can't handle any more," Jade cried.

"Trust me," Noah grinned.

Jade sighed playfully and said, "Okay, but when can we come back here?"

"Tomorrow, if you'd like. I left the house completely empty aside from this room so you could decorate. I wanted this place to feel like your home."

"Thank you, Noah. Really...I'm so in love with our new home," Jade said in awe.

"I'm glad. We can come back here tomorrow and start picking out furniture and stuff."

"It's a date," Jade laughed gleefully, grabbing Noah's hand and allowing him to lead her out of the house.

"Congratulations!"

Jade stopped in the restaurant's entrance and smiled as she shook her head. Darlene, Mia, and Kenyon were sitting at a table close to the door, grinning at Noah and Jade as they walked in the restaurant.

"You guys knew about this?" Jade asked exasperated.

"Girl, please," Mia waved Jade off as she got up to give her a hug. "Noah couldn't have pulled that off without us."

"Hey," Noah laughed.

Jade giggled, "How did you even know I would say yes?"

There was a collective scoff as Kenyon and Darlene got up from the table to congratulate the couple.

"Girl, we all knew you would say yes," Darlene smiled. "Congrats, sweetie. Welcome to the family."

"Thank you, Darlene," Jade replied genuinely.

"Call me mom," Darlene winked at Jade before giving her son a hug. Jade's heart swelled as she realized that she had a mother again. She knew that if her own mother was alive, her and Darlene would be fast friends. Jade had faith that her mom was looking down on her, proud of the direction her daughter's life was heading.

"Come on, babe," Noah reached out for Jade. "Come sit. I know you're tired."

Thankful, Jade took his hand and allowed him to lead her to the table. She was honestly ready to fall asleep right there, but the giddy feeling she had was keeping her awake and engaged in the conversation with her people.

"Did you like the nursery," Mia asked from next to her as her eyes lit up.

Realization hit Jade as she asked the question she already knew the answer to. "You decorated it?"

"Yup," Mia stated proudly. "It was really down to the wire, too. I wasn't sure if I would need to get pink and brown stuff, or blue and brown, but I made it work. I was really happy your stubborn ass agreed to have a gender reveal party because this was the end goal the whole time."

Jade pointed a finger around the table and said, "Y'all are sneaky."

Everyone laughed and continued to talk while Mia nudged Jade and whispered, "Hey, isn't that Noah's ex?"

Jade whirled around in her seat and looked towards where Mia was pointing. Sure enough, Alana was sitting at a table with an older man that looked to be her twice her age. Jade snickered, "Yeah, that's her. Looks like that ass beating you put on her knocked Noah right out of her mind."

"Guess so," Mia giggled.

They turned their attention back to their own table and Jade asked, "Hey, Mimi. Something has been bothering me."

"What, Mouse?" Mia asked in concern.

"What are you going to do now that Noah and I are moving? You know you're more than welcome to come with us, but I wasn't sure what your plan was."

Mia blushed profusely as she bit her lip and said, "Uh, well... yeah. I actually do have plans to uhm..."

Overhearing the conversation, Kenyon interrupted and said, "She's moving in with me."

Both Noah and Jade's mouths dropped while Darlene laughed knowingly. "I knew y'all would get together, eventually. Ain't no way y'all argue that damn much and not have feelings for one another."

"When the hell were you going to tell us that y'all were even dating?" Jade barked.

"See? I told you she would be mad," Mia whined as she looked over at Kenyon.

"Mad?" Noah asked. "I'm pissed. After all that shit y'all pulled trying to push Jade and I together and you two carry on a secret relationship? Not fair."

"Okay, but in our defense, you guys are engaged with a baby on the way, so it worked out," Mia said nervously.

"Nope," Jade admonished. "You are never living this one down, Mia Reyes. I'm going to need full details later."

"Fine," Mia huffed.

"Man, all that matters is that you're happy," Noah conceded.

"And that you don't hurt my best friend or I'll hurt you," Jade said sweetly as she gazed at Kenyon who put his hands up in mock surrender.

"I have no intentions of hurting her," he said with a laugh.

"Good," Jade smiled.

The waitress came to their table and took their drink orders. When she walked away, Jade sat back and wiped a tear away from her eye as she watched her family interact. If she had been told a year ago that this was where her life would be, she would have laughed until she was blue in the face. After her parents died, it was as if good things no longer happened to her, but finally, she was living the life she deserved with the people she loved. It was surreal to her most of the time, but that was exactly why she enjoyed sitting back and relishing the moment because she knew all too well that happiness could be snatched away as soon as it was obtained.

She laid a hand on her baby bump, and then a moment later, Noah laid his hand on top of hers. This was it. Their family. They smiled at each other, knowing that this was all they needed in life, nothing else mattered. Love was the key to happiness, and they each had enough of that for each other to last several lifetimes.

EPILOGUE

CHRISTMAS MUSIC COULD BE HEARD THROUGHOUT THE HOUSE. It was packed with people and the holiday spirit was overwhelming. The date was December twenty fifth, and the energy was magical. The holidays in New York were the most wonderful time of the year for most people, and this year, Jade was amongst them.

As she sat in front of the mirror and reflected on the rollercoaster her life had taken her on over the past year, tears freely fell from her eyes. Just a year ago, she had spent countless nights in the freezing cold, praying that she didn't die. Some of them all by herself until she met Mia. Now, she lived in a stunning home with her soon to be husband and their adorable six week old son, Roman David Bennett. Named after Noah's brother and Jade's father. Darlene liked to call him Murph, though. As soon as he came out of the womb, she swore that he looked exactly like her late husband.

Everyone else called him Ro, and he was the light of their lives and the center of attention in whatever room he was in. The fights that Kenyon and Mia would have over who got to hold him were ridiculous. They spoiled Ro rotten, and there wasn't a moment where he wasn't in somebody's arms. He hadn't even slept in that crib in his nursery. Instead, Noah and Jade kept him in a bassinet next to their bed, but if either of them were awake, then he was in their arms. Jade would stay entertained for hours at a time, just staring at her sweet baby, marveling at the fact that he was hers. She was forever thankful for how her life turned out.

Jade grabbed a tissue from her vanity and dabbed at her eyes just as Mia walked in the room. Jade smiled at her best friend when she saw her. She was stunning in a long tight fitted dress that dipped low at her cleavage. The dress flared out at the bottom, giving it a mermaid effect, and it was made from silk. The deep red color was striking against Mia's tanned skin and wavy brown hair that fell over her shoulders and down her back. She was absolutely gorgeous, and Jade couldn't have envisioned a better maid of honor for her wedding.

Mia tsked when she saw Jade crying and said, "Now you know if Ryder was still here she would beat your ass for this."

Jade giggled as Mia took the tissue from her and finished drying her best friend's eyes. Jade knew that Mia was telling the truth. They had met Ryder a month ago when they had their makeup and hair trial with her and Jade had instantly fell in love with her fiery spirit. Ryder was a no bullshit kind of woman and most likely would cuss her out for crying and ruining her makeup. Jade thanked God that she wasn't there to witness it. Ryder was already on a flight back to California to be with her, husband, daughter and newborn son.

Ignoring Mia's fussing, Jade grabbed her friend's hand and said, "Mimi, you look so beautiful."

Mia's features softened as she squeezed Jade's hand, "And you look gorgeous."

Jade's smile grew as she looked into her best friend's eyes. "Can you believe that we met only a year ago at a homeless shelter?"

Mia shook her head, "First of all, that seems like lifetimes ago. Second of all, we really were a hot mess back then, weren't we?"

Jade laughed, "Yeah, but for good reason."

"Yeah," Mia nodded sadly. She hadn't given up on reaching out to her parents. In fact, she and Kenyon made a trip to Florida so that Mia could try to see them. When they got to her old house and knocked on the door, her mother peeked out the window and refused to let her in. It broke Mia's heart that her parents hated her so much that they wouldn't even have a conversation with her.

Mia had cried the whole way home while Kenyon held her and tried his best to comfort her. He knew that she missed her parents and there wasn't anything he could do to fill that void for her, but he cared enough about her to try. Mia appreciated his efforts, and that trip only brought them closer together. They didn't have that Noah and Jade kind of love that consumed them. Instead, they had that slow burning kind of love that took its time and they were okay with that for their own reasons. Kenyon had never been in a relationship before and he didn't want to fuck things up with Mia, while she had been in many failed relationships before, the last one leaving her homeless. Mia wanted to take her time and be fragile with Kenyon because at the end of the day, he was her best friend and she never wanted to lose that.

Seeing that Mia was getting caught up in her thoughts, Jade brought her back to the present. "Hey, I'm proud of you. You do know that, right?"

Mia smiled, "And I'm proud of you, Mouse. No more is the shy woman scared of the world. In her place is a confident, woman who is an amazing mother and will be a great wife."

"Okay, but let's take the focus off me for a moment," Jade laughed.

"Said no bride in the history of brides," Mia teased, pointing out Jade's white dress.

Jade laughed, "Fair, but still...I want to say this. I've spent a lot of time praising Noah for everything that he has done for me and I feel like I've done you a disservice, Mia. From day one you have been my rock through this whole journey. We have literally shared a single piece of bread in order to subside hunger pains. We have battled the cold with only each other to keep us warm, and we endured those nasty ass shelters. I wouldn't have survived without you, sis, and that isn't even mentioning how you fought for me against Elijah. I love you so much and I am so grateful for you. Look at you! In a loving relationship—"

"We are *not* in love," Mia interrupted.

"—and working a bomb ass job as an executive accountant. You're smart as hell and a beast with numbers and you're the best auntie the world has ever seen," Jade continued, ignoring Mia's interruption. "You had nothing, and you made it into something amazing. You deserve the world, Mia. Don't forget that. I'll always be here for you, boo. Whatever you need, I got you."

Tears filled Mia's eyes as she listened to Jade speak. She had to grab her own tissue so she could prevent the tears from ruining her makeup. Being reminded of everything her and Jade had been through was emotional. They were some strong ass women and had been through hell and back. It was rare that two women connected in the way that Jade and Mia had, but they would lie down and die for each other and they wouldn't change that for anything.

There was a knock at the door, interrupting their moment, and Darlene poked her head in the door followed by Kenyon.

"Wow, you are both beautiful," Darlene gushed as she walked into the room.

Kenyon followed behind her with Ro tucked into his arm. He was sleeping peacefully and Jade's eyes lit up when she saw him. She got up from her chair at the vanity and strutted over to her child.

"Hi, mommy's baby," she cooed softly as she looked down at her son. He had dark curly hair and a bunny nose. His skin was a milk latte color and his cheeks were so fat, Jade had to kiss them any time he was within three feet of him. His Navy blue tux was so adorable on him, and he even had a dark red bowtie. Noah got it custom made just for his son of course, and Jade just wanted to eat him up. He was the cutest baby she had ever seen, even if she was biased. Not only that, he was a good baby. He only cried when he was hungry or uncomfortable. Other than that, he was really laid back like his daddy.

"Hey, now," Kenyon waved her away. "Don't wake him. I just got his lil' ass to sleep. Besides, you're wearing the hell out of that dress, sis. I wouldn't want him to get baby drool all over it."

"Fine," Jade pouted and Kenyon laughed as he leaned in to give her a hug.

"Relax. You can have him after the ceremony," Kenyon grinned as he pulled back.

Jade's pout morphed into a smile as she asked, "Have you seen him?"

"Duh, I'm the best man. I've been with him all morning."

"How does he look?" Jade asked eagerly.

Kenyon cocked his head to the side and asked, "You really want me to describe how my best friend is looking in his tux?"

"Yes, please!" Jade quipped.

"Hard pass," Kenyon grumbled as he moved passed her and towards Mia.

Jade heard him say something inappropriate to Mia and tuned them out. Those two were something else now that they were dating. The bickering had lessened while the sexual tension had grew. Noah and Jade found it extremely uncomfortable to be in the same room as them sometimes. They weren't ashamed to make out with each other right in the middle of dinner in front of Noah and Jade. It was cute how much they liked each other, but they needed to learn how to reel it in a bit.

Luckily, Darlene started talking to Jade, so she didn't have to listen to the two lovebirds in the corner.

"Jade, baby. You are absolutely stunning. Are you nervous?"

"No, mama," Jade beamed. "I'm just ready to see him."

"He's ready to see you, too," Darlene smiled as she flattened down Jade's dress around the middle.

Her dress was simple, but stunning. The long sleeves were made of lace that swooped down her neckline and stopped at her chest. It was a tight-fitted dress with a simple diamond belt at the waist. The fitted bottom flared out in the back into a long train and Jade opted to wear simple white flats instead of heels. Her curly hair was pinned back and to one side and her makeup was perfection in soft gold colors. She was happy as hell that her dress fit since she could only do one fitting, being pregnant up until one month ago and all. Jade snapped back down to her original weight of one hundred and twenty pounds. Her breasts were a lot fuller and her hips a bit wider, but she was glad to have her body back.

Jade looked in the mirror one last time before turning to Darlene. "Okay, I'm ready."

Darlene smiled. "Let's go get you married, then."

"Here's your bouquet, Mouse," Mia grinned as she handed Jade the beautiful bouquet made up of dark red roses.

"Thanks, Mimi," Jade smiled.

Kenyon moved ahead of the ladies and said, "Ro and I will be down there already. We'll see you at the altar."

"Thanks, Kenyon," Jade beamed at him.

"See ya, baby," Mia blew him a kiss before he left the room.

"Alright, girls. Everyone is seated. I'll go queue the pianist. Once you hear the music, Mia come on down. Jade follow after."

"Okay, mom," Jade said.

Darlene kissed Jade lightly on the cheek, careful not to mess up her makeup, before leaving Mia and Jade alone. Mia busied herself with Jade's train, making sure it was straight and spread out evenly. Suddenly, the music started, and Mia straightened up. "That's my queue."

"See you down there," Jade grinned. "Love you."

"I love you more, Mouse," Mia said before opening the door and stepping out.

Jade counted to ten slowly, barely able to contain her excitement. On the other side of that door and down a few stairs was Noah, and she was more than ready to jump in his arms and never leave for the rest of her life. All the bullshit that she had been through made it worth this moment right here. The abuse, the rapes, the homeless-ness...hell, even the cold she had to endure. It all made her one thousand times more thankful for the life she had now and the people that were in it.

She willed herself not to cry as she finally reached ten and slowly opened the door. She walked down the hall of their side of the house and opened the final door that would bring her to the banister where the stairs were. She took a deep breath and opened the final door, and tears instantly flooded her eyes. Her home was beautiful. Red roses were everywhere and filling the air. They decorated the banister along with mistletoes and gold ornaments. The wide windows in every direction showcased the falling snow outside, creating soft white pillows on the ground. The sun was falling, and the sunset was magnificent against the snowy scene in their backyard. Jade peeked over the banister as she walked and saw her family and friends looking up at her.

Tears fell as she slowly descended the stairs and took in the scene before her. They had transformed their large foyer into a winter wonderland fit for any wedding. A large Christmas tree sat in the corner with enough gifts to make a small village happy, which was exactly what they intended to do. They asked all of their guests to bring toys for children versus wedding gifts for them. Kenyon and Mia would bring them to homeless shelters across New York while Noah and Jade were on their honeymoon. Since they just had a baby, they put off going out of the country for their honeymoon. Instead, they were going to a luxury cabin in Colorado, and they would take Ro with them. It would be quiet and peaceful, and their family would have a chance to spend quality time together.

They set several chairs up on either side of the foyer, creating an isle down the middle. As she walked passed her friends from the architect firm, Cassy and Kai, and several of Noah's friends and distant family, she smiled politely, but kept her eyes on Noah. He was so handsome in his navy blue tuxedo and dark red tie. Of course it fit him like a glove and his thick beard had grown out a bit and was sexy as hell. His tears matched her own as they stared into each other's eyes. They'd known each other for only a year, but that year had changed both of their lives forever. Neither of them knew what love was until they met each other and it was an overwhelming feeling.

When she finally reached Noah, she leapt into his arms without thinking. There were some laughs and some *awws* echoing throughout their foyer, but it was as if they were the only two in the world in that moment. Noah held onto Jade tightly as he cried like a damn baby. He was so overwhelmed by emotion, and he was a little embarrassed by it. He kept his head buried in her shoulder until his tears slowed some before pulling back and kissing Jade on the cheek. When they finally separated, Mia slyly handed Jade a tissue from behind her. Jade laughed as she dabbed her tears away and the officiate started the ceremony.

Noah and Jade barely paid attention as they got lost in each other's eyes. The only time they broke eye contact was when their son woke up in Kenyon's arms and started crying. Jade knew that he was getting hungry, but he would have to wait for a few more moments. Always the prepared grandma, Darlene rushed over from her seat a few feet away and grabbed her grandson with a bottle in hand. Normally, Jade would insist on breastfeeding her son, but now was not the time. Her son was her world, but her husband was her universe, and this moment was theirs.

They focused back on each other just as the officiate said, "Can we please have the rings?"

'Oh, shit," Kenyon exclaimed as he rushed away from the altar and towards Ro. He patted the baby down for a moment and then breathed a sigh of relief when he found the rings tucked into the baby's jacket pocket.

"Sorry about that," Kenyon grinned cooly as he made his way back to the altar and placed the rings in Noah and Jade's hands. "Seems we had a runaway ring bearer."

Everyone in the room laughed as Kenyon took his place behind Noah. The officiate had Noah repeat the vows after him, and as he did, he slid Jade's wedding band onto her finger. A fresh wave of tears spilled from her eyes as she realized that it was her mother's ring. She looked up at Noah with watery eyes, and he grinned back down at her.

Thank you, Jade mouthed, not even bothering to wipe the tears away. This was exactly what she needed to make this day perfect. A reminder that her mother and father were with her, watching over her, and proud of her. Her heart couldn't be any more full than it was in that moment.

It was Jade's turn to say her vows, and she did so while looking Noah in the eyes, conveying her love to him with every word that she spoke.

"Do you take this man as your husband, to have and to hold until death do you part?"

"I do," Jade said through her joyful tears.

"I now pronounce you husband and wife. Noah, you may kiss your bride," the officiate smiled.

"Finally," Noah said as he palmed the back of Jade's head and drew her into him. Jade melted into the kiss as Noah parted her lips, giving her an unspoken promise of what was to come later.

When they pulled apart, Jade felt dizzy and Noah had to steady her. "Don't worry, baby. I got you."

"I know," Jade replied, unable to contain her smile.

"I love you, Mrs. Bennett."

"And I love you, Mr. Bennett."

The End

MORE TITLES BY CYN ALEXANDER

Formerly known as Queen Pen

Full Novels

Dust 2 Diamonds: An Urban Fairytale
The Baddest of Them All: An Urban Fairytale
Lil Red Ryder: An Urban Fairytale
Rebel & Her Beast: An Urban Fairytale
A Fairytale Wedding: An Urban Fairytale

Short Stories
The Third Wheel

Collaborations
Should've Thought Twice - By Queen Pen & Queen T

UPCOMING FROM CYN ALEXANDER

Lyric & Rhyme: The Intro

Book One of the Lyric & Rhyme Series

Caught off Guard: A Game of Love

Book One of the Game of Love Series

STAY CONNECTED WITH CYN ALEXANDER

Facebook: Cyn Alexander
Instagram: @Author.Cyn.Alexander
Twitter: @Qu33nP3n
Snapchat: @Lillady92
For signed books please visit:
www.kingdomlitpublications.com